SHE WAS SOCIETY'S CHILD,
A BEAUTIFUL PAWN
IN THE HANDS OF
A RUTHLESS TYCOON,
DETERMINED TO BUY
RESPECTABILITY
AT ANY PRICE....

Meagan McKinney

Lions and Lace

Island
BOOKS

Island Books

Published by
Dell Publishing
a division of
Bantam Doubleday Dell Publishing Group, Inc.
666 Fifth Avenue
New York, New York 10103

ISBN: 0-440-21230-8

Printed in the United States of America

Published simultaneously in Canada

May 1992

10 9 8 7 6 5 4 3 2 1

OPM

To all the nieces and nephews:
Jewel, Jessie, Callie, Anna Grace, Sam and Jack,
and Zachary Steingrimur

And to Maggie Caruso and Genny
We'll see you in heaven, dear friends.

Acknowledgments

First, I'd like to thank my cousins Anna and Morton Delson, who've always made Manhattan a more wonderful place than it already is. Thanks goes also to my agent, Pamela Gray Ahearn, who's worked so hard on my behalf and had to work especially hard for this one. My appreciation to the institutions who keep the past alive: the New-York Historical Society, the Museum of the City of New York, the New York Public Library, the Newport Historical Society, Columbia University, and the A. B. Freeman School of Business Rare Books Library.

Special thanks to dear Turlogh O'Faolin for so generously sharing his vast knowledge; to Jill Barnett, who finds brilliance even when, alas, there is none; and to my editor, Damaris Rowland, who showed faith and enthusiasm. I couldn't have done it without all of you.

Lastly, regarding all things Gaelic, thanks to the grandnephews of the Irish writer Liam O'Flaherty: to Danny and Patrick O'Flaherty, owners of the best Irish pub this side of the Atlantic. I invite all my readers to have a pint and hear them play "Bridget O'Malley" at O'Flaherty's in the French Quarter of New Orleans.

Lace

Society was based on a sort of untitled but
long-established social hierarchy, from which
all random elements were rigorously excluded.
It held many attractive people, good-looking,
agreeable, well-dressed women and men, but as
a society it seemed flat and arid, a Sahara without lions. . . .

—Mrs. Winthrop Chanler,
Memoirs on New York Society

1

Of course it was raining.

From the filmy web of lace at the bedroom window, Alice Diana Van Alen looked down at Washington Square, made dark by looming nightfall and the storm. Below, rain pounded the streets, scouring the herringbone pattern of the paving stones; above, wind kicked at the skeletal trees in the square, causing the gaslights of the street behind them to blink through the shaking claws of their branches. Not a soul was about. Even the hack stand stood empty, all its cabs dispersed to carry pedestrians caught in the bad weather.

She stared out the wet windowpanes, hugging herself as if she were cold. The storm was an omen. But even believing this, she could not change her mind. She was going to the ball tonight.

A small wry smile touched her lips. The dream she'd had last night was an omen too. She hadn't had it in such a long time, she'd almost forgotten about it. Then, with tonight's worries on her mind, she must have conjured it from her deepest thoughts. The dream was always the same, and even now she found it hard to resist its images.

Succumbing to it, her green eyes warmed, and her face took on an ethereal expression, as if she were far away.

A heavy burst of rain pelted the window and thrust her thoughts back to reality. Disgusted with herself for daydreaming at such a crucial hour, she turned from the window to head toward her lace-draped dressing table. But the opulence of her bedroom, especially in contrast with her reverie, almost repulsed her. The bedroom was beautiful, appointed with all the luxuries a wealthy young woman could wish for. Just looking at the dressing table proved that. It was kidney-shaped and so heavily festooned and skirted in costly French lace, it appeared upholstered. Its tufted pink velvet seat waited for her like a throne, but she was suddenly reluctant to go to it. Her surroundings were a shocking contrast to the simplicity and charm of those of her dream.

The white clapboard house was what she always dreamed about. And she had dreamed about that house last night. It was a house so spare and modest, most in her social circle would be embarrassed even to dream about such a dwelling, let alone wish to live there.

But wish it she did. Fervently. She loved that little white house perched atop the green grassy hill and gleaming beneath the blue sky. She had never been to such a house, but she thought about it so often, she could almost smell the scent of apple blossoms that surely drifted on the breeze from the orchard, and she could almost hear the snap of clean linens she pictured fluttering on the line behind the house. She loved the place, not so much for what it was but for what it contained.

She closed her eyes, willing herself to stop her thoughts. It wouldn't do to linger in reveries. They weren't destined to come true. Wishing for them would only cause unhappiness. She opened her eyes, intending once more to take her seat at her dressing table, but the wealth of her bedroom again seemed to overwhelm her.

She glanced around, hating the oppressively large cabbage roses on her wallpaper, the gaudy chintzes covering the furniture, the heavy rose velvets and silk fringes swathed across her Duncan Phyfe bed. It was all wrong. Though she'd grown up in this room, she knew it wasn't right for her any longer. Now she wanted other things, things like green hills, blue skies, white houses. Him.

Her eyes darkened. He was always there in her dream, an ever-present spirit—dark, overpowering, unreachable. He took the form of a handsome man who leaned indolently against one of the whitewashed porch supports, arms crossed against his chest, staring at the landscape behind her. In her dream she would watch him from the bottom of the hill, unsure of who he was yet desperate to see the details of his face, obscured by the distance.

As had happened before, her desire to see this man overtook her, and she began to climb the hill, negotiating the grassy bank with difficulty in her satin gown. She clutched at her skirts to lift them free, but soon the heavy figured satin fell like water through her hands, and she lost her hold on it. With every step, her gown seemed to grow several inches longer, as if it were purposely trying to trip her, and it grew unimaginably heavy, as if lined with stones, not crepe. Soon the bustle at her back became like two great hands pulling her down the hill, keeping her from what she wanted most. The pearls at her neck weighed her down until she began drowning in this sea of satin and jewels.

In the end, unable to move, she could only look at the man on the hill, her arms outstretched, imploring him to save her from the quagmire of her wealth. But he didn't come down and rescue her. With a cry of anguish, she watched as he turned.

"Don't go," she cried, her voice desperate and low.

But he would never hear her.

"I need you," were the last pitiful words on her lips before the man disappeared into the simple white house, and she would violently awake, overwhelmed with bitter regret for something she would probably never have.

Her face became taut with emotion. The dream's end was like a nightmare. She hated to recall it. Unconsciously her hand went to the pearls at her neck, and she lifted them as if they were too heavy.

"Miss Alana?"

Startled, Alana turned from the window and found the person who had called her by the diminutive of her name. Her maid, Margaret, stood in the center of the room holding out her evening cape and long satin gloves.

"Miss Alana? Are you ready?" Margaret asked tentatively.

Alana stepped into the cape. "Has the carriage been ordered?"

"Yes, miss. I had Kevin do it. I figured the footman'd keep his mouth shut better than t'at butler o' yourn, Pumphrey. T'at one's too quick to answer to your uncle."

Alana nodded, sensing the maid's fear by her heavier-than-usual brogue. "Good. Uncle Baldwin must never know I'm going to the Sheridan ball."

"Not as I've told him."

Alana smiled and looked at Margaret. "With the rain, I was sure this evening was doomed. But now I feel much more optimistic. If all goes well, the only way Uncle Baldwin will find out that I attended the Sheridan debut will be to read it in tomorrow's *New York Chronicle*."

"We've done our best to keep quiet."

"I'm grateful for that, Margaret. You tell Kevin that too." Alana pressed the girl's hand and took the gloves from her. She was about to put them on, but the maid's expression gave her pause. Her heart quickened. "Is there something wrong?"

"Well, no, miss . . ." Margaret gave her a sheepish glance.

"What is it?"

"I promised them I'd tell you this, miss," she blurted out. "What I'm tryin' to say is just t'at I, well . . . we . . ."

"Yes?"

"Me and Kevin and Katie and McDougal—well, we all want to thank you, miss."

"Thank me?" Alana looked puzzled. "But whatever for?"

The maid's words seemed to tumble out before she could

stop them. "We know why you're not supposed to go to-night, Miss Alana. We know it's on account of the Sheridan lass bein' Irish. You're standin' up for her, and we want to thank you. Me and me husband, Kevin, never left County Wexford until the year before'n last. So it means a lot to us, you going to t'at ball tonight."

Margaret's words left Alana speechless. She stared at the maid, groping for a correct response. There were several things she could do and say, from what she probably should do—chastise the servant and remind her of her place—to what she wanted to do—hug the little maid and ask her to pray for her this night.

"You're welcome, Margaret," Alana finally whispered as she pulled on her gloves with embarrassed haste.

Equally embarrassed, Margaret gave her a swift, nervous curtsy and nearly ran out of the bedroom.

When Alana had decided to attend the Sheridan ball, she'd never thought about the fact that Mara Sheridan was Irish. She'd met the sixteen-year-old girl one afternoon last fall in Central Park and had liked her instantly. The first time she'd encountered Mara Sheridan, the girl had stopped east of the Green in her elaborate basket-phaeton and publicly accused a hackney driver of maltreating his animal.

The invitation to her debut had arrived, and Alana viewed it as nothing more than another social obligation. She knew little about Miss Sheridan, but during their brief sojourn across the Mall, she'd found her genuinely guileless and sweet. Unlike the things she'd heard about her brother.

Everyone in New York talked about Trevor Sheridan. They said he was one of those rich, vulgar, self-made men so new to Manhattan who ran over everyone in their haste and greed for more dollars. There'd never been a kind word spoken about Mara Sheridan's brother in her circle, but of course, as Alana knew so well, the Knickerbocker set was hardly the place for charity.

Her lower lip twisted in derision. Oh no, exclusivity was

the thing foremost on the minds of the Four Hundred, certainly not charity. She knew that better than anyone. Mrs. Astor kept exclusivity in front of her like a shield that would protect her from the "unacceptables." It was the final irony of the Van Alens' glorious existence that if Mrs. Astor were to find out their secret, New York's exalted social matriarch would find she'd embraced just what she'd been trying to run from—scandal. Vulgar, sticky scandal.

But to protect herself, and mostly to protect those she loved, Alana played the game. In some ways it wasn't hard for her. With her Knickerbocker heritage that could be traced back to Petrus Stuyvesant himself, Alice Diana Van Alen was the jewel in the crown of hyphenated New-York. But when that well-bred veneer was stripped away, Alana knew she was only a girl playing desperately at charades.

Against her will, her gaze slid over to the ruby-velvet-framed Sarony daguerreotype of her sister that she kept next to her bed. She stared at it, an inexplicable panic running through her veins. She hated this game of exclusivity, hated it enough to run from it screaming. She lived a lie. She socialized with those who would be the first to ostracize her should they know the truth about her and her family.

Alana's gaze focused on the picture of her sister once more. To shield her sister, she played the wretched game. But even making that sacrifice, she found she could do it only to a point.

Her thoughts turned again to the Sheridan ball. She knew quite well that Mrs. Astor and the other Knickerbockers weren't blackballing tonight's affair simply because they disliked Mara Sheridan's brother—it was doubtful any of them had even met Trevor Sheridan. Alana certainly hadn't. The real reason was the despicable one Margaret had just stated. The Sheridans were Irish. Good enough, perhaps, to scrub the chamberpots or hand the master his trotters should he want to run them along Harlem Lane. But not good enough to socialize with.

Alana stared at her reflection in the mirror. The yellow satin Doucet gown was just right to attend a young girl's debut. The strings of pearls roped around her neck were costly yet restrained. Mrs. Astor would be proud of how she looked tonight. Yet appalled. The matron had heard the rumor that Alana was going to attend the Sheridan ball, and at their last collision Mrs. Astor had made it clear she expected Alana to stay home this evening. Now all of society was holding its breath to see if Alana would defy her and attend the ball. Alana took one last glance in the mirror and smoothed the swag of jonquil satin around her hips. She would.

Her coffee-colored satin evening cape had slid off and now billowed at her feet. She picked it up and struggled in her tight sleeves to throw the garment over herself, unwilling to inconvenience Margaret to return and help her. *The* Mrs. Astor wouldn't have cared. She would have called the maid back without hesitation, but after Margaret's painful confession Alana couldn't bear to embarrass her further this evening.

Suddenly there was a loud pounding on her door. Before she could take another breath, the voice of her uncle shouted behind the locked door. "Alana! Open up! I know what you're doing, and I won't have it!"

Terror seized her. She froze. The voluminous cape fell once more to the carpet. Her uncle's pounding echoed that of her heart. Like a convict facing the gallows, she steeled herself for the worst. Didier had somehow gotten wind of her rebellion, and now he thought he could crush it.

But she wouldn't let him. She walked regally to the door and opened it.

There stood her uncle, Baldwin Didier, furious. He walked boldly into her room, his brilliant blue eyes taking in her ball gown. "What's the meaning of this?" he demanded. "How dare you disobey me?"

With a nonchalance she did not feel, Alana swept past him and sat at her dressing table only to peer nervously at his reflection in the glass. Uncle Baldwin was in fine form. Past his prime, he was still well maintained for his fifty-odd years. With his handsome gray Van Dyke beard and those astonishingly vivid blue eyes, Alana was always surprised by his striking appearance. "Commanding," was what her aunt had said the day she met him so many years ago. But along with that word, came the haunting words of a maid who'd once worked in her aunt's household: "He's the kind of man a lady begs for as a suitor," the elderly servant had noted, "then runs screaming from on the wedding night."

Didier moved toward her. Alana watched him as a vixen watches a marauding hound. When he rested his hands on her shoulders, she could hardly breathe she was so frightened.

"You're not going out this evening."

"I am." She tried desperately to keep the fear out of her voice. "I know what you're going to say, Uncle, and I won't listen. You'd best return to your hotel because I won't disappoint that girl. I'm attending the ball tonight, come what may."

"Mrs. Astor doesn't approve. You will not attend."

Anger burgeoned in her chest, threatening to overflow even the tight corseting beneath her jonquil gown. "I refuse to be Mrs. Astor's handmaid."

"Oh you do, do you?"

She froze. He pulled her roughly to her feet.

"You will do as I say, Alana. Need I remind you that your position in this community is my lifeblood? How do you think I make a living?"

She didn't even react. She'd heard this speech before, and while it sickened her, it strengthened her. His abuse brought out a resilience in her she'd never known she had. Struggling to be released, she retorted, "Mother and Father wanted me happy, not chained to a lawyer's pocketbook like you've done."

"My attorney's fees don't make me nearly the fortune

I've made on the exchange since becoming your guardian, and I'm not going to let you threaten that."

"I may do as I like. I've my own money—"

"And, as you well know, it's been given to me to hold in trust. So keep me happy, Alana. I don't want to consider you *and your sister* another one of my bad investments." He shoved her aside and sat on the nearby banquette beneath the window.

She didn't like him threatening her sister. "Bad investment," she muttered icily. "Is that what that painted woman you keep at the St. Nicholas Hotel is called? Or has another one taken her place by now? There've been so many."

"Watch it, my dear, your Knickerbocker class is showing," he said, a nasty twist to his lips.

"Someone in this family has to show some."

He bolted from the chair. "And I'll be damned if you'll soil it tonight by going to some potato-grubbing Irishman's house!"

"You don't even know these people! How can you speak of them like that?"

"Trevor Sheridan's a gutter-licking mick, and don't I know it. I've lost enough money to him and his damned Northwest Railroads."

"I don't care how much you've lost to him," she said quietly. "And I don't care if the Sheridans are Irish. Mara Sheridan's only sixteen. Won't anyone take pity on her? Don't you know how this could destroy a young girl—to have no one show up at her debut?"

"Let someone else take pity on her. You have a different task."

"What task is that?"

"To flaunt all that costly, protected virtue of yours and keep me in good stead with your peers." He grabbed her arms again, this time bruising them viciously. "So you *will* play handmaid to Mrs. Astor, and you *will* do as I say, or your sister won't find me so merciful."

"Oh God, how my aunt must be turning in her grave that she let you into the family," she spat, her eyes tearing from the pain of his grip on her arms.

"On the contrary, she's rejoicing that she left someone to take care of you. I'm all the family you've got left, Alana." A cruel light appeared in his eyes. His gaze wandered over to the daguerreotype on her night table. He released her arm and went to pick it up. "But I forget about Christabel." He fingered the portrait, his once handsome lips curled in amusement. "How is your sister? Have you visited her recently? Of course you have. You're quite religious about it, aren't you."

Alana remained mute. He knew she didn't talk about her sister. It was too emotional for her to speak of it. She lived a lie about her family. The Knickerbockers believed that all her family had perished in a housefire three years ago. No one knew the truth—not her beaux, not her "friends," not even Mrs. Astor. Only Didier knew what had happened to Christabel. And that terrible fact kept her protected and vulnerable at the same time.

Didier glanced again at the picture. "She looks so happy here, doesn't she? How long after this was taken was she put in the madhouse? Has it really been three long years?"

Alana tried to turn from him.

He wouldn't let her. "Answer me," he insisted. "She looks very happy in this picture. How happy do you think Christabel would be in a public institution, not that nice clean private home that coddles her so?"

"She won't be put in a public institution," she lashed out.

"And how will you afford her care if I no longer permit it?"

"I shall hire a lawyer and fight you!"

He shook her. "With what? Your fortune's under my control. You think I'd give you money to use against me? Think again."

"I won't be blackmailed by you any longer! I'm going to the Sheridan ball, and my sister won't be threatened!"

"Your sister's care is shockingly expensive. How will you pay for it if I cut you off? Your parents, God rest their souls, didn't realize when they died that they were to leave you with such a burden as your dear sister's care."

"You're the burden to me, not Christabel!" She struggled against him. To grip both her shoulders, he released the picture, and it shattered on the floor. Alana was furious as she looked down upon her sister's fractured portrait.

"You will stay in tonight," Didier stated. "And since no one else is showing up at that party, I don't think it necessary to send your regrets."

His words appalled her. Though he was probably right that no one would show up at Sheridan's ball, she didn't want to believe people were so cruel. Yet the evidence seemed irrefutable. Young Mara Sheridan would be destroyed by this blow.

But Alana was not so cruel, and she would not contribute to society's cruelty. She said, "I'm going tonight."

"You're not."

"I am." She lifted her head and leveled a challenging gaze at him. "I'm going because of Mara Sheridan, but mostly I'm going for myself, and to defy you *and* Mrs. Astor."

"I see." Didier took a calm step backward. Without warning, he raised his hand and hit her hard across one cheek.

She moaned and took her face in her hands. No one had ever hit her before. The shock of it was more debilitating than the pain.

"Do not defy me, Alana," he whispered as she sank to her dressing-table bench, her palm gripping her throbbing cheek. He'd hit her so hard, she felt nauseous. She didn't know whether she was going to faint or have to run for her washbasin.

"I'll stop by tomorrow to see how you're faring." Didier spoke calmly, as if she were facing him, not hurt and crumpled on her bench. "We'll take my curricle out after tea."

"I'm going to the ball tonight," she said, making one last attempt at defiance.

"You're not," he said. His eyes lowered to her back where her corseted curves seemed to beckon beneath the jonquil satin. "Oh, the price of avoiding vulgarity," he whispered, sliding a hand to her small bound waist. She bolted away from him, and reluctantly he left, locking the door firmly behind him.

It was several moments before Alana could gain her bearings. Her head ached abominably, and her vision was still not steady. She looked around the room, its oppressive opulence making her long for the simple white house in her dreams. She would find that man, and when she saw his face, she would know him instantly. He would be the man she could share her troubles with, and her triumphs. He would love her, and together they would build a life. It would all happen one day, she vowed, taking what comfort she could in her reveries. One day she would find happiness, despite Baldwin Didier.

Yet as much as her spirit rebelled, the locked door was her ultimate defeat.

She made a miserable figure as she picked up her sister's shattered picture. Margaret soon knocked softly on her door, whispering hushed inquiries about her well-being and begging her to let her in. Helpless and angry, Alana rested against the dressing table, her eyes unable to shed tears. Her only solace was her sister's daguerreotype, and she hugged it to her bosom, unmindful of the way the glass shards caught in her bodice.

Somehow, some way, there was an escape from the hell her life had become. But try as she could, she couldn't think of one. There seemed to be no other option but the one her uncle presented. Her sister's care was frightfully expensive, more than she could ever hope to earn. And the thought of her sister being reduced to public care and all the horrors that brought with it was unendurable.

Inconsolable, Alana rested her throbbing head against

the dressing table. Her sister had been destroyed by their parents' death. Alana had been grateful for the home in Brooklyn that took such wonderful care of her. Even their uncle had agreed it was the best place for Christabel, considering the alternatives. Now Christabel at least lived out her youth in a tranquil environment, well sheltered from the madness their uncle had created around her.

In the mirror Alana glanced at the ornate expensive drapery at her windows, then at the red mark Didier had left on her cheek. It was ironic, but for the first time in her life she wondered if Christabel wasn't the lucky one.

Lions

Were he not a supreme scoundrel, he would be
a great man.

—George Templeton Strong
(on Boss Tweed)

2

Wall Street called him the Predator. No one knew if
Trevor Sheridan was hated more for his wealth, which
seemed to multiply as quickly as the Irish tenements
springing up north of the Manhattan toe, or if it was the
fact that he was a son of Erin, an enterprising phoenix
newly risen out of the ashes of his impoverished homeland.
Regardless, New York's elite publicly shunned him. Yet as
Knickerbocker society pushed the Predator away with one
hand, certainly the other hand was outstretched like a beg-
gar from Five Points in the hope that where Trevor Sheridan went in the exchange, they might follow and be the
richer for it.

Tonight the Knickerbockers had Sheridan very much on
their minds.

The Predator had them on his mind also.

"Do you think they'll come?" Eagan Sheridan asked his
brother as the two men stood in the dining room of the
house on Fifth Avenue. Mara's debut was to start in less
than an hour, and the table had been set for fifty guests.
Cobalt-colored Stiegel glass goblets and eighteen-karat-
gold-painted Limoges porcelain graced the table. The
ten-foot centerpiece consisted of 370 pale-pink tea roses
interspersed with bouquets of lily of the valley topped off
by an elegant ice sculpture of entwined swans. In the cor-

ners of the room, as a rather defiant gesture, topiaries had been set up in the shape of shamrocks. It was a breathtaking display in a breathtaking room, for the dining room was an exact copy of the one at Blenheim, except that in the Sheridan dining room, unlike Blenheim's, the heavy dentil moldings and priceless pink Numidian marble were real, not trompe l'oeil.

The master of all this splendor remained silent as he walked around the table, giving it a last critical study. His gait was as stiff and formal as the ever-present ebony and gold lion-ornamented walking stick he always used.

Eagan watched his older brother, worry etched on his handsome, boyish features.

"I suppose the question should be what if they don't come?" Eagan prompted, obviously trying to get a response, any response, from his brother.

"Is Mara dressed?" Sheridan finally asked, the table having passed his inspection.

"Mara? She was dressed a month ago. I've never seen her so excited." Eagan stared down at the glass of V.S.O.P. brandy he held in his hand. "I wonder, Trevor, was this . . . debut a little hasty?"

"Other girls have debuts. Look at the Varicks, the Biddles, the De Witts."

"Yes, but—"

"Yes, but those ladies have no association with the Irish shanties on Eighty-ninth Street," Sheridan finished bitterly for him. Quickly, as if he regretted his honesty, he looked at his brother's casual attire and said, "Are you dressed, then?"

Eagan slowly shook his head, but unable to put his fears to rest, he whispered the dreaded words again. "But what if they don't show, Trevor?"

Sheridan released a disgusted sigh. He stared long and hard at the shamrock topiary as if trying to think of the appropriate words. When they wouldn't come, he cursed.

"I don't give a damn about Caroline Astor!" he proclaimed, twisting his walking stick in his hand.

Eagan only nodded as if cheering him on. By then, Sheridan need no prompting. "Her and that precious following of hers! Who do they think they are?" He whipped around and faced his brother. "But God grant me mercy, Eagan, what was I to do? Will it hurt Mara more if no one shows up tonight or if she were denied a debut altogether?"

"I don't know, Trevor. Right now, I really don't know." Eagan whispered.

Sheridan glanced at his brother, obviously struggling with his anger. The two men stared at each other for a brief tormented second, then Trevor moved away as if unwilling to discuss the evening further. With a fatalistic shrug of his shoulders, Eagan returned to his brandy while his brother made one last survey of the glorious room.

To the casual observer, the two brothers might look very much alike. There were eight years between the two, Trevor being older, but there were still many similarities. They were both tall, broad-shouldered, and uncommonly handsome. Yet for all their similar physical attributes, the brothers didn't quite match. Whereas Eagan was rakish and charming, Trevor was intense and grim, a man whom it was said horded his smiles like he horded his gold. Eagan had brown hair; Trevor, black. Eagan had eyes as green and wild as the Emerald Isle; Trevor's were hazel, unusually dark, with an almost permanent wrathful expression. Though they had both been born in Ballinlough, County Roscommon, Eagan had been in New York since he took his very first steps. He exuded an ease and enthusiasm that was confidently American, while Trevor did everything with rigid, studied calculation. Even his accent was cultivated, a self-conscious, almost painful cloaking of his impoverished past.

"I've got to finish dressing," Sheridan said, his words cutting the silence between the two men like a blade. "When will you be ready?"

Eagan only raised his empty glass and smiled. "Give me a refill, and bring on the Four Hundred."

Sheridan lifted one eyebrow. "I suppose you're guzzling our best brandy."

Eagan laughed. "It's better than drinking that rotgut you keep in your rooms. Look around, Trevor. Look at what your money has bought you. I think by now you can afford better than cheap Irish whiskey."

"Brandy or *poitín*, I can't tell the difference." Sheridan dismissed him by walking away but then thought of something and turned. "By the way, it was Chateau Margaux you recommended for the wine tonight, wasn't it?"

"Yes, that was it."

An inkling of relief crossed Sheridan's face; he would have let no one but Eagan see it. "Good. It needs to be right. This evening everything needs to be right."

"Another would have done, Trevor."

Sheridan gave Eagan a slight smirking smile. "Yes, but then why did I pay for that expensive education of yours if you can't direct me in choosing our wines?"

Eagan suddenly softened toward his brother. "Despite my days at Columbia, Trevor, I truly don't know as much as you."

If they'd been ten years younger, Sheridan might have affectionately mussed Eagan's hair. "Of course you know more than I. What's the use of university, then?"

"There are things only life can teach you," said Eagan.

"But those things you don't ever want to learn."

After that morose statement, Sheridan lightened. "Your education will prove much more useful, I think. With that degree from Columbia, perhaps your daughter won't have Mara's troubles." He turned to depart. "I'll see you in an hour, Eagan. Don't be late."

Eagan watched him go, his expression burning and full of pride. If ever a brother looked up to another, Eagan looked up to his. "Trevor," he called, unable to stop himself, "I want you to know, if none of them show up tonight, I say we Sheridans go out tomorrow and lynch every one of them—just like they done in Galway."

Sheridan turned and looked at Eagan. The Predator only nodded.

An hour later Sheridan knocked softly on the white gilded doors of his sister's suite. In seconds the double doors were flung open, and a girl of sixteen took Trevor by the hand and pulled him laughing into her room.

"How do I look?" she asked, pirouetting before him.

Mara was beautiful. She had inherited the Sheridan good looks along with the stunning coloring of the Black Irish. She had masses of shiny raven-hued hair, skin the color of rich cream, and warm sparkling sapphire eyes made even bluer by the costly gown she wore. Her dress was ice-blue satin with the pattern of swallows set free at the hem appearing to fly to the heavens. Done in the Renaissance taste, her large puffed sleeves were slashed, revealing undersleeves of brilliant magenta. With her hair still unbound and cascading down her back, she was a Raphael madonna brought to life. She looked exactly like the kind of maid that knights of old had dreamed of and bled for. No one was more proud of her tonight than her eldest brother.

"Trevor! Trevor! Come see! Shall I wear the pearls in my hair or simply this *boring* wreath of artificial flowers that Peg wants me to wear?"

Trevor looked at the scowling elderly maidservant behind Mara and began to chuckle. "So she's been a handful, I see," he said to the maid in his native Celtic tongue.

Peg answered him back in tart Irish Gaelic. "Aye, sir. I think she'd be better tamed with a whip and a chair."

Trevor tipped his head back and laughed, much to Mara's ire.

"What are you two scheming about?" she asked, traipsing over to her dressing table. "You know it's rude to converse in a tongue that the third party doesn't understand."

"And where did you learn this?" Trevor asked in English.

"In Mrs. Mellenthorp's *Lessons to Young Ladies.*" She took the little red book from her dressing table as if it were her Bible. "Here it is, Trevor, on page fourteen. 'Rudeness is to be tolerated only in others, never in oneself.'" Mara opened her eyes wide. "Oh dear, I suppose *I* was being rude in pointing out that *you* were rude." She scowled and began thumbing the pages of the book as if to find another passage to prove her point.

"Enough of Mrs. Mellenthorp for tonight." Trevor took the book from her. He took in the picture of her in her womanly finery, and a sad smile appeared on his lips. "No more short dresses for you, isn't that right, Mara? After tonight, you'll be a lady, and you'll wear only ladies' clothes."

Mara smiled back, then impetuously hugged him. "Thank you for the beautiful gown, Trevor. I love it every bit as much as you said I would."

"So I'm not the beast you claimed I was last winter."

Mara gave him an impish grin. "Oh yes you are." She turned to her maid and explained, "You should have seen him, Peg, in Paris, sitting before Monsieur Worth at seven Rue de la Paix. Monsieur Worth was showing Trevor all his magnificent gowns." Mara began to imitate the rotund couturier. She took her alpaca lap rug from the chaise longue and swept it before Peg for her inspection.

"Is this to your liking, Mr. Sheridan?" Mara asked, artfully imitating Worth.

"Too low-cut!" Mara answered out of the corner of her mouth, lowering her voice to mimic her brother.

"And how do you fancy this one, sir, if I may ask?"

"Too sophisticated!"

Mara mimicked exactly Worth's supercilious expression. Disdainfully, she asked, "And this one, Monsieur Sheridan, if you would be so good as to give your opinion?"

"Not *RED!*" she boomed out her brother's reply, nearly choking with the effort not to giggle.

Peg turned away, her shaking shoulders betraying her laughter.

Trevor only scowled and took the alpaca rug from Mara's hands. He mocked, "So is this how you thank me for that costly gown?"

Mara turned again to Peg. "Oh yes, and I almost forgot. Once he'd finally decided on a gown, Monsieur Worth assured Trevor again and again that he would pour his entire soul into the effort of clothing me. But when Trevor was handed the bill, do you know what he said?"

Peg shook her graying head.

"He said, 'Mr. Worth, I see you place too high a price on your soul.' "

Mara fell back on the chaise hysterically giggling while dear old Peg hid her crooked smile behind a discreetly mitted hand.

"Very good," Trevor said dryly.

"Miss, you're wrinkling," Peg admonished when she saw the master's face.

Mara sat up and rushed back to her dressing table, nearly tripping on the long satin skirt.

"Will she be ready soon?" Trevor asked Peg in Gaelic.

"As soon as I can tame that hair," the maid answered briskly, also in Irish.

"Dearest brother?"

Trevor slid his gaze back to Mara. "What, you minx?"

"Shall I wear the pearls in my hair tonight or this sad little bit of lily of the valley . . . or those diamonds you keep in the vault downstairs for when I marry?" In the looking glass, Mara's eyes clearly reflected her preference.

"The flowers, I think." Trevor took the lilies from her and handed them to Peg.

"Not even the pearls?"

"The pearls you can wear *after* you come out." Trevor smirked. "The diamonds won't see the light of day until you're a married woman, so"—he held up his hand, already seeing her plotting to wear them—"don't let's speak of them again, shall we?"

Mara heaved a great dramatic sigh of despair, but then, in spite of herself, she wrapped her arms around her brother and gave him a loving hug. "I forgive you for being such a beast, Trevor. But only if you forgive me for being so greedy. I just want tonight to be perfect." She rested her dark head against his chest, and a furrow appeared on her sweet youthful brow. "I'm such a ninny. But I've such a fear that I'll do something wrong. And I couldn't bear it if none of the young gentlemen asked me to dance tonight."

Trevor stiffened and looked down at the beautiful young girl in his arms, his precious little sister. A crushing ache appeared in his hazel eyes. He touched her wild black locks, then held her to him fiercely.

"Why, Trevor, what is this?" she asked when he finally pulled free.

"I want you to never doubt that I'd do anything for you, Mara. I want tonight to be as glorious as your dreams. I've done everything within my power to make it that way."

"I know that. But why do you speak so solemnly?"

He smiled, but it never quite took the melancholy from his eyes. "Am I being solemn?"

"Yes, terribly solemn."

"Well, you know how I am. I'm never quite as much fun as Eagan."

"Nonetheless, you're just as dear to me."

Trevor stared at her for a moment, as if flashes of their mother, or something deep and close to his heart, had touched him. Yet his stiff, formal manner soon returned. He kissed Mara's hand and motioned for Peg to take over. After giving explicit instructions to Peg to use her Irish-born common sense and not to listen to a word of Mara's on how she would like to wear her hair, he sauntered to the doors, leaning on his walking stick. He turned one last time to find Mara and Peg already in a battle of wills over the powder pot. He smiled and appeared reluctant to leave.

Especially while Mara was still so full of happiness and her eyes still shone with the anticipation of the night ahead.

The Louis XIV clock in the Sheridan drawing room chimed eight times, and with each bell, the sound seemed to echo endlessly through the enormous mansion until the final sound was like a distant moan of despair. Precisely on the hour Eagan came down the stairs, his face jolly for the moment. Mara was on his arm, her hair finally dressed in a modest falling chignon with lilies of the valley strewn through the twists at the back of her neck. She looked lovely, but Trevor did not look at her. He asked their butler if he would bring Mara a sherry on this fine occasion, and once the sherry was brought and Eagan's glass refilled with V.S.O.P., he left the conversation to his brother.

The worst moment came when the large ormulu clock on the mantel chimed the half hour. Mara still waited for her guests, the hope burning in her eyes, dimmed only slightly. Trevor kept his gaze on the fire and his glass of liquor, hardly bothering to address his brother or sister.

By nine o'clock even Mara knew there was something wrong, yet she refrained from speaking her worries. Her conversation with Eagan drifted to a morose silence, and all three of them waited. For what, they weren't sure.

When the clock chimed ten o'clock, the drawing room was a tomb. No one spoke. Eagan slouched over his glass, an unusual frown marring his handsome features. Trevor still stood at the mantel, his face a cold emotionless mask. Mara stared at her hands. But when the final bell chimed, she couldn't bear it any longer. She stood up and slowly took the flowers from her coiffure. In defeat, she walked to the door, her every step like a death march.

"Mara," Trevor finally whispered, making her stop. "I will avenge this if it's the last thing I do." He delivered this promise with as much hot fury as cold vengeance.

Mara turned, her beautiful young face far less innocent than it had been only two hours earlier. "No, Trevor," she said, her voice trembling with held-back tears. "Remember what Mrs. Mellenthorp said: 'Rudeness is to be tolerated only in others, never in oneself.' " She met her brother's eyes and suddenly burst into tears. She ran out of the room, leaving a trail of crushed flowers in her wake.

The only sound left was the tap of a walking stick as Sheridan made his way through the cavernous foyer. Eagan stayed behind in the drawing room, finding cold solace in another glass of brandy, but Sheridan was not to be comforted that way. He entered the dining room, still decorated in anticipation of the dinner that was to be held there. Surveying the room, his gaze rested upon the shamrock topiaries that now seemed to mock him, their shapes taking on nearly mythical proportions in the abandoned grandiose room. A dripping noise drew his attention to the expensive table arrangement. Atop the center, the swan ice sculpture, once a masterpiece, was now a melted, grotesque caricature of its former self. The roses and lilies surrounding it drooped almost imperceptibly, yet Sheridan noted their defeat, and his face hardened further.

He stepped up to the table and touched the rim of a cobalt goblet. But when he looked down at it, something inside him must have snapped. He must have been reminded that this was a goblet that should have been raised in toast to his sister, not sitting unfilled at an empty table in a desolate room. Without warning, his rage overcame him. Abruptly he raised his ebony walking stick and smashed it down on the table, breaking crystal and china in its wake. The Limoges porcelain clattered to the marble floor, and the roses and lilies were ripped apart from the force of his blow. He moved down the table and took particular vengeance on the wine goblets, shattering them one by one like clay pigeons, his expression frighteningly calm and deliberate.

When the last cobalt goblet was destroyed, the last piece of Limoges cracked beyond repair, the last pink tea rose lying limp upon the floor, Trevor straightened and stared down at his hand that clutched his walking stick. It dripped blood from a dozen tiny cuts, a casualty of his violence and the flying shards of glass. He looked down at the carmine spots on the damask tablecloth. They were like virgin's blood on bedsheets, a final metaphor for Mara's lost innocence. Tormented beyond salvation, vengeance burning in his dark eyes, Sheridan decided on his retaliation. He shouted for his butler.

Whittaker arrived, his professional demeanor not shaken by the violent destruction of the dining table or the crunch of priceless crystal beneath his polished shoes. After all, he was an English butler, trained to remain above the master's tantrums.

"What may I do for you, sir?" Whittaker bowed.

"Get me this evening's guest list." Sheridan didn't even look at him, his gaze riveted vengefully on the shamrock topiaries.

"Very good, sir. Thank you very much, sir." He bowed again and mechanically went to retrieve what the master desired, the smile on his aging lips the only hint that he was not as detached as he appeared. Whittaker, with his scrupulous British background, was, of course, very much a believer in the Mellenthorp Rules of Etiquette. But he knew what went on in his domain. He, like the rest of household, knew that Miss Mara was upstairs in her bedchamber crying her eyes out. So he carried out the master's request with even more efficiency than usual, for in spite of his skills at the gentle art of buttling, Whittaker still believed that there was indeed a time and a place for revenge. And that time had most certainly come.

3

The Commodore Club was busy that noon. Old rich men sat in the library in burgundy leather chairs reading the latest edition of the *Bankers' Magazine*. Hopeful investors crowded around the ticker-tape machine next to the concierge, praying that silver or Erie stock would rise and thus pad their incomes.

The Commodore Club was the watering hole for Wall Street, one of the few places where old money shook hands with new. Though the Knickerbocker society wives wouldn't dream of taking tea with those beneath their social position—even if those not of their set possessed five times their wealth—the Knickerbocker men, while in the Commodore Club, behaved by no such rules. They easily mingled with the nouveaux riches if only to gamble and increase their bank accounts. (After all, those Knickerbocker wives with all their rules and airs of superiority were quite a dull flock, and mistresses *were* getting expensive.) Even old William B. Astor himself consorted easily with the young and mighty of Wall Street. At the Commodore Club, he even asked to be called Backhouse because it was his middle name, but more importantly because Mrs. Astor, once they had been married, had asked him never to use it again. It reminded her of "all sorts of vulgarities."

So the established and the interlopers alike took their cigars and brandy at the Commodore Club. They con-

versed about bulls and bears, but mostly they talked about
the Predator. They discussed in infinite detail how he had
fared in the Comstock Lode and if his investments in the
Marine Bank would prove astute. True, most wouldn't invite Trevor Sheridan to dinner, nor would they expect their
wives to associate with his family. Yet for a tip on the exchange, all would gladly have shared their mistresses with
him, and perhaps, if the financial reward were worth it,
they might have even lowered themselves to laugh over one
of his crude Irish jokes.

Today the Knickerbockers were willing to laugh. Tomorrow they would not be.

Appearing unconcerned with the speculation around
him, the Predator sat in the corner of the dining room
eating, of all things, corned beef and cabbage, with his
younger brother. Every now and again a gentleman would
look up from his table and glance at Sheridan, then, seeing
no profitable activity, return to his meal. This continued
through Sheridan's enjoyment of a large glass of the club's
best brandy (upon Eagan's insistence) chased with a pot of
strong coffee.

The atmosphere in the dining room was sizzling. Everyone, of course, knew about Sheridan's sister's failed debut,
but that was quickly overshadowed by the fact that it was
Tuesday. And Tuesday was the day that the Predator *bought*.

James Fitzsimmons entered the room, and all eyes fell
upon him. He was Sheridan's workhorse. One could set
one's watch by James Fitzsimmons. Every Tuesday afternoon at precisely two o'clock he entered the club's dining
room and walked to the Predator's table. There the
Predator would write out his order on a napkin, and James
Fitzsimmons would then leave for the exchange, the napkin
in his hand coveted by everyone in the room.

The Predator wrote, and eyes followed his hand as if
they might decipher the movements and reveal those hal-
lowed words: *silver bullion, Western Union, Chesapeake Railroad*. Whatever it was, the Predator was almost assured of

making a fortune, and those lucky enough to be holding on to his coat tails would profit beyond their wildest imaginings.

Sheridan finished his order with a flourish and handed it to Fitzsimmons. Fitzsimmons bowed and turned on his heels.

Then the unthinkable happened.

Some thought Lady Luck had just landed sweetly in their laps when they saw that napkin slip from Fitzsimmon's hand. The linen square fluttered to the ground, the scribblings in black ink available to anyone within sight of it. There was one huge intake of breath as they strained to read each line. Then Fitzsimmons retrieved it. He shoved it in his pocket as if the entire incident had never occurred. At the far end of the dining room the Predator hardly lifted his head. To all appearances, he hadn't even seen Fitzsimmons drop the thing. Men suddenly began rubbing their hands.

One by one, they left the dining room, each with a different excuse, each with the same destination and the same name on his mind: *Jubilee Patent Laces.*

Eagan, of course, had seen the napkin drop. He paled and almost jumped from his seat. If not for his brother's discreet hand on his arm, he would have sprinted across the room and taken the napkin back. Eagan looked down at his brother's hand and said, "Trevor, they've seen the bid. We've got to tell Fitz not to put the order through."

"Wait," was all Sheridan offered.

More men cleared the room. Soon the only ones in the dining room were the Chinese busboy and old Cyrus Field, too blind and deaf to notice anything around him but the strip of beef on his plate that his manservant sawed into gummable scraps.

"Jesus, Trevor, what the hell are you doing? That stock'll be worthless if you *and* the rest of this room buy it," Eagan whispered.

"It's Jubilee Patent Laces."

Eagan looked as if he'd just been slapped in the face.

"That's not worth the paper it's printed on. Everyone knows that. Jubilee's going into receivership any day. Are you out of your mind?"

Sheridan stood as if he hadn't heard him. "What do you think, Eagan, if we give Fitz the day off tomorrow? He's done well for us today, wouldn't you agree?"

Eagan looked up at his brother and narrowed his eyes. "What'd you do here? You just—just—?"

"Fitzsimmons won't be bidding for me today," Sheridan commented, "though I doubt any of our luncheon partners will notice. Not in their haste to get their bids in for Jubilee."

With realization dawning on him, Eagan couldn't help but see the flaw in his brother's plan. "But not all those men who ran out of this room toward Jubilee were invited to Mara's debut, Trevor. You've gone and ruined men who have no business with us."

Sheridan whipped around and bitterly whispered, "You know what they're calling Mara today after her disappointment? The Irish whore. I was told that several men in this club were betting which one could take her to mistress. If I ever get their names, I swear they'll be dead before they see another day at the exchange."

Rage and disbelief crossed Eagan's features. Numbly, he stood and looked out the bay windows across Broad Street to the exchange. "You were too easy on them, then," he said.

"I'm not through yet."

Sheridan turned to go. He ambled out of the dining room, and the only noise besides old Cyrus Field in the corner busily masticating his beef was the distinct click of a walking stick on marble.

"Bless me, Father, for I have sinned."

Hearing these words, the old parish priest, who had been listening to those very same words for at least six hours, suddenly sat up straight. His rheumy eyes widened, and he stared at the tiny mesh window that separated sinner from priest in the narrow oak confessional. He couldn't see through the black screen, but he didn't need to to know who the speaker was. He knew that voice as surely as he knew his amber-beaded rosary. It was Trevor Byrne Sheridan, *the* Trevor Byrne Sheridan of Wall Street, the Sheridan Bank, and several railroads and silver mines that he couldn't begin to name. But more than that, it was the Trevor Byrne Sheridan whose gold had roofed the chapel last winter, the sole means of support for the parish's orphans' home in Five Points, the man who the bishop once said owned nearly a quarter of Manhattan, including the costly dirt beneath St. Brendan's.

Old Father Donegal nervously replaced his steel spectacles and began listening as if the bishop himself were at his shoulder.

"It has been a year since my last confession." Sheridan's shadow moved as if he were lowering his head. "I am treating men unfairly, Father. I'm depriving them of their money. For this and all the sins of my past life, I humbly beg forgiveness."

"You've stolen from them?" The priest mopped the sweat from his balding head. The last thing he wanted to hear was that the orphans' home in Five Points was being run on thievery.

"No, Father. I'm not stealing their money. I'm simply making sure they have less of it. I know this must be a sin, and while I *must* do it, I seek God's forgiveness."

"Tell me what you're doing to these men," the priest asked, curiosity getting the better of him.

"It's a long story."

"Begin, and you will find forgiveness."

"Three days ago in the Commodore Club, I was having my lunch. The exchange was busy that day. I made sure it became even busier. . . ." And so the confession went until Sheridan the sinner felt himself confessed.

"What shall you say to me, Father?" Sheridan finally

asked when he was through. "What shall be my penance for these sins?"

The priest had lived a long time, but he'd never heard of such schemes. He had no idea that so much money changed hands in one day. In his amazement, he mumbled, "For your penance, say one hundred rosaries."

"*One hundred* rosaries?" the irate voice boomed at him from the confessional window. "There is no other way?"

Father Donegal nearly slipped from his hard oak seat. "Exactly how—how much money did you plan on depriving these men of?"

"All told, about three million dollars, I think."

The father was too shocked to even close his mouth.

"I'll say *three* rosaries. One for each million. Will that suffice?"

The priest nodded lamely, then remembered himself. With as much confidence as he could muster, he squeaked, "You cannot bargain for your soul, my son. You must also make a good act of contrition. You must pay these men back."

"That's impossible, Father."

"You must pay restitution."

The shadow paused. Quietly he said, "I shall give the bishop the same sum that I plan to remove from the pockets of my enemies. He may use it toward St. Patrick's. I see fourteen years of building, and still Bishop Hughes's dream of a cathedral for New York is not realized."

The priest nearly choked.

"Shall it be *three* rosaries, Father?"

The good Irish priest bowed his head in a silent prayer. "Yes," he gasped like a sinner.

"Thank you, Father."

"But you shall give some of that money to St. Brendan's."

"Of course," Sheridan finished smugly.

"*Ego te absolvo.*" The priest made a sign of the cross.

The door to the confessional swung open. The shadow

slipped out and using a walking stick, moved to the front pew, the Sheridan pew, and began his penance.

Father Donegal slumped back down on his seat. Another sinner was at the window with the endless words "Bless me, Father, for I have sinned . . ." The housewife-confessor went on to say that she'd been coveting her friend's new gas stove, but he hardly heard her. In only a few minutes, he'd saved the bishop's cathedral, the orphans in Five Points, and Trevor Byrne Sheridan's soul. Now, that wasn't bad for a day's work.

The Knickerbockers fell just like the expensive German lead soldiers they bought for their little sons at Schwarz Toys. One by one, the families of the invitees to the Sheridan debut found themselves inexplicably in financial ruin. If Sheridan couldn't lead them astray in their stock purchases, he discovered what sound investments they did have and created the worst of all catastrophes—rumor.

Prosperous Bouwerie Iron Works tumbled to ruin when it was whispered that cheap tin was secretly being unloaded in the yards upon nightfall. Likewise, the Knickerbocker Savings Bank teetered on the precipice of disaster while it was being bandied about that its investments in the Hudson Railroad had faltered. In the end, foolishness and greed brought the Knickerbockers down, not Trevor Sheridan. Again and again they fell victim to the exchange's moody mistress, Illusion of Value.

The final coup for Sheridan came on a stormy April day when the season's last snowfall powdered Central Park. He was sitting by the fire reading the evening edition of the *New York Chronicle* when Eagan burst into the room still wearing his overcoat, its shoulders dusted with snowflakes.

"Good God, have you heard the news?" Eagan shut the doors behind him.

"You didn't even allow Whittaker to take your hat." Sheridan commented over his newspaper.

Eagan pulled the black top hat from his head and let the

snow on its brim melt on the hearth. "I just came from the Commodore Club. You wouldn't believe the frenzy down there. The markets have gone mad. Every hansom cab from as far as Forty-second Street is lined up taking chaps to the telegraph office. They're wiring to Chicago—and you won't believe what they're trying to corner."

"Commodities. Potatoes and cabbage, to be exact."

Eagan stopped. "How did you know that?"

Sheridan lifted one brow, then leisurely returned to his paper. "Rumor has it blight may come early to Ireland this year."

"Blight—already? I don't see—" Eagan stopped. He looked at Sheridan, then nearly choked on his own laughter. It was several minutes before he could collect himself to utter a simple sentence. When he finally could, all he said was *"Potatoes? Cabbages?* Goddammit, Trevor, I'd have never believed it, but you *do* have a sense of humor."

Trevor ignored his brother's roundabout praise and asked, "Would you hand me that list on my desk?"

Eagan took the sheet of paper off the heavy ornate desk. "What's this?"

"Check off the names De Harinck, der Burch, and Wynkoop." Sheridan watched while Eagan did it. "Now," he said, "are there any more names left?"

"Just the name Van Alen."

Sheridan eased back in his chair and resumed reading. Quite off-handedly, he murmured, "Oh yes, I forgot. Check that name off the list too."

4

Alana hardly noticed the covert glances of the servants as she was helped from the Van Alen brown coupé. If it hadn't been raining so hard, she might have felt a tingle of foreboding at their wary gazes, but as she was escorted by umbrella to the front door of her residence, her thoughts were elsewhere, preoccupied with another impending disaster.

Tonight had been another tedious Monday soiree at Mrs. Astor's. For an evening that should have been made for pleasure, "pleasurable" was hardly how Alana would have described it. Mrs. Astor spoke incessantly of "that wretched Irishman" and "his vile manueverings," while the men holed up in the library right after dinner, uttering oaths, she imagined, that could have put Mrs. Astor's groom to the blush.

The Knickerbockers had been hit hard by Sheridan, the man they too now called the Predator. But their financial ruin didn't compare to their outrage at being humiliated. Some Knickerbockers, Alana had heard, were even being chased by debt collectors after losing enormous sums in speculation. That was unheard of in her circle, and it would have amused her—the picture of all that old money being chased down by such a common vulture, the bill collector—if she weren't another ready victim for the Predator.

She was a Knickerbocker too. She'd meant to attend Mara's debut, but Sheridan didn't know that, and though he'd left some of them alone—the Astors because it was said he admired Willy B. and because he wanted to ensure there was some society left for Mara to be accepted into—Alana wondered if the Van Alen money wasn't just a matter of time.

In her heart she truly understood the reasons for Trevor Sheridan's wrath. The cruelty of Mara Sheridan's failed debut still stabbed at her too. But as much as she empathized, Trevor Sheridan's vengeance had been too strong and too sweeping to condone. She had a sister and loved her as well, but only a madman would go to such lengths to destroy the people he blamed for hurting his sibling's feelings. So she'd reached the conclusion that either Trevor Sheridan was a madman or there was something about Mara Sheridan's debut that cut into him more than just its lack of attendance.

Now, disembarking from the carriage in the pouring rain, Alana felt weighted down with worry. The evening had been torture, and while she dreaded feeling Sheridan's wrath upon her shoulders, it had been all she could do not to say something inflammatory at Mrs. Astor's—to blame those licking their wounds in Willy B.'s library for their own misery. She hadn't because she knew she couldn't. Didier made it all too clear to her that, for her sister's sake, she must keep her standing in society. Yet she longed to lash out, and tonight, seeing all those hateful people who had so callously crushed the hopes of a sixteen-year-old girl, she'd found it difficult to restrain herself.

Tiredly she allowed the butler to take her cape and shake off the raindrops. Pulling on the fingers of her skintight kid gloves, she began on the fifteen buttons at her wrist and slowly strode through the carpeted foyer. She walked unmindful of the glittering blue eyes that watched her from the double parlor, unaware how the gaze ripped down her figure, taking in every detail of her costly appearance, from the pale-peach satin of her gown to the strands of pearls that were woven into her chignon at the back of her neck.

The sight of all these expensive trappings so enraged the onlooker that he rose, knocking his cognac from its perch on the arm of his chair.

"Alana."

Hearing her uncle's angry rasp, Alana turned sharply to find him at the entrance to the double parlor. Didier's menacing figure stood in the shadows cast by the gasolier. He had frightened her before, but now his very quietness terrified her. Without guessing, she knew he'd come all the way from his hotel on Fifth Avenue to talk about Sheridan. He'd come to tell her she was ruined. And though her first reaction was unadulterated panic, her next was a strange relief. At least now the ax had fallen, and she could begin picking up the pieces.

"Uncle Baldwin—what are you doing here at so late an hour?" she asked, though she hardly needed to. From the corner of her eye she glanced at the servants who had helped her from the carriage. Margaret's husband, the footman, Kevin, quickly averted his eyes, and even Pumphrey, a master of butler's detachment, looked anxious to be excused. They'd known something was up. They'd also known it was bad.

"Come in here," Didier instructed, ingeniously hiding his drunkenness with precise speech and impeccable attire. Even his dark-blue cravat was as straight as a pin.

Alana braced herself for the worst. Her uncle was furious. Sheridan might be the cause of their troubles, but somehow she knew she would pay. She knew from the glitter in those magnificent ice-blue eyes.

She handed her gloves to Kevin, and to the man's credit he looked as if he just might step forward and block her way, disproving Mrs. Astor's theories that there was no chivalry in the working class. Yet just when he was about to move, Alana covertly shook her head and brushed past him. "I must handle this," she whispered in passing. The next time she glanced back, Pumphrey was nodding Kevin in the direction of the basement kitchen.

Alana stepped into the parlor and watched her uncle pull together the enormous pocket doors that shut them off from the foyer. With any other person this wouldn't have frightened her, yet she knew from their last encounter that Baldwin Didier was unlike any other person. Her stomach lurched, and her palms began to perspire, but she faced him with cool green eyes. "What is so pressing at this hour that you've come all the way down from your rooms to speak to me?" She wanted to get through this as quickly as possible. The bruise he'd left on her cheek still smarted when she touched it, and it was still a trick to hide it with powder. Her insides coiled with anger every time she thought of it.

"Sit down." Didier's glance went to the old Belter settee her parents had bought during better times, times that now seemed bitterly distant.

"What must we discuss at this late hour?" She reluctantly sat on the edge of the settee, still ready to stand and fight.

"You may dispense with those nice manners, Alana. You can't afford them anymore."

Her uncle stood over her; she could smell the spirits reeking on him and on the carpet behind him where his cognac had spilled. He had many vile faults, but she had to admit she had never seen him drunk. Not in the three years he'd held her trust fund.

"I'm ruined, then?" she asked, a wild surge of panic rushing through her.

"That's right. You're poor. I bought into the Hudson Bank. They went under today—" he brutally took her chin in hand and spoke very well for one so drunk—"my money with it. They went bust when Sheridan demanded their note. I've lost everything. And now even the almighty Van Alens have lost their last gold dollar."

She tried to pull out of his grasp, but it was impossible. Momentarily overwhelmed, she released a small moan and inwardly cursed the Sheridan name. The Irishman had been thorough in his rampage. Now she too was a casualty, and the thought made her swing between outrage and helplessness. She had wanted to go to that ball! And because of that, she had almost believed Trevor Sheridan would leave her alone. But he hadn't. In his strange obsession to avenge his sister he had raked her fortune clean just like the others. Yet in her case she hadn't a soul to help her recover. No relatives except the charlatan standing before her.

Shattered, she had barely recovered from that knowledge when another terrible thought overcame her. "Oh God, how shall we take care of Christabel?" she whispered.

Didier's grasp tightened. "Forget about Christabel. She can go to the state. I want to know what *you* are going to do. You owe me, Alana."

She looked up at him, knowing she had never seen him so enraged. "What are you talking about?" she gasped.

"Your expensive upkeep! Those clothes! This house! Who do you think has seen to these things all these years!"

"That was your job. I had a trust fund for these things," she answered, a wary expression on her face.

He grew purple with anger. "I had control of that fund, and if it had been my choice, I would have taken the entire thing and left you and that loon of a sister of yours by the wayside!"

She couldn't hide her shock. "How can you say such a thing? You had a duty—"

"Duty be damned!" He let go of her chin. With the force of his release, she fell backward. He leaned close, and his voice was ominous. "It was to my advantage to keep you in society. So I paid for the pretty things you wear and see around you now. But now I've nothing. Do you understand me? Nothing! You owe me for being so charitable!"

She stared up at him, truly believing he'd gone mad. His words made no sense. While it was true she had never liked her uncle, until the night of the ball, she had done her best to think well of him, mostly because of Christabel. After the fire it was her uncle who had held things together. He had been the one to find the "country estate" for her sister.

He'd even talked to the police. But the man who towered over her now had no redeeming characteristics at all. Whatever goodness there had ever been in him was truly gone.

"I owe you nothing, Uncle," she said numbly. "Our parents provided for my sister and me, and provided well." She stood. "We've had a tragedy here tonight. But this isn't solving it. I must ask you to return to your hotel."

He swung his arm around her torso, and she felt every rib being squeezed to cracking. "You speak so well and so haughtily, but tell me how you're going to rise above this, Alana. Tell me how this fine little Knickerbocker is going to like sweeping streets to keep food in her mouth."

She wanted to beat him. With clenched teeth, she said, "Let go."

"You are the cause of all this!" He shook her.

"Not I! I wanted to go to that ball!"

"I did the right thing! How did I know Sheridan would do this?"

"Well, he has done it, and perhaps there's some good to come of this." She shot him a look of contempt. "I see you now, Uncle, for the vile creature I've always suspected you were. So leave me alone and never come here again."

He laughed. "And how will you get along?"

"Tomorrow I shall speak to Mr. Sheridan and make him see reason. He cannot mean me harm when I've meant him no harm. I met his sister, Mara. I didn't want to see her hurt."

Didier stared at her for a moment. "You think that potato picker's going to have mercy? And why on you, Alana? Don't you think to get back their millions, they'd all claim they were going to attend Sheridan's ball?" His eyes inventoried her finery: the Worth gown, the matching beaded slippers, the Dutch West India Company pearls. Disgust plain on his face, he pulled her to her feet. "How are you going to convince him? Shall you go in the expensive attire I've bought you and prostitute yourself?"

His words, his very being, disgusted her. Unwilling to address such a loathsome question, she pried his fingers from her bare arms.

"How will you convince him?"

"I shall appeal to his better nature."

"Sheridan has none."

"He must if he cares so deeply for his sister," she said, her voice cracking.

"But not for you, Alana. He'll have no mercy on you." With that, he pushed her back onto the settee. His hand pulled agitatedly on his Van Dyke beard, and he began cursing. "I've spent a fortune keeping you up. Is this why I did it? To be a pauper?" He looked at her gown again, and it only inflamed him further. "All my plans are ruined by this! What good are you when all the people I've tried to impress are ruined too? What's left for me? You and your goddamned costumes have cost me my last gold ten piece, and now I haven't anything to show for my investment!"

"I am not an investment!" she retorted angrily. "These gowns were bought with my money. *My* money, do you hear?"

He grabbed her. A guttural cry escaped her lips before he shook her violently. "But you haven't any money now, Alana! Shall you try a week on the streets at Gotham Court and see how you like that?"

She pulled away. If he could, he would have hurt her, but this time she vowed to do anything she could to stop him. Prying his fingers from her, she couldn't stop herself from saying, "If I haven't any money, then I'll no longer need you telling me what I must do. Leave, then. I demand that you leave!"

Furious, Didier raised his hand to strike her, but she refused to flinch, even blink. She couldn't struggle from his strong hold, but even though he could hurt her physically, her spirit, astonishingly, remained unbroken.

Her defiance made him falter but only until her words registered. Then a wild glint appeared in his eyes, and he lowered his hand. He took in her rich, luxurious clothing and released a laugh. The sound chilled her to the bone. Before she could guess what he was thinking, he grabbed her hand and pulled her to the parlor doors. He shoved them aside and dragged her through the foyer to the front door.

"What are you doing?" she cried out, becoming hysterical.

"I'll tell you what to do, all right! One last time, you'll do as I bid, and I'll get even with you and that rag-picking Irisher!"

"What are thinking of?" she gasped, fighting to keep the front door closed.

Without warning, he stepped toward her and ripped the strands of creamy pink pearls from her chignon. She moaned from the pain, but he ignored her. The costly pearls went into his pockets, and he dragged her out the door into the rain, her flaxen hair swirling freely around her like a milkmaid's.

"You must be mad!" she cried, drowning in the cold pelting rain.

"You want to appeal to Sheridan's better nature?" Didier grunted, dragging her to the street. "Fine, then. Go ahead. Now's the time. He's ruined me, and I can't afford you anymore. So let him take care of you!"

"This is insanity!" She grasped at any straw. "You're the one who will be hurt by more scandal! If you continue with this behavior, my reputation will mean nothing! Your business dealings will die!"

Her uncle didn't react. As if he weren't listening, he pulled her down the brownstone's stairs and out to the curb to look for a hired hack.

He was beyond reasoning, so she again tried to free herself, believing if she could just get back to the house, perhaps Kevin would help her. But in her struggle to get free she slipped on the wet cobbles and fell bruisingly against him. She looked up. The rain was coming down in dark, blurring torrents, but his eyes still had the power to hold her.

"You and Christabel ruined everything for me," he hissed. "God, how I've wanted you both off my back these three years since your parents were killed. I've tried to be patient—tried to hold on. No longer. No longer!" He shook her hard. "Without any more money, you're ruined, no matter what I do now. My last connection with the Knickerbockers is gone, so it's just that the final humiliation should be yours and Sheridan's!" He stared down at her, his gaze, brilliant in the refracting light of the rain-covered streetlamps, pinning her in place like a doe frightened by the sudden flare of a torch.

"Don't do this," she said, her face porcelain-pale. "Don't humiliate me like this. I'll never forgive you."

A lone hack turned the corner onto Washington Square. Didier glanced its way and rasped, "With that money gone, I haven't a hope in hell. You'll do as I say."

Panicked, she suddenly possessed the strength to pull away. She got free from his hands and ran halfway to the marble stairs of the brownstone before her wet satin train tripped her. Without pause, Didier lifted her and slammed her into the seat of the hack before she could catch her breath.

"I swear you will pay for this!" she ranted while Didier held her and knocked on the cab to get them going.

Eyeing her with that hellish stare, he swayed and said, "This is merely payment for all the sacrifices I've made on your behalf."

"Sacrifices?" she panted, furious and desperate. "It's I who've made the sacrifice! You've taken my money—you've lost it and spent it on whores! If not for Christabel, I should see you in prison for all your wrongdoings!"

At the mention of prison, Alana thought Didier might actually kill her. He looked as if he wanted to put both hands on her throat and press until she no longer breathed. But his joy seemed increased in proportion to her fear, so

he quieted and stared him straight in the eye. He returned
er stare, and her mouth filled with the metallic taste of
error.

"Alana, go ahead, drive me over the edge. I'm halfway
here already," Didier said, his voice reed thin.

"Burn in hell!" she rasped in a ragged breath.

He laughed, and it was a horrible sound, but she was
ever to know what he might have done because right at
hat moment the cabbie stopped the hack and called out,
Thirty-third and Fifth!"

They could hear the muffled thumps of the driver scram-
ling off his seat in the pouring rain to open the door. Her
ncle threw some coins on the ground and dragged her
way before she could plead with the driver to help her.
midst the rain-muffled curses of the hired driver, Didier
orced her to the porte cochere of a huge mansion that took
p the entire city block. It was too dark to see whose house
was, but from its chateau-like proportions, Alana knew it
idn't belong to a Knickerbocker. Knickerbockers never
isplayed their wealth like this—it was much too ostenta-
ous.

"Be nice to Sheridan, Alana." Didier laughed. "Why, he
ight even think of an arrangement where he'll pay for
hat sister of yours." He slicked the rain off his face with his
and, and with a sheet of water beating down on both of
hem, he dragged her up marble stairs to an enormous pair
f brass doors that looked as if they'd be more appropriate
or a Roman coliseum.

She turned to him and made her last plea. "By all that
ou hold sacred, Uncle, stop this! If you cease now—"

"Give me your hands." Didier took them before she
ould pull back. He removed his cravat and began winding
around her wrists. She tried to claw at him—anything to
scape this mad, irrational act he was determined to do—
ut it was no use. She could barely see him in the dim, rain-
hadowed lamplight from Fifth Avenue. When she struck
ut at him, her thinly slippered feet slid on the slick marble

stairs, and she nearly lost her balance. With tears of rage
and frustration mixing with the rain on her cheeks, she
struggled as he lashed her hands to the railing. A low, piti
ful moan escaped her lips when he stepped to the hug
bronze doors and pounded on them.

She cried out to stop him, but to no avail. He pounded
again and shouted his message. "Sheridan! Sheridan!" he
screamed in a blind, drunken rage. "Come out, Sheridan
See what you've bought for all your troubles!"

"Stop this! I beg—" she cried as the bronze doors slowly
opened. In the driving rain it was hard to make out the
figure, but the man appeared to be elderly and dressed in
butler's attire.

He gave her drunk uncle a glance that should have sent
him scurrying back to the rathole from which he came
"Yes, *sir*?" the butler seemed to say, though Alana found it
difficult to hear him with the rain pounding the pavement
all around her.

"Sheridan! Sheridan! You tell him I want my money
back! I want it all back!" her uncle screamed.

"And the young lady?" the butler asked.

Didier faced her, and Alana gave him such a look of
loathing, she knew she would never hate anyone as she
hated Didier at that moment.

"The girl is Sheridan's problem! He's left me no money
to take care of her now!" Didier grasped the aged man by
the lapels. "By God, you tell Sheridan he's going to pay for
all the misery he's caused me! I'll go to my grave before I'll
let him off the hook!"

"Remove your hands at once," the butler appeared to
say.

Alana let out a muffled sob, and Didier shot her a venge
ful glance. But with no other course left to him, he released
the butler and stumbled back, skidding on the slick wet
marble.

As much as Alana resisted, she couldn't stop herself from
pleading, "Please don't leave me like this!" But the word

were as useless as she had feared. Didier staggered through the porte cochere and disappeared into a hack he hailed from the avenue.

In desperation, she hung her head and gave vent to her tears, bitterly noting that the rain washed them from her cheeks as fast as they spilled from her burning eyes.

"Miss?"

She looked up and found the elderly butler out in the rain futilely holding a large black umbrella over her soaked figure while he tried one-handed to untie her. It was then she had the misfortune to look toward the open bronze doors.

In the years to come she would always remember her first sight of Trevor Byrne Sheridan. He stood in silhouette. She was not privy to the details of his face, but he left a deep and lasting impression on her. He held a walking stick, an unusual accouterment for such a tall, muscular form. His straight, formal figure was pleasing, yet his stance left her feeling as if a frigid wind had just passed through her heart. He crossed his arms and tipped his head back to look down at her as she almost knelt on the wet marble stairway, and in the shadows he looked every bit as cold, dark, and forbidding as the night that mercilessly pelted her with rain. And she knew then, with a truth that pierced her very soul, that the devil before her now was sure to be worse than the one who had just left her behind.

5

Alana repressed a shiver by sheer will. She was freezing, but she did her best to hide it by crossing her arms over her chest and taking long controlled breaths. Her gown was dripping wet, and the blackguard who sat silently behind his huge overly carved library desk didn't even offer her a wrap.

She stared at Sheridan, anger, humiliation, and determination burning within her. Her uncle's actions had cut her to the quick. What was worse, the Irishman knew it. Shuddering, she remembered how he'd looked at her when his butler had led her into an awe-inspiring marble foyer. The expression on his face was unforgettable, an odd marriage of pity and satisfaction. It was obvious that he saw her as a hated Knickerbocker and found great amusement in her downfall. But the pity was far harder to take. When his gaze had lowered to her wrists, red and scraped from the bindings, she wanted to run from him in shame.

Yet now, sitting in the Irishman's library, she swore to endure. Though she held herself together with the thinnest shred of dignity, she kept Christabel in the forefront of her thoughts to strengthen her. She had to save her sister—with as great a need as his when he had sought revenge for Mara. That above all else, she reminded herself, was important.

But the Irishman was a more than worthy opponent.

With his piercing dark stare and cold manner, he inspired a fear in her that her uncle never had. She believed she knew how far Didier would go to achieve what he wanted, yet of this ominous man sitting in front of her she knew nothing. She was at his mercy, and her future and her sister's rested upon his whim, doom or salvation awaiting them as Trevor Sheridan chose.

Alana watched him shuffle papers on his desk, her shame enormous. Ever since Sheridan had led her to his library, she'd forced herself to put up her Knickerbocker facade, if only to retrieve some of her pride. Now she sat mutely across from his desk, thinking with shattering clarity about what her uncle had done to her. If she'd come to the conclusion that her uncle was a devil, then the dark, emotionless man in front of her was Satan incarnate. Her uncle had proven himself to be so lacking in character that he was unworthy of cleaning the Van Alen chamberpots. But in truth, the Irishman Trevor Sheridan was the real source of all her trouble. Her uncle had thrown in his share of the kindling. She would never forgive him. But she couldn't escape the fact that it was the Irishman who had sparked the fire in the first place.

While she churned with these thoughts, she leveled a cool green stare at Sheridan. She knew she must appear an ice princess on the outside, yet on the inside, when she thought about being tied to this man's banister like a runaway slave before the war, she burned with humiliation.

She looked across the desk. The man's attitude toward her bedraggled presence seemed as cold and professional as if he were dealing with one of his bankers. She watched him, and her anger produced another silent thorn. She wondered how the man could be so emotionless and calculating. He'd taken all her money and now didn't even possess the grace to offer her a shawl.

She studied him more closely. Her host, if that was what this devil could be called, was finely attired in black trousers and a burgundy silk paisley waistcoat. Her unexpected appearance had caught him unawares because his shirt was missing its starched collar, and the stud was gone at the throat, revealing a mass of dark chest hair. His head was bent as he perused a document on his desk, and the flames from the gas lamp lit the planes of his profile. He was a handsome man. His hair was cropped, and she thought the color was black, yet it was difficult to tell in the dim gaslight. He wasn't looking at her now, but from the first time their gazes had met, she had known that particular dark-hazel color of his eyes could only be from his native Erin.

An uncontrollable shiver caught her, and she wrapped her palms around her upper arms in a futile attempt to warm herself. This seemed finally to gain his attention. He looked up from the paper he was reading, and his gaze ran down her soaked Worth gown, taking particular note of the way the sodden peach flowers wilted at her décolletage and the defeated way she grasped her limp *ciel*-blue satin train. All at once the silence became deafening.

"Miss Van Alen?" he asked rhetorically, shattering the library's tomb-like quiet.

She didn't answer, giving him a frosty leaf-green glance that belied the blush of shame pinkening her cheeks.

As if expecting her to be difficult, he checked the paper before him and began to recite from it, his pronunciation almost artificial in its exactness. "You are Miss Alice Diana Van Alen, of Thirty-eight Washington Square. You are considered to be one of the foremost treasures of the city of New York. Your family has had a box at the Academy of Music from the beginning of time, even before the illustrious Caroline Schermerhorn got her clutches on old Backhouse. Your ancestors were shareholders in the Dutch West India Company, and you can trace your family all the way to the Schuylers, the Philipses, the Van Rensselaers—even Peter Stuyvesant." He looked up. "Have I the right woman, then? Am I correct?"

Alana felt the sudden heat of anger. Instead of shivering, she boiled. The man looked at her as if she were some kind of dead poet whose meaningless life could be summed up in a paragraph.

"No, you are not correct, Mr. Sheridan," she said in a tone that could cause frostbite. "He signed his name *Petrus*. I am related to *Petrus* Stuyvesant."

"Of course. My mistake." Their eyes met for a moment, and as if to taunt her, he took the paper from which he'd read her biography and made a display out of changing *Peter* to *Petrus*.

She stood and leaned over the great rosewood desk separating them. With a boldness she could hardly eke from her chilled, trembling body, she reached out and crumpled the paper. When she straightened, she dared him to complain.

He looked almost surprised. One eyebrow lifted, and the first glimmer of interest sparked in those dark hazel eyes.

"Mr. Sheridan, we obviously have no need for an introduction," she said now that she had his full attention.

"That's true," he agreed with a dark little smile. "I've known who you are for some time. And now I expect you know who I am."

She didn't know why his words threatened her, but they did. She groped for the words that would extricate her from this mess. "In any case, I must tell you you've done a terrible thing here—"

"*I've* done a terrible thing?" he interrupted, incredulous. He chuckled, and if she hadn't been so desperate, she would have picked up her train and left in a huff. "Let me tell you, Miss Knickerbocker, I've never hitched a woman to the front of a townhouse like she was a Broadway horsecar."

Too embarrassed to begin to address her uncle's hellacious behavior, she blurted out, "You've taken away the Van Alen money unjustly, Mr. Sheridan. And I wish to make you understand that. I must have my money returned."

A grim smile lifted the corner of his mouth. "Your uncle has controlled your money for several years now. You dare beg for that . . . *man?*" he said as if he were having a difficult time characterizing Didier as a man.

"How do you know so much about me?" she asked in a small voice.

"Shouldn't I know you? You're society, after all. And isn't that the point of that little clique—to be exalted by the masses?" He almost laughed, "Well, madam, you should consider yourself honored. You've personally felt the fervor of my exaltation."

"I meant you no harm," she said passionately. "And in truth, I did you no harm, so I would like the money you took from me. I must have it."

"What do you mean you did me no harm?" He sat back as coolly as if he were discussing the day's trading.

She put both hands on his desk and leaned forward. "I mean that I would have attended your sister's debut but was restrained from doing so. Therefore, you must return my money. You've made a tragic error."

He laughed, a shockingly joyless sound. "Do you know how many times in the past weeks I've heard that, Miss Van Alen? My God, I'd need an accountant to keep track of all the excuses."

"But in my case it's the truth," she said, sure she could make him believe her.

He only laughed harder. "There must be a mockingbird in this room. Doesn't the Manhattan aristocracy have any originality at all?"

"But I truly meant to attend," she answered, panic rising in her breast because he didn't believe her. "I *wanted* to attend."

A sardonic smile played on his lips. "Ah, finally something new. Congratulations, Miss Van Alen, you're the first one who's said *that.*"

She shook her head, desperate that he believe her. "I met your sister Mara in the park several months ago. She'll tell you I wanted to attend. I believe she liked me every bit as much as I did her."

He lifted another paper from his desk, a long list of names, and he paused. "These are all the people my sister thought liked her. Do you know how many of them attended her debut?"

Sickened by what the answer might be, Alana said nothing.

Without a word, he rose and walked stiffly to the fireplace. He tossed the list into the fire, and as it burned, she saw his knuckles whiten over the gold top of his walking stick that he never seemed to relinquish.

Their eyes met, and she could hardly look at him for the fury in his gaze. "I know none of them came," she whispered, her heart aching for some inexplicable reason. Suddenly she was as desperate to soothe Mara's ills as her own. "But perhaps those people on that list are not worth all this trouble, Mr. Sheridan. Have you thought of that? And does Mara want you to do all of this? Cause all this trouble? I think not. So I wonder whether you're doing this for Mara . . . or for yourself."

"I don't give a damn about people like you, Miss Van Alen. I never have." He eyed her coldly. The walking stick tapped a muffled staccato on the thick carpeting as he left the fire. "But you cannot convince a sixteen-year-old girl that people like you are meaningless. You and your cronies are gods to my little sister, who's too young and naive to know better. So for now, if she wants you, I'll truss up the lot of you and serve you upon a platter if I have to to make her happy."

She sank to the chair, pulling aside her damp bustle. A tiredness seeped into her limbs, and for a moment she wearily lowered her head.

He watched her, a gleam of triumph lighting his eyes. "Are we through? May I send my carriage around to take you to your home, Miss Van Alen?"

His voice had a finality about it that sparked one last flame within her. She raised her head, and anger gave her the strength to continue. "No, we're not through." She got to her feet and faced him, this time without the safety of the desk between them. "I must make you understand, Mr. Sheridan, how important it is that you make reparation in my case. You've wrongly taken my money, money that I need quite desperately." She hoped she was being strong enough. To make her point, she tipped her head back to look him in the eye, now realizing how short she was compared to his great height. She was shocked at how he intimidated her.

"You're not the only Knickerbocker in straitened circumstances," he answered easily. "Why should I help you?"

She opened her mouth to say "Because of my sister" but stopped herself. Instead she stared imploringly into his eyes. "I have to have it. Others depend on that money. Others not so fortunate as you, or even I."

"Mr. Baldwin Didier?" He stepped to his desk and picked up another paper. "Ah yes, that's the name of that gentleman who was so kind as to leave you on my stoop. Is he not so fortunate as we? I must tell you, I wouldn't have guessed that, especially when he left you in the rain tied to my banister."

His words appalled her. She began shaking again, and something terrible inside her burned when she thought how Didier had humiliated her. But her uncle wasn't the only one responsible for her downfall.

She met Sheridan's amused eyes. "I must have my money, Mr. Sheridan. It was unfair of you to take it from me, and I promise you I won't leave here until I convince you to return it."

"Well, I'm sorry, Miss Van Alen, of the *Petrus* Stuyvesants and Thirty-eight Washington Square, you'll have to do better than that to convince me." He leaned on the baroque edge of his desk.

She felt as if she were falling into a great vat of oil, that if she didn't grab something quickly, she and her sister would drown in it. Impulsively she reached out and grasped the satin lapels of his waistcoat. "See here, Mr. Sheridan," she gasped, "I'm sorry for Mara. Truly, heart-wrenchingly sorry! But my God! What is it that's made you perform this act of insanity? We all have those we care about! We can't ruin everyone who might have slighted them!"

Anger hardened his expression. He looked away and said, "For some uncharacteristically foolish reason, my sister believes your set worthy of her company." He turned back to her, and the vengeance in his expression took her breath away. "Mara is a beautiful, warm, and caring young lady. The Knickerbockers will accept her, or I'll use my last gold coin and my last dying breath to see that they do."

Alana was left almost speechless. Sheridan's ferociousness to protect his sister stunned her. If she weren't careful, Alana knew, she'd be lucky to retreat from this man unscathed.

Calming herself, she changed tack. Softly she said, "Both of us would benefit greatly if we could change the situation. You must see that, Mr. Sheridan. Yet the fact is the Knickerbockers don't like you, and whether the reasons for that are right or wrong, we both have to live with them." Despite herself, she began to plead, "So I beg of you—listen to reasoning. You've wrongly taken my fortune, and I must have it back. I must!"

He looked down at her small hands grasping his lapels. That one glance made her want to tear her hands away in fear. She saw something then that she'd never seen in the men in her set. There was an earthiness about this man, perhaps because he'd been spawned from the gutter, but that earthiness didn't translate into the image of gentle, pastoral nature. When Sheridan looked at her as he was looking at her now, she thought of a lion raging bloody fights for territory or subduing lionesses in the primeval need to procreate. This Irishman personified nature in all its dark, magnificent fury, and she knew she'd never come up against such a force before. When he covered her trembling hands with his large ones and stared down at her, a taunting quirk to his lips, it was all she could do not to turn and run.

"You feel like ice."

"Let me go," she whispered, unable to meet his eyes.

He refused. Instead he looked down at her wet gown, appearing to take great interest in the way the satin draped across her shoulders. It sent a fiery tingle down her spine. She'd never been perused like this before, as if the man were trying to see her without her clothes, trying to see deep inside her—no doubt all the way to where he thought her barren little heart lay.

Her reaction, though she tried to hide it, obviously pleased him. A small dark smile touched his lips, and he said, "Your dress is quite beautiful, Miss Van Alen. I must compliment you on the color. It's the exact color of your skin. You hardly look clothed at all. . . ."

She blushed all the way to the tips of her toes. If her mission with this man hadn't been so serious, she might have slapped his face for such a familiarity. "My dress is not the subject of this discussion."

"Of course. We were discussing your fortune . . . or lack thereof." He forced her gaze to meet his. "But first tell me—do all you hoity-toity hyphenated New-Yorkers behave in such a ludicrous manner? Demand reparation in drenched Worth gowns? Leave your relatives on strangers' doorsteps? Interesting behavior for society folk."

Embarrassment rose again to color her cheeks. She gave him a censorious look. "My uncle is a vile man, Mr. Sheridan, and you lower yourself when you taunt me with his wretched behavior." She stared at him, and her mouth went dry. His hands were like fire around hers, and she wondered if that was because she was so cold or he so scorchingly hot.

"Tell me why he did what he did."

His touch affected her so much, she could barely whisper. "He was drunk. Your ruining us made him go crazy. He thought if I were humiliated, he might gain some kind of revenge."

"And was this revenge also?" He released her, and one warm finger trailed down the soft inside of her arm.

She looked down and saw the bruises Didier had left there. She covered them with one hand, unwittingly showing him the bruises on her other arm. "Please, Mr. Sheridan," she began quietly, her insides dying with shame.

He ignored her and touched her cheek, the one Didier had bruised the night of the Sheridan ball. The powder she had used to cover it must have washed off in the rain, and she cringed at what a sight she must present to this man. While his touch was gentle, she couldn't bear to feel it. He was only pointing out another facet of her degradation.

She pulled away his hand and said, "I must ask you to return my money. I'll leave your home and never bother you again. It's not an enormous sum."

"I know it isn't, Alana."

She wondered how he knew they called her Alana, but he already knew so much about her, she didn't bother asking him. With defeat settling around her shoulders like black laurels, she made one last humiliating confession. "My uncle is my curse, Mr. Sheridan. So you see, your revenge lacks the sting it might have had. What was done to me tonight is punishment enough. You needn't add to it. Return my money, I beg of you. I must have it."

"If I do, it'll be as if I'd given it back to your uncle."

"But even so, my uncle still pays for Chris—" She stopped herself.

His curiosity obviously piqued, he said, "Pays for what?"

She pulled back, but he gripped her hands anew. Still, she wasn't going to tell him about Christabel. And as quiet as they'd kept things, she knew her sister wasn't in that little biography he'd been reading. "Cease this torture, Mr. Sheridan. Tell me what I have to do to get my money back, and I'll do it," she said, shame and fury battling within her.

"My requests would definitely offend you."

He held her gaze. He wasn't smiling. Any other man might have smiled then, even leered. Sheridan looked grave. His coolness scared her. It wasn't that he was unaware of the connotation of his words. On the contrary, his brief heated glance at the flesh pushing over her bodice proved that theory false. Yet he was a master of detachment. His studied nonchalance made her think he was waiting to see which would offend her the most—his "requests" or the fact that they were made by a common Irishman.

"Give me back my money," she whispered, an edge to her voice.

A dangerous glint appeared in his hazel eyes. She didn't know what he was going to do next. She knew only that she was vulnerable to him. They both knew it. She was exhausted, cold, wet, and near despair. He could do anything now, ask anything of her, and if he were crafty enough, probably force her to comply.

She suppressed a shiver and lowered her gaze. She looked down at her skirts and for the first time noticed how the wet peach satin clung to her hips and thighs, outlining her shape. Despite the sculpturing of her undergarments and the layers of artfully draped silk, she looked almost naked.

She raised her face to his, desperation etched into her expression. But just when she expected him to lay his cards on the table and shock her with his demands, he did the most extraordinary thing. He merely touched her arm and glanced again at the bruises on it. Incredibly, he seemed to soften. "Why do you need that money so desperately, Miss Knickerbocker?"

She stared at him, tears glistening in her eyes. How could she tell him? How could she reveal such a terrible, personal thing to this rude, arrogant man? Her lips couldn't form the words.

He released her and walked once more to the fire. He said, "You may go, Miss Van Alen. Forgive me that I don't summon the butler, but at this late hour—"

"Are you not going to return my fortune?"

"Return your fortune?" He smirked. "No, I'm not going to return your fortune. You Knickerbockers owe Mara something for your bad behavior. Now you'll take your punishment and like it."

Her fury exploded. She wanted to hurt him and said the first thing that came to mind. "This won't solve a thing, and do you know why? Because your fate is written in stone, Mr. Sheridan. No one has ever changed Mrs. Astor's mind about who the Four Hundred should be. And your filthy manipulations will never make her!"

He grabbed her so abruptly, her teeth shook. "Nor my filthy money. Isn't that what you think?"

"Yes," she hissed.

"And if I want acceptance, then I'd better damned well go back to the Irish shanty from whence I came—is that right, Miss Knickerbocker?"

She couldn't answer him for the sob that was rising in her throat. She loathed contention, yet this man could bring out the very worst in her.

Disgusted, he pushed her away. "I'll get Mara into that little society of yours, I swear upon my grave I will!"

"You will never convince Mrs. Astor! Their rules may seem cruel, but they're ironclad. You have to be born into that set. Don't you understand that?" She was no longer taunting him. She was trying to reason with him. She could see the anguish the Knickerbockers had caused, but Sheridan's pain seemed better ended by giving him the brutal, heartless facts, no matter how unacceptable they might be to either of them.

Yet it seemed to make him only more implacable. "There are other ways, and I'll find them."

"There are no other ways. By marriage or by birth. That's it!"

He looked as if he might go mad. The truth of her words seemed to frustrate him beyond endurance, and she realized that he had rarely been confronted by such a problem as this—one for which money was no cure.

There was a brief second when he seemed almost ready to let her go, perhaps even to return her funds. He didn't look defeated. In fact, after meeting Trevor Sheridan, Alana couldn't imagine defeat ever crossing those stern features. Yet he was at an impasse. The enormous power his wealth lent him wasn't going to move the obstacle; there was nothing he could do about the Sheridan birthright. He and his family were outcasts in society, and as much as this might be unpalatable, it was also an indisputable fact that he had to know no one could correct.

A log tumbled in the fire. A shower of brilliant orange sparks danced up the chimney, and the flames were resurrected, given one last breath before their final death. She caught herself staring longingly at the hearth, again reminded how weary she was and how cold and damp her clothes were. She must have been looking for a while, for suddenly she realized the room had become ominously quiet. Even the fire had ceased to crackle, surrendering its life with a low hiss.

A tremor went through her. Without glancing at him, she knew he was staring at her, knew it as well as she knew her heart was beating, though she could not see that either. With a reluctance born of fear, she slowly forced her gaze up to meet his.

There was a most astonishing gleam in those dark hazel eyes. An idea was forming in this man's mind, and she knew it was trouble. Sheridan, with his genius for manipulation and revenge, was almost an unconquerable foe. As he watched her like a starved lion viewing his feast, a feast he'd never seen the possibility of or the necessity for, she knew without a doubt that all her problems had just multiplied.

" 'By birth or by marriage' did you say?" he asked, his eyes narrowing.

"If—if you think I might find a husband for Mara, I wouldn't know how," she stuttered, backing away from

him. That had to be what he wanted—Mara's marriage to a
Knickerbocker. Still, she didn't like that glint in his eye by
half.

"Mara must only marry for love."

"If you care for her, that's the only way." She stared at
him. Why didn't his answer ease this overwhelming, inexplicable panic?

"But *I* don't have to."

She swallowed, her throat suddenly dry. "You don't have
to what?"

"If I had a Knickerbocker wife, Caroline Astor would be
forced to accept Mara."

All the blood drained from her face. She shook herself,
unable to believe where his thoughts were going. "You
must be joking. You aren't possibly thinking of asking *me* to
marry you?"

He paused and with a wry twist to his lips said, "I've no
thoughts of *asking* you at all."

She should have been relieved, but with that dark penetrating stare not wavering from her face, she could hardly
think to take her next breath. "What are you planning,
then?"

"Perhaps a wedding . . ." Pensively he walked to his
desk. He smoothed out the crumpled paper that held her
biography and read it over again.

"Whose wedding?" she asked, desperately trying to hide
the anxiety in her voice.

"Alice Diana Van Alen . . . one of the treasures of New
York . . . of Washington Square and *Petrus* Stuyve-
sant . . ." He finished the biography and glanced up.
Their gazes locked.

"My God, what are you saying?" she finally whispered,
her very soul crying out in horror.

"I think I need a Knickerbocker wife. I think that's the
answer to this perplexing problem."

Her heart skipped several beats. She couldn't reconcile

herself to what he was implying. Finally she asked what she knew she must. "So you *are* asking me to marry you?"

"Not *asking.*"

She stared at him, unable to accept that he might abuse his power this way. Her shock was so great, she could barely choke out the words. "You're—you're *telling* me to marry you?"

"Are you in the position to say no?" He almost laughed when his gaze raked down her sodden, ruined dress.

She turned from him, unable even to think. Every part of her seemed to have gone numb. This was like living a nightmare. The picture-perfect ending to a hellish night. She didn't want to ponder how far he might take this crazy idea because if her experience was any indication, the answer was as far as he wanted to go. Trevor Byrne Sheridan didn't retreat. That thought alone made her want to faint, to succumb to blessed darkness.

"Surely you're not serious," she whispered, horrified.

"No?" He picked up her crumpled biography and studied it with rapt attention.

"You can't be," was the answer she clung to. This was madness. Utterly untenable, even from his point of view. After all, he was surely a papist, and she was most definitely not.

He met her stare again. "This could be the best business decision I've ever made. I understand your uncle Baldwin Didier got rich off your connections, even if he did lose it all in the end."

She angered. When would someone look at her and see something other than a way to make himself richer? "Marriage is not a business decision," she stated frostily.

He almost laughed. "I beg to differ, Miss Knickerbocker. In your crowd, it's all business, right down to the pedigree."

She was growing hysterical. If this man was becoming set on this insanity, she could see a long and difficult fight ahead, one she desperately wanted to avoid. "I was taught to believe marriage involves people and their emotions, not money and a ticker tape."

"Must it?"

His question left her astonished. She finally found her tongue and spoke slowly, as if that would make him understand. "Marriage is for a lifetime. There are things involved in marriage that cannot be compared to business—"

"Such as?" He cocked one eyebrow, and for the briefest of seconds she could see the little hustler he must have been when he was a boy, the little hustler that had made him the enormously wealthy man he was today.

She groped for an answer. Finding one, she held on to it like a lifebuoy. "Children," she gasped. "They're a consequence of marriage and cannot be treated like a business."

He walked over to her and ran his finger beneath her chin, his touch raising her anxiety to dizzying heights. "I can see to it we won't have any children."

She closed her eyes and tried to calm herself. It was useless. "This has got to be some terrible joke. You cannot be serious. We don't love each other. We don't even know each other."

He smiled darkly. "Think about it, Alana. The irony is priceless. You're the purest of Knickerbocker bloods. It's only fitting that you should be the sacrifice for what was done to Mara."

"But I wanted to attend her debut, I tell you! My uncle locked me in my bedroom!"

His answer was a disbelieving smirk, and he put a quick death to that topic when he said, "You know, the more I think about it, the more this arrangement suits me."

"Marriage is not an 'arrangement'!"

"Ours will be."

"But it only suits you! What about me? I don't want to marry you!"

"You don't want to marry a mick, is that what you're thinking?"

The bitterness in his voice threw her. Cautiously she

shook her head. "It doesn't matter that you're Irish, Mr. Sheridan. I won't marry any man I don't love."

"Can you afford the luxury of refusing me? Where's that desperate woman who needed her pitiful fortune returned?"

"Why would you want to do this? Is getting Mara a place in society so important to you that you're willing to sacrifice so much for it?"

He gazed at her in her damp, clinging, peach-colored gown, and that lion in him didn't even attempt to hide the base desire for what he saw. His words came slow and easy. "Where's the sacrifice?"

For the first time she knew his guard had slipped. She heard the brogue in his words, the softest of sounds, not entirely unpleasant. Instead of saying "Where's the sacrifice?" he'd said "Whare's the sacrifice," rolling in an extra *r*. She didn't want to think about the reason for his slip, but while he stared at her in all her ruined finery, there was no hiding from the lust burning in his eyes. She threw her arms across her chest and backed away like a frightened kitten.

"You don't like some Irisher looking at you that way, do you, Miss Knickerbocker," he said, tormenting her.

All the years of training to play society belle came back to her. She painted on her most frigid facade and gave him a stare that told him exactly what she thought about his looking at her that way, and it had nothing to do with his being Irish. "I'm not about to be bought and sold this way, no matter how terrible my circumstances," she retorted, angry at him for treating her like some kind of expensive whore and angry at herself for weakening toward him when he used that seductive brogue.

"Think about why you need your money back. Will that convince you?"

"No!" she burst out. Then her thoughts turned to Christabel. But she couldn't completely martyr herself for her sister, no matter how much she loved her. Yet when she pictured her sister sitting in the filth of Bloomingdale Asylum, where she'd have to go when the money ran out, it nearly drove her insane. "No—" she choked, wanting to fight him.

"Then you can go back to your uncle, penniless as before."

"Why must you do this? It's madness. Find a more willing girl. You could marry anyone!"

"If we Sheridans could marry anyone, we wouldn't be in this fix, now would we?"

She met his glance and couldn't stop herself from surrendering a small moan. "What if I can't help you? You will have married a stranger for no reason."

"You can help. I bet Mara will be married within a year if you guide her." His stare never wavered.

She turned away. There was no possibility that she could go through with this crazy idea. She couldn't marry this stranger and throw away all her future happiness. Sheridan wasn't the man for her, the man in her dreams, the one who lived in that simple white house she could never quite reach.

"I'll give you an annulment as soon as Mara is happily married. And of course I'll see to it that you'll never want for anything again," he promised softly.

In some ways his offer was the worst thing that had ever happened to her; in others, it was the best. She couldn't picture herself married to this enigmatic stranger standing before her, but the appeal of his money and the worry that would be off her mind because of it was almost too sweet to resist.

Yet resist it she must. It was a terrible idea, necessitating things she couldn't even foresee now. He spoke of an annulment, but what if that wasn't possible? She knew a consummated marriage could not be dissolved that cleanly. She looked at him, and the thought of consummating their marriage made her blanch. What if their separation required a divorce? She couldn't live out the rest of her life as a divorced woman. The shame it would bring to her family name would be beyond bearing.

No, she could not marry this stranger. Even though it would remove her from Didier, and allow her to take care of Christabel as long as Christabel needed it, she couldn't do it.

"This won't work. Don't you see? I can't make Mara fall in love with a Knickerbocker," she whispered.

"You won't have to. I want Mara to be happy, and I'd rather she see your peers for the shallow persons they are. I believe in my sister. She'll fall in love with a good man, be he a Knickerbocker or not."

She couldn't hide her bitterness. Facetiously she asked, "But what if she gives up on you and this entire mess and retires to a nunnery? What then, Mr. Sheridan? Shall we be stuck with each other for all eternity?"

He smiled, displaying even white teeth that hinted at carnivorous appetites. "That's up to you, Miss Van Alen. Put my sister on the right path, and you'll have your freedom quicker than you can blink."

She grasped one last straw, desperate for anything that would get her out of this man's clutches. "My uncle is my trustee. He must approve my marriage—it's stipulated in my parents' will. He won't be convinced of this crazy plan. He hates you."

Sheridan laughed. "After what he did to you tonight, Miss Van Alen, I've no doubt he'll sell you. And the best part of it is, I'll wager he takes my very first offer. Now what do you say to that?"

She stared at him, her face pale and disbelieving.

She didn't say a word.

6

The next few hours were almost as bad as the previous ones. The more time Sheridan had to think about the marriage, the more he seemed to embrace the idea. Alana did her best to reason with him, but he could not be moved to change his mind. For some strange reason at which Alana could only guess, his sister Mara took precedence over both their needs. Sheridan was determined to right the wrong done to her, no matter the cost.

Alana's frustrations mounted the more she pushed against Sheridan's implacable will. Her choices were to fight or run away, but neither seemed viable. She was no match for this iron-willed Irishman, and where could she run in the middle of the night, soaking wet and without a penny to her name? Not to Washington Square, for even to walk back to her home would mean risking her life. New York had never been a safe city. There had always been the poor and the desperate, and even in her posh neighborhood it didn't take long to walk from the Bowery. And she wouldn't turn to Didier. After what he had done to her, she swore on her grave she would never have anything to do with him again—even if that meant she must marry the Irishman.

The seriousness of her situation began to sink in. She was sadly lacking in alternatives. Her only consolation was that she had time, and she prayed that Sheridan would eventually see the folly in his plan. And if that didn't happen, she prayed she would find a way out before he dragged her off to a Roman church.

Not long after she and Sheridan had reached their impasse, the butler entered and led her out of the library like the doomed to the gallows. She thought she'd be shown to a waiting carriage and be driven back to Washington Square. Instead the austere butler brought her to an upstairs chamber that could have served Marie Antoinette—if the cherubs painted on the ceiling and the rose velvet upholstery were any indication. She was obviously expected to relax there, an impossibility considering her situation. Yet as desperate as she was, cold and weary, she could hardly think of anything except how wonderful it would be to be warm again.

But to her astonishment an army of maidservants arrived in the rooms, ready to attend to her toilet, and Alana found herself rebelling again. An elderly woman who introduced herself as the housekeeper tried to take her into the satin-draped dressing room where a French porcelain tub was filled with steaming rose-scented water, but Alana adamantly refused it. She was neither mistress nor guest in this household. It would be difficult enough borrowing one of Sheridan's blankets to place over her shoulders; she was definitely not going to let down her guard enough to bathe, not in this man's house.

In the end, however, she capitulated. Not because she trusted Sheridan and not because her desire to fight him had been tempered but because upon her refusal of help, the flock of maids just stood there adrift without new orders, looking at her in her torn and dirtied peach satin gown as if she were some pitiable street urchin. Disgusted with herself and the entire situation, Alana finally removed her ruined gown and sank into the tub, her pride stifling an unwilling sigh of pleasure. She had surrendered, but only for the moment, she told herself. When she had regained her strength, she would fight again.

She was given a girl's pink wool robe that had to be Mara Sheridan's, for it was a shade too small. Alana put it on, waiting for the return of her dress that she assumed had been taken to the laundress.

Once her hair was coiled in a chignon at her nape, she perched uncomfortably on a gilt fancy chair, making every effort to avoid the room's enormous rococo mirrors. Their reflection didn't lie, and every time she peeked into one, she saw an overwrought girl with a pale face and a slightly bruised cheek. She didn't even have face powder to hide behind.

Exhausted, she battled the urge to sleep and pondered her situation until she felt she would go mad from a lack of ideas. But there was nothing she could do until her gown was returned, so she waited, fighting off unconsciousness like a boxer who'd received a knock-out. She was nodding off for the third time when the elderly housekeeper addressed her again. "Would you like to retire, miss, or should you like me to send the girl for your breakfast?" The woman clasped her hands, obviously anxious to please.

Alana sat up straight and looked at the woman. What was going on? The servants were acting as if she'd just moved in. She answered cautiously, "Please don't trouble yourself further. I know you must have other duties to attend to."

"I've been given specific orders to see to your needs first. Mr. Sheridan himself gave the orders to me."

Alana was completely taken aback. Collecting herself, she said, "May I have my gown now? I must speak to Mr. Sheridan before I depart."

"I'm sorry, miss, but Mr. Sheridan's unavailable. He's making arrangements for the wedding."

Alana felt as if she'd been struck. "The wedding?" she repeated, incredulous. "So soon?"

"He's gone to see your uncle."

A wild surge of panic raced through her. Sheridan's scheming was not to be underestimated, and already he was going forth at full throttle. Facing that fact, a wild desire to fight him overcame her, but the same rhetorical question kept reverberating through her mind: What could she do?

Alana closed her eyes, wishing fervently that she could just give in to the desire to sleep and then awake to find she had had a nightmare. Her thoughts darkened even further and turned to Sheridan. What was he saying to Didier? Was he exchanging bank notes, buying her as if she were some stock on the exchange? Was he gloating over this latest coup, or was he waiting to see her again to gloat? Moaning, she knew only one thing. If she didn't find a way to extricate herself from this mess in a hurry, she just might awake to find herself married to the man.

Morning broke over Washington Square in a bath of orange sunshine. It tinted the naked trees in the park and glittered off the oily street stones until they appeared like jet. The hurdy-gurdy man was already about, calling out in a strong Italian bass while an old gnome-like woman swept the curbs, singing a blasphemous rendition of "Amazing Grace."

The cacophony of the city had begun again, made complete with the clatter of the wheels of an expensive black landau as it stopped at number 38.

Sheridan stepped from it, his eyes narrowing in the intense sunlight. He viewed the prepossessing brownstone with a jaundiced gaze and wasted no more time. His walking stick clicked on the steps, and he rang the bell.

A butler answered the door, obviously surprised by Sheridan's early call, even more so by the Irishman's dark, commanding stature.

"I'm here to see Didier. Tell him to meet me"—Sheridan entered the foyer, surveyed his surroundings, and pointed his walking stick toward the parlor—"in there."

Pumphrey had never been so abused. Or so intimidated. He cleared his throat and said, "I'm sorry, sir, but this is the Van Alen residence. If you desire to see Miss Van Alen's uncle, he has rooms at—"

"I know where his rooms are," Sheridan snapped. "And I also know he's here—taking inventory, no doubt, while the mistress of this house isn't around to stop him." He nodded again to the parlor. "You tell him to meet me in there. Right away."

Pumphrey appeared as if he wanted to object once more, but he took one long look at the Irishman's thunderous expression and thought better of it. He quit the room, anxious to be gone.

Alone, Sheridan stepped into the Van Alen parlor and glanced around. The room was handsome, the furniture expensive. Still the decor bowed to the dictates of proper society. Nothing was *too* new. The Knickerbockers considered newness the height of vulgarity. Even their daughters were taught to place their costly Worth gowns in the attic for a season or two, as if to cure them of their immediate stylishness.

With a mild disgust marring his handsome features, Sheridan sat on the rosewood settee and waited. He didn't have to wait long. Didier soon appeared at the faux-walnut doors, hungover and ill at ease. When he set his gaze upon Sheridan, it was as if all of last night's activities had suddenly came back to his memory. Didier fastened his shirt collar, looking like he'd just been dragged from bed. He smoothed down his Van Dyke and finally summoned the courage to say something. "Where's Alana?"

"Why do you ask?" Sheridan stared at him.

"She's my goddamned niece, that's why. I want to know where she is."

"Your concern is impressive, Didier. I see this will cost me more."

Didier looked like a cur who had suddenly discovered a rat in his doghouse. "What does that mean?"

"Exactly what I said. I'm here to pay you. I want to purchase your good blessings. Your niece and I plan to marry."

If he'd just been told the Commodore had died and he had inherited all the Vanderbilt millions, Didier couldn't have been more surprised. His notorious blue eyes nearly popped from their sockets. "What did you say?"

Sheridan studied his well-groomed nails. "Your niece, whom you so graciously introduced to me last night, and I have decided we want to be wed. We'll need your blessing."

The first gleam of wariness shadowed Didier's gaze. "What are you up to, Sheridan?"

"I want an entree into society, and Alana, as my wife, will do that for me. She and I will be wed next Saturday." Sheridan turned his dark hazel eyes upon Didier and looked as if he were using every ounce of strength to control himself. "That is . . . with your permission, of course."

"You're tricking me, aren't you, Sheridan," Didier countered. "But your trickery's not working, because I haven't anything left after that last bout. The Van Alen money's been depleted. I don't have a penny."

"Who knows that better than I?" Sheridan lifted one eyebrow and laughed.

If Didier had been a brawler, he'd have punched him.

Sheridan returned to the subject. "In any case, I'm not playing around. I want to marry your niece. And I'll need your blessing to do it."

Didier stroked his beard down one side with his knuckles, the other with his palm. He stared at Sheridan, unsure.

"Are you going to give it to us or not?"

"Permission to marry? Not without a damned heavenly settlement." Didier appeared smug, obviously thinking he'd cornered the Irishman into revealing his scheme.

But Sheridan was ready for him. "Splendid," he said. "I'm glad we're down to business." He pulled out a gleaming black leather portfolio and thumbed through the bank notes in it. "How much, then?"

Didier swallowed, his bleary eyes unable to tear away from Sheridan's portfolio.

"How much, boy-o?"

Sheridan's slang did the trick. Didier's angry gaze met the Irishman's. "One hundred thousand dollars."

"That much?" Sheridan asked, unmoved.

"That'll teach you that I won't be insulted by some shoddy. Not in my own house."

Sheridan stood and angrily grasped his walking stick. But he composed himself before he spoke again. "I'll give you fifty thousand. Not a penny more. And I suggest you take it. If you don't, Caroline Astor will hear where your niece spent all of last night. She won't be worth fifty thousand then, I wager."

Didier paled.

"Is it fifty thousand or not?"

He gave Sheridan a contemptuous stare. "Still trying to buy your way into that crowd, aren't you, Irisher."

Sheridan's face became taut with anger, but he calmly dangled the portfolio in front of him. "Is it fifty thousand, or do I go elsewhere—to a lawyer perhaps? I think he might find ways around the stipulations in that will."

Didier's expression boiled, but he held himself back. He stared at the portfolio and finally succumbed to his need for money. Obviously despising the Irishman, he nodded for Sheridan to hand it to him.

Sheridan dropped it at his feet. "Twenty-five thousand now," he informed him. "The rest when the wedding is over."

Didier looked as if he were having apoplexy. With obvious relish, he said, "I think I should have more money if I have to sacrifice her to a dirty mick like you."

One hand slammed him into the white marble mantelpiece. Sheridan and he came face-to-face. "Listen to me, boy-o," the Irishman quipped. "I shouldn't have to pay dogs like you, but more's the pity, I'm forced to." A murderous gleam sparked in his eyes, and he twisted Didier's collar. "Or am I?" he whispered, making Didier whiten at the suggestion.

"Let me go," he rasped, taking in Sheridan's enraged features. There were a lot of stories about this man, some that he'd been raised on the street, roving with a gang of boys who'd performed all sorts of treachery in their efforts to get by. Knowing this, Didier wasn't about to test Sheridan's fighting skills, especially when the Irishman had pinned him to the mantel without dropping his ever-present walking stick. "I said, let me go," he repeated, his voice becoming shrill.

Sheridan stepped back. He glanced around, as if trying to cool that quick Gaelic temper. "There are conditions to my giving you that money, Didier," he instructed in a monotone. "First, you're to show up at the wedding, and you'd better learn how to play-act because everyone had better believe you bless this union."

Didier nodded reluctantly.

"Second, you're to leave New York after the wedding. I won't have you spreading any vicious rumors that I paid for my bride."

"That's ludicrous! Where will I go?" he protested.

"To the devil if it were up to me." Sheridan gave him another frightening glance, and Didier wiped the defiance off his face.

"The third condition is the most important." Sheridan turned grave and pinned his opponent with his dark stare. Didier, unable to help himself, squirmed. "After Saturday, your niece is to be my wife. And as my wife, I find I'll have the duty to keep her away from harm. That being so, if you come within a mile of her, if you ever raise your hand in anger to her, I will kill you. I will strike you down dead. Have I made myself clear?"

Didier sputtered, giving Sheridan a guilty glance. "Are you saying I've hurt the girl? She's lying, I tell you!"

"Your niece hasn't said a word to me. That's just my policy."

"Christ, you must be out of your mind. You don't even know this girl you're marrying. Why would you make such a statement?"

Sheridan took a moment to stare at the gold lion's head of his walking stick, then quietly, in a soft brogue, he answered, "I saw bruises on your niece last night. After me father died and we came here to New York, I saw bruises like that on me mother. It makes me crazy to see that on a woman. Do you understand? It makes me *crazy*."

Didier licked his lips in fear. "All right."

"Good."

Business finished, Sheridan quit the parlor without the civility of a farewell. Didier scooped up the black portfolio and followed him, counting bank notes. Outside, he finished counting and began to laugh. He feathered the edges of the notes with his thumb, reveling in the sound. Brazenly, he called as the Irishman ascended to his carriage, "The joke's on you, Sheridan! I must tell you, I would have taken a lot less for her!" He hugged the portfolio to him and laughed.

Sheridan only turned and smiled. Before he disappeared into the landau, he said, "On the contrary, Didier. You see . . . I would've paid a lot more."

Leaving Didier dumbstruck, Sheridan knocked on the landau's door. The driver cracked the whip, and the carriage sped away.

7

Alana had never slept in satin sheets before. She hadn't wanted to sleep at all, but she'd felt foolish when the servants had left her and she sat all alone in the huge rose velvet chamber perched on a tiny gilt chair. Unwillingly she'd lain on the bed, thinking that when the laundry maid returned with her dress, she'd depart to seek Sheridan. But now, after she'd obviously slept for many hours, she was even more uneasy with her foreign surroundings, uneasy even with the sensual slippery satin that enveloped her. Something had gone wrong. The light filtering through the ornate rose drapery at the window told her it was late the next day. The maid had never returned with her dress. Or had she come and gone, laying out the gown on some chair?

Alana sat up and pulled together the sides of Mara's robe, which she all too generously filled out. She looked down and still couldn't completely close the deep slit of the robe's bodice. Forgetting her modesty for the moment, she stood and surveyed the room, but there was no peach satin gown anywhere. Distressed, she was just about to search the adjoining dressing room when the chamber's door flew open. Certain it was the laundry maid, Alana looked up expectantly.

The Irishman walked in as if the room were a men's club. Shocked to her core, she scrambled to close her bodice.

he was unsuccessful. Mara's little pink robe wouldn't close. She skittered backward, unsure where to hide. Before he could take two steps, he was in the room, the door closing behind him.

"How dare you come in here when I'm not dressed!" she gasped while he laid his walking stick by the fireplace and nonchalantly seated himself on a velvet settee.

"Your clothes are on their way." His gaze flickered to her, lingered on her state of dishabille, then reluctantly tore itself away. In a quiet voice he said, "I thought you'd be in better spirits after some rest. I can see now I was mistaken."

"What time is it?" she asked, giving him a desperate glance. He was in dinner dress, not a good sign.

"It's almost five o'clock in the evening."

"Good God." She bit her lower lip. She was ruined. She had lain in this man's house and slept while her reputation tumbled to the gutter.

He looked at her. As if against his will, his gaze traveled to that parting of the robe where her bosom was crushed between her crossed arms. "No one knows you're here, Alana. I've made sure of it." He looked away as if she were some kind of temptation he savagely wanted to resist. "One of your gowns—a more appropriate one than the one you wore here—is being sent over. When it arrives, you can go back to Washington Square. I've made it . . . all right for you to return there."

"What do you mean, 'all right'?" She didn't know what he was talking about. Were these crazy wedding plans now a thing of the past?

"I mean that you're free of your uncle. He won't be . . ." Sheridan looked as if he were searching for the right word, "bothering you any longer. He's agreed to leave you alone."

"You paid him, then?" she accused in a trembling voice. "You *paid* him for me? You still believe this wedding is going to happen?"

"It *is* going to happen." When he looked at her, she couldn't stop the tears from falling onto her pale cheeks.

"And my uncle accepted your terms?"

He nodded.

Feeling utterly destroyed, she turned from Sheridan so that he wouldn't see the tears cascading down her face. She had somehow hoped that her uncle would stop him. Now that Didier hadn't, now that he'd proven once and for all that he was a knave, she felt as if the ground had been taken from under her feet. The final blow was her uncle's. She couldn't believe that he would sell her to this man.

"You're better off."

Sheridan's words were meant to comfort her. If she hadn't known better, she would have sworn she'd heard that brogue again, a clear signal that her tears had touched him. But she did know better. A man who could pay another for a wife would be quite unmoved by a woman's tears. "I will not marry you." She wiped her cheeks with her palms and faced him again. "You might have paid my uncle for his blessing, but I'm the one who must walk down the aisle and say the vows. And I won't. And no one in New York has the power to make me."

"Alana, your defiance is admirable, but pointless." Sheridan pierced her with that dark gaze, "You will marry me. And next Saturday, no one in New York need make you, for you'll do it of your own free will."

"I won't," she countered, her eyes flashing like emeralds. His offer of wealth might have been tempting, but Christabel was cocooned in terrible secrets. Even to maintain her sister, Alana couldn't reveal them to Trevor Sheridan.

"You will. I'll see to it."

"Do it, then." Her eyes clashed with his. It was a long moment before he was the victor.

"I know you need money," he said, his voice coaxing and deceptively soft. "And I know you need it more than just to live on. So why, Alana? Tell me. I can be ruthless. Is preserving your independence worth enduring my wrath?"

"It is, and I'll go to my grave before I'll tell you why." She was heartened that Didier in his last despicable act had kept their secret. Once Sheridan flashed his bribe, she suspected Didier hadn't wanted to spoil it all by informing him of his fallen soon-to-be sister-in-law.

"But you do need money." He rose and went to her, the noise of his walking stick on the polished floor a brilliant form of torture. "You need money desperately. I can see it on your beautiful face. It's something that goes beyond your own needs. If you had to, love, I believe you'd whore yourself for it."

Her self-control broke. She raised her hand to slap him, but he caught it in midair. He pulled it down to her side and roughly pulled her to his chest. He finished by saying, "But then, no doubt a girl like you'd rather whore yourself than marry the likes of me, now wouldn't you?"

She stared up at him, too angry to think about her state of undress, too angry to think of anything but how much she hated this man.

"Go on, answer the question," he prompted contemptuously.

"I won't marry you," she choked out, fighting back tears of rage. "I won't because I despise you. You play with people's lives like it was a game of chess. But I'm no rook to be moved as you see fit. I've a mind of my own. I'll move where I like."

"You need that money, Alana," he whispered against her hair, stifling her rebellious movements in the steel of his embrace. "You need it so badly you can taste it. And what's it for? Morphine? Gambling? Do you lovely little Knickerbockers have the same dirty vices we navvies have? Well, I don't care why you need it. As my wife, you may have all the money you can use. All you have to do is speak two little words. Say 'I do' Saturday, and you'll never want for it again."

"You make everything sound so—disreputable," she cried, her nails scratching down the black worsted of his evening coat. His offer was terribly tempting. She only wished she could believe him.

"I don't care why you must have that money, Alana. I just want you in that church."

She paused and thought about it. How wonderful it would be to have Christabel's future secure. With this man's limitless funds, she would never have to worry about her sister's expensive care again. Her only worry would be for herself, and as she looked up into Sheridan's taut, hard features, she was again overcome with doubt. She was crushed in his arms, her petite stature hardly a threat to his tall, muscular one. And in this stance she couldn't ignore the requirements of marriage, particularly the physical requirements. "I won't marry you because I won't live with you as your wife," she finally said.

He shook her gently. "You needn't think of that. We'll get an annulment."

"I can't risk that," she moaned into his chest. "I won't do it."

"You will, sweet lady. You'll right the wrongs done to Mara, or I'll hunt you down like a fox in a meadow and see that you never enjoy a moment of peace again." His hand brushed down her hair, belying the harshness of his words.

She spent her remaining tears and finally looked up at him, her eyes accusatory. He met her glare and lowered his gaze, a spark flaring in his eyes when he found what he'd been searching for. Her mind filling with dread, she looked down and saw what had captured his attention. Mara's chaste pink robe had proved otherwise. In her struggles it had parted, revealing not only a lush portion of one breast but the rose-colored edge of one nipple. "You promised an annulment. An *annulment*," she whispered harshly, betrayal written upon her every feature.

A small pulse throbbed at his temple. His jaw clenched, outlining every strong muscle. At that moment she seemed to be asking something that he wanted to refuse. But slowly, regretfully, reason seemed to take hold of him again. He nodded, his arms fell away from her, and she stumbled back, clutching at her bodice.

"I'll keep you informed of the wedding plans. I'll send word to Washington Square." His gaze again flickered to her chest where the valley between her breasts was lush and deep. He continued. "Your uncle's behavior last night is knowledge only you and I possess. Therefore, you'll return to your home this evening unsullied by past events. Since this is to both our advantages, I suggest you behave for the rest of the week in your usual lady-like manner. Saturday we'll wed, and then you may embark upon your new career as my wife."

"I'll find a way out of this, Mr. Sheridan. I swear I will spend the entire week scheming to be free of you."

He walked to a green *bonheur du jour* and took a newspaper off a tray that had been brought while she slept. He handed it to her, letting her read the *New York Chronicle*'s shocking evening headlines:

WEDDING OF THE CENTURY!!!
THE MRS. ASTOR SWOONS IN NEWPORT!
KNICKERBOCKER TO WED FENIAN SATURDAY!

Seeing her shocked face, Sheridan smiled. "Try" was all he said.

The next day, a pale and drawn Alana received callers in her parlor. They came in droves after reading the headlines announcing the upcoming nuptials. Alana expected them. After the announcement of her marriage in the *Chronicle*, her only surprise was that her "friends" had waited long enough for breakfast to be over before showing up at her door.

Didier was not among them. He had yet to show his face at Washington Square, and Alana had heard from the servants that he'd been forced to lower his living standards from the Fifth Avenue Hotel and move to lesser quarters. Yet Didier's whereabouts interested her little. There were far too many other worries, the first the incessant flow of gossipy well-wishers who rushed to leave their calling cards. If Sheridan thought she might try to flee, his fears could be put to rest; she'd never get through the line of carriages that had formed in front of her house.

Ostensibly, her visitors were arriving to pay their respects to the bride-to-be. Yet in the fifteen minutes allotted for a formal call, they tried tactfully to pry all sorts of information out of her about her hasty engagement to the Irish financier. One matron was even so bold as to ask if her corset had changed sizes recently.

Feeling as if she were fighting a war, Alana dodged their questions and innuendos as if they were bullets. She didn't confide in any of them since she didn't trust them, so she spent all of Wednesday in the parlor fending them off, her only weapons wit and evasion. But on Thursday morning, when the Astor carriage stopped at number 38, Alana almost admitted defeat. All night she'd tossed and turned trying to think of a way out of the financial catacombs in which the Irishman had put her. She was exhausted and running out of ideas, and she was now going to have to defend her situation to the very woman who had been the cause of it.

Yes indeed, it was a perfect time to receive a call from *the* Mrs. Astor.

Alana watched as Pumphrey entered the parlor with Mrs. Astor's calling card on a salver. The white vellum card was completely folded in two, a rather dramatic gesture of disapproval in the language of calling cards. Alana merely stared at it, not needing to read the name engraved upon it.

"Miss?" Pumphrey raised his eyebrows, waiting for her instructions.

"Send her in," she said.

Caroline Astor did not enter a room in a flurry of sable

and diamonds, as one would expect of *the* Mrs. Astor. Instead, it was almost as if the room opened itself to her and bowed. Her omnipotent presence filled the space before her first gleaming black boot touched the Persian carpet. By her very height she threatened; what was worse, she knew it. And today she looked as tall as Alana had ever seen her. She was like a general who upon his first taste of great power had suddenly become a dictator. And Caroline Astor loved being dictator. A cut-direct from her, and one became social anathema.

"Mrs. Astor," Alana said evenly, rising from the ruby tasseled cushions in the window seat, "how good of you to call on me."

"Alice dear." Caroline Astor took Alana's hands and squeezed them. She didn't smile.

"We've been having a dreadful bit of rain, haven't we? I'm so glad to see the sun finally out." The motions, well choreographed from the previous day of visitors, were mechanical. Alana showed the matron to a Thonet chair and began to count her fifteen minutes. But when Caroline Astor began removing her gloves, Alana's heart almost stopped beating.

When her parents, who were close, personal friends of the Astor's, had died, Caroline Astor hadn't called long enough to necessitate the removal of her gloves. It was not done, except under very serious circumstances. This had to be a catastrophe.

"Darling Alice, we've a lot to discuss and not much time to do it. I don't want to be seen lingering here. It would not do." The matron removed a diamond hatpin the length of a saber. She took off her hat of handsome ochre-colored moire and revealed a smooth dark brown coif. Caroline Astor had to be forty, yet she sported not one gray hair.

Wigs, Alana thought in a moment of uncharacteristic ungraciousness.

Unable to read thoughts, Mrs. Astor placed her hat upon a table and like the commander she was, got right to the point. "Alice, the reason for your engagement eludes me. I must tell you what a shock it was to hear of it."

Alana lowered herself gingerly to the edge of the tufted Belter settee. She wanted to answer that she too was shocked to hear of it. Instead, she said uneasily, "It's quick, I grant you."

"Your mother was a Schermerhorn, my second cousin, I think, once removed. Am I correct?"

Alana nodded.

"That almost makes us relatives, then, doesn't it?" Mrs. Astor smiled.

Alana nodded. *No, that most definitely makes us relatives,* she thought, but in her mood she wasn't about to protest the distance Mrs. Astor had put between them.

"Alice—*Alana,*" the matron quickly corrected. "That's what your mother called you, wasn't it?"

Alana nodded, hating this attempt at familiarity. She didn't want to be reminded of her mother. Not today. It had been almost three years, but the fire that had taken her parents and, in essence, her sister, was still vivid in her mind.

"She wouldn't want you to marry that . . . Irisher, Alana. You know that."

The question ripped into her very soul. No, her mother would not want her to marry Sheridan, and that was why she didn't want even to consider his offer. Her mother had married for love and surely expected her daughters to do the same.

But things had not turned out as expected. And first and foremost her mother would have wanted her to care for Christabel.

"My mother and father would not have forbidden me to marry Sheridan if I loved him." Alana gave her the most truthful and intentionally misleading answer she could. Mrs. Astor would not ask if she loved Sheridan. That was entirely beside the point.

The matron did not look pleased with Alana's answer.

Like a general redirecting the troops, she took another course. Her face softened, and she grasped Alana's hands. "The Van Alens have such a grand history." Impetuously, with genuine feeling, she said, "There aren't many of us old New Yorkers left. You can't do anything foolish, Alana. There won't be any Knickerbockers at all if we don't preserve ourselves. You know our motto: *Nous nous soutenons.* 'We support ourselves.' *Ourselves,*" she emphasized.

Alana stared down at their clasped hands, all the emotional turmoil she'd suffered the past few days rising to the surface. Caroline Astor had caused her problems. This very attitude of self-preservation and exclusivity had thrust her into Sheridan's lion's den. And though the Irishman was the most ostensibly wicked soul in all of this, there were others.

With as much conviction as she had in her heart, Alana said, "These parvenus are going to get in—it's an inevitable eventuality. All this trouble—for what? Something that's going to happen, no matter what you do. Trevor Sheridan just wants to speed things up."

Mrs. Astor dropped her hands. Her eyes narrowed. "That man is . . . *crude*, Alana."

Alana wanted to nod her head in agreement. Sheridan was certainly that. Peeking out from beneath his stiff formality lurked a hedonistic spirit, born of the streets or born of Erin, she did not know. She only knew that it was there, pacing beneath his veneer like a giant cat in a cage. "What you mean is, that man is *Irish*, and you cannot accept that." Alana saw no point in avoiding the obvious.

Mrs. Astor closed her eyes as if praying for strength. "They're out there. Right now, Alana. Shall I show them to you?" The matron's eyes flew open, and she stared at her. "There are Irishmen right now working on the Nicholson pavement on Mercer Street. Shall we drive by them? Is that what you want for your husband, a man no better than a common laborer? A man most likely blessed with the manners of an animal, who strays from woman to woman, leaving evidence of his prurient behavior in the city's orphan asylums?"

The last thing Alana wanted was to defend the man. Sheridan was causing her so much anxiety, she wanted to curse him from the highest summit. But the fabric of her character would not allow her to do that in this instance. If the attack on Sheridan had been personal, she might have applauded it. That arrogant, manipulative devil deserved a good dressing-down. But when criticism of him was stated like this, simply because of his background, she couldn't abide it. "Trevor Sheridan is not a shantyman. You cannot compare him to the brawling, drunken louts you see paving the streets."

"He's not a shantyman now, but he was once," Mrs. Astor pointed out, annoyance coloring her pugnacious features.

"Even the Astors were poor once." Alana didn't want to get into this battle, but now that she had parried, she saw by Mrs. Astor's face that there was no turning back.

Anger created two cherry-colored spots on her cheeks. "The Irish drink," the matron snapped.

"Knickerbockers drink—some even too much," Alana answered, thinking of the night her uncle thrust her into this tangle.

Caroline Astor was not a woman to dally around the point. She looked Alana in the eye and said, "The girl Mara, Sheridan's sister, was born in New York. When the Sheridans immigrated through Castle Garden, they were listed as a widow and two young sons. There is only one conclusion to be drawn from that."

Alana didn't want to show it, but there was no hiding her shock. She could hardly believe it. Mara Sheridan, with her lovely piquant face and her stunning black hair, was nothing like the image of illegitimacy Alana had conjured. She thought back to that beautiful young girl she'd met in Olmsted and Vaux's Greensward months ago. Bastards didn't wear blue velvet cloaks that matched their eyes. Bastards were gangs of dirty boys forced to haunt the Lower East Side, picking pockets before supper and making it impossible for even a gentleman to roam the streets at night without a pistol. They certainly weren't sweet young girls taking buggy rides in Central Park with an army of postilions and grooms.

But one thing was now stunningly clear. She knew why the Irishman had been so insanely protective of his sibling. If Christabel had been born illegitimate, Alana knew she herself would have fought for her acceptance to the death. Strangely, she almost admired Sheridan now. Though he loomed a nearly unconquerable foe, as a brother, he was almost a saint.

"That bothers you, doesn't it."

Mrs. Astor's words snaked into her thoughts. Alana looked up, the shock on her face replaced with anger. "Even a bastard has feelings," she said quietly. "Even Mara Sheridan, if she was indeed born on the wrong side of the blanket, deserved better treatment than she received from you at her debut." She had wanted to say those words to this woman for weeks. Now, even with everything going awry in her life, it felt good to say them.

"*You* could have attended, my dear. But, alas, I know you did not, and I wonder if that didn't put you in the situation you're in now." Caroline Astor's next words were razor sharp. "Everyone knows the Van Alen fortune is only a million. Why, that's hardly respectable poverty. Oh yes indeed, I think Mr. Sheridan could do a lot of damage to you. If he took away your funds, I think you could be 'persuaded' to marry him."

Alana bit back a retort. After all, she was never going to convince anyone that she'd meant to go to Mara's debut, and the matron's assessment of her wealth, even delivered in that insulting tone, was absurdly generous. She had nowhere near a million to inherit, not now, with Didier's hands too long in the till. Also, Caroline Astor spoke the truth. Sheridan *was* doing a lot of damage to her. At wit's end, she stood and hoped the matron would take her cue.

Mrs. Astor remained seated. "Alana, dear, you must hear me out. I don't want you to ruin your life. You've always attended my annual January ball with the other Four Hundred. Why, I even wanted you to help entertain the Duke of Granville when he arrives. I've some regard for your mother, Alana. I feel I must save you."

"Please—" Alana began angrily.

"No, hear me out. If you've found yourself in a pinch, why can't you marry Anson Vanbrugh-Stevens? He's mad for you. His family's got sterling connections—why, he's even one of the Patriarchs, and he's filthy rich."

Alana wanted to laugh. Anson Stevens was the poorest choice for a husband she could imagine. It was true he'd been paying her calls for over a year now and had even escorted her to several soirees when her uncle could not attend. He was handsome and possessed all of the qualities Mrs. Astor spoke of, but he was untrustworthy. He cheated at cards, and there were even rumors that he'd been known to snip tendons in other men's trotters to win races. The idea of telling him on their wedding night that he had a mad sister-in-law in Brooklyn was ridiculous. The only reason she'd allowed his escort was that he never asked questions about her. In all the time she'd known Anson she couldn't once remember their conversation ever steering away from his favorite topic—himself. The world revolved around Anson Vanbrugh-Stevens, and while that was fine for a beau, it would never do for a husband. Alana almost smiled. Anson was so wrapped up and coddled by his wealth that if told he must tie his own shoelaces, he would no doubt faint. The shameful news of Christabel would probably kill him.

"I can't marry Mr. Stevens—" Alana began.

"You must. Why have you always been so cold to him? He loves you dearly."

Again Alana wanted to laugh. Anson Stevens loved her

about as much as he loved the trotters he ran on the Boulevard. As bad as Sheridan's offer was, she at least had no illusions. She wouldn't be going into a marriage believing herself to be a wife when in fact she was in a caste somewhere below a set of matched bays.

"Alana, I want you to listen to reason." Mrs. Astor stood as if it were finally time to leave. "This wedding with this Irisher is ridiculous. You won't be marrying that man on Saturday, and that is final. If you need someone, I shall summon Mr. Stevens to your side this very day." She placed her ochre moire hat at a discreet angle on her head and jabbed it with her diamond hatpin. "These people don't know their place. It's time we told them where it is. Our families have deep roots in Manhattan. We cannot taint them with impurities."

Alana stared at her, suddenly imagining what this tall, stately woman would do if she ever heard about Christabel. One response she was sure of: The fact of Mrs. Astor's relation to their mother would be buried so deeply, a well digger wouldn't find it.

"Now, is this clear, Alana?"

Alana hardly heard her. She was pondering Sheridan's offer. If he let her keep her secret, it became very simple, really. She would have the wherewithall to take care of her sister without prying questions. He would have entree into this vile society in which even she could find no redeeming value.

"You won't be marrying that Irishman on Saturday, now will you?"

And it really might not take that long to get Mara well entrenched. She was Irish, and she was young, but she was fetching and uncommonly pretty. And the Knickerbocker men were so much less obsessed about family lines than the women.

"You're touched, child, if you think any good can come of being such an upstart."

After a season or two, she and Sheridan would have a

quiet annulment. She could move to a country house in Brooklyn just like the one in her dream. She could be near her sister and escape all this unhappiness.

"You aren't going to marry him. I forbid it!"

Alana looked up, her face as pale and beautiful as alabaster. She paused, hardly able to believe the decision she had finally come to. Slowly she said, "You must know, Mrs. Astor, that I've thought this out and I think there may be no other way for me but to marry Mr. Sheridan."

"This is madness! You will not do this!"

Alana smiled bitterly. "Madness must run in the family, then."

The reference was lost on Caroline Astor. Astounded, the matron gave her a no-one-uses-that-tone-to-me look and without another word departed. Watching her, Alana was left with only one thought: Now she'd gone and done it. This was most definitely war.

Terms of Surrender

Late suppers . . . rich wines . . . low voices
. . . are dangerous.

—Junius Browne, *The Great Metropolis:
A Mirror of New York* (1869)

8

Pumphrey entered the parlor not ten minutes after Mrs. Astor departed with the news that Sheridan had sent over a few necessities for the wedding. Alana was beginning to fear the Irishman could read thoughts. She hardly had time to take a deep breath before an army of delivery boys trooped through her foyer laden with purchases from Ladies Mile on Broadway. There were yards of creamy white satin from Arnold Constable and Lyons lace from the Lace Room at A. T. Stewart's, all chosen for her wedding gown. The trousseau "A" was delivered from Lord and Taylor, consisting of fifty-one pieces of undergarments and silk negligées; there was a complete suite of emeralds from Dreicer on Fifth Avenue; and to add insult to injury, her diamond engagement ring from Mr. Tiffany's store on Union Square was delivered not by her fiancé but armed courier.

Alana stood mutely by as the boys were instructed by Pumphrey where to deposit their goods. But as soon as they were taken care of, the door chimes rang again, and Pumphrey announced the appearance of Madame LaBoeuve, the couturiere from James McCreery who was to make her wedding gown. And right at this lady's heels was a footman in the Sheridan green and black livery with a note from the Irishman himself.

Alana took the letter from Pumphrey and closed herself

off in the parlor. She wanted no one to see her face while she read it. It was bound to be upsetting. Slowly she thumbed open the envelope and read:

Miss Van Alen,
I want you to dine with me at Delmonico's this evening. Lorenzo Delmonico will show you my table. Be there at 6pm. We have much to discuss.

                                                        Trevor Sheridan

PostScript—wear my ring.

She closed her eyes, infuriated. So she'd received her marching orders, she thought bitterly as she crumpled the note in her hand. The postscript was enough to make her rip the thing into tiny bits and crush them beneath her slippers. The cad was referring to the engagement diamond, of course, the one so lovingly delivered by the last messenger. How coldly logical he was to ask that she wear it in public. She would then be branded as Sheridan's chattel, pure and simple.

Her idea to marry him began to wear away. Caroline Astor was no longer around to get Alana's back up, and suddenly the thought of tying herself to this man seemed impossibly stupid. The speed and control with which he tried to manipulate her was daunting. Though she had seen some reason in this absurd plan before, when she thought of that postscript, all she could see was red.

"Pumphrey," she said as she crossed the parcel-laden foyer, "have the coupé brought around at five thirty. I must go out tonight."

"Very good, madam." Pumphrey bowed, his face professionally clear of expression.

Alana dismissed him with a nod and ascended the stairs to her bedroom. She wouldn't be late for this dinner— especially when she was not going to be wearing that vulgar ring.

* * *

The Van Alen brown coupé made the short trip up Fifth Avenue in quiet Knickerbocker style. Tucked inside the cab, Alana watched the cast-iron storefronts and marble palaces roll by, awash in the lavenders of a cool spring twilight. The ride was pleasant, this part of Fifth Avenue still unmarred by the relentless web of telegraph lines that plagued Broadway, but Alana hardly noticed as the carriage turned right at Fourteenth Street toward Union Square. Her mind was very much on the Irishman.

The coupé halted at the old Grinnell mansion where the former owner of the famous clipper ship *Flying Cloud* had once lived. Delmonico's, with its distinct white-and-scarlet-striped awnings, now operated there as New York's unrivaled eating establishment. The restaurant had become the ultimate rendezvous of society where the Family Circle and Assembly Balls were held, even Ward McAlister's brainchild, the Patriarchs' Ball. A steady stream of celebrities passed through its doors, and Alana had dined there many times, but always in the company of an escort. This time she was alone, and she couldn't help an uncontrollable shiver as her driver assisted her from the carriage.

Once inside, the owner and maître d'hôtel, Lorenzo, immediately recognized her. He was a pleasant balding man with a fine set of muttonchop whiskers. With a polite bow, he said, "How very good of you to join us this evening, Miss Van Alen. Please allow me to take your cape and show you to your table."

Alana smiled and nodded. She would have greeted the man more personally, but for some reason, once she'd stepped inside Delmonico's, anxiety had taken control of her voice.

Lorenzo removed her coffee-colored evening cape without further ceremony and handed it to a nearby servant. "I beg you to allow me to escort you, Miss Van Alen. Mr. Sheridan is waiting in the private saloon."

"A private saloon?" she asked, her heart stopping in her

chest. She hadn't counted on this. At the very least she'd expected a public table where he could show off that ring that was supposed to be encircling her finger.

Once again he'd pulled the rug from beneath her. Perhaps it was only logical that he take a private room. He was no doubt prepared for a refusal. They had much to discuss, and to do it in the main dining room would be difficult, but her rationalization sounded false even to her ears. There definitely was logic in this plan, but knowing Sheridan, she wouldn't know what it was until after the fact. The only thing she knew for sure was that the thought of being alone with Sheridan in one of those luxurious, well-couched decadent rooms, rooms she'd heard whispered about behind fans, made her want to retrieve her cloak and flee.

"I know Mr. Sheridan awaits your arrival with great anticipation." Lorenzo smiled a handsome Continental smile that would have comforted her if she hadn't noticed his gaze on her hands. He was obviously searching for a ring, some telltale sign that all the gossips, all the newspaper articles, were correct and that indeed a Knickerbocker was going to lower herself to marry a common Irishman. When he didn't find one, he seemed disappointed, as if he had an army of relatives in his kitchens just waiting for his exclusive report.

Unnerved, Alana hid her hands in the folds of her dinner dress and stared at him. Lorenzo Delmonico, in the grand tradition of restaurateurs, remembered himself at once and suavely offered his arm. She almost didn't take it, but knowing she would have to face the Irishman here or in an even more public place, she reluctantly did.

They walked through the main saloon filled with diners, cigar smoke, and laughter. Their footsteps echoed through the enormous empty ballroom, its Saracenic splendor now ghostly without other inhabitants. Lorenzo took her up a flight of stairs carpeted in ruby wool. He opened an ornately carved walnut door, and its occupant, the infamous Trevor Sheridan, stood to greet them.

His gaze met hers, and again she was struck by his eyes, an uncommonly dark hazel. They seemed even more stern than usual, and, panicked, Alana looked behind her, as if Lorenzo might offer her reassurance. But sensing the tension, Lorenzo had already departed, closing the door behind him.

She took a deep breath and turned back to Sheridan. Dressed in a black evening swallowtail coat and trousers, he looked more handsome than any other man she had ever seen. The starched turned-down points of his shirt collar accented the masculine contours of his face to perfection, while the white barrel-knotted bow tie was just enough out of fashion to be tasteful. If this had been any other meeting on any other occasion, Alana could have almost enjoyed being in the company of such a magnificent example of manhood. But she couldn't escape the fact that he was a terrible force to reckon with, and staring at him now, his face lean and determined, she could see why William Astor had always referred to him by his Wall Street nickname, the Predator.

"You look beautiful tonight if I may say so, Miss Van Alen" were his first words. His gaze flickered over her attire, but in that brief glance he seemed to catalog everything: her evening gown of brilliant arsenic-green taffeta; her bodice done in the Elizabethan taste, outlined with chains of tiny black chenille balls; her bosom, discreetly adorned with a necklace of jet set in Etruscan gold—an odd piece, especially since she was no longer in mourning.

His eyes fixed on the necklace until she felt forced to cover it with her hand. When she had dressed for this evening, she felt it was the most appropriate piece of jewelry, considering her situation. He seemed to find the irony in it too, but he didn't smile, especially when he looked at her left hand. Predictably, his next words were "Where's your ring, my dear betrothed?"

She opened her purple-beaded purse and dug inside it.

When she retrieved his ring, she stepped forward and laid it upon the white linen tablecloth.

A scowl marred his fine Irish features. "Why aren't you wearing it?"

"I think that's obvious."

Anger began to simmer beneath his calm facade. "I see."

"Is our business concluded, then?" She looked around the intimate saloon, anxious to depart. In Sheridan's company the room only seemed to grow smaller.

"You're already here, Miss Van Alen. Why not have dinner?" He smiled, and a tingle of warning went down her spine.

"I really don't think—"

"Where's the harm?"

She looked at him, remembering similar words. "Whare's the sacrifice?" he'd said with just the slightest hint of accent, allowing her a brief peek into his real self. But he wasn't letting her peek now. She heard no trace of an accent.

"No, really. I've imposed upon you enough." She closed her purse and looked to the door.

"Perhaps I might contemplate the return of your fortune. Would you dine with me then?"

She looked up and found him standing next to her. The thick ruby carpet had muffled the sound of the walking stick he never seemed to be without. "Shall you give it back to me?" she asked, stepping back, his height again intimidating her.

"Perhaps. Let's discuss it."

He held the rosewood-and-velvet dining chair for her. She paused, a warning bell sounding in her mind. But the lure of the return of her money was too much. She slowly sat, being careful not to wrinkle her train or crush her bustle.

He seated himself on the burgundy moire banquette at the opposite side of the small table. The banquette ran along the entire perimeter of the room. There were also

several gold-fringed ottomans, and she could finally understand why Mrs. Varick had once likened the private rooms
at Delmonico's to small brothels. This little saloon was
suitable for any kind of intimate activity.

"You do look bewitching tonight. I don't lie when I say
that." His voice interrupted her thoughts. She looked at
him, the corner of his mouth lifted in a wry smile. "I can
finally understand why the Knickerbockers prize you so
much, Miss Van Alen. You're everything they aspire to be.
You're lovely to look upon, intelligent, and scrupulously
well bred. What more could they desire in a young
woman?"

"Money, I'm afraid, and alas, because of you, I now have
none."

"You could have more than you ever dreamed about if
you married me. I've a fortune few can equal."

"Your wealth is notorious in New York, Mr. Sheridan."

"Trevor. My name is Trevor."

She hesitated, but for some reason, perhaps because of
the seductiveness of his dark gaze, she complied. "Trevor,"
she said softly.

The use of his Christian name seemed to please him.
The shadow of a smile crossed his face, and satisfied, he
placed his napkin on his lap.

His confidence annoyed her. Once and for all, she decided to nip his aspirations in the bud. "I won't marry you,"
she said, looking him straight in the eye. "You've caused me
a lot of trouble, Mr. Sher—*Trevor*." To make her point, she
picked up the enormous Tiffany diamond ring and dropped
it onto the gold charger at his place. It made a metallic
sound as it fell.

He smiled down at it, but his eyes had turned cold. "The
ring doesn't suit you? I paid five thousand for it."

"Five thousand is an obscene sum for a ring, Mr. Sheridan, and your vulgarity in telling me its price is only sur-
passed by the way in which it was delivered."

The simmer began to boil. "You criticize my wealth,

Miss Van Alen, yet I wonder how you will feel a month from now when you're selling that exquisite dress you wear to the rag merchant."

A dark depression settled around her, but it wasn't for fear of losing her family's money or the dress she wore. It was for Christabel. "I have beaux, Mr. Sheridan. Haven't you ever thought that if I become desperate, I might marry one of them?"

His smile didn't reassure her. "Yes, I've heard about your beaux, Alana, particular that Stevens lad. And I tell you what—if you marry one of them, you can count on me ruining the lad the second you whisper 'I do.' "

She blanched. The option of marrying Anson was no option at all, but it unnerved her that this man had every avenue blocked. Perhaps the best she could do for Christabel would be to marry Trevor Sheridan, and she had almost convinced herself of that this afternoon with Mrs. Astor. But every time she thought about crossing that line and accepting this man's crazy scheme, all she had to do was look into those dark vengeful eyes and know she couldn't be so foolish. It was wrong. All wrong. No matter how logical his plans sounded, her heart rebelled. She didn't love him. And he was very dangerous.

"I should go," she whispered, wanting to end the discussion.

She was just about to rise when he grasped her hand from across the table and held it as in a vise. "Listen to me. You've got more trouble than you know if you refuse my proposal. I'll make sure of it."

She pulled on her hand. To her dismay, it didn't budge from his warm grip. "No, you listen to me, Mr. Sheridan. I've already got more trouble than *you* know of. So you needn't cause me more."

"Stay." He held tight.

"Let go of me." She glared at him.

Looking as if that were the exact opposite of what he wanted to do, he released her. He took a second to tame his temper, then said to her retreating back, "If you leave here with your cheeks so red with indignation, they'll see you in the main saloon, and it'll only cause more gossip. They'll know I got the better of you."

She spun around and faced him. The gall of it was that it was true. They would see her in the main dining saloon, and there wouldn't be a soul who wouldn't be out on calls tomorrow snickering about her fleeing Delmonico's. They'd deduce that Trevor Sheridan had the ability to incite passion in her, and that was the last thing she wanted.

She resumed her seat, her gaze furious. She stared at him, and her frustration grew. The silence was so oppressive that she was almost glad when Lorenzo brought his waiters to serve them their meal. The beef was delicious, the sauces delicate yet flavorful, but Alana might as well have been eating cardboard for all the enjoyment it gave her. Dessert was an assortment of ice creams—raspberry, bourbon, chocolate—but they were soup by the time the waiter took them away untouched.

When they were finally alone again, Sheridan stood and walked to a lace-covered rosewood table. On it was a brandy decanter and two crystal brandy snifters. He poured two healthy drinks and put one in front of her. She thought he would take his place but saw that he had to retrieve his own glass. Again she found it unusual that he would hold on to his walking stick for that small trip.

When he sat again, he laid the ebony walking stick across the table, the gold lion's head burnished in the dim light. She looked up at him and again thought of lions.

"Miss Van Alen, I wanted this to be gentle, but the more you refuse, the more cunning I'm forced to use." He took a sip of the brandy and made a face as if the liquor didn't quite suit him. "Now I see I'm at the end of my rope. I must either convince you to agree to marry me before you leave this room tonight or consider my plans ruined. Is there any way we might come to an agreeable settlement without the use of more distasteful methods?"

His words were intentionally ominous, and they produced the desired effect. Dread weighed upon her chest. But they didn't produce the desired result. She summoned all her courage and with soft but unyielding words took her final stand. "My life is not yours to do with as you wish. It was not yours to ruin after your sister's debut, and it's not yours to use now as a means of gaining what you really desire: an entrée for Mara into society. It will be very difficult for me, now that I've been hurt so much by your manipulations, but somehow I will get through it. Somehow I'll find a way to hold things together. In the meantime, I wish your sister well, Mr. Sheridan. She's a lovely girl, and I didn't like seeing her hurt. I understand things better now, and I see how much you care for her and want to protect her. You're a good brother to do so much for her, but I can't let you continue at my cost."

He listened to her, his strong well-shaped fingers stroking the lip of his snifter. When she was through, he seemed truly pained to say what he said next. "Alana—I'm going to call you that because soon you'll be my wife—I'm not accustomed to failure." He paused and looked down at his vest. From the watch pocket, he removed his gold watch and checked the time. He replaced it slowly. "It's now ten o'clock. At ten thirty an old priest will arrive here from St. Brendan's. I intend to convince him to marry us here, tonight. What I've told him is that if I don't marry you immediately, I'm going to take you to my bed without benefit of marriage."

The color drained from her face. She stood, knocking the chair over. "You—you cannot *think* that!"

"That is my plan. We're to marry officially and publicly at St. Brendan's Church Saturday, and to assure that you will be there and not stand me up in front of your peers, I'll have you become my wife tonight." Sheridan was calm. "You see, I've thought of everything."

"You haven't!" she cried out, gripping the edge of the table as if she were reeling from his blow. "What if I don't show up on Saturday! I could still humiliate you, and if you force me into this tonight, I swear I will do just that!"

"My humiliation will be your humiliation, as my wife. Remember that. If you don't show up Saturday, I'll simply announce that we couldn't wait and that we were married here, this night."

He had indeed dealt her a shattering blow. She lowered herself to the banquette and put her shaking hand to her lips. "No one is going to show up at that wedding—you know that. If you couldn't get them to your sister's debut, why would they attend your wedding, and at a Catholic church at that?"

He took a deep gulp of his brandy, as if he were unused to savoring a liquor's flavor. "You do yourself an injustice. They'll come to see one of their own marry me."

"They won't! Don't you see? They'll simply shun me as they have you. And then this will be for naught! Don't you see how impossible this is?"

He shook his head. "It's not at all impossible. I have one trump card you forgot about. It's stipulated in your parent's will that when you marry, William Astor, Jr., is to give you away. So you see, if he's forced to be at your wedding, his wife will be too. And if Caroline Astor is there, then everyone will be there."

Alana closed her eyes, an all-encompassing dread seeping into her soul. She'd forgotten about that clause in the will. It had seemed so incidental when Didier had read it in the parlor that rainy afternoon following her parents' burial. William Astor had been there, out of respect for her father. Caroline had been absent, of course, the reading of wills too morbid a task for her to attend. Alana recalled that when Mr. Astor had left the town house that day, he'd placed a kiss on her forehead and told her how honored he would be to perform such a noble task. She had smiled, barely hearing him, for at that time she'd been too numb to register anything. But never in her wildest dreams could she have imagined this eventuality. She wondered how

William Astor felt about his promise now. She didn't wonder how his wife felt about it.

Sheridan's voice intruded upon her thoughts. "I've thought of everything, Alana. You see, you have no choice but to marry me and cooperate."

She looked at him, wild-eyed. Grinding her fists into the burgundy moire, she said, "I won't do it. When that priest comes here, I'll tell him everything—how you're forcing me, how we plan on an annulment. He won't marry us then."

"But you won't do that."

"And why not?" she shot back at him. "I've lived nineteen years free. I'll do anything to see that I get nineteen more!"

"You won't do that, Alana, because I know you have a secret, a secret that makes you susceptible."

She paled further. Their gazes locked, and she could barely whisper, "How do you know that?"

"I don't know what it is." His voice took on an odd soothing quality when he added, "Nor do I care what it is. But whatever, I know you have one, and I'll find it out and see it smeared across tomorrow's headlines of the *New York Chronicle* if you don't cooperate tonight."

She felt like a mouse caught in a bear trap. Her insides roiled with fury and fear. "Even if I have been hiding something, how do you think you could find out what it is?"

"If Tuesday's headlines announcing our marriage didn't tip you off, let me just tell you. I own the *Chronicle*. And I've men in my employ there who are trained to delve into people's lives and find their secrets. They'll find yours, and when you read about it, it'll sound so bad, you'll wonder how you lived with it all these years."

She could feel herself beginning to break. Tears came to her eyes, and her voice started to tremble. "The *Chronicle* is too respected a newspaper to waste space on such things. When your reporters find the reasons for what I hide, they'll only bore their readers by divulging it."

Sheridan put his elbows on the table and leaned toward her. "If you haven't guessed, as most have, Alana, journalists are the greatest fiction writers of our time. Believe me, when they find out what you have to hide, they won't bore the *Chronicle*'s readers."

She turned away from him just as a tear slipped down her cheek. She tried to stem the flow, but he had her beaten. There were no other arguments she could use. He hadn't overlooked one detail. She was going to have to marry this man, and though it would probably ruin her life, the choice was now either Christabel or herself. She was left with no choice.

Her shoulders began to shake with silent sobs. She wiped at her tears but new ones sprang forth. There was so little she wanted out of life, it was difficult sometimes to accept that she would never have it. She thought of that man in her dream, and that simple white clapboard house. That was all she had ever longed for. But her shadow man, the man whose face she could never quite see, had never appeared. He'd been replaced by this bitter wealthy Irishman sitting behind her.

"It's not a death sentence, sweeting. You'll get your annulment, and a fine pot of gold to boot." After those words, a hand rested on her shoulder, obviously to comfort her.

She pulled away from it as if it were the devil's own. "I'll get an *annulment*, do you understand? You're not to touch me! Ever!" She shot him a scathing, contemptuous glance.

At her rejection, his cheeks tautened with anger. He muttered, "Of course. You wouldn't want a common Irisher to soil those fine lily-white Knickerbocker thighs."

Whatever semblance of composure she had left snapped when she heard that crude remark. Unable to stop herself, she stood and took the closest thing, an empty water goblet, from the table. She meant to throw it at him with all her might, but he grabbed her wrist and forced her to drop it. The goblet fell noiselessly to the moire banquette, but she twisted to take another one from the table.

She understood only later what happened. He pulled her
to him to prevent her from hurting him and inexplicably
lost his balance. Suddenly she found herself toppling forward, his superior weight dragging them both to the ruby
carpet. She landed with a thud on his chest as his ebony
stick fell to the floor next to them.

Panting with anger, she raised her head from his chest
and glared at him. She would have accused him of purposely creating this mischief if she hadn't seen the expression on his face. His face had paled, made paler still by the
evening shadow of beard on his jaw, and his eyes fixed on
the gilt ceiling, their expression glazed with what could
only be described as suppressed pain.

She couldn't understand what could make him react this
way. She was certainly not such an overly voluptuous
woman that her weight falling upon him would cause such
a reaction. And when she'd fallen, she was sure she hadn't
landed on any vulnerable parts.

She looked down at him again, and this time he was
staring back. His face had regained some of its color, and
now she wasn't sure she had seen anything in those eyes but
detachment and arrogance. She struggled to sit up, and her
gown slipped provocatively from her shoulder. His eyes followed, and as if reacting to instinct, his hand, warm and
strong, reached out and caressed the fragile flesh of her
shoulder.

The shock of his skin against hers was electrifying. She
took a sharp intake of breath but didn't pull back. When
she looked down at him, he was staring at her gown, especially where her bodice met her sleeve, revealing a portion
of one breast, and he studied its fullness with great relish.
The undisguised, barely controlled lust on his face was
something she'd rarely been exposed to, but while part of
her feared it, another part, the part that for some reason
was not in a terrible hurry to pull up her sleeve, tingled
with a charge that was very much like desire.

"It's a hard bargain you make after all, Alice Diana Van

Alen," he whispered, his gaze locking with hers. "And I'm wondering why no one has taken you to wife before now."

There was a long pause as they stared at each other, his question unanswered, especially because a knock sounded at the door. Shocked, Alana tried to scramble from him, but he held her where she was. Sheridan called "enter," and instantly Lorenzo Delmonico appeared with a portly aging priest at his side.

When they saw Sheridan and Alana seeming for all the world to be tumbling about on the floor, the old priest dropped his jaw and gaped like a schoolboy, and Lorenzo's eyes nearly popped out of his head. The restaurateur looked torn between wanting to stay and hear the sordid explanation and taking the stairs two at a time to the kitchens to relate this choice bit of scandal right away.

"Your guest has arrived, Mr. Sheridan," Lorenzo said elegantly, trying to appear as if it wasn't at all unusual to speak to a patron lying prone on the carpet. "Shall I bring more wine?"

Mortified, Alana looked down at Sheridan. She'd expected him to look as ashamed as she was, but he flashed her a Cheshire-cat smile, and his dark eyes gleamed with amusement. She knew then she was doomed. Discovering them like this, the priest would have no choice but to marry them and save them from the wicked sins of the flesh.

With amazingly strong arms, Sheridan lifted her from him and took his walking stick. He rose to his feet stiffly, then held out his hand and helped her. When she stared mutely at the old priest, Sheridan discreetly reminded her of her state of dishabille by pulling up her sleeve and covering her bared shoulder. His hand felt like fire, and she colored from the tips of her toes to her ears.

"Will you be so kind as to allow us our privacy?" Sheridan asked Lorenzo pointedly.

Lorenzo, remembering himself, said, "Of course, sir," and left the saloon. He looked disappointed. If he were not the professional that he was, Alana was convinced Lorenzo would have been on his hands and knees outside the door trying to listen through the keyhole.

"Mr. Sheridan, I believe now what you told me. You must marry this girl . . . before you pay with your soul." The priest's words were like a death sentence.

Alana began to deny what he thought, but Sheridan interrupted her. "We want to be married immediately, don't we, love," he said, daring her to disobey.

She remained mute.

"Can you perform the ceremony here, Father?" Sheridan turned to the priest.

Father Donegal looked supremely uncomfortable. It was bad enough trying to convince this powerful man to stay on the right path while in the shadows of the confessional. Face-to-face, it was difficult to summon the courage. "I've already waived publishing the banns for your marriage on Saturday, Mr. Sheridan. If I marry you tonight, I'll have to answer to the bishop. He'll be most displeased."

"It's marry tonight or my soul be damned. Look at my bride-to-be, Father. Can you blame me if my will is not my own?" Sheridan was being really wicked now. Alana looked at him, dismayed that he would so mislead a priest. But when she met his gaze, she was left with the feeling that he was not being entirely untruthful.

Father Donegal glanced at Alana's mussed hair and sumptuous gown. His gaze finally rested on her face, but then he quickly looked away as if he were thinking thoughts he shouldn't. "You must not make me anger the bishop," he said.

Sheridan's words were coaxing and slick, like silk over steel. "Perhaps I know a way to soothe the bishop's ire. I see construction on the cathedral has resumed. Will the bishop accept another donation for St. Patrick's? I, more than anyone, want to see him made archbishop."

The priest looked pained.

"You may tell him I'll have my bank officer visit him

omorrow." He looked at Alana. "But tonight I must marry his girl."

It was a bit of a moral dilemma, but politically there was no alternative. The bishop must have his cathedral. And he must feed the orphans at Five Points. "Shall there be another gift to St. Brendan's?" he asked.

Sheridan nodded.

"I'll marry you, then," the priest conceded.

"Excellent." Sheridan smiled, and Alana was struck by what a handsome rogue he really was. And he was a rogue, or his enjoyment was entirely at her expense.

"Are you ready now?" Father Donegal removed a small Bible from beneath his cassock.

He opened it to the Sacrament of Marriage, but before he could stop herself, Alana cried out, "Wait."

Sheridan pulled her back and said to the priest, "If I may have a word with my fianceé, Father?"

Father Donegal nodded and Sheridan took her to the opposite corner of the saloon. He whispered, "What's it to be, Alana? The front page of the *New York Chronicle*? Believe me, I probably could leak a thing or two to the *Times* and the *Herald* if that would be to your liking."

She hesitated, desperate to fight what was happening yet powerless to do anything about it. After a moment, she nodded, but before she allowed him to lead her back to the priest, she grasped his coatsleeve and said in a trembling, angry voice, "I'll marry you, Mr. Sheridan. But under these conditions only: that I be allowed my own money and that my withdrawals not be answerable to you. And you must promise that from this day forth, whatever secrets I possess are mine and are never to be asked about or inquired into. Do you promise?"

"I promise," Sheridan answered easily.

She lowered her head, relieved that he had promised, furious that she was being forced into this. Numbly she allowed him to lead her back to the priest. Lorenzo and a busboy fresh from Sicily were summoned to be witnesses, and after they were sworn to secrecy, Father Donegal resumed his position in front of the couple and began.

"What is your name, child?" he asked.

"Alana—" She faltered, still not believing that this was happening. "Alice Diana Van Alen."

Father Donegal stared at her. "You're not Catholic, are you, Miss Van Alen?"

She shook her head. "My family has always belonged to the Reformed Dutch Church."

"I see." He lowered his Bible. "Then I must ask you to swear in the name of Jesus Christ our Savior that you will raise the children of this union as Catholics."

Alana swallowed, her numbness melting into panic. She wanted to cry out that there were to be no children of this union. And now she was being forced to promise before God that she would raise her babies in a religion completely foreign to her. "I do so swear," she whispered, unable to look at Sheridan.

Satisfied, Father Donegal began the rite, but Alana hardly heard him. His words were like a stream, one running into another, merely background noise for the war being fought inside her.

She was totally numb by the time she was required to whisper, "I do." She heard Sheridan quickly say, "I do," and the next thing she was conscious of was his taking her left hand and slipping onto her finger that vulgarly large diamond from Mr. Tiffany's store.

The priest then blessed their union, and Sheridan lowered his head, brushing her lips with a light, perfunctory kiss. When he straightened, she finally found the courage to look at him. What she saw didn't comfort her. His dark eyes shone with triumph, and there was a new possessiveness in them. She suddenly knew she'd been a fool to do this. He'd been impossible to defy when she'd been a woman of independence. Now that she was his wife, her very soul was his to mold and use as he wished.

With that thought heavy on her mind, she took an un-

nscious step backward. The priest made a rather jovial
:mark that if she was looking for her bridegroom, he was
. the other direction. Lorenzo laughed, and the busboy
:hoed him, though it was obvious he knew not a word of
nglish. But her panic wasn't soothed. She felt as if she had
st been bound to the devil. She couldn't take her eyes
om Sheridan. In his satisfaction, he almost looked as if he
:ere gloating. And he had every right to. His mastery had
:orked. Everything had gone like clockwork. She was this
an's wife now, legally and before God.

What on earth had she done?

9

Later that evening the black and green Sheridan carriage pulled up in front of the brownstone on Washington Square. It was not even midnight, but to Alana it seemed she'd left for Delmonico's a lifetime ago. Now, whether she liked it or not, her life was changed forever.

The carriage lamp cast a circle of light into the interior of the vehicle. Sheridan sat on one tufted brocade seat, and on the opposite side, as far away as she could get, Alana sat on the other. They had both been quiet on the ride down Fifth Avenue. After the priest left their saloon, Sheridan had summoned her wrap, and they departed without any exchange of words. What was there to say? The ceremony had brought no happiness, no reason for joy and celebration. For Sheridan, there would only be the cold satisfaction of a job well done. Alana had even less. She'd not been the one scheming. She'd been the prey caught in the net, and now that she'd been taken captive, she felt nothing except heart-wrenching bitterness.

The driver dismounted and held open the door. Sheridan got out first and assisted her. She didn't expect him to walk her to the door, nor did she want him to, but he did. He opened the tiny porte cochere and allowed her to step inside. Pumphrey should have met them at the front door, but when Sheridan had sent the brown coupé back to the town house, the butler obviously thought she'd be home much later.

The gaslights were dim in the enclosure, and Alana, typical of her class, didn't possess a key to unlock the front door. She glanced at Sheridan and was unnerved to find him staring at her. She reached up to pull the chain that rang the doorbell, and the diamond ring on her hand flashed before her eyes. With trembling fingers, she removed it and held it out to him. "I believe you'll need this again for Saturday," she said, not looking at him.

He glanced at the beautiful ring in her palm. Quietly, he said, "I'll get another one for the ceremony Saturday. Keep this one on. It's your wedding ring."

"Don't buy another one. We won't be married that long." She held out her hand.

He still refused it. "The ceremony Saturday won't make us any more married than we are tonight. This evening bound us together as man and wife, and that is your wedding ring. Keep it on."

His insistence irritated her. As if she were a servant, she answered, "Very good, *Mr. Sheridan.*"

"*My pleasure, Mrs. Sheridan.*" He smirked, and she was left speechless. The name shocked her. No one had spoken it before now, and it brought home the reality of her situation.

Numbly she pulled the chain to summon Pumphrey and be rid of Sheridan. If she had less than two days of freedom, she was determined to spend as little of it as possible with this man. Pumphrey opened the door, one side of the collar of his jacket turned up as if he had donned it in a hurry. He looked surprised to see his mistress with Sheridan. Alana couldn't blame him. The only man he'd ever seen her with had been her uncle. She'd never invited any of her beaux to her house, not even Anson Vanbrugh-Stevens. After the fire, she'd insisted on her privacy.

She turned to excuse Sheridan, but to her dismay, he walked right in as if he were the master of the house. She stood speechless for a moment, then collected herself and said begrudgingly, "Pumphrey, would you please ask Hazel to make us some coffee? We'll take it in the parlor."

Pumphrey nodded, his eyes flickering with surprise. Alana relinquished her wrap, and the butler left the hall stealing covert glances at the Irishman who the newspapers proclaimed was to marry his mistress.

Alana looked at Sheridan. She knew she should be gracious and ask him to accompany her into the parlor, but she couldn't quite summon the necessary words. The best welcome she could give him was to nod slowly toward the parlor.

He sauntered into the room and sat on the Belter settee as if he had been there before. His walking stick was nonchalantly laid to rest on its rococo arm, and he made a point of watching her lower herself to the Thonet chair.

It was at that moment that the evening got the best of her. Unable to stop herself, she commented frigidly, "It's customary in New York for a *gentleman* to remain standing until all the ladies have found their chairs." She was being a pill, and she knew it, but if she had had to marry this man the least he could do was treat her with courtesy and pause before he took ownership of her mother's settee.

Sheridan lips took on a sarcastic twist that any other person might have mistaken for a smile. He answered acidly, "What a coincidence. That's how we do it in County Roscommon. Except where I come from, it's customary for a lady to invite her gentleman friend into her house with a kind and gracious word, not just a nod of that cool blond head."

Feeling upbraided, she retorted, "You can't expect me to welcome you into my house as if we were courting, can you?" Her voice rose. It was the culmination of a bad night in a week of bad nights, and she was ready to snap. "After all, now that we're—" She heard a noise in the foyer. Whoever was there had suddenly stopped, probably having heard her distraught tone. The footsteps resumed, and soon Pumphrey entered with their coffee. He set the silver tray upon the Phyfe card table and discreetly rolled the faux-walnut pocket doors together, leaving them alone.

In a harsh whisper, she said, "You can't expect me to take to this situation with immediate grace, Mr. Sheridan. When I went out tonight, I had no idea this would happen to me. I thought there'd be time—"

"Time to back out, *Mrs. Sheridan?*"

She colored. There was that name again. Mrs. Sheridan. "Don't call me that," she asked softly.

"All right, Alana, then you call me Trevor."

There was a challenge in his voice and insistence. But there was also something else, a strange wistful note that caused an unexpected tingle down her spine.

"You're my wife now," he said, the planes of his face hardening. "Is it too much to ask that you at least give the appearance of it?"

"This isn't going to work . . . *Trevor,*" she said, his name sounding foreign yet oddly comfortable on her tongue. "There will come a day when you'll regret this hasty wedding. Despite what you think now."

"I can't imagine a circumstance that would make this situation disadvantageous," he answered, nearly gloating. "I have everything in place."

"You'll live to rue this day. You've interfered with too many lives to remain unscathed. Someone will avenge all your wrongdoing."

His gaze captured hers. "And will that someone be you?"

Yes! she wanted to cry out, though she doubted that she would ever possess the cunning to outfox him. Instead, she said gravely, "If I'm not the one to do it, you'll pardon me if I laud the person who finally does."

He suddenly laughed. "Such ominous words. Yet you should be on your knees giving thanks that I've taken you out of a bad situation."

She turned ice cold. "I could handle my uncle without your manipulations."

His eyes flickered down to her arms, the bruises now healed. "Of course," he answered sardonically.

Angered, she stood and walked to the coffeepot. Pouring them both a cup, she handed him his without a word.

When she resumed her seat, he looked at her at length. "I must tell you that tomorrow you've got to decide what servants you're to bring into my household. Also what belongings. You won't be coming back here after Saturday. If you're to get Mara into society, I insist you be under my roof as soon as possible."

Her eyes widened. She hadn't given much thought to giving up her household. Of course, she would have to do that now, as this man's wife, but the thought of losing everything familiar was unbearable. Panic seized her again. This wedding had been too quick. She'd not been able to think out all the sacrifices she'd have to make.

Where's the sacrifice? Sheridan's words echoed in her thoughts. She looked around her, at her mother's dear Belter sofa and the Duncan Phyfe mahogany card table that had been in the family almost three generations. The table's base had been carved as an American eagle spreading its wings, and she remembered with aching clarity how her father had once referred to it as Phred, making a joke out of the fact that when the Van Alens had bought the table so many decades before, the cabinetmaker who'd made it was then only an unpretentious Scotsman named Duncan Fife.

Unexpected tears threatened her eyes. She had had no attachments to the furnishings in her house. If anything, she rejected them and thought of other possibilities, as her dream of the simple white house proved. But that was before Trevor Byrne Sheridan had thrown his mighty fist into her life, destroying everything she'd hoped for and believed in. It was easy to reject the old Knickerbocker life when she thought she was destined to marry another Knickerbocker and lead what would be to her an ordinary existence. It was not easy to leave these old pieces of furniture that had her family's glorious history worn into every scratch in the priceless mahogany and upon every shiny piece of velvet upholstery when she knew she was giving them up because fate had dealt her a terrible blow.

A cold ball of emotion lodged in her throat, warning of hot tears to come. But she couldn't allow herself to cry, not in front of this man. Not again. Not after what he had done to her tonight. So she swallowed them, controlling herself like an expert. If the Knickerbockers had taught her one thing, it was how to put on a facade at a crucial moment.

"We'll honeymoon in Newport," Sheridan announced in a deep, rumbling voice.

She glanced at him; he was staring at her. His accent had filtered into his words, surprising her. Had something thrown him? Perhaps her coolness unsettled him. Perhaps despite her efforts, he'd seen her distress over their marriage and found it moved him more than he'd expected. Perhaps there was, after all, a humane man beneath that cold exterior. But when her stare met his and she looked deep within his eyes, she found nothing but defiance and the well-rehearsed self-confidence of a conqueror who was utterly convinced he had made the right decision.

He continued, this time in flawless English. "The season's just starting. You'll have time to get better acquainted with Mara. And to introduce her around."

"In Newport?"

He nodded.

She'd almost asked why his sister was coming on their honeymoon, but their marriage was a sham, executed for the sole purpose of benefiting Mara. Why wouldn't his sister come along? Mara might as well start her social conquests right away. If the truth were known, Alana was almost glad the girl would be in tow. Then she wouldn't be alone with Sheridan. "What does Mara think of our marrying?" she asked, suddenly wanting to know all the details that had led up to this catastrophe.

Sheridan finished his coffee. "She's confused by it, unsure how she might have motivated it. I haven't told her anything, and I would consider it wise if you kept silent on the matter as well."

Alana heard the threat. She whispered, "What does she think of me?"

"She speaks kindly of you." A strange emotion caught in his voice. "She, of course, speaks kindly of everyone."

Alana didn't argue. It fit well with what she remembered of Mara Sheridan. She glanced at the man who was now her husband, sitting uncomfortably on the settee that was too fussy and delicate for his large frame. His dark, angry eyes and unyielding expression gave her only one thought. If Mara Sheridan personified a saint, her brother Trevor did a magnificent job of negating his sister's goodness. He unbalanced her altruism and then some, tipping the scales toward wickedness.

"You've a lot to do tomorrow. I'll leave you." He stood and grasped the gold lion's head of his walking stick. "Send a list of the things you want. And the names of the servants you would keep."

Alana nodded numbly. She had a lot to do tomorrow, but first and foremost was a trip to Brooklyn to tell her only blood relative that she had married the night before.

Sheridan paused as if he were not sure how to phrase his next words. "Alana, I understand there were some beaux who fancied you. I expect tomorrow you owe it to them to tell them of the finality of our arrangement."

She nodded, and her bleak expression made him cynically add as an afterthought, "Take heart. If you're careful with your words, you may persuade them that though we're married, their cause is not lost."

Her mouth dropped open, she was so completely taken aback by his words. Her entire definition of marriage was undergoing a metamorphosis tonight. A husband didn't suggest things like that to his wife, not in the way she understood things. And though she didn't love this man whom she now had to call husband, his words were so crushing, they made her want to put her head into her hands and cry. Sheridan spoke vows to her one minute and the next encouraged her to string along other prospects until she might be free to consider them. It broke her heart to think of how she used to imagine marriage. Her fantasies had been nothing like this.

"Good night, Alana. I'll see you at St. Brendan's."

"Good night," she answered stiffly, unable even to look at him. She heard the pocket doors open. Before the front door had even shut behind him, she threw herself on the Belter settee and wept inconsolably.

10

The next morning Alana took the carriage to South Street, as she had done a hundred times before. The ferry across the East River was prompt, and the Van Alen brown coupé ambled off the ramp at the new Fulton Ferry Terminal at precisely noon. It took longer than expected to leave the dock area because of the work being done on the bridge. Already several blocks had been leveled to accommodate the bridge's tower and approach. Workmen were everywhere, many of them Irish.

Stopped in traffic while mules dragged huge granite stones to the construction site, she heard several of them shouting to one another in Irish Gaelic. Every now and then she'd hear part of a sentence in English. "Me mudder's cumin' ta Castle Garden" or "T'ere's the divil ta pay if we ain't done in time," all spoken in a thick Irish brogue.

Discreetly, she lifted the lace curtain from the window of the coupé and watched them. In truth, there wasn't a lot to recommend these men. They certainly didn't possess Trevor's handsomeness. They had wide florid faces and short stubby bodies worn down from years of impossibly hard work. A group standing in the distance covertly passed around an indigo glass flask while the foreman oversaw the unloading of a dray. She recalled with biting clarity Mrs. Astor's words concerning the "Irishers" who worked on the streets. These men seemed to live up to every conception of the Irish she'd ever known and the words *Irish Need Not Apply* echoed back to her from a thousand signs she'd seen in the past.

But suddenly a man caught her attention. He was a worker listening with quiet intensity to the foreman as cranes lifted the stones off the cart. The man looked up, and Alana saw the same rebellious dark eyes that her husband had and the same lean, hungry expression on his face. The two men couldn't be related, but Alana couldn't get the picture of Trevor out of her mind.

Quickly the stones were unloaded, and traffic once more began moving, but from the hidden veil of lace at her carriage window, Alana watched the dark-eyed Irishman go back to his job, shovel in hand, as he and the others dug the deep pit that was to serve as the foundation for the bridge tower. It was terrible work this man had, and just from looking at him Alana could see his intelligence was wasted by the drudgery of the shovel. "Irish spoons" she'd heard shovels called before. She now knew why.

Letting the curtain fall back, she leaned against her seat. That man with his dark eyes and angry defiance wouldn't leave her mind. She hoped he made it—that the soul-stripping toil and tedium of his work didn't break him, working for pennies a day, a slave to the shovel. She was amazed anyone could overcome such odds, yet some had.

Her thoughts wandered to her husband. Trevor Sheridan had risen from the streets. Picturing him now as she pictured that worker, filthy from head to toe, a desperate edge to his expression, she suddenly understood a part of him. She could hardly imagine what he'd had to do to get where he was today, and as she thought of the chances against his succeeding, she was filled with a grudging, solemn admiration.

She gazed past the curtains and found they were already far into Brooklyn's countryside. Sheep grazed to her right, and to her left the claylike soil was already tilled and ready for spring planting. As usual, the closer she got to her sister's asylum, the more the pain seared her heart. It was terrible what the Irish had to do to survive in this new country of theirs, but poverty wasn't the only prison, as Alana well knew. She sat in her velvet-upholstered coach, the agonies of the past engulfing her as if she were reliving them again. Prejudice and poverty were tragedies, but there were other kinds of tragedy. As the carriage turned right at the sign quietly announcing entrance to the Park View Asylum, Alana found Tragedy's arms around her once again.

The nurse in her blue-and-white striped gown, white apron, and cap met her at the end of the drive, an unusually bright smile pasted upon her lips. She greeted Alana almost too warmly and took her hand.

While they walked the long glass corridor to the back of the home, Nurse Steine filled her in on her sister's progress. "She's having a good day, Miss Van Alen. See for yourself. Out there, by the duck pond. See? She's feeding the ducklings." Nurse Steine stopped and pointed through the glass atrium.

Alana's gaze followed, and she saw Christabel's figure on a green cast-iron bench, her flaxen hair blowing in the soft wind. Her sister made a heart-wrenchingly lovely sight. She'd recently turned sixteen and was becoming quite a beauty. Her figure was petite and well formed, her face as flawless as the face of the Madonna in the *Pietà*. And until she went to her grave, Alana would believe her sister was as beautiful inside as out. "Thank you. I'm so glad she's happy today." Alana looked at the nurse. "I'll go to her—"

"Wait, Miss Van Alen, if you will."

Alana paused.

"She's been having nightmares again. She's trying to remember the fire. I'm afraid she may ask you about it, and I strongly suggest you redirect her."

Alana nodded. When the nurse turned to leave her, she asked a question that had long been heavy on her mind. "I'm not a physician, Nurse Steine, but wouldn't my sister be better off remembering what happened that night? That might heal her better than any medicine."

"Killing one's parents is an ugly crime, Miss Van Alen. The shock of the truth could destroy her."

"Or set her free." Alana became insistent. "I keep saying this, but I'll say it again: She is not guilty. We must keep that foremost in our minds. If Christabel could remember the circumstances of the fire, we might be able to finally convince the police chief that the fire was indeed an accident."

"And what if it's otherwise? Can you accept that? Or is it better to live in this limbo?"

There was no softness in Nurse Steine's words. Alana attributed her callousness to years of working with grief-stricken relatives. "I know in my heart my sister did not commit the crimes of which she's been accused."

The nurse stared at her, a patronizing smile on her large mouth. "Miss Van Alen," she said, "you were very lucky that Park View was offered as an alternative to jail. Your sister's youth and the fact that your uncle lined the police chief's palms with bank notes, placed her in a fine institution. I think it best not to rock the boat. We know what's right for your sister. Your uncle is happy with us. Can't you be also?"

"You've been kind to her, I know that. I'm not suggesting that—"

"Then visit your sister, Miss Van Alen." Nurse Steine again pointed to her sister at the end of the sweeping lawn that led to the pond. "You've precious little time with Christabel. Should you spend that time with me?"

Frustrated, Alana nodded mutely. She'd had this discussion many times—with her uncle, with the police chief, with this nurse. At the beginning she'd been much more passionate, much more outspoken, much more hopeful. But given the same answers and alternatives again and again, she now felt as if she were merely playing out a recurring dream.

"Go see your sister, Miss Van Alen. I'll instruct your driver to have the carriage pulled around in an hour."

The nurse's words were civil, and the woman had always been kind to Christabel, but Alana would never like her. There was something about her she didn't quite trust. With that thought on her mind, Alana opened the wrought-iron door of the atrium and went to seek her sister.

"Christal?" she said softly when she had crossed the velvety lawn. Using her sister's nickname again, Alana said, "Christal, have you forgotten me in just two short weeks?"

Christal turned around, and her sky blue eyes filled with delight and pain. She rose from the bench and threw her arms around her. Alana hugged her as she always did, desperately, tightly.

"Oh, Alana, I was thinking of you today," Christal whispered against her hair. "Remember how father used to take us to Loft's confectionery? I've such a craving for licorice right now, I don't know if I can endure it."

Alana smiled. Reluctantly she pulled back and looked at Christal. Her sister was wearing a pale blue taffeta gown that exactly matched her eyes and a basque of plum velvet trimmed with fringe along the corset. She looked beautiful, far too beautiful to be imprisoned in this home with no one to ever see her.

"Come sit with me a minute. It's such a warm, lovely day, is it not?" Christal led her back to the cast-iron bench. They both sat, and the fluffy brown ducklings gathered at their ankles looking for bread crumbs.

"I'm so glad you're in high spirits today, Christal," Alana began, unsure of how to approach the subject of her marriage. "I've something to tell you and—"

"It's not bad news, is it?" Christal interrupted, her luminous eyes shadowed with fear.

"Of course not." Alana took her hands and held them to reassure her. She considered her marriage bad news, but for Christal it was salvation, and for that reason alone Alana was determined to show she was happy.

"Why, that's a diamond ring," Christal murmured, staring down at her sister's hands. "Have you gotten engaged, then?"

Alana opened her mouth to respond, but the words escaped her. She hardly knew how to begin. "I'm not engaged, Christal. It's much more than that." She paused, knowing what she had to say would come as a shock. "I'm already married, in fact. Last night I was wed."

Christal's expression was an odd mixture of joy and wounded feelings. She whispered, "That's wonderful news. I'm so glad. Truly I am. I wish you every happiness." Her eyes turned toward the pond so that Alana could not see how hurt she was. "I know I'd never be allowed to attend your wedding, Alana. I understand why you didn't tell me. I just wish I was involved in your life—even just a little bit." A small frown furrowed her brow. "I don't even know his name, do I?"

Alana impulsively gathered her in her arms. She was close to weeping. "You *are* my life, Christal. Not a minute goes by that I don't think of you. Don't ever think that while you're in this place, I plan on forgetting you."

"But you should forget me." Christal began to tremble. "Good heavens, what does your husband think?"

"I haven't told him," Alana answered defiantly. "And I'm not going to tell him. Someday I'll get you out of this place, Christal, and I'm not going to air the family's dirty laundry for any stranger to see."

"This man is no stranger. He's your husband. You'll have to tell him one day." Christal tried to hide a shudder. "Did you marry Anson, then? I know he was calling on you a lot."

Alana stiffened. How could she explain everything that had happened to her? "I didn't marry Anson," she answered slowly. "I married an Irishman named Trevor Sheridan. And the reason I didn't tell you, love, is because I didn't even know this man myself until last Monday. It's a very complicated story—"

"An Irishman?" Christal exclaimed. "Do we know any Irishers?" Her eyes lit up with a deliciously scandalous idea. "Did you marry one of the help, then?"

Alana laughed. Her sister wasn't being malicious. On the contrary, Christal's limited experience was simply catching up to her. Her naiveté was charming, and Alana wished desperately that she could be there tomorrow at St. Brendan's for her wedding. "Trevor Sheridan is as far from being a servant as Caroline Astor is," she said, still smiling. "In fact, he's got millions and millions. I'll be able to take care of you forever, Christal. We'll buy a little farmhouse here in Brooklyn when I get you out of here, and we'll spend the rest of our lives there without a care in the world. I can already see it. It'll be atop a grassy green hill, with newly whitewashed clapboards, just a simple house. . . ." Alana became so caught up in her imaginings, she didn't see the strange look her sister gave her until she had almost gone too far.

"But you're married now, Alana. What can you be thinking of?" Christal frowned.

"Oh, but that's not—" Alana began, then stopped herself. She couldn't tell Christal about her arrangement with Sheridan. Her sister would see quite clearly that Alana had sacrificed herself. Then Christal would feel guilty, and Alana couldn't bear that.

"I don't know what I'm saying." Alana released a forced laugh. "I've been married so short a time, I can't think straight."

"He must be a generous man to let you come here and tell me about your wedding when you should be on your honeymoon." Christal's eyes glistened with happiness. "Tell me he's a fine man. You deserve a fine man."

Alana stared at her, unable to answer for a moment. She couldn't explain that her honeymoon hadn't yet begun or that her "real" wedding had yet to take place. It was so terribly complicated, and from Christal's expression, all her sister really wanted to know was if she was happy. "He's

everything I want," she whispered flatly. It was true. As true
as her logic could make it.

"Oh, I'm so glad. Now you'll have children. They'll heal
all these wounds I've caused. I know they will." Christal
hugged her again and Alana numbly accepted it, glad that
her sister couldn't see her face.

When they parted, Christal suddenly looked tired, and
Alana knew she should leave. She gathered her steel-mesh
purse and straightened her kidskin gloves, but before she
stood from the bench, Christal said, "Did Nurse Steine tell
you I've been having dreams?"

Sorrow filled Alana's eyes. Her heart grew heavy. "Don't
let's talk about it. It's such a beautiful day."

Christal tried to hide her torture behind a pale, beautiful
face. Her hand shook as she placed it over her sister's. "No.
I must tell you, Alana. Someday I'm going to remember
what happened. I must remember. I *must*."

"They say not to. My darling, don't do this to yourself.
You're so young, I can't stand it that you've got this weigh-
ing on your mind."

Christal broke away. She swallowed, and Alana could see
tears glistening on her cheeks. "In my dream I went so far,
I could feel my hand burning." Christal looked down at her
palm. She wasn't wearing gloves, and Alana saw the unusual
scar that had convicted her sister in the eyes of the police
chief who'd investigated their parents' death.

The scar on her palm was in the shape of a rose, the exact
pattern of the silver repoussé doorknobs that graced their
parents' bedchamber. When her parents had burned to
death in their bedstead and the door of their bedroom had
been found locked, all evidence had pointed to Christabel,
then only thirteen. The police had found her hiding in her
wardrobe, obviously having escaped the blaze from the
ledge outside her parents' room. She was so traumatized
that to this day Christal had never regained her memory of
what had happened that night or why she'd been in their

parents' bedroom during the fire that had at one point raged so hot, the doorknobs had become like cattle brands.

With vile clarity, Alana remembered how kind Didier had been afterward, settling their parents' will, financing the repairs to the house on Washington Square. He'd seemed genuinely shocked by what had happened, especially at Christabel's fate. Alana would never forget his face when the superintendent of police told him about the incriminating burn on Christal's hand. Didier had been so moved that he'd personally convinced the superintendent to show mercy on Christal because of her tender years and pleaded for her to be put away at Park View instead of jail . . . or worse. He'd been beside himself to protect the unsullied Van Alen name and he'd done a magnificent job of wiping up the tragedy behind him. It was the last kind act she'd known him to do. And if Didier hadn't had an alibi of being seen at the Academy of Music that night, Alana might not have believed, as she'd been forced to, that her parents' death was nothing but a bizarre accident.

"Don't let's speak of it now, Christal. You look so tired, this can't be good for you," Alana whispered.

"No, I'm going to remember, Alana. It's my only hope."

"Christal—" said Alana, her voice breaking with emotion. She couldn't stand to see her sister in such pain, her dear little sister who had gone with her to Loft's confectionery all those years ago and with wide eyes had surveyed the rainbow of gumdrops and chocolates, only to agree with her older sister that the licorice was best. There were all kinds of misfortunes in this world, and poverty was definitely one of them, but at that moment, if working with a shovel would have eased her sister's plight, Alana would have dug until her hands bled.

"Please go now, Alana." Christal wiped her cheeks and stood. She crumbled her remaining bread crumbs for the ducklings still gathered at her feet. "I really am tired, and you've been here too long. You mustn't make your husband impatient on my account."

Alana stood, wanting anything but to leave at that moment. "Let me help you to your room."

Christal shook her head. "You can't help me with any of this, Alana. In the end, I'm the only one who can do it."

"Please don't upset yourself." Alana went to take her hand, but Christal brushed it away.

"No, Alana, you must leave now. I can't be responsible for taking you away from your husband. He's already been so kind to let you come. You must tell him how grateful I am"—Christal's voice shook—"and you must promise me that you'll tell him that I said he's wed the most brave and dear lady in all of New York."

Alana began to weep, and unwilling to upset her sister further, she ran up the hill toward the front of the asylum and her waiting carriage. Christabel didn't watch her go. The ducklings still gathered at her feet, and she stared down at them with the tragic face of a doomed Ophelia.

Alana's eyes were red and puffy from crying when the coupé stopped in Washington Square. Despite the clamor for her attention to the upcoming wedding, she went directly to her room and stayed there, ignoring everyone from the delivery boy to sweet-tempered Margaret. She wanted desperately to cheer herself. In the past she'd always found a way to do it, but this time she wondered if she would ever smile again. The tears still streamed down her cheeks every time she thought of Christal.

Her sister's plight had always affected her, but today something inside her broke, and now the dam no longer held. Perhaps it was the strain she'd been under, perhaps tomorrow's impending ceremony, but Alana knew in her heart that it was neither of those things. Seeing Christal as she had today was what was breaking her heart. Her sister's attempt at bravery in the face of such monumental sorrow made Alana ashamed for ever having indulged in a moment of self-pity. Her troubles, even Sheridan's forced marriage, seemed inconsequential compared to Christal's. As she wiped her tears again with her damp handkerchief wadded tightly in her hand, Alana swore with all the power of her soul that someday she would see her sister out of that place and restored to the life she'd been meant to lead.

A knock interrupted her solitude, and Alana was tempted to ignore it. But when the couturiere, Madame LaBoeuve, called to her in a desperate plea for her to try on her wedding dress so that it could be finished by morning, Alana took pity on the woman, wiped her eyes, and opened the door.

She looked nothing like a joyful blushing bride, but Alana didn't care. Ignoring the curious stares of Madame LaBoeuve's seamstresses, she stepped out of her carriage dress and stripped down to her pink silk corset and chemise threaded with matching pink ribbons. Madame LaBoeuve and her seamstresses went to work expertly pinning and basting the satin gown, all of them very noticeably trying to ignore her red eyes and tear-stained cheeks. Alana knew she should care what they thought of her, but at that moment she just wanted to be left alone.

She should have known she wouldn't be so lucky.

Not a second had passed after Madame LaBoeuve placed the last straight pin when Alana's maid, Margaret, could be heard protesting vehemently outside the bedroom door. All eyes turned, and to Alana's horror, Trevor Sheridan suddenly appeared with Margaret near hysterics at his coattails trying to bar him from the room.

"The man won't listen, miss!" Margaret shrieked. "Shall I fetch Kevin to throw him out? What shall I do?"

"Whatever is this about?" Alana gasped, feeling as if she were naked beneath Sheridan's stare with just the loosely basted bridal gown held to her bosom.

"I've never seen such a beast of a man—to barge into a lady's boudoir!" Margaret squealed.

Sheridan ripped his gaze from Alana, flashed a dark smile down to the little maid, and said for her ears only, *"Go dachta an diabhal tú."*

Margaret's eyes widened, as if to say the language, if not the words, were familiar.

"You don't know what I've said, do you, Pegeen?" Sheridan inquired, vaguely annoyed.

Warily, Margaret shook her brown curls.

"The English take you, then, if you don't know the tongue of your motherland. Go on! Go back to the kitchens. Leave. All of you," he suddenly commanded to Madame LaBoeuve and her army of seamstresses. "I want to be alone with my"—his gaze again traveled to Alana, who stood in the brightness of the windows clutching her bridal gown—"fiancée," he finished with an amused glitter in his eyes.

"This is outrageous behavior," Alana protested, his gaze making her heart thump wildly in her chest. "You can't come into my bedroom! It's not done!"

"It's now done," he answered succinctly as the last little seamstress scurried past him. Even Margaret had disappeared, running back to her Kevin, no doubt, to see what kind of Gaelic curse Sheridan had placed on her brow.

"Have you no decency? What gives you the right to barge into my bedroom like this?" she hissed when they were alone, unable to believe the gall of the man.

"I'm your husband. That gives me the right."

"But no one else knows we've wed. You've shocked my servants."

"Let them be shocked." He walked closer and suddenly saw her red-rimmed eyes. "You've been crying," he stated flatly, the expression in his eyes the only hint of his interest.

Anger colored her all the way to her temples. She turned her face from his and said in a low, vengeful voice, "Why shouldn't I cry? I've a lot to cry about."

Her sister's situation was killing her, but he didn't know this, and when she looked at him again, it was obvious he had mistaken her tears as a sign of her shame over their marriage. If it were possible for a man to freeze, Trevor Sheridan had done just that. He was never a terribly warm man, but in seconds his manner and attitude suddenly changed from neutral to menacing. With stiff, formal steps he went to a chintz-covered chair by the fireplace. He sat as if defiantly claiming his territory and laid his walking stick like a rapier across his lap.

She strode over to him, nearly tripping on the long bridal train. "If you wanted to speak with me, you should have waited for me in the parlor. Why have you barged in here like this?"

"I don't wait in parlors." His eyes were as cold as she'd ever seen them. How such a dazzling combination of gold and green and brown could so suddenly turn to ice was beyond her ability to comprehend. "You're my wife," he rasped. "You'll see me now."

His words sent a chill down her spine, but she found them all much more preferable to the word *wife*. He made it sound like a curse. "This was not a part of our bargain," she whispered harshly. "I didn't agree to allow you to invade my privacy whenever you thought it might convenience you. You must leave this minute."

He stared at her, his gaze unwillingly flickering over the white satin that was taut against her breasts. Nonetheless, his expression remained dispassionate. "Would you have rather I sent my attorneys here instead? I wager your privacy would have been more violated with a dozen lawyers crawling around this room."

"Your lawyers would have at least waited for me in the parlor."

"I'm not sure about that. They're a very excitable group. When I informed them I had married, they fell over themselves to try to see you. Apparently they don't like anyone encroaching upon my estate."

"Well, they're intelligent men. I certainly intend to have some recompense after what you've put me through." She thought of her sister's bills. Those lawyers wouldn't find a way to circumvent what she had due.

He shook his cursedly handsome head. "I've told them

about our agreement. But for you to get anything, they insisted that you sign these papers immediately. They were about to come when I told them I'd bring them to you myself."

"How gracious of you." She couldn't keep the acid out of her words, especially when she saw how premeditated this was. He'd come instead of his lawyers just to see the irritation spark in her green eyes.

He smiled cynically, coldly, and reached into his breast pocket. He took out a thick sheaf of paper and laid it on the table next to him. "Have you a pen?"

"What am I to sign?" A small frown appeared on her brow.

"This stipulates the funds I am giving to you. Is ten thousand a month sufficient?"

The blood rushed from her head so quickly, she nearly fainted. Calculating quickly in her mind, she realized even if they were married for only a year, she'd have enough money to take care of Christal forever if necessary. Suddenly she was feeling more optimistic.

"Are you agreeable to that, Alana?"

She looked at Sheridan and nodded. Finding a pen and ink at her escritoire, she brought them over to the table and signed all the pages he designated. She wanted to read what she was signing, but there were so many *hereins* and *moreovers* that the words became like Greek. There were three pages devoted just to "the definition of authenticity of signature," whatever that meant.

Disgusted, she blotted her signatures, and he placed the papers back in his breast pocket. "I can already hear the sighs of relief at Glass, Goldstein, Sach et al." That cynical smile again graced his lips.

"Now that the majority of your money is safe from my greed, will you excuse me?" She raised her eyebrows and pointed to the door.

He looked in no hurry to depart. His gaze again lowered to her wedding gown. Even in pieces it looked impressive.

The satin clung and draped just where it should—at her breasts, at her waist, along her derriere. His eyes warmed, and he seemed to hesitate. "You haven't told me what you want sent over. This house goes for sale tomorrow." His lips quirked in disgust. "I suppose you'll insist on keeping that annoying maid of yours?"

"Margaret's been with me since the day she arrived at Castle Garden. I wouldn't think of putting her out on the street."

He rolled his eyes. "So be it. When they arrive tomorrow, tell them my butler Whittaker is the one they must answer to."

"Whittaker. You've an English butler, then?"

She'd made the comment with the most benign intentions, mostly because she was curious to know a little about the situation in which she was destined to find herself tomorrow. But Sheridan did not find the comment so innocuous. He grew still; his hands tightened on his ebony walking stick. "This isn't Ireland, now is it?" he said caustically. "We're in America, and the British can work for the Irish for a change when the Irish can pay for it."

"I meant only that—"

"I know what you meant."

She put her hands out in supplication. "No, really—"

He stood, and the words died on her lips. He was mistaking her comment for something she hadn't intended, something cruel and vicious. As much as she didn't like the man, she didn't want him thinking that of her. Yet his attitude was infuriating. He was always so anxious to jump to the worst conclusion.

"The wedding is to be at nine o'clock," he explained in a frigid, perfunctory manner. "I don't want anything to delay it. Lent is over, and the priests have too many to marry. I can't reschedule."

"If only I'd been thrown to you during Lent. Then I wouldn't be in this mess."

A black smile touched his lips. It never came close to

those eyes. "You can cry some more, wife. It's not bad enough you've married an Irisher, but you've got a Catholic one as well."

"Stop it." Her chest heaved with suppressed anger. "Not everything I say is a premeditated slur against your background."

"Forgive me if I find that difficult to believe."

"No, I won't forgive you." She pulled up her train and followed him as he walked to the door. "I can't live as your wife and guard my tongue against any and every phrase that might be taken in the wrong way. You can't burden me with that too."

"Yes, and as you've just pointed out, I've already put a lot of burdens on you."

She grabbed his lapels and forced him to look at her. She whispered harshly, unwilling to let the servants hear her, "You have burdened me, and don't you ever forget it! You've forced me into a loveless marriage. You've taken away all my money. You've nearly ruined me with scandal. Yet for the last time I shall say this: You misjudge me when you twist my words. I don't care that you're Irish, and upon my grave, I swear I meant to attend your sister's debut. So knowing that fact, you will now and forever treat me accordingly!"

He hesitated, and for one precious second he almost looked as if he believed her. But not totally. His ire raised, he cupped her jaw and forced her to look at him. "I hate to blacken that snow-white soul you'd like everyone to see, Alana, but you've all the selfish reasons in the world to say such things to me. No, you're just like the rest of those Knickerbockers. You care about the 'purity' of those around you and little else."

"Yes, I care about that! But it's the purity of their hearts I judge them by, and I've seen well enough of yours to know you haven't a clean spot on it!" Angry that he'd so upset her, she released a moan of fury and pried his fingers from her chin. But before she could get them off, a pin along the seam of her bodice jabbed at her and viciously pulled along the tender flesh next to her breast. She tried to grab it, but the seam was underneath her arm, and she couldn't see well enough to find it. In agony, she reached around until she felt a strong hand on her arm and another at the seam searching for the pin. When Sheridan had several pins taken off, revealing a good portion of her pink silk corset, he finally found the offending object hidden in the pink-ribboned edge of her chemise. He removed it, then took out his handkerchief and pressed it to the edge of her breast to absorb the tiny drop of blood before it stained her delicate undergarments.

"I can do this now," she said stiffly, embarrassed that he'd seen so much of her corset.

He nodded and allowed her to take his handkerchief. Surely it was her imagination, but when he removed his hand, it brushed lightly against the side of her breast, and she could have sworn that it trembled.

"Your handkerchief," she whispered when she no longer needed it. She thrust it into his palm, a small crimson dot the only evidence of her wound.

He stared at the drop of blood, then at her as she clutched the sides of her seams together to preserve her modesty. That mysterious Irish fire burned again in his eyes, and as if he were afraid of being burned, he glanced down at the red drop and said cruelly, "Funny. It's not blue at all. In fact, it looks remarkably like Irish blood. Who'd have thought?"

His sarcasm cut her. "We both bleed," she answered quietly. "I think it wise neither of us forget that."

He pocketed the handkerchief. "I'll see you in the morning."

"In the morning," she nearly sobbed before he walked out the door.

11

The day of Alana's wedding arrived, and she thought it fitting that it was still dark when she arose to dress. Madame LaBoeuve, looking ten years older than when she'd first shown herself at Alana's door, appeared with her dress at precisely six o'clock. The gown was now finished, with a pointed basque-waist richly oversewn with passementerie of pearls that must have taken an army of seamstresses all night to attach. Her skirt was satin, looped up in back to reveal an underskirt of Duchesse lace. It had a simple virginal veil of silk tulle that covered her face and tumbled to the floor elegantly behind her. Everything from the rose-point lace of her gloves to the satin of her shoes was the tender color of snow in candlelight, even the bridal bouquet. Sheridan had delivered orange blossoms.

Her attire was exquisite. No cost had been spared. But Alana could find no joy in it. As Margaret tightened her white damask corset and handed her her silk garters, all Alana could think about was how much this day should have meant to her, how much it would have meant to her if she'd been in love with her bridegroom. A painful longing tugged at her heart, but with it came the doomed acceptance of what was to come. She had to marry Sheridan. Everything she cared about depended on it, yet that thought was little solace as she picked up her bouquet and smelled the fresh sweet scent of orange blossoms. In years to come that innocent fragrance should bring back vivid memories of a joyful day. But already her wedding day was something she wanted fervently to forget.

She was dressed before the first blush of morning painted Washington Square. She couldn't sit easily because of the yards of fabric of her heavy satin train, so she stood at the window and watched the emboldened sunlight stride across the park, her breakfast still untouched on the tray on her desk.

She did her best not to think of her dream, the white clapboard house and the faceless man who always turned away just when she called out to him. It had always been doubtful she would meet that man. Still she thought about him, especially this morning while she hung between two worlds, one she desperately wanted to exist and one that tragically did.

"It's time, miss. Your uncle's downstairs. Oh, miss, you do look beautiful!" Margaret dabbed her eyes. "You're so lovely, I'm sorry I won't be there."

Alana turned from the window and forced herself to smile. "But if you leave now, I'm sure you can find room in the pew with the other servants."

"How can I, miss? After what I did to your dear Mr. Sheridan?" Another bout of tears threatened Margaret.

Alana gathered her bouquet, unable to meet Margaret's eyes, especially after those last words. "You didn't know the man barging in here yesterday was my hus—" She coughed, unable to believe her near mistake. "Fiancé," she corrected quickly.

Typically, Margaret could go from tearful contrition to heated indignation in lightning speed. "But the man should know better! You weren't married yesterday! He had no right to come into your bedroom!"

Alana smiled uneasily, thinking just how much right Sheridan did have in the bedroom. "Please fetch Kevin and go to the church. It won't be the same if you're not there."

"Oh, miss, can it be that you're a bride today? Wasn't it

only yesterday when you and your dear sweet sister were wearin' short dresses?" Margaret's gaze wandered to the daguerreotype of Christal, and she threatened to cry again. "What a shame the poor lass died so young."

"I wish she could be here," Alana whispered, tears filling her eyes too. She looked at Christal's picture, and a devastating regret tightened in her chest.

Margaret wiped her eyes for the last time. "Here, look what I've done now. I've made you glum. And this is such a wonderful day! Oh, miss, I wish you every joy! How I'd love to see you say the vows."

"You must be there, Margaret." Alana went to her desk, and from a tiny silver Le Roux box she took out enough coins for a hackney coach. "Go on. Put on your finery and take this. You'll be there before I am."

Margaret suddenly turned shy. "I couldn't, miss. How could I pay you back?"

Alana almost laughed. With as much dignity as she could summon, she said, "Marrying the man that I am this morn, I don't think we have to worry about these few coins. In the future I suspect there'll be more of these than I'll ever know what to do with."

"May the Holy Mother Mary bless you, miss. For all that you've done for us." Embarrassed, Margaret scooped up the coins and curtsied. She was gone before Alana could say another word.

Despondent once more, Alana looked at the picture of Christal, and her heart broke again. She gathered her voluminous satin skirts, walked up to the velvet-framed daguerreotype, and touched the glass that had just been replaced. She kissed her sister on the cheek. "Someday, Christal," she whispered. "Someday I'll find the way to exonerate you, and then I'll dance at your wedding."

Reverently, she placed the daguerreotype in the stack of boxes by her door that were to go to the Sheridan mansion. She took an encouraging breath and walked out of the room.

Her uncle met her in the foyer, and her eyes told him exactly what kind of cur she thought him. She frostily accepted his hand as he helped her to the carriage, thinking how different the situation was from the last time he'd put her into a carriage. Yet how alike it was. Again he was taking her to Sheridan. Again she didn't want to go.

In oppressive silence they rode up Fifth Avenue. The crowds grew thick as they passed the Sheridan mansion and thicker still as they approached the church. The Four Hundred were as close to royalty as New York had; there were almost a thousand people outside the church watching the display. The crush of carriages was phenomenal, and they lined up along Fifth Avenue like shiny black top hats all the way to Fifty-fourth Street. There were so many of them, the bridal carriage had to wait for almost half an hour for all the guests to pull up and disembark.

At last, it was time.

William Backhouse Astor, Jr., descended the marble steps of the medieval-style church and assisted her from the vehicle. Although most believed him not to be the illustrious figure his father had been, Alana still thought he was dashing. He wore morning gray, his tall stature complemented by the swallow-tailed coat and top hat. His enormous black mustache was fashionably curled like the horns of a water buffalo until it grew into his substantial sideburns. Though she could tell he was disturbed by the publicity of this wedding, he offered his arm with staunch politeness. His face was drawn as if he didn't particularly relish the task before him, and Alana would always wonder if this was because of the row caused by her notorious husband or his notorious wife.

In the vestibule two tiny pages dressed in black-velvet Gainsborough suits lifted her train. The organ began Handel's *Water Music*, and suddenly she found herself walking down the aisle, her hand lightly resting on William Astor's arm as she headed for that dark, forbidding man who stood bleakly before the altar with the bishop.

With every step she wanted to run in the other direction. Their marriage at Delmonico's had been short, and she'd been so numbed by the whole ordeal she could hardly remember it. Now, however, everything struck her with cutting clarity: the shocked crowd, most of them Protestant members of Grace Church, the metropolis's most exclusive court of heaven, scandalized to be sitting in what they believed to be a pagan place of worship, silent as she and her escort passed row after row of pews; the frigid stature of Mrs. Astor who refused to turn and look at her; the rakish young man, a younger copy of Sheridan, who nonchalantly eyed her with approval as he stood next to his brother; and Mara, Sheridan's choice for maid of honor, who walked just ahead of her down the aisle, heart-wrenchingly lovely in a pink satin gown inappropriately innocent and short for her womanly sixteen years.

But if there were only two things she would remember of this day in the years to come, it would be the overpowering sweet citrus scent of orange blossoms and the look on Sheridan's handsome face when their eyes at last met. She would never forget that look.

Her bridegroom's eyes glittered with conflict. He was triumphant. The gleam in the gilded depths of those hazel eyes told her so. Yet there was something else there, something she couldn't quite name that ate at his glory and took one cutting edge off the sword of his victory. Perhaps it was a tiny glimmer of guilt for what he had done to her, perhaps it was only a sudden jab of doubt that maybe this marriage was not destined to be the simple bargain he'd planned. She didn't know. She only knew he'd seen to it that their marriage was even now rock-solid in the eyes of his church and the law. There was absolutely no turning back.

William Astor left her at Sheridan's side and returned to the pew where his wife stood. Alana finally noticed that Sheridan wore morning gray also. He had on a dove-colored frock coat and dark-gray striped trousers. His cravat was pearl, his shirt blinding white, a startling contrast to the black hair that had been slicked back with Macassar oil. This had the stunning effect of making his shoulders look even broader, the lines of his face more austere, his eyes arresting, his gaze inescapable.

She somehow had the power to tear her gaze away when the bishop made his exhortation. Finished, the bishop then turned to her bridegroom and boomed out his words as if he wanted to make sure there could be no one in the church questioning this lawful union about to take place.

"Trevor Byrne Sheridan," said the bishop, his face grave and deadly serious, "wilt thou take Alice Diana Van Alen, here present, for thy lawful wife, according to the rite of our holy Mother, the Church?"

His chin lifting in defiance, Sheridan said in a deep, confident voice, "I will."

The bishop nodded resignedly and turned to her. "Alice Diana Van Alen, wilt thou take Trevor Byrne Sheridan, here present, for thy lawful husband, according to the rite of our holy Mother, the Church?"

Alana's heart seemed to stop in her chest. The entire church seemed to still and lean forward to listen. The words were so simple, and though she knew they wouldn't change a thing, whether she uttered them or not, in this huge Gothic church with the presence of both God and man casting judgment upon her, it seemed blasphemous to speak anything but the truth. She glanced at Sheridan, and he was as still as a statue. His gaze burned into her as if daring her to defy him. "I will," she whispered, dooming herself into making those words the truth.

The bishop took her trembling hand and placed it in the bridegroom's. Sheridan's was warm and strong, and its strength seemed to seep into her and keep her standing.

Sheridan made his pledge in his usual assured, stiff manner. When it was her turn, her voice quavered and fell, the emotion she felt coloring every word until she ended with the hushed phrase "until death do us part."

They knelt, and Alana trembled a smile at Mara while the girl valiantly tried to assist her with her enormous train.

"I join you together in marriage, in the name of the Father, and of the Son, and of the Holy Ghost. Amen." The bishop sprinkled them with holy water, then began the Blessing of the Ring. When he was through, he sprinkled the ring with holy water in the form of a cross and handed it to Sheridan, who took it and turned to her.

Like thunder and lightning, their gazes met. She stared hard at him, and even through the mist of her veil, her eyes were reprimanding and beseeching. His held only defiance and an iron-hard determination that said, "I *will* do this."

She looked down to remove the diamond from her finger so he could place his wedding ring there, but before she could do it, his hand stopped her. He took the ring the bishop had blessed, a perfect circle of sapphires, and placed it on the finger with the diamond, saying, "With this ring I thee wed, and plight unto thee my troth."

She glanced down at her hand laden with both his costly rings. "Now you're married to me twice," they said to her, making the panic inside her begin to swell. She looked at him and saw him take off a heavy gold Claddagh ring, in the shape of two hands holding a heart with a small crown over the heart. As if performing an old Gaelic tradition, he turned the ring so that the heart no longer faced outward, as if to symbolize the intimacy and fidelity of marriage.

The bishop began his nuptial blessing, and his every word drove another knife of guilt into her heart. ". . . to be so inseperately bound to him, that Thou didst give to her body its beginning from his body—thus teaching us, that it should never be lawful to sever that which it had pleased Thee to form out of one substance. . . ."

She couldn't even look at Sheridan. The betrayal of those words made her want to cry out and run down the aisle, fall to her knees, and beg forgiveness. How could he stand so quietly and listen when he knew they were making a mockery of them?

She muffled a sob. The bishop continued his blessing, placing his hand upon her crown. ". . . do Thou graciously look down upon this handmaiden. . . . May she please her husband, as did Rachel; be prudent, as was Rebecca; long-lived and faithful like Sara. . . . May she be fruitful in offspring: be approved and innocent. . . ."

A tear slipped down her cheek. She cared not a whit if Sheridan saw it. He was a cad to have done the things he'd done to her, and worse for bringing her to this church to make a pledge that held no more weight than dust.

"You may kiss your bride, Trevor Sheridan. You've now earned the right."

Before she could take a breath, Sheridan lifted her veil and placed his finger beneath her chin. He bent to kiss her, but her instincts overtook her and she unconsciously pulled back.

It was the wrong thing to do. She doubted anyone in the pews could see what had happened, but Sheridan had. To him, her rejection had been loud and clear, and those dark hazel eyes nearly spewed fire. His arm went around her. She couldn't utter a moan. His mouth slammed into hers, and she felt the searing scorch of his tongue as it forced its way between her teeth. His arm grasped her waist and lifted her clear off the floor to the gasps of shock and amazement of the guests in the pews.

Next to her, Mara released a giggle. But Alana hardly heard it. Her face flushed with anger, and her ears rang with fury. She wanted to beat him from her, but she couldn't in front of this crowd. His tongue burned against her, a delicious combination of velvet and steel, and the unwanted desire for him that rose in the pit of her belly made her even more furious.

Finally the scandalized bishop bade Sheridan stop. Trevor reluctantly released her, but before they turned to face their guests, the bishop whispered to him, "I caution you to control those passions, my good man, or you'll one day find yourself in the fires of hell because of them."

Sheridan, with his usual irreverence, said, "To hell or to Connacht, Father?"

He took her hand and placed it on his arm. The color was still high on her face when they turned and faced the congregation. She wanted to rub her lips, to wipe the kiss from them, but that wouldn't wipe it from her mind. His behavior was calculated to shock everyone, including her. She had expected her anger. What she hadn't expected was the desire that had rushed through her veins. It unsettled her so much that when Mara stepped forward to take her bouquet—for only a bride could wear orange blossoms, and now she was a married woman—Alana gave her a blank look. When she finally understood what the girl wanted, she gave her the bouquet and immediately felt Sheridan's hand tighten upon her arm. He escorted her down the aisle to the music of "Lullay My Liking."

It was not until he had deposited her and her train into the carriage and climbed in beside her, his walking stick resting on his lap, that she dared confront him. "Nothing like this was to go on. You promised me," she snapped.

"And what has you so upset?" he asked as the carriage started up amid the cheers of hundreds. "I thought everything went as planned. Even that old witch Caroline Astor was there, albeit scowling." This last comment made him chuckle.

She found no humor in it. "She had a right to scowl about this unholy union. That your priest could marry us, knowing these lies!"

"The bishop knows naught of our 'arrangement.' Although I suspect he wonders how I was able to persuade you to the Catholic altar."

"With blackmail and bribery! What a wonderful start to a marriage." She couldn't keep the bitterness from her voice.

"Ours is no marriage," he corrected, his words like icicles in her romantic heart. "It's an arrangement with specific duties which you are to perform. For both our sakes, I suggest you do them expediently."

"Your sister's entrée into society is my only duty. Remember that the next time you think to do what you did in church. I promise you you'll get no further. You'll not get the chance to consummate this marriage." Angrily, she crossed her arms over her chest and glared at him.

A shadow of a smile lifted the corner of his mouth. "Mrs. Sheridan, my kiss in church was no attempt at a consummation. That won't give you children. That's something else entirely."

Her cheeks flamed with embarrassment. There was no civil answer to what he had just said, so she fixed her attention on the passing crowds on Fifth Avenue. Until they reached the Sheridan mansion, she didn't look at him again, which was fortunate, for if she had, she would have found him staring at her, his gaze unwavering and inexplicably hungry.

12

The reception was held in the Sheridan ballroom, where Mara was to have had her debut. The people who had been invited then were for the most part the ones who attended now. They ate upon the gold Limoges porcelain and drank from the cobalt Stiegel goblets, were duly impressed by the fourteen-carat-gold chargers, and in general gazed in awe at the Sheridan wealth until their eyes fairly popped from their heads.

Alana could hardly endure the three-hour wedding breakfast, beginning with Mr. Napoleon Sarony making a daguerreotype of the wedding couple. Her nerves were frayed to virtual ruin during the fifteen minutes they stood for the picture. In it she demurely looked down at the clasped hands of her and her husband. She felt anything but demure with Trevor beside her. Though she couldn't move, she couldn't even dare look at him, still she knew with every sense he was there. She felt him like a pulsating force, a force at once great and terrible. There was no escaping him, especially when his hand had a steely velvet grip on her own, when his breath tickled hotly upon her ear, when his scent, a seductive blend of bay rum and adult male, grew to such an obsession that she could taste it on her palate.

After that torture she sat next to her husband, eating nothing and drinking every time her champagne glass was filled. The morning had shaken the very foundations of her beliefs. The bishop's words still haunted her, her vows still rung hollow in her ears. She had promised to be this man's wife, promised him all her wifely duties until death took her away. And it was all a lie. Her marriage was nothing more than a farce, a one-act play.

She peeked at Sheridan covertly as he laughed at something his brother had said. Sitting at the bridal table overlooking his guests, he appeared like a king viewing his kingdom. His satisfaction was almost palpable, and she despised him for it. Yet for all that he had done to ruin her, she despised him more for that kiss in the church than all the rest combined. That kiss had stepped over the line from the impersonal to the intensely personal. For one brief second he had clasped an emotion she hadn't wanted to give him. If he ever did that again, she was afraid he'd hurt her so badly, he'd make what he'd already done look like child's play.

He turned to her and caught her staring. Their eyes met, and a current passed between them. She wanted to be hostile, but it was impossible when his gaze probed so deeply, she felt as if he had passed through her soul. She sat, motionless and silent, helplessly trapped in the web of his stare, but too quickly the magic wore off. An arrogant smile graced his lips, and she ached to slap it off.

"We leave at noon. Let Mara show you where to change your gown. Shall I summon your maid?" he asked with false solicitation.

"Yes," she whispered angrily, and began to stand. He stopped her.

"My bride hasn't had a toast yet."

"That isn't necessary," she quipped.

"I insist."

She sat down and saw Sheridan glance at his brother. Eagan rose and lifted his glass. The entire room went silent as he spoke.

"An Irish marriage is renowned for being a long one."

He solemnly turned to Alana and raised his glass higher. "I predict this one shall endure for eternity. To the bride!"

Everyone, no matter how reluctantly, said, "To the bride!" and sipped champagne. Alana only grew more pale. She'd just been pummeled with another curse, another lie. Again she wanted to put her hands over her ears and run away.

Sheridan stood; the crowd hushed. He raised his glass and looked at her. His gaze held her so tightly, she felt as if she were the only one in the room. "Where I come from in Ireland, they've had many a famine, and we've a toast to the bride that loosely translated says 'May she always have potatoes.'" In a deep, compelling voice, he looked at her and said, "To my bride, Alana. *Go mbeidh fatai aice go brach.*" He raised his glass higher and scandalously added, "*Erin go bragh!*"

There was a split second of disapproving silence before William Astor raised his glass. As if to taunt his wife, he said loudly, "*Erin go bragh!* God bless you, Alana!"

Everyone followed in the toast, even a sour-faced Mrs. Astor, and the room again buzzed with talk.

Alana stood and tried her best to smile. She was moved by his toast, moved by the history and the pain that was behind it. Sheridan had had the character not to mock her with pretty words, yet she was unnerved by his foreign Gaelic tongue, as she could see most in the room were.

Slowly she lifted her glass to the crowd and looked across the sea of faces. It was her wedding day, yet there were none in the room she considered friends. Didier sat at the table with the Astors, a false beaming smile upon his face, handsomely paid for, no doubt, by her husband. Caroline Astor nearly spewed venom from her eyes, though her expression was one of dignified serenity. So many faces were familiar, yet those who loved her were not there. With tears suddenly springing to her eyes, she hastily lifted her glass to the sea of faces and drank. She didn't look at Sheridan. Mara helped her with her train, and she went upstairs, thankful for the blessed respite from all the prying eyes including her new husband's.

"What do you think of my bride, Eagan?" Sheridan asked in the quiet of the library while Alana was upstairs changing into her traveling suit. The guests still drank in the ballroom, waiting to send off the bride and groom before they too could take their leave. Sheridan had slipped off his frock coat and stood before the fire in his shirt, his black brocade vest and his gray striped trousers. Relaxed with his brother, he didn't use his walking stick, resting it against a velvet ottoman.

"Having seen her, I understand a few things now." Eagan sipped his brandy with the casual air of one who always has a glass in his hand.

"Like what?"

Eagan grinned like an urchin running from the whip. "Like why you insisted upon marrying her within a week. She's bloody beautiful."

A cynical smile touched Trevor's lips. "Aye, Knickerbocker cold, but Knickerbocker beautiful."

"She's any kind of beautiful, and don't deny it. You haven't taken your eyes off her since she walked down the aisle."

The muscles in Sheridan's jaw tensed. "You are mistaken in that."

Eagan sipped again, unperturbed by his brother's mercurial mood. "I'm actually jealous of you, Trevor. Your wife has the face of an angel, and if you look lower . . ."

Sheridan's head snapped up. He shot Eagan a glance that made the words die on his brother's lips. Turning back to the fire, he said, "Don't be too jealous of me tonight. I wager it won't be quite what you imagine."

"On the contrary, my imagination is limited. I'm the untalented one in the family, remember?" Eagan finally smiled again. "Why are you going to Newport with her? Why don't you sail to Alexandria? Egypt's becoming quite popular, you know. All that sailing time and that long ride down the Nile, if you grasp my meaning."

"Newport will suffice."

Eagan conceded that with an understanding nod. "So when will you return?"

"Two weeks." Trevor hesitated with his next words as if he were already expecting what was to follow. "And I'm going to bring Mara with us. She'll come up later with the rest of the servants."

Eagan choked on his brandy. He gave his brother a disbelieving stare. "You *are* joking. You're going to take Mara on your honeymoon?"

"I want her to get to know my bride."

"Shouldn't *you* get to know your bride?"

Sheridan's gaze flickered to the fire, unable to meet his brother's eyes. "I'll have time for that."

Eagan's stare grew more hostile. "What are you playing us for, Trevor? Do you think we're fools? What are you up to?"

Sheridan didn't answer.

Eagan took a long drink from his glass. Coolly he said, "I see now. You don't love this girl. You're using her for Mara's sake. You should have let me in on this." He smirked. "But of course you wouldn't consult *me* on something this important. Oh, it's all right for me to pick out the wine or have a philosophical conversation on Euclid's *Elements*, but to have a hand in anything of real importance—"

"That's not true," Trevor snapped. "You're the one with the university. But what have you to do with my choosing a wife?"

"I would have talked you out of something this crazy." Eagan shook his head. "What does the woman you just married think of all of this? Does my sister-in-law have any regard for you, or have you forced her into this? Does she think we're all just a bunch of stupid micks like the rest of them out there?"

"I don't know what she thinks of us, and I really don't care." Trevor's expression hardened.

"Does she even know, then? Or does she actually think you have some regard for her?"

"Alana knows."

"Mara?" Eagan asked.

"How do you explain an arrangement like this to Mara?"

Eagan snorted in contempt. "Don't you think she's got brains in her head? She'll figure something's not right. She's got to suspect already, with you dragging her along on your honeymoon."

"Well, I'll never tell her, and neither will Alana." Trevor looked at him and waited.

Eagan shook his head in disgust. "*I* won't tell her, Brother, if that's what you want. But Mara'll find out sooner or later, and when she does, don't be surprised if she doesn't handle it well."

"She won't ever know."

"How can you do this?" Eagan's voice was full of disbelief. "How could you marry that woman and say those vows and not accept her as your wife?"

"We won't live as man and wife, and when Mara has her place in society as she deserves, Alana and I will get an annulment."

"An annulment," Eagan scoffed. "I give you a week before you get beneath that woman's petticoats."

"The devil bite your tongue!" Trevor lashed out in Gaelic.

Eagan smiled, seeing he was getting to him. "So you're worried. As you ought to be. You married her, Trevor. She's your wife now, not an opponent on the exchange. You won't extricate yourself from this one easily."

"She'll not be livin' with me as me wife!"

Sheridan's brogue was out in full now, and Eagan judiciously decided it was time to retreat. "Fine. If that's part of your bargain, you live by it." He took another sip from his glass. "But I see one big problem. If you don't treat that beautiful woman like a wife, what will you do if a man comes along who wants to?"

Sheridan didn't answer. He jammed his arms into his frock coat and snatched up his walking stick. He gave Eagan a murderous look before slamming out of the room.

"Your hair is so pretty. It's just the color of butter. I wish I had such pretty tresses." Mara stroked the brush through Alana's hair while Alana sat at Mara's lace-festooned dressing table. The maids bustled in the background, packing away the bridal gown and laying out her traveling cloak.

Surrendering to the relaxing pull of the bristles through her scalp, Alana closed her eyes and said, "You mustn't wish for that, Mara. You just might get them. And believe me, with my hair, you wouldn't have turned all those heads at the reception. Your coloring is ever so much more stunning."

"Those people really only want ladies who look like you."

Mara's voice was so wistful and brave, it was like a knife turning in Alana's gut. She opened her eyes and looked at Mara in the mirror. Her gaze fell again on the girl's gown, and she knew she would have to ask Mara about the short dresses in the not-so-distant future. At sixteen, a girl didn't usually go about in short dresses. Alana had known some Southern girls who'd come up from Atlanta, and much to Mrs. Astor's disapproval, they'd been in long dresses at fourteen.

"Mara," she said gently, "you mustn't believe such things, because they're not true. You're a lovely young woman, and any man would be proud to have you on his arm."

Mara glanced at her, her beautiful blue eyes filled with undisclosed hurt. "Thank you for saying so, Alana," she answered quietly. Then, with the impulsiveness of youth, she wrapped her arms around Alana and said, "Oh, I was so happy when Trevor told me you were to be his wife! When we met in the park, I liked you, and now I see you're as wonderful as I thought you'd be. And only someone wonderful could ever marry dear Trevor!"

Mara hugged her, and Alana felt paralyzed with emotion. She wanted to share in Mara's joy, but that was impossible when the girl was being duped. Anger burned within her at Trevor's deception, even to his beloved sister. She stroked Mara's dark head and said haltingly, "You're generous to say that, Mara, especially when you have every reason to hate me. I didn't show up at your debut, you know."

Mara smiled. "Oh no, Trevor told me why you didn't come. I was so sorry to hear how wicked your uncle has been to you. I wouldn't have invited you if I'd known he would lock you in your bedroom."

Alana stared at Mara, doing her best to mask her disbelief. "Your brother told you that?"

Mara nodded grimly. "He didn't want me ever to think bad things about you. But I wouldn't have, even if you hadn't wanted to come to my debut. If he wanted to marry you, I would have loved you like a sister, which, really, you are now, aren't you?"

Alana again felt tears moisten her eyes. She couldn't believe how trusting Mara was, or how guileless. It pained her all over again that the Four Hundred had hurt this girl so badly. Without thinking about it, Alana hugged Mara, suddenly wanting very much to be her sister. "I did want to be at your party," she whispered. "Always believe that."

"I know," Mara answered. "Trevor told me so."

They broke apart, and Alana laughed as she wiped the tears from her cheeks. She couldn't believe Sheridan had told Mara what he had. It was the truth, but she knew very well he thought it a lie. He was definitely a perplexing man.

"Mrs. Sheridan? It's almost noon," one of Mara's maids said softly, holding Alana's blue velvet traveling cape on her arm.

Hurriedly, Alana pinned her hair into a sleek chignon at the back of her neck. She stood and appraised herself in the mirror. Her traveling suit was appropriately somber yet rich. It was a midnight-blue brocade with just a whisper of a bustle and train. The skirt opened up to reveal an underskirt of gold taffeta pleating with gold cording and tassels adorning the shoulders in the popular military style. She was pleased. Now all she needed was a sword and a shield, and she would finally be ready to face her nemesis.

She kissed Mara on the cheek. "Your brother cares for you dearly. More than you may ever know."

Mara smiled and clasped her hand. "I've needed a friend in this men's club my brother thinks is a home. I'm so glad he's fallen in love with you."

The words made Alana cringe inside. Woodenly, she nodded and departed for her bridegroom's side.

Alana descended the grand staircase as the guests spilled out into the huge marble foyer. Halfway down, she stopped and let Mara pass her. When all the unwed females had taken their places at the bottom of the stair, Alana turned and tossed the bouquet. There were cries and exclamations while the orange blossoms sailed through the air, and Alana prayed Mara would be the one to catch it. But she missed her mark entirely, including all the unwed females, for to everyone's disappointment, the bouquet flew across all the outstretched hands to a gentleman lounging in the door to the library. Alana turned around to see Eagan reach out and catch the bouquet just in time to keep his drink from being spilled.

There were some soft moans of despair, then laughter as Eagan waved the thing mockingly at the bride. "Is this good luck or bad?" he called to her.

She smiled. "For an eligible bachelor, most definitely bad luck. This means you'll be married within the year."

Eagan juggled the bouquet as if it were a hot coal.

"Oh no you don't!" she shouted to him above the laughter. "You have to keep it now. It's your cross to bear."

Eagan balanced the thing in his hand. His smile looked

more like a grimace. "But marriage! The good Lord help me! I never thought my cross would be this heavy!"

She laughed and was just about to begin her descent again when her gaze was riveted to the front door. Sheridan stood by himself, his face hard and humorless, his eyes dark and directed restlessly at her. Her smile dimmed. His gaze made her catch her breath. "Neither did I, Eagan," she whispered to herself as she descended the staircase.

Amid a shower of rice and rose petals, Sheridan led her to the white-swathed carriage that was to take them to the new Grand Central Depot at Forty-second Street. For the benefit of the cheering crowd, she gave her uncle a cursory farewell and waved to those familiar faces who were old acquaintances of the Van Alens. Eagan paused at the carriage and gave her a brotherly kiss on the cheek.

Her last good-bye was to the Astors. William kissed her soundly, and she and Mrs. Astor embraced because society expected it. But getting in a last blow, the matriarch parted from her and in a voice that was only loud enough for the Sheridan brothers to hear, she said succinctly, "I'll never forgive you for doing this, Alice."

Alana felt her anger rise like mercury in July. It was bad enough that the matron's comment was intended to offend her husband, but Eagan, a brother-in-law she hardly knew, was a target as well. That made her furious. Unable to stop herself, Alana retorted confidently, "I beg to differ, Mrs. Astor. You forgave Caroline Slidell Perry, and she married a Jew. Now what *was* August Belmont's name back in Germany? Oh yes, Schönberg, wasn't it?"

After that dressing down, Alana took Trevor's hand and ascended the carriage. When Alana looked back, Caroline Astor stared after them, tight-lipped with fury. Eagan only added fuel to the fire. Left standing next to Mrs. Astor, he mutely offered the stunned matron his orange-blossom bouquet for solace. When Mrs. Astor didn't respond, Eagan nodded understandingly, then thrust his drink at her instead, as if to say "You certainly need this more than I."

While Alana watched, Caroline Astor finally looked at him and with an enormous "hrrumph" that Alana thought she could hear over the cheering crowds, Mrs. Astor took her husband's arm and departed. Eagan began to laugh, and if Alana hadn't known better, she would have thought William Astor's shoulders were shaking as he led his wife away.

"Why did you do that?"

Alana whipped around and faced her husband. The confines of the carriage were diminished by half when those unusually colored fascinating eyes were trained on her. Thinking of what was ahead brought a new attack of nerves. They had a day's train ride to Newport. The thought of spending that much time alone with Sheridan, alone with that dark piercing stare, caused a shiver to run down her spine. "She deserved it," she answered quickly, looking away.

"The witch well deserved it. But I'm left to wonder why you of all people were the one to speak up."

The steely sarcasm in his tone set her teeth on edge. No matter what she did, he wouldn't think well of her. She was a Knickerbocker, so she was anathema. She retorted, "Because you're Irish doesn't make you a villain, and because Caroline Astor is a snob doesn't make her a witch."

"That woman is the sole reason behind Mara's failed debut. Hanging's too good for her."

She shifted on her seat to face him. It amazed her how angry he could make her. As quick as the strike of a match. "How can you say such a vile thing? Caroline Astor may not be the most perfect person, but she's not evil incarnate. She loves children, did you know that? She's funded I don't know how many asylums to house the abandoned wretches you Irish have left on the streets. Why, I've seen tears in her eyes for those pitiful creatures. That's the woman you just wanted hanged."

"If there were ever tears in that woman's eyes, they were crocodile tears. And if she contributes to an orphan's care—

well, I say a guilty conscience can move mountains." His jaw tautened.

She locked gazes with him. "It's women like Mrs. Astor who've seen to it that your children of Erin suffer a little less. You owe her better than that."

"If given a just and equal chance, we Irish could take care of our own," he growled ominously. "And it's people like Caroline Astor who keep us down."

"Perhaps. But some of your plight's your own doing. It's not all Mrs. Astor's."

"You offend and defend that woman in the same breath. So is she sinner or saint?" he scoffed angrily.

"She's both, just like we are."

"Speak for yourself."

She narrowed her eyes. "I don't consider you, above all, a saint, sir."

He leaned back on the burgundy velvet squabs and rolled the gold head of his walking stick in his fingers. Tersely he said, "Neither do I. So beware."

The gist of what he said hit her like a boxing glove. Her mouth parted in surprise, but she had no retort. What could she say to a man who had just proclaimed himself a sinner only? She sat back, uneasy, and watched him like a trapped rabbit. Relieved to find that unsettling gaze directed to the outside, where the omnibuses spilled out of Vanderbilt Avenue onto Forty-second Street, she breathed a sigh of relief and looked out the window at Commodore Vanderbilt's folly.

The locals dubbed it "The Grand Swindle Depot" because it was so poorly planned that pedestrians were forced to find their way through a massive tangle of switching tracks, locomotives, and cross streets at the risk of life and limb. In spite of the criticism, it was still a handsome sight. *NEW-YORK & HARLEM R.R.* blazed across the three towers of the terminal on Forty-second Street, and the building's Second-Empire-style architecture was considered by some the best in New York.

They pulled up to the carriage entrance and dis-
embarked. Trevor showed a pass to one of the attendants,
and they were then quickly escorted through the terminal
to their platform. The trains awaited beneath steel-and-
glass vaults behind the depot. It was easily the largest covered space in the country, and though she'd been there
several times before, Grand Central never failed to impress
her with its enormity.

At first Alana thought this trip would be much like the
ones she'd taken on other excusions to Newport. But as she
held on to her husband's arm, she could see it was destined
to be quite different. They were traveling on one of the
Vanderbilt lines, yet not in a private compartment, as Alana
usually went, but in Sheridan's private Pullman car that was
just now being hitched to the rest of the train. As Trevor
oversaw the loading of their luggage and servants into adjoining cars, a polite elderly porter helped Alana up the
steps of the gold and green Pullman. Once inside, she was
aghast at the luxury. Deep maroon watered silk draped the
span of windows across each side, tied at intervals with
heavy gold cording. Velvet of the same deep purple-red hue
covered the tufted sofas, arranged as if in a parlor. The
woodwork was polished mahogany and brass, the black,
gold, and green needlepoint carpeting tailor-made for the
Pullman, its border incorporating Irish motifs such as the
harp and the shamrock and the Connacht shield that proclaimed the home province of the Sheridans. In the corner
sat an ornate but friendly pot-bellied stove stoked up for
the journey to Rhode Island.

Alana needed no encouragement to sit by the stove. The
Pullman wasn't cold, it had been too well-prepared for that,
but the enormous wealth it boasted seemed to chill her to
the bone. She looked around and thought of Sheridan's
massive mansion on Fifth Avenue. His home in Newport
was supposedly as awe-inspiring, designed by Hunt entirely
in marble. She again thought of her dream, and if before

she'd felt suffocated by her wealthy background, now she was drowning in it.

Her husband entered the car and made himself comfortable on one of the sofas at the opposite end of the stove. It took another ten minutes for the train to lurch to a start, and during that time neither spoke a word. At the wedding she had felt his eyes upon her constantly. Now, in these close quarters, he treated her as if she were invisible.

A billowing cloud of steam rose from both sides of the car as the train pulled out of the station. Through it she could see people on the platform waving good-bye to loved ones in cars behind them. No one waved at the Sheridan Pullman. The train left the huge sooted glass vault, and suddenly they were in sunshine, heading north toward Yorkville.

Alana tore her gaze from the window, by some instinct sure Trevor had been watching her. But when she looked at him, his head was buried in the evening copy of the *Chronicle* as he analyzed the stock-market section. The front page, emblazoned with the details of their wedding, lay discarded on the needlepoint carpeting.

"Do we take the regular route to Newport, or can your money get us there faster?" It wasn't the most gracious of questions, but for some irrational reason, the front page lying crumpled at his feet irked her.

Slowly he looked up from the paper. "Did you say something?"

The train gave a little jump, and her well-corseted breasts bounced with the movement. Though it was so quick she thought she might have imagined it, she swore his gaze flickered involuntarily to her chest. "I asked how long is the ride?" Hating herself for her self-consciousness, she crossed her arms over her bosom as if to ward him off.

"The usual time. Haven't you ever been to Newport?" He looked away, dismissing her. She almost smiled. His accent had filtered in again. Every now and then the veneer cracked. Still, she wondered if she would ever entirely see that man he took such pains to hide.

"I thought with all your millions, you had a way of getting us there faster." She dismissed him too and looked out the window.

"When there is a way that's faster, you can be sure I'll be one of the first to know about it."

"And sell stock in it, and make another trillion zillion dollars," she said under her breath.

He gave her a sharp look, then surprised her with a chuckle. "Have you a problem with that? It's the American way, after all. And you, Miss Knickerbocker, an American of Americans, should be in favor of such things."

She raised her eyebrows and looked at him. "On the contrary, I've heard earning money on the exchange is usually less than honest. Even my uncle said that most of it should be illegal, selling stock you don't even own, printing stock that you know has no value—"

"So men should merely take their inheritance and live off that—is that what you suggest?"

She frowned, angered that he twisted her words. She was not the cold-hearted statue he believed her to be. "There's no shame in family money honestly earned," she said quietly.

His lips tightened in disgust. "I know this hypothesis might come as a shock to you, my girl, but what does one do if there *is* no family money?"

The derision in his voice cut her like a knife. She knew he hated her. He couldn't have played with her life as he had if he had any regard for her feelings, but she'd thought he considered her better than a half-wit. "What do you think I am?" she whispered. "Unthinking? Unfeeling? Do you think I'm so shallow that I believe everyone is rich and privileged? Do you think the plight of the poor has escaped me? Or when faced with it, that I call out, 'Then let them eat cake'?"

"You've never been poor. You've no right to judge me, to

even speak of such matters." He callously forced his attention back to his stock reports.

Wild, hot tears sprang to her eyes, a product of the long, trying, disheartening day. "It's you who judge me, sir," she said before standing and weaving her way to a sofa at the other end of the plush car. She looked out the window and saw that they were well past what used to be the shanty-town of Bloomingdale. Their route would take them along the former Bloomingdale Road to Harlem Heights, across to Kingsbridge, finally picking up the route of the old Boston Post Road.

She snapped open her steel-beaded purse and searched for a handkerchief. One would hardly know she was crying. Her tears came in silent restrained shudders—she'd been well schooled in hiding her pain.

She dabbed her cheeks. He said she had no right even to think of the poor, but she did think of the poor. There were advantages to being poor. Life was more simple. There were no pretentions, no hiding. If one was lucky enough to have friends, they accepted you the way you were and didn't wait in the shadows to pounce on the slightest imagined irregularity.

She watched the barren landscape pass by—muddy, graded, treeless farmland that speculators were already sectioning off for town homes. The monotony of the view allowed her to escape into a favorite daydream. She imagined life as another girl, one with far less money and far more friends. Her pleasures would be simple. They would have to be. In that kind of life, she'd have to make herself content with things like a warm fire and good company. And content she could have been.

She gazed at the little pot-bellied stove and thought of her shadow man. He was the kind to relish a good fire on a cold day, the kind to like a fire best with his lady by his side. She longed to be that lady, to simply sit with her dearest by the fire and enjoy his good company. If only she could picture the shadow man's face. If only he had one.

She looked up and saw Sheridan. His expression was tense and defensive. He stood and walked toward her, intent upon the champagne bottle resting on the bar. He passed her as she discreetly wiped the tears from her eyes. She didn't want him to see her cry. He should never again know she was that vulnerable.

Covertly she watched as he poured himself a glass of champagne and tossed it down, nearly in one gulp. Dissatisfied, he pulled a cut-crystal decanter from behind the bar and poured himself a healthy dose of the pale amber liquid. Still not saying a word, he tossed that down and poured another.

She watched him at the bar, and her irritation festered. She almost envied him. Being a woman, she wasn't allowed the same escape he could seek in spirits. For her to pour herself a drink would be too bold, and inwardly she cursed the suffragists for aligning themselves with the temperance movement. But the more she thought, the more bold she became. This man had forced her to marry him, and she had no reason to impress or obey him. Their marriage was in name only. She was to take care of his sister's social career and nothing else, so what would he care if she privately had a drink and drowned her sorrows as he was drowning his?

She stiffened her spine and made the decision. The ride to Newport was already proving overly long. He could go to the devil if he didn't like it. His anger would be only a distraction.

He watched her as she stood and sauntered to the bar. She didn't dare look at him with her red-rimmed eyes, but she cursed that piercing gaze that she felt follow her every movement.

"If you wanted champagne, I would have brought you some," he commented dryly, looking down at her.

"I don't want champagne, thank you." She found a glass and lifted the stopper of the decanter he was drinking from.

"You don't want that," he stated abruptly, obvious disapproval on his face.

Her rebellious streak surfaced. The suffragettes were fighting for the right to vote, but she wished that they could fix it so that when a lady drank, she could do so without being thought an adventuress. "This shall do just fine for my needs." She ignored his stormy expression and reached for the decanter.

Without warning, he took it from her grasp. "You won't like this." His brow darkened. "And is it your usual course to belly-up to the bar and pour yourself a drink?"

Her green eyes glittered with both mirth and fury. So he thought her a tippler. She almost wanted to laugh. Fine. Let him think so. "Worried?" she taunted. "After all, you don't know much about me. I could have all sorts of vices."

He ran his thumb over the lion's head of his walking stick. She didn't know why that action sent a thrill down her spine. "True. But then so could I." That dark smile appeared again.

Instinct told her it was best to ignore him when he was in this confrontational mood. She reached for the decanter once more, but he pulled it away again. "I tell you, you can't drink this."

Her temper flared. He was such a hypocrite! Typical of his sex, he thought it fine to allow her some wine in Delmonico's because it suited him to muddle her thoughts, but now she didn't possess the right to have a drink on her own.

"If you sit down, I'll pour you a glass of champagne."

He sounded as if he were talking to a child. He would allow her, would he? Impetuously she said, "I'd like something stronger. I'll have what you're drinking."

He opened his mouth to speak again, then suddenly thought better of it. Something began to amuse him. "You want this *poitín?* What's in this decanter? Fine. You may have it." He took her glass and poured, his brows rising with the level of liquor. Smugly he presented it to her.

"Bottoms up," he announced, a small smile lurking on his handsome lips.

"Bottoms up," she repeated and took a huge, numbing sip.

The fires of hell flared in her throat. She wanted to cough, but she was so overcome by whatever it was she'd drunk, she couldn't breathe. After a heart-stopping moment, she sucked in a breath, and her eyes teared. She began to cough at exactly the moment he began to laugh.

"Here, have another." Trevor brought her the decanter and filled her glass to overflowing while she desperately tried to breathe. It would have been comical if she hadn't been so angry. "What—are you trying to do—kill me?" She coughed, furious green sparks flaring in her eyes. "What—is this?" She held out the vile glassful of liquor.

"Good Irish whiskey, home-distilled in Bandit's Roost, one of my very own haunts. Don't tell me you don't like it?"

"It's poison!" she rasped.

"If you drink too much of it . . ."

"You drink this stuff, *willingly*?"

"It's the only stuff tha' can knock me flat on me ass." He smiled wickedly. " 'Ave anoother." He reached for her glass, obviously enjoying himself, and at her expense.

She pulled her glass away. "I don't want to be knocked on my—" her hand flew to her mouth, "bottom!" she finished, her cheeks growing warm.

"What are you? Fearful you might grow to like the stuff? Well, don't worry. It's cheap and plentiful where I get it, so enjoy."

"Good heavens! No one could grow to like this nasty brew! It's worse than hair tonic!"

"And how would you know? Is that what you Knickerbocker ladies do when you're hard up for a drink—swill the hair tonic?" He put his head back and laughed.

He'd insulted her, and she should have been angry. But within the haze of that initial gulp of spirits, she found herself entranced, struck by how truly handsome he was when he was in good cheer. Mesmerized, she studied him. He had all of his brother Eagan's rakishness, only Trevor's was less obvious and to her infinitely more seductive.

Even the train worked against her at that moment. The smooth ride disappeared with a sudden lurch, a lurch that propelled her into his broad chest, her pliant bosom crushing against him. The laughter died on his lips. Their gazes locked in one electrifying second, then Alana felt the ground fall out from beneath her. Deep in those restless eyes, his invitation couldn't be missed.

The worst of it was she wasn't saying no.

They were so close, she could feel his breath against her hair. He was obviously trying to control some impulse and obviously failing. He lowered his head, and she wanted to cry out, to refuse this strange longing that seemed to be driving both of them, but she didn't utter a word. This desire blossoming within her had been sleeping for years, and if she were truthful, the only time it had ever stirred was that night she'd first come face-to-face with this dark Irishman.

Like a salve for her burn, his lips came down on hers. It felt so good, she wanted to sigh her pleasure and relief, even as her mind drummed a warning. His arm slid down her waist, and he drew her nearer. He kissed her just as he had in church, but now there were no spectators to rush them, and he took his time, letting his mouth pull on hers until he went deeper and broke the barrier of her lips. His tongue was still a shock to her, and her instincts told her to pull back. But always the master of the situation, he put his hand beneath her chignon and stopped her. He drove further, and any thoughts of leaving him seemed to be gone from her head. Reason told her unequivocally to pull away, yet her hand moved up his starched white shirtfront and gently touched his cheek, clearly conveying her approval.

He seemed to like this almost too much, for his kiss became even more ferocious until she was bent back against the bar, accepting thrust after thrust of his tongue with the delirium of an addict. His hands caressed her corseted rib cage, but longing for something more substantial to fill his palms, he pushed them up until he almost reached her bosom. When he'd just reached the bottoms of her breasts, a warning went off in her head, one loud enough for her to hear. Wild, irrational panic beat through her veins, and she ripped her lips from his.

Panting, she stared at him, unable to believe what he had almost done. They stood suspended in their embrace, the only movement the erotic rhythm of the train beneath their feet.

When he straightened, reality came down on her like a bucketful of water. She was arched against the bar like a trollop, her head wantonly lolled backward, her lips eager for another kiss. Horror filled her expression, not because he had kissed her but because she had wanted so desperately to be kissed. And by this man. A man who hated her.

He looked down at her, studying the self-loathing that played across her features. Misreading the reasons for it, he wiped his face of any emotion and retrieved his whiskey. Then, as if he couldn't help himself, he said in a thick, earthy, contemptuous brogue, "So, Miss Kickabocker, is that what y' foin ladies do when yer hard-up fer a man?"

She could have slapped him. Betrayal crossed her face, hurt too, but she quickly covered them both with a cold mask of ice. As if she were the Queen of England, she turned and regally walked back to the sofa, not saying a word, her cheeks and eyes saying too much.

She stared once more out the window, and a silence came down on the Pullman. Numb, horrified, and too proud to lick her wounds, she sat like a mannequin posed at a funeral. She tasted whiskey in her mouth, and the thought that the whiskey could have come from him only unraveled her further. A shaking hand ran over her lips as if to draw the taste away. It persisted, cruelly reminding her of that kiss.

They were in the countryside now, well past 125th Street. Some would have been cheered by the old colonial farms and neat white pickets that ran for miles. The two in the private Pullman that bulleted north along the tracks were not. He sat drinking silently in the corner. His wife stared sightlessly out the window, inconsolable with the knowledge that her new husband had the ability to make her feel things that could only cause catastrophe.

13

At eight that evening a friendly black porter served them a multicourse dinner that Alana hardly touched. It took all her courage to sit across from Sheridan at the Pullman's cramped damask-draped dining table after that kiss. Excusing herself early, she sat uncomfortably in one of the velvet sofas until the clickety-clack of the train lulled her to sleep.

The locomotive lurched to a halt well after midnight. She awoke and looked around, unsure of the time or where she was. The Pullman was dim, lit only by the gaslights of the platform. Sitting up in the darkness, she pulled away whatever was covering her and looked for Sheridan. He stood across from her, alert and intense, staring out the windows, the gaslights silhouetting his profile. Her thoughts were still jumbled from sleep, so she just watched him, unable to ask if they were in Newport.

Even in the darkness, he was compelling, an unlikely combination of the forbidding and forlorn. When she saw his lonely formal figure absent-mindedly clutching that lion-headed stick, she felt a strange impulse to put her arms around him. Yet another part of her wanted to flee. He had the unique ability to cause irreconcilable conflict. He was one of the most unfeeling men she had ever met. On the other hand, there was something about him that moved her, that connected with her so deeply, he seemed to possess the power to mold her like clay. His cold contrivance of this marriage had proven that. There was every reason, from the callous to the kind, not to marry this Irishman, but she had gone through with it. His manipulations had been brilliant, yet if she examined it more closely, she wondered if there wasn't another reason she'd agreed to it, the same reason she hadn't fought when he'd kissed her.

A blush came to her cheeks as she thought about that kiss. She longed to say she'd hated it, but that would be foolish when her actions had so clearly stripped away that lie. She'd all but made a wanton of herself. Anson had tried to kiss her like that once, but when his tongue had run along her closed teeth, she'd wanted nothing more than to make him stop, and she had. With Trevor, even in the church, she'd felt something else entirely. The desire not only to continue but go further had been almost uncontrollable. When his lips touched hers, a strange kind of magic happened. Suddenly she'd felt like a some kind of wild animal who at last recognized her mate.

But, she reminded herself, taking one last look at his dark figure, this marriage was nothing more than a contract, an impersonal, calculated business transaction the likes of which he made every day on Wall Street. If she failed to remember that and got her emotions tangled up with him, she had no doubt at all he'd treat her like any other stockbroker. He'd crush her. Indeed, he already had.

"Newpaht! Newpaht!" the carman cried in a Boston accent when he stepped into the Pullman. The black porter went ahead of him and turned up the gaslights.

It took Alana a moment to adjust her eyes to the light. Then she looked down and saw what had been covering her. She'd thought it was some kind of light blanket, one she couldn't recall pulling over her. To her dismay she found it was a man's black frock coat. She held it out to see if it was true. It was indeed her husband's frock coat.

"My coat doesn't bite," Trevor commented.

She looked up at him, unsure of what he meant. Then

she realized how she was holding his coat. "It was kind of you—" she began helplessly, but he turned from her.

"It's late. Our carriage is waiting. Let's be off." He stepped to her and shrugged into the coat, a tight, hostile expression on his face.

She opened her mouth, desperately wanting to say something, to thank him or deny what he thought. But she took one look at his face and decided against it. There would be no changing his mind tonight.

"I'll need my cloak," she mumbled, looking around for it. He nodded to the porter who stood ready by the door, her blue velvet cloak in hand. She stood, and the porter walked over to drape it over her shoulders. Footman and servants had been helping her with her cloak as long as she could remember, but suddenly she didn't like the foreign hands upon her. It now was her husband's task to place her cloak around her shoulders, and as the porter did it, she looked at Trevor, longing shamelessly etched on her face.

Bellevue Avenue was quiet as their carriage rolled along, headed for Fenian Court, Sheridan's mansion. When she'd been a girl, she and Christabel had spent many a happy day walking along Bailey's Beach searching for seashells or just sitting on the cliffs at Brenton Point watching the surf toss upon the rocky black coast.

Ten years ago Newport had been an entirely different town. Gingerbreaded houses with wide breezy verandas lined Bellevue, and in June enormous powder-blue hydrangeas bloomed everywhere, giving the town a homey atmosphere. The resort was favored by Southerners, who came north to escape the sweltering heat back home, and summering Bostonians who wanted a more social atmosphere than Cape Cod.

But everything was quickly changing. The donkey carts and picnics of summer were fast being replaced by the societal stratagems of the Four Hundred. If democracy was forced upon them in Manhattan for the sake of husbands' business dealings, it was not in Newport. Wives were the unquestionable rulers of this land, and with their husbands' money, the skeletons of monstrously huge fifty-room "cottages" were already obscuring the ocean view.

From the carriage, Alana looked at the looming shadows of the mansions, impressed with their size yet saddened by what they represented. The old Newport was going the way of the cow pastures along Bellevue, and an even more rigorous round of exclusivity was coming. She tired of the game. It was all a facade, anyway. She knew better than anyone else that behind all the pretentions lay an appalling amount of insecurity and just plain fear.

It was ironic to discover that Fenian Court was the most pretentious of them all.

They turned left and trotted down a drive sentineled by budding elms. Fenian Court, the fabled manse, lay ahead, its Louis XV styling apparent even in the gaslight. Tons of marble had been imported to build the Petit Trianon lookalike. It had every French rococo detailing: Hardly a straight line wasn't forced into a curve; everything that could be gilded was. Even the stairs sweeping up to the house were a cliché—marble, with a curving wrought-iron banister iced by gleaming bronze handrails.

The size was breathtaking. She'd heard the Sheridan "cottage-by-the-sea" consisted of seventy-eight rooms, not including the outbuildings, such as the boathouse, stables, and garden houses. From the moment Alana had heard about it, she'd amusingly dubbed it "Bold Fenian Court."

Their welcome was as well rehearsed as a ballet. The majordomo took her cape; the secretary handed Trevor the closing ticker tape. Sensing her fatigue, the majordomo expedited her to her rooms. Trevor was asked if he wished to send any telegraphs. When she was led away, her husband gave her a stiff bow, dismissing her with what appeared to be utter indifference.

Hurt despite telling herself otherwise, she went to her suite, walking through marble corridors fit for Marie Antoinette. But she was unable to comprehend the majesty of the interior because of her exhaustion and her roiling emotions. So much had happened to her today, and no matter how she rationalized that this marriage would be only a memory in as little as a year, her instincts told her that her life had irrevocably changed course.

Her bedroom, contrary to what she'd seen of Fenian Court, was decorated in refreshingly restrained tones of rose and ivory. Left alone by the majordomo, Alana sought out her dressing room but was undecided which door it was. There were several nondescript doors to her left, then a pair of ornate gilded doors to her right. Believing the gilded ones led to her dressing room, she flung them open, only to discover that her husband's room lay beyond.

When she saw the room was empty, she let out an audible sigh. The last thing she wanted was to stumble in on that cold Irishman while he was preparing for bed. She was about to leave when suddenly it struck her how different Trevor's room was compared to the rest of the house. Standing in the middle of an ancient Tabriz carpet, she looked around, curious about the master's domain. A cheerful fire blazed in the hearth, taking away the chill of the May night. The mellow walnut paneling added more warmth, and during the daytime there would be a breathtaking view of Rhode Island Sound from the eastern windows. The drapes were a rich but plain brown linen dobby; the blankets, a striking heavy wool tartan. In the privacy of his quarters, the ostentation had disappeared, replaced instead with handsome simplicity and no-nonsense function.

Her gaze wandered back to the fireplace. A chair of gray-blue leather awaited its owner with the morning's neatly bound *Chronicle* resting on the ottoman. The master's walking stick leaned casually against the arm. Her eyes widened, and she took a protective step backward. She'd never seen Trevor without that stick in hand. If he'd laid it down, then he must be—

"What are you doing here?" a familiar voice barked from across the room.

Stunned, Alana looked up to find Trevor standing in a doorway holding a towel as if he'd just finished washing. He'd stripped down to his trousers, and two of the top buttons were undone. Naked, his chest seemed even more broad than in a shirt. Droplets of water glistened like sweat against the dark hair sprinkled down his front.

When he saw where her gaze was drawn, he rubbed himself down with the towel. "I asked what you're doing here," he snapped, tossing the towel on the bed.

"I—I—" she stammered like a fool.

Hesitating, as if he didn't really want to do it, he took a step toward his walking stick and defied her to speak. His jaw was so tense, it looked as if it might crack. He strode to the fireplace, each step more awkward and difficult than the last.

"Why, you're hurt," she whispered, shocked by the discovery. Her instincts drove her to his side to assist him. This made him so angry that if he'd been one fraction less the gentleman he was, she wondered if he wouldn't have struck her.

"Get away from me," he snarled, grabbing his stick.

"But you're hurt," she repeated, her hands falling helplessly to her sides.

"I'm not hurt," he bit out. "I hate to inform you, my girl, but you can add 'gimp' to your husband's other sterling attributes."

She let this news sink in as he clutched the lion-headed stick and strode to another corner of the room. Watching him, she finally saw that what she'd mistaken for stiffness and formality in his bearing was not that at all but a physical dependence on that stick. Now she could see that he leaned too heavily upon it, used it overly much for just a fashionable accouterment to his attire. Though he hid it well, there was no disputing the evidence of what she'd just seen. This big, strong, intimidating man was a cripple.

"Is that why you fell in Delmonico's?" she asked quietly, remembering how she'd thought she'd been the one to put them in the predicament the priest had found them in. Now she could recall her legs entangled with that walking stick.

"Yes," he answered, his back to her as he looked out at the blackness through the windows, the lighthouse on Sachuest Point the only break in the inky nightscape.

She nodded, though he couldn't see her. "As much as that scene benefited you, I didn't think you had planned it."

"No."

"How—"

Before she could get the words out, he whipped around and faced her. "What business is that of yours?" he asked, a nasty tone to his voice. "And what business do those idiot servants have putting you in that goddamned room connected to mine so that you can wander in here and dare ask me these questions?"

His tone tore her to shreds. "I think they believe I'm your wife." She could barely choke out the words.

He calmed, but a muscle still clenched his jaw.

"Haven't I a right to know what affects you?"

His dark green-brown eyes filled with contempt. "Are we to share this marital bed?" He tossed a glance at his heavy Jacobean-revival bedstead. "Are you going to live with me as my wife?" He snorted in disgust. "No, that's not the bargain we made. You're no more my wife than my mistress back in Manhattan is. So you've no right to know anything about me."

This last revelation about his life nearly knocked her to the ground. Her horror and surprise was beyond her ability to hide. "You have a mistress?" she gasped. "Even now?"

"Why should I not? Have you intentions of taking her place?"

"But you're married!" she cried out, unable to believe this man. That he could retain a mistress now meant he truly had no respect for the vows he'd spoken just hours earlier. And no respect for her.

"In theory, I'm married. In blood and heart and hand, I'm no more married than Eagan."

She stared at him, betrayal and rage crossing her features. Her feelings boiled up until they were almost out of control, but she managed to cover them with her Knickerbocker coolness. It was almost jealousy she felt, she realized after reining in her anger. But she could not be feeling jealousy because that was completely illogical. To be jealous would mean she had some feeling for this man who stood before her, and she had none. Nor would she, ever. "I see," she stated, her voice even and cold.

He looked at her rigid, defiant figure, and the muscle in his jaw relaxed a bit. "We can each have our vices in this marriage, as long as they're carried out in a discreet manner."

"You certainly have yours," she whispered, unable to stop herself.

He walked up to her, anger driven deep into his face. "What does that have to do with you?"

He took her arm, and she tried to jerk it away. Unsuccessful—his grip was like a manacle—she quieted but refused to meet his eyes. "This has nothing to do with me," she hissed. "And if you ever catch a man making love to me, you tell yourself the same thing."

"You almost sound jealous. Perhaps it was that kiss on the train—"

"I should have never let you kiss me! I should have slapped you instead!"

He released a black little laugh. "You'd dare slap me? What, and ruin those frigid, well-schooled little manners? Oh, no, sweeting, you wouldn't do that. You haven't the passion for something like that."

His sarcasm drove a hammer through to her heart, destroying her facade of detachment. Before she knew what she was doing, her hand came up and did exactly what he had taunted her to do. When she lowered her hand, her palm stung from hitting his face. Her only satisfaction was that his cheek had to sting worse.

She expected many things then. She certainly expected the burst of Irish temper, even half-expected to be slapped back. What caught her by surprise was the arm that encircled her waist, pulling her against him. His other hand held his cane, but by all evidence, he didn't need it, gauging from the strength of the arm that held her. She struggled against him; his arm held her like an iron band.

"Let go of me," she gasped.

He pulled her farther against him. Her hands reached up to push him away, but when they met with the warm muscle and crisp hair of his chest, they seemed to lose much of their strength. She could hardly believe a man could be so supple and yet so . . . hard.

Obviously angered, obviously relishing the thought of frightening her, he spoke down to her as if she were a truant child. "Let me explain something to you, Alana. This is a business deal. You do something like that to me again, and I'll see you pay with your little marble Knickerbocker ass."

"You provoked me." She struggled in his embrace.

"Yes, and you provoked me."

"I've never done that!" she retorted, clawing down his warm chest.

"Shall I show you?" he whispered, letting go of her waist and running his hand up the curves of her side. He grasped her jaw and tilted her head up. When she met his gaze, she was caught.

Her lips parted softly as he lowered his. She should have screamed in defiance, but as she well knew, his kisses had the effect of a drug. The more he kissed her, the more she wanted to be kissed.

His mouth was almost upon hers, and she unconsciously lifted her head to meet him. Her lips seemed to ache with the need to feel his pressing against them. Her mouth felt empty and unfulfilled, longing against her will for the caress of his tongue. He was just about to give her everything she so mindlessly desired when a noise came from behind them. Trevor's head snapped up, and a scowl washed away the restless desire on his face.

"Oh! The saints preserve us! I'm so mixed up in this huge house! Forgive me, miss—er—*Mrs. Sheridan!* I was lookin' for one of your trunks! Me heavens, I didn't know!"

Feeling as if she truly had been drugged, Alana stumbled from Trevor's hold and turned to Margaret, who stood beyond in the rose and ivory bedroom. The little maid's cheeks were bright red, and she looked around the room as if searching for a place to hide.

"It's all right, Margaret," said Alana, her voice still thick with desire. "You've done nothing wrong," she finished, giving Trevor an embarrassed glance.

"I'll wait for you in the dressing room, miss, er, Mrs. Sheridan." Margaret curtsied and ran for the nearest door. When it happened to be the water closet, Alana thought Trevor might explode. He took an angry step toward her bedroom, but Alana put her hands on his chest and stopped him. Margaret, fully flustered now, curtsied again, her cheeks like fire. She took one look at her new master's face and ran to another door. This time finding the dressing room, she shut the door behind her with a slam of relief.

In the ensuing quiet, Alana discovered her hands once more on Trevor's chest. She pulled them away as if touching a hot iron. Her palms curled as if hurting, or holding the sensation.

"Good night," she said softly, and turned to walk away.

He touched her arm. "Do you want me to move you to another room?"

She didn't know why this offer wounded her. Perhaps it just further chipped away at her beliefs in marriage, but somehow when he'd said the words, they stung in a more personal way. "If you find it necessary. But I can promise you I won't bother you again now that I know this is your bedroom."

"I could bother you, you know."

"I trust you," she whispered.

"That's your first mistake."

She looked up at him, startled by his candor, but there seemed nothing left to say, so she retired to her bedroom, shutting those intricate gilt doors firmly behind her.

Margaret had already laid out a peignoir on the massively draped Louis Philippe couch when Alana joined her in the dressing room. Both women were too embarrassed to converse, so Alana obediently slipped into the sheer bit of peachy froth that was a part of her bridal trousseau. Though she wasn't disturbed by letting Margaret see her in such attire—her maid had seen her naked every day she'd been with her—Alana was still disturbed by the alluring gown. When she peeked into the cheval mirror, she could see her nipples, covered only by a mist of peach silk. Trevor had picked out her trousseau. He'd certainly done a fine job, leaving her with no modesty.

" 'Tis a good thing you're now married, ma'am. It surely ain't fittin' for a young miss to be wearin' such a thing." Margaret shook her head at the spectacle in the mirror.

Alana nodded her agreement and dismissed her for the night. Morning was almost here. It had been an incredibly long day, and she was glad to go to bed, even more to cover her nakedness with the heavy satin quilts. When Margaret had turned the gaslights out and departed, Alana thought she'd go right to sleep, but she didn't. She stared through the darkness at those enormous gilded doors to Trevor's room and thought about the man on the other side. He wouldn't come to her room. She couldn't imagine their ever becoming so intimate. If anything, they were too much alike. They were both restrained and logical. And logic told her now that falling in love was not part of their arrangement.

But no matter how she tried to deny the strangeness of the situation, she tossed and turned and stared at the gilded doors. Again and again she pictured him standing just beyond those doors, his hand raised to grasp the doorknob, his face taut with determination. If he came to her that night, there were a thousand scenarios, everything from the crude to the sublime, that could be played out between them. Lying in the darkness, with dawn just tipping the horizon, it seemed she thought of them all, but not one came to fruition. In the end she fell asleep, depressed with the knowledge that her wedding night had come and gone. And never had she imagined it could be so lonely.

"But I don't want to go to Newport! Why is Trevor making me, Eagan! It's his honeymoon. I feel so stupid tagging along!" Mara made this announcement just as her trunks were being carried down the huge marble staircase of the Fifth Avenue chateau. The extra servants were already at Grand Central, and the Sheridan Pullman was again ready for another trip north.

Mara looked at her departing trunks in disgust. She turned to her brother. "I know you know more about this than you're telling me, Eagan, so confess now or it'll go hard with you." She knitted her dark brows together and gave Eagan such a wrathful expression, he couldn't help but laugh.

"Mara, me sweeting," he said, putting his arm around his sister's shoulder and leading her into the drawing room, "let me tell you a few things about Trevor's marriage. The first is, Trevor doesn't know what's good for him. Did you know that?"

Mara shook her black curls.

"And did you know that Trevor is somewhat less than perfect—yes, even in spite of the fact that he is related to me?"

"Oh, you're just teasing me." She pushed him away. "You're not going to tell me a thing—"

"Oh, yes I am, sweeting. You sit there like a good girl, and I'm going to tell you everything you need to know about your trip to Newport and Trevor's marriage."

"All right, tell me," Mara demanded once she was seated.

"Do you like Alana?" Eagan began.

"Yes. She's very nice."

"I agree."

Mara started to say something, but Eagan held up his hand. "Mara, our brother's marriage is in trouble, and we might be the only ones to save it."

Mara gasped, despair clouding her piquant features.

"There are things you don't know about our brother." Eagan turned from her to impress her with the gravity of the situation. Yet a wicked twinkle appeared in his amused emerald eyes when he peeked at her. "I tell you this because it may help you help him."

"What don't I know about Trevor?"

"He's shy." Eagan had to bite his lip to keep from laughing.

Confusion crossed her face. "Trevor is *shy*?" she repeated incredulously. She looked around as if trying to comprehend what he had told her. When Eagan still hadn't turned around to face her, she suddenly became wise. "Oh, you goose! You're pulling my leg. Trevor isn't shy!"

Eagan collected himself, though it took a will of iron. He whipped around. "But he is, Mara, and it's going to ruin his marriage. You've got to believe it. I'm counting on you to help him. You've got to make sure when you're in Newport that he and his bride spend every living minute together, or he may never get over this 'affliction.' "

"Eagan, Trevor isn't shy! He's made all this money, and he sees men at the exchange all the time—"

"But it's *women* that put him into a fright. He's deathly afraid of women."

"But I saw him with that actress friend of his, Miss Daisy Dumont, once. He was a bit drunk at the time and didn't notice that I was in the library. He pulled her in there and kissed her. Eagan, I recall quite clearly that he was not shy. Why, without even asking her permission, his hand went up unhesitatingly and squeezed her—"

"Forget that you even saw that!" Eagan snapped, horrified that his virginal little sister could be so knowledgeable about such activities, especially in the household. "Why didn't you tell someone about this?"

Mara looked a bit surprised. "Who was I supposed to tell?"

"Well, you should have told *someone!* No doubt seeing that—" he began to stumble over his words, "well, seeing such a thing, no doubt, has brought many unanswered questions to mind—"

"No it hasn't."

Eagan looked as if he were totally stumped, as if he didn't know whether to be relieved that she wasn't pelting him with awkward questions or terrified that she might know more than she should. A faint blush came to his face when he realized that Trevor might not have been the only culprit to give Mara a show. Unable to inquire about that, he brushed the topic aside altogether and began anew. "Forget about Daisy Dumont, Mara. She's not of the same class as Alana. You see that now, don't you?"

To his inexpressible relief, Mara nodded.

"Fine, then you can see how our brother Trevor could be suddenly struck by a paralyzing fit of shyness around a woman as refined as Alana Van Alen?"

"I suppose," she answered slowly.

"That's why he's bringing you up there, don't you see. He's afraid to be alone with her."

"Do you really think so, Eagan?"

God forgive me, Brother. I know not what I do. Eagan nodded with utmost conviction.

"Then what should I do to help him?"

He hid his winner's smile behind a cough. He sat down and put his arm around her again. "Mara, sweeting, I've thought about this all day. Here's what you should do. . . ."

14

Alana didn't see her husband the next day or the day after that. She'd heard that Trevor liked to take long walks on the beach, but she never chanced to see him. He walked only at dawn and dusk, an inappropriate time for a lady to be out walking.

She occupied herself with writing Christal about the wedding and reading a volume of Civil War poetry, *Drum-Taps*, penned by an obscure battlefield attendant named Walt Whitman.

By evening, however, she was bored. Their honeymoon was to last two weeks, even three, and Alana began to wonder how she would fill the countless hours before they returned to Manhattan. It was May, and since the season had hardly begun in Newport, she could count on getting at most a couple of invitations to balls. Mara had yet to arrive, and there was no one except Margaret to talk to. While Alana loved her maid dearly, they had only so much in common; their conversations were beginning to repeat themselves. Alana had already walked the grounds and attempted to explore the endless maze of the house. With no companionship, the days stretched before her like a cavernous yawn.

A welcome diversion came when Trevor sent a rather abrupt note asking her to dine with him in the dining room. She'd been taking her meals in her suite, and now she actually looked forward to the "outing." She dressed with care in an elegant forest-green cut velvet and the family pearls, but when she arrived in the dining room, she almost longed for the intimacy of her vast suite of rooms.

The dining room was an enormous gilded jewel with paneling from a seventeenth-century French chateau. She entered, and Trevor stood, greeting her in a perfunctory manner, his expression blank. She moved toward him, but then her gaze roved down the eternal stretch of table to the opposite end where a footman held her chair. The footman seated her, and she felt ridiculous when she tried to look at Trevor a mere fifty feet away, her view obstructed by eight brilliantly lit gold candelabra that did nothing to add warmth to the cold marble room. Dinner was served promptly, and Alana ate in silence, unwilling to make herself look like a fool by attempting to shout conversation.

It was almost a relief when dessert was served. She was uncomfortable eating beneath the gaze of two oversolicitous footmen, and her dinner partner sat so far away, he might as well have been back in Manhattan.

She had just dipped her spoon into the custard when Mara burst into the dining room, her traveling cape still around her shoulders. "Hello everyone! I'm here at last!" Mara skidded to a halt when she saw her brother at the end of the long table. She turned in the other direction, as if she were watching lawn tennis, to find Alana sitting stiffly at the other end. "Good heavens! It *is* true!" Alana heard the girl whisper to herself before Mara ran to her and gave her a kiss on the cheek. "Hello, dear sister-in-law! How has Newport been? I can't wait until we have time to get to know each other." Mara went to the other end of the table and kissed her brother. "Trevor! No, don't get up, Brother mine. I've eaten, and when you and your lovely wife are through, I'll see you in the library for tea. I'm off now!"

Mara was gone before Alana had time to put down her spoon.

"What was that all about?" Trevor's voice echoed off the

marble. In the distance she could see his footmen shrug as if they were used to their young mistress's flights of fancy.

Unable to endure the last of this dinner, Alana abruptly stood and waved to Trevor. "If you don't mind, I'd like to freshen up before the evening continues," she called in as loud a voice as she could without cupping her hands and shouting.

Trevor stood and nodded. Only after she was out of sight did he resume his seat. Or take his eyes from her figure.

Alana was longer than she thought she would be. She found the great marble staircase all right but then made a wrong turn and wandered on the second floor through several sitting rooms, a billiard room, even an unused nursery, the wing that held the bedrooms escaping her. She finally stumbled on the servants' stair and startled a laundry maid from whom she procured directions to her suite. Once there, Margaret helped her with her toilet, and she rushed back downstairs, afraid she might be missed.

She shouldn't have rushed. From the entrance to the library a warm family scene greeted her, the likes of which she hadn't seen in years. Trevor tended the fire, laughing at something Mara had just said. Mara sat on the sofa, her hands acting out her conversation like any other sixteen-year-old.

". . . and did you see all those important people in St. Brendan's, Trevor? Father Donegal said he'd never seen a wedding like yours in his entire lifetime."

"More's the pity he's an old man, then. Fadder Donegal will be seein' many a weddin' like mine in the future, I'll wager."

Alana stood there, entranced by her husband's soft, lyrical accent, a nice sound—natural, relaxed, seductive. He rarely revealed it, and she knew if she hadn't been eavesdropping, she wouldn't have heard it. Feeling like an intruder, she watched the easy camaraderie between brother and sister as they conversed. Part of her wanted to make her presence known and be included with them, but part of her hesitated, afraid that there was no place for her. It was clear that the Sheridan family was very tightly knit. She was the stranger, a foreigner to both of them, to be guarded against and held at a distance. Backing into the shadows, she decided it might be wise to depart.

But Mara's voice suddenly chimed, "Alana! You're back! We wondered where you had gone!" And then there was no graceful exit.

Alana plastered a smile on her face and stepped through the doorway. Unwillingly, her gaze riveted to her husband, and he stared back at her, assessing her with that dismissive yet probing stare.

Mara ushered her in. Feeling awkward, like an interloper, Alana said, "I hope I'm not interrupting." She noticed that Trevor agitatedly fingered the lion's head on his cane and that gesture could mean only one of two things—how much he disliked her knowing his affliction or how much he disliked her intruding presence. She didn't know which bothered her more.

Forcing her gaze from him, she found the nearest chair and groped for something witty to say. "So, Mara, has New York missed its most infamous couple yet?" She started to laugh, but when she glanced at Trevor, the laughter died in her throat.

Displeased by her comment, he took a seat by his sister on the sofa, all the while gracing Alana with that dark, hostile stare. Unnerved, Alana returned his stare but leaned back in her chair as if bracing herself. He believed everyone outside his family was the Enemy. She wondered if he would ever change his mind about her, his own wife.

Mara leapt to her feet, unexpectedly interrupting this silent exchange. Misreading the situation, the girl exclaimed, "Oh dear, what am I doing! Alana, you must sit next to your husband!"

Alana's jaw dropped. She couldn't even think of a protest before Mara had her by the hand and pulled her to the sofa. "No, no, it's all right, Mara. Sit next to your brother,"

Alana told her, desperate to avoid her husband's attention and more important, that bleak, belligerent manner of his.

Mara shook her head. "Oh, I couldn't keep you apart. I know how much you must long for each other."

Alana felt the heat of a blush rise to her cheeks. She couldn't look at Trevor.

"You do?" he asked, his voice at once incredulous and suspicious.

His little sister hid a smile. "Well, I can *imagine*. After all, I'm sixteen now. I've at least read penny novels, you know." Mara all but shoved Alana onto the small sofa next to her brother. Appearing satisfied, Mara took the big leather chair opposite them and stared at them, dreamy-eyed.

Alana could feel the blood drain from her face. *Chagrined* was hardly a strong enough word to describe how she felt, being forced to sit right next to Trevor on the postage-stamp-size sofa. His proximity was more than unsettling; in fact, she felt a rush of panic whenever she thought of it. Desperate to cover this, she said nervously, "So, Mara, tell us about your trip."

"You may hold hands if you like." Mara smiled. "Oh, I know Mrs. Mellenthorp might not approve, but she's not here, now is she?"

"Mrs. Mellenthorp?" Alana questioned, looking for salvation from Mara, who only gave her a sweet smile. Finally she braved a glance at her husband, but he didn't answer either.

He looked as if he might throttle his sister. "Mara—" he rumbled ominously.

But Mara interrupted. "Hold your wife's hand, Trevor. You must go about as if I'm not even here. I don't want to think I'm keeping you apart."

"You aren't keeping us apart."

"But I am. I shouldn't be here. Eagan told me so."

"Eagan, eh?" Trevor scowled, his expression more enlightened.

"Please hold Alana's hand, Trevor. There's no need to be shy."

Shy! Alana almost cried out in dismay. Before she could, Trevor roughly snatched up her hand resting on the cushion next to him. But she might as well have been a tree trunk for all he seemed to notice. He refused even to look at her.

"Wonderful," Mara said, sitting back in her chair, that same romantic expression on her face.

"Tell us about your trip, Mara," he demanded testily.

Mara rambled on about her delays in Narragansett, the footman forgetting one of her trunks, while Alana sat like a statue, her hand captured beneath the lion's paw. She was moved by the strength, the warmth, the anger, of the hand holding her own, and she was almost afraid to glance at him for fear he'd read more in her expression than she wanted.

"But I want to hear how you've been, Alana." Mara turned to her. "Do you like Fenian Court?"

Alana took a deep breath. It was difficult to make conversation when her mind was so focused on the man next to her. His hand wrapped around hers like thick molten steel. His leg grazed hers, and though there were yards of batiste and silk velvet between them, she was sure she could feel every tense muscle in his thigh. "Fenian Court is certainly beautiful, but I never expected it to be so huge." Alana released a nervous laugh. "I confess, I find it impossible to get around this place."

Mara smiled. "And how about my brother? Please don't tell me he's abandoned you for all that ticker tape of his. I'll be terribly disappointed if he has."

"Well, I . . ." Suddenly Alana felt Trevor squeeze her hand. He was coaching her; he wanted correct answers. She knew he didn't want to educate his sister on the more jaded aspects of their marriage, yet the pressure on her hand annoyed her. She was no child needing to be tutored on the ways of polite society. She knew how to behave without his prompting. He squeezed more tightly. She rebelled. "Well, yes, he's impossible too."

Alana's statement caught everyone off guard. Suddenly Mara laughed, and Alana would have laughed too, but she feared Trevor might break her hand.

"Fine, but don't either of you forget that the impossible is my trademark." He spoke to both girls, but it was obvious he directed the warning solely to Alana. She stiffened to pull away. He only gripped harder.

A mischievous smile touched Mara's lips. "But tell me, Brother dearest. When may I expect a niece or nephew?"

Trevor looked at Mara as if she had just asked him to jump over the moon.

Alana might have blushed, but she suddenly remembered the interminable dinner at that long table and decided it was her turn to torment. She dug her fingernails into his callused palm and gave him her softest, most alluring smile. "Yes, my love," she said wickedly, "I've been wondering that myself. Do tell us."

He gave her a sideways glance that would have quelled an entire army. Squeezing her hand tighter, he said, "That's up to you, sweet wife. Whenever you desire a babe, let me know, and I'll make sure you have one."

If she had any doubt about his sincerity, one look into those eyes told her otherwise. Turning away from his sister's gaze, he gave her such a hot, openly lustful, punishing look, it took the breath from her lungs.

She removed her nails from his palm and reluctantly conceded defeat. Thinking he'd let go, she was stunned to find his grip closed like a shackle. Her gaze slammed into his, and they looked at each other for a long burning moment while neither of them backed down.

"Shall I play some romantic music?" Mara looked at their linked hands approvingly. "I know. We need a waltz. I'll play one for you, Trevor." She breezed to the ebony Steinway in the corner and began to play from memory.

The exquisite notes seemed to float from the girl's well-trained fingertips.

" 'Blue Danube,' " Alana whispered, recognizing the Strauss waltz. She peeked at Trevor. There was pride in his eyes as he watched his beautiful, accomplished sister play. But while the music swelled, something flickered in those eyes, something very like sadness. When she saw how he clutched that gold-tipped cane, she suddenly knew why. It was a tragedy that her husband liked waltzes. He would never dance to one.

The music mellowed him, for as Mara continued to play, Alana looked down and found his thumb gently stroking her knuckles. The gesture was absent-minded at best, but the gentleness of that touch, especially in contrast to his strength, sent a warm shiver through her body. It shouldn't be happening, but she enjoyed sitting, listening to Mara's music, feeling his hand wrapped protectively over her own. She wondered if there would be many evenings like this. If there were, she thought as she looked up at her husband, she might be in danger of caring for this man too deeply.

The tender moment ended. Mara finished her piece, and the silence must have made Trevor conscious of what he was doing, for he ripped his hand away.

Alana looked at Mara, a sadness of her own in her eyes; she was made painfully aware of how cold her palm was without his. "That was lovely," she said, desperate to retrieve some normalcy in the situation.

Mara shook her head. "If Eagan were here, he could sing, and then we'd have a truly fine evening. You must hear him, Alana. He has such a handsome voice."

"I'd love that. As soon as we return to New York, we'll have to ask him." Alana smiled, and Mara returned it. Alana was struck by how pretty the girl was, and when she looked down at Mara's short dress, a gray silk poplin, she made a mental note to speak to her about her dresses tomorrow.

Mara stood. "Well, it's been a long day for me, and I know you two must be anxious to be alone."

His sister's comment seemed to snap Trevor from his pensive mood. He looked up sharply. "Before you retire, hooligan, I want you to know I'm planning a trip on the *Colleen* tomorrow."

"What—what is the *Colleen*?" Alana asked, groping for any conversation that would keep Mara from leaving them alone.

"Oh, you must see her," Mara exclaimed in a reverent voice. "The *Colleen* is Trevor's yacht. She's won trophies and everything. Sailing her is beyond anything—it's like waltzing on clouds."

Alana glanced at Trevor. Mara's choice of words was inadvertently insightful. Trevor Sheridan couldn't waltz, so he sailed, and no doubt sailed the best and the biggest yacht to make up for any other deficiencies, imaginary or not.

"When shall we go, Trevor?" Mara asked.

"Tomorrow morning. First thing."

"I can't wait. I love you both!" The girl quickly said her farewells and left the library.

Trevor stood, and Alana rose, inexplicably sorry to see the evening over so quickly. "Let me see you to your room," he offered in a perfunctory manner.

"No. Please. If you don't mind, I'd like to stay here a moment longer." She walked to the cheery fire and warmed her cold hands. Fenian Court's library, as she had discovered, was one of the best rooms in the house. Here there was no gilding, no "Louis" influence at all. Heavy masculine design predominated, with English wainscotting, and leather chairs around the fire, the perimeter of the room lined with screened bookcases of walnut. The only concession to opulence was the custom-loomed carpeting in a deep forest-green. The room reminded her of Trevor's bedroom.

"I hope you'll be good to Mara and see out this arrangement."

Trevor's statement fell on her like a dead weight. She

turned from the fire and locked stares with him. "Your sister is a sweet child. Why wouldn't I be good to her?"

"Perhaps in defiance of me."

She took a fortifying breath. She was never going to convince this man she was human, that she could feel empathy and pain just like those he loved. "Believe it or not," she said coolly, "I'm going to do everything I can for her, in spite of you."

"Good." His eyes gave her a slow, ominous perusal. "Because you must know I won't allow you—or anybody—to hurt her again."

She stared at him and with aching clarity remembered that debut. But Mara was not the only one hurt that ill-fated night. She herself had paid a dear price for that social shunning, and the irony was that she was probably the only one who would have attended it. Yet now that debut ball seemed a lifetime ago. Disheartened, she said, "I've never hurt your sister. I know you'll never believe that, despite telling your sister otherwise."

"I think it's important that she think well of you." His voice lowered in a threat. "I want her to trust you, if I dare."

"How can you expect her to trust me when you won't?"

"Except for the matter of how you treat my sister, it's not necessary that I trust you."

A lump came to her throat. She could hardly say what she felt she must. "I'm your wife. You're my husband. Is that bond not worthy of trust?"

"In a true marriage, yes."

She looked away to the fire, unable to meet his gaze. She couldn't understand why his words hurt her so. All he said was correct. But ever since she'd been thrown at him, her emotions had ceased to follow logic. "I'm surprised you aren't relishing the task of defaming my character to her." She gave a dark laugh. "In fact, it seems at odds with your previous behavior that you should be so anxious that Mara and I be friends."

Sheridan appeared hesitant to explain. When he did, his words were cautious and few. "Mara has rarely known much female companionship. She's never had a mother. Our mother died upon her birth. I believe it would do her good to have some womanly guidance. . . . But only from a sympathetic source," he added, the accusation all but said.

She took a deep breath, her emotions almost out of control. In a shaky voice, she said, "Contrary to your beliefs, I'm not some marble-hearted creature who cannot be kind unless forced to be. Mara has my every sympathy. Why, she's the exact same age as my sis—" She stopped with a sharp intake of breath.

"Your *sister*?" he finished, noting her reaction.

"Good night." She picked up her skirts to make a hasty retreat. She wasn't going to answer him. They had struck this deal with the promise that he would never inquire about her. He would keep it, or he would have his annulment right now.

"Wait." His tone stopped her more than the word. As if he realized he had overstepped his bounds, he came to her side and said simply, "Promise me you will never hurt Mara. If you make that promise, I'll believe you."

"I won't hurt your sister, I promise you," she whispered, her eyes suddenly filling with irrational tears.

He searched her face a moment. Then, appearing satisfied, he pulled back and walked stiffly to the fireplace. She started to leave, but his voice stopped her once more. "I meant to tell you, Alana—an invitation from the Varicks arrived today. They're having a ball tomorrow at Maison-sur-Mer."

"Then rejoice. Your plan is working."

"Yes," he answered, not hiding his bitterness. "We Sheridans would never have been able to procure an invitation from that family before my marriage to you."

A deep melancholy seeped into her heart at those words. Their marriage was rolling right along the agreed path. But the calculation depressed her. It left no room for anything else. The bishop's words came back to haunt her, and she thought about her marriage vows. For some wild reason, her impulse was to treat this marriage with the gravity God and the law proclaimed it was due. But every time she entertained that thought, he came along and drove it into her heart that this was a business transaction. And nothing more.

But that kiss on the train had been something more. And there had been something more in his room that night when she could have sworn he wanted to kiss her again. Yet if she knew anything about this man, he was ready to die for his convictions. And his convictions about her obviously told him that because of her privileged past, she was not capable of caring for another and therefore unworthy of his regard.

"Well, I've got a lot to do tomorrow, so . . ." She turned to leave.

"One last thing. I want you to do something for me."

She paused. "And what is that?"

He didn't answer her immediately, clearly unsure of how to begin. "I want—I want you to speak to Mara about her inappropriate dress."

Alana had been thinking the same thing. She almost pointed that out to him, but she kept her mouth closed.

He said, "You know why she's wearing those short dresses, don't you?"

She nodded, hating the pain she heard in his voice, hating the unmistakable accusation. "I know," she whispered.

With that understanding past them, he dismissed her. "All right. You can go." He suddenly gave a sarcastic laugh, clearly noting her anxiety to be gone from him. "In fact, *run* if you must."

His words cut her like a knife. She stiffened. Then, unable to help herself, she did run, all the miles to her lonely suite of rooms.

Engagement

. . . thus keeping out the "new people"
whom New York was beginning to dread
and yet be drawn to. . . .

—Edith Wharton,
The Age of Innocence

15

It was a beautiful day, blue-skied and breezy, a perfect morning for a sail.

Alana shoved aside the heavy draperies and threw open the casement windows, breathing deeply of the sea air. An unexpected moment of optimism hit her, and she smiled, for a second believing that perhaps, just perhaps, all was not lost. If she, Mara, and Trevor had a few good days in New-port, even just sailing around on the *Colleen*, then maybe Trevor and she might find a common ground. For reasons she couldn't quite articulate yet, Alana suddenly felt the strange desire to make the vows they had spoken in church not such lies after all.

"What should I wear to sail, Margaret?" she asked when she turned from the windows.

"White linen, definitely," Margaret announced.

"All right. Get out a white linen gown—and perhaps that blue straw bonnet—you know, the tiny one with the polka-dot ribbon?"

"Yes, Mrs. Sheridan."

Alana turned back to the windows, the draperies swaying with the brisk sea breeze. In the distance, at the end of Fenian Court's docks, the *Colleen* had been taken from the boathouse and now rocked with a dozen deckhands who were preparing her to sail.

Excitedly, she pictured herself at the bow, the breeze

freeing her hair and whipping at her skirts. She imagined
Trevor next to her pointing out some of the landmarks of
the coast while Mara and she laughed at their attempts to
keep their hats on in the wind. It would be a wonderful day.
More important, it would give her the chance to enter that
sacred ground the Sheridan family was built upon and be
included.

Margaret handed her the white linen dress. She couldn't
get it on fast enough.

"Is she ready?" Trevor asked his first mate when he
walked to the end of the docks and surveyed his prize. The
Colleen was indeed beautiful, 150 feet of polished brass and
teakwood. She was renowned for being the fastest yacht on
the eastern seaboard, and if anyone doubted it, they had
only to peek inside the *Colleen*'s trophy room.

"Trevor!" Mara called from the bow, pretty in a short
pink linen gown piped with navy-blue ribbon. "Do you
want me to have a servant fetch Alana? She hasn't arrived
yet!"

The first mate assured Trevor they were ready to sail.
Trevor nodded and walked up the gangway.

Mara ran to meet him. "Should I send for her?" she
asked.

Trevor gazed grimly toward the house. "Did she tell you
she was coming along?"

"I just assumed she was. Didn't she mention this morning whether she wanted to go?"

He didn't look at her. "She didn't mention it."

"Oh. Well, perhaps she was too tired." Mara's face fell.

Trevor didn't answer. He just stood staring at the house,
deep in thought.

"Was she still sleeping when you left, then?"

"I don't know, Mara. Because she's my wife doesn't
mean I can read her mind," he snapped.

"I didn't ask whether you could read her mind," she said

quietly. "I asked whether she was still sleeping when you came down here."

"I don't know." He gave a curt defiant nod to the first mate, who had signaled him. "Look," he conceded testily, "you've got to understand, Mara. Your sister-in-law comes from a very different world. Ladies like her don't necessarily want to go yachting, with sea spray making their gowns limp and the wind spoiling the arrangement of their hair."

"But Alana's not like that." Mara grew solemn. "Is she?"

Again Trevor looked at the house. "I announced our sail last night. The only reason she's not down here"—his voice grew dispassionate—"is because she doesn't want to be down here." He nodded to the first mate and said, "Cast off." In ten minutes they were well into Rhode Island Sound.

Anticipation sent Alana almost running out the French doors and down Fenian Court's sweep of lawn to the crest of the hill where she could see the docks. Holding on to the tiny straw hat perched artfully on her head, she scanned the docks searching for the enormous yacht that had been there only minutes before. It was gone.

Her smile faded as she held her hand to her eyes to scan the sea. Out in the sound, unmistakably, was the *Colleen*, cutting through the blue waves like a glorious white phantom.

Her heart sank.

The hand that had shielded her eyes lowered to her lips. They had left without her. She felt something tighten in her throat, and she desperately denied how she was feeling. Her mind told her there were a million reasons for their leaving without her if she only took the time to think about it. But no matter how rational she tried to be, there was no avoiding the reason that hurt her the most. They'd simply sailed off without giving her a thought. They had not wanted her.

But Mara wouldn't have done this. Last night she'd made a point to include her. It was Trevor. He was the one to exclude her. Alana felt a coldness in her heart when she wondered how long she would have to pay for failing to attend Mara's debut. Trevor had done this to make her hurt as Mara had.

Her shoulders slumped at the thought. Trevor wanted her as an ornament on his arm to further his sister's social aspirations. He wanted her womanly advice for Mara. But he didn't want her to be part of his family. She was to do her duty, and he was to live his life, and never the twain should meet.

Tears threatened her eyes, but she swallowed her hurt like a bitter pill. Trevor had set boundaries for their marriage, and perhaps it was just as well. In the end, when the annulment came, it would make things more comfortable. She wouldn't have to worry about becoming too fond of his family, and more to the point, she wouldn't have to worry about becoming too fond of him. For a brief second, guilt had weakened her into almost wanting to believe in those marriage vows, no matter how false they had been. But no longer. Let him treat her as if she possessed no feelings, and she would show him that she didn't. She would be cool, dutiful, and polite. Nothing more.

Yet as she looked out at the exhilarating form of the *Colleen* skimming the high waters of the sound, her eyes glittered with unshed tears. She pictured Trevor, relaxed and happy, perhaps standing at the bow letting the salt wind bite at his hair, and the pain stabbed her as never before. Her husband didn't want to share such pleasures with her. She had married a man with a heart of stone. He wanted business and only business, her needs be damned.

Unable to stop them, she let tears roll hot and bitter down her cheeks. They'd barely been married, and already Trevor had wounded another place in her heart, not even giving her time to scar.

Dejected, she left the bluff, putting what armor she had

into place to protect her from further blows. The next time, she vowed, brushing away her tears with a violence she hadn't known she possessed, next time, she wouldn't let herself care enough for him to hurt her again. If he thought he'd married an ice maiden, he was in for a surprise. He didn't know what cold was.

Late in the afternoon, Alana decided to forgo being entombed and depressed in the mansion. Recovering her composure, she took a walk on the immaculate grounds of Fenian Court, enjoying their green beauty and defying anyone to be better company than the birds and Roman statuary.

But to her surprise, Mara found her. She came running from the direction of the house, and Alana supposed the *Colleen* had long been in port. "Did you have a nice morning, Alana?" Mara asked as she caught up with her, slightly out of breath.

"I did some needlework. I was just taking some air—"

"May I go with you?"

Alana smiled. She could never blame Mara for anything her villainous brother did. "Of course." Affectionately, she slipped her arm in Mara's.

"Have you seen the gazebo?" The girl brushed back an unruly lock of black hair that had escaped her chignon.

Alana was struck by the fetching sight she made. "No. Where is it?"

Mara pointed to the ocean, a liquid jewel of blue in the late afternoon sun. "Out there. Don't you see it?"

To the right of where the ocean broke into a frothy white upon a pile of rocks, where the bay swept in calm and undisturbed, there was a gazebo at the end of a long dock.

"You have to go through the boathouse. But the water's almost always calm in that part. I assure you it's quite safe."

"Then let's go." Alana started for the gazebo. It was just the place for her to bring up the subject that Trevor wanted her to clear. They could have a private conversation, and

Alana could approach Mara with the sensitive topic of those juvenile short dresses.

The open-air gazebo was fashioned in the Chinese-Chippendale manner that was becoming all the rage with the upcoming American centennial. Once they'd gotten through the enormous boathouse where Trevor kept the *Colleen* and traversed the length of the long pier, the two women easily made themselves comfortable on benches well cushioned with chintz-covered squabs. Conversation turned to the weather and how beautiful Fenian Court looked from the sea, a great white marble monolith rising from perfectly clipped green hills. Chatting easily with Mara, Alana gazed through the pierced fretwork of the gazebo, surveying the wild beauty of the sea, and she was sure this would be her favorite place forever.

"Is something bothering you, Alana? You seem . . . preoccupied."

Alana looked at Mara, surprised at how astute the girl was. There was a directness about her that Alana found refreshing, in contrast to the circles she had recently come from. Alana wasn't used to such forthrightness, this Sheridan trait. The Sheridans, for all their money and possessions, had a surprising lack of pretentiousness. "Oh no, I'm fine, Mara," she answered, putting a bright smile on her lips. She still hurt from being left behind on the sail, but she put those feelings aside, unwilling to burden Mara with them. Besides, they were here to solve Mara's problems, not her own.

She entered the subject lightly. "We're going to the Varicks' tonight, did you know that?"

Mara nodded and tossed the riotous curl from her forehead. "Yes. You and Trevor will have a wonderful time, I'm sure of it."

"You're coming too. Didn't you know?"

"I—I really don't think I should go. . . ." Mara's eyes darkened with pain. Their glistening sapphire color now almost matched the sea.

"Mara, it's important that you go. I want to introduce you to my acquaintances. I know Trevor wants you to attend."

"Forgive me. I just couldn't." Mara looked away, forlornly gazing out to sea.

Alana didn't answer. Instead she thought hard about what she had to say. Mara was lovely in her pink linen gown, but the gown was too young for her. She should be wearing something more mature, like what Alana wore. After her disappointment, she'd changed out of the white linen into a spring-green taffeta. The gown was simple, yet it reached the ground and even trained behind her in the current taste. "Mara," she began with difficulty, "you're getting too old to wear short dresses. I think it's time you wore some of the gowns your brother purchased for you from Worth. I understand they're all just sitting up in your room, still in their tissue, packed away in trunks."

A tear escaped those wild blue eyes. Mara wiped it away with a vengeance. "I don't want to. Am I so terrible, then?"

"No, you're not—"

"I've decided I'm not going to be a lady. I'm going to remain a girl forever." Mara had a defiance in her eyes that was shockingly like her brother's.

Alana scooted closer to her on the cushions. She took her hand and squeezed it. "Whether you've had a debut or not, you're not going to remain a girl forever. You've already 'developed' out of the gowns you have. I know it's difficult, particularly after your debut, but you must accept it."

"I'll have others made." Mara looked down at her bosom. "I'll hide everything. I'll—" Suddenly she burst into tears.

Alana wrapped her arms around her and let her cry onto her shoulder. "I know," Alana cooed softly into her hair. "I know," she whispered, thinking how painful this age was and how any trauma made it doubly so. She thought of herself a few years ago. She'd been secure then, nestled within a tight and loving family. Then everything she had thought to be true proved otherwise. Tears sprang to her eyes, in part for Mara, in part for Christal, in part for herself.

Alana looked down at the blurred image of Mara as she wept on her shoulder, and she couldn't stop herself from comparing her to Christal. Both girls had been forced to question everything around them at a tender age, even their self-worth. As Alana hugged her, she became even more determined that both Mara and Christal would overcome their circumstances and thrive. They must. "Mara," she said gently, "the world is not always kind. But you can't let it defeat you. You must go with us tonight. I promise you, Trevor and I'll do everything we can to make sure you aren't hurt again."

"They'll call me a biddy, just like they call all their Irish serving girls," she sobbed.

"No they won't. They wouldn't dare." Especially not now, Alana thought derisively, after they'd personally felt the damage the Sheridan wrath could bring upon them.

"I'm afraid. What if the women laugh at me? What if the men won't ask me to dance because I'm—I'm Irish and not good enough?"

Alana kissed the top of her head and hugged her. "Things are changing, Mara. I promise you they'll be polite. And I think when those young men see how pretty you are, they might see being Irish as not such a liability."

"Is that why you fell in love with Trevor? Because he is so handsome?" Mara sniffed and accepted the handkerchief that Alana had tucked into her sleeve.

Taken aback, Alana only said, "Trevor is certainly handsome."

"Would you love him if he were not?"

Alana's brow furrowed as she parried this question. Mara wanted assurance, and yet it was impossible to answer her when the first supposition was wrong. She didn't love Trevor. "Your brother is your brother, Mara. It's difficult to separate all the things that make up Trevor Sheridan."

Alana looked at her and said what was honestly in her thoughts. "But I will confess this. Though Trevor is an uncommonly good-looking man, there's also a force about him that I find I'm drawn to. If he were less handsome, I have to say I'm not sure I would feel differently about him."

"I knew you loved him! I knew it." Mara impulsively wrapped her arms around Alana and hugged her tightly.

Alana remained motionless, despising the falsehoods she and Trevor were building around them. "I trust we may go back to your bedroom, then, and decide which lovely Parisian gown might be correct for tonight's ball?"

Mara pulled back and wiped her eyes. "I'm still afraid." She looked up at Alana, and trembled a smile. "But I think you know best, so I'll do it."

"Growing up's not always so terrible, I promise you." Alana gave her a fragile smile. In her experience, the only good thing about growing up meant an increased ability to numb the pain. But she didn't see such a bleak existence for Mara. Somewhere there was a knight in shining armor for this wild, beautiful spirit.

"Alana, do really think one of the gentlemen will ask me to dance tonight?" Mara tossed her such a worried look, Alana couldn't help but laugh.

She pulled that rebellious jet curl and said, "Truly, Mara, the only problem I see for you, my girl, is which one to choose."

Alana was dressing for the ball when a knock came from the large gilt doors separating the master's suite from hers. It was silly, but upon hearing it she and Margaret stopped in their tracks as if the sound had summoned the executioner.

"Shall I open the door, mum?" Margaret whispered.

Alana paused, still smarting from what had happened that morning. But she'd had all day to prepare for seeing Trevor again, so she pulled on her veneer of ice and said,

"Please do," annoyed that her maid was so intimidated by the master, she felt she had to whisper.

Margaret went to the door, and Alana glanced at her reflection in the pier mirror. She was glad she looked cool and unapproachable. Her gown was an elaborate peacock-blue silk pulled up on the sides with large chartreuse bows and silk bouquets of deep-pink roses. Her slippers were peacock-blue shantung and peeked out beneath a frothy white Guipure lace petticoat. The dress had a tournure that was far more elaborate than for daytime, but she'd already sat once, and the bustle was not unmanageable. The only thing left to do was to braid and pin her hair into a coif, for it hung down her back in a thick buttery stream. Not bothering with it now, she nodded to Margaret to open the door.

As expected, Trevor stood there, already dressed in his evening finery of a black swallow-tailed coat and white piqué vest. He was impossibly handsome in formal attire, especially when that hard mouth quirked in greeting and those eyes locked with hers, leaving her slightly out of breath. Before she could avoid it, she was stung by the thought that this was how he must look when he took his mistress out.

He entered her bedroom as if it were his domain. Surprise and something she almost wanted to believe was approval gleamed in his eyes as he took in her appearance. He especially noted her hair, free and cascading down her back in odd contrast to her rich, complicated clothes.

"Would you have me be waitin' for you in the dressin' room, Mrs. Sheridan?" Margaret peeped, nervous in the master's company.

Both of them looked at the little maid as if they had almost forgotten she was there. Trevor smiled, a little wickedly. "I don't think your maid likes me, Alana. She's always skittering away whenever I enter the room."

"Oh, *no*, sar! You're a fine master, you are!" said Margaret. Nonetheless, she took a step backward.

Trevor laughed, clearly enjoying himself at Margaret's expense.

The cad, thought Alana. "You're excused, Margaret. Why don't you go on downstairs and have some supper. I'll do my own hair tonight."

Margaret nodded, then looked at Trevor.

"That's right. Run along, Pegeen," he said, using Margaret's Irish pet name affectionately as if he were suddenly sorry he'd caused the little maid anxiety. "In fact, there's a surprise for you downstairs. Your husband, Kevin, just arrived. I heard you were pining for each other, so I summoned him from the house in Manhattan. Go to your true love and put the blush of an Irish rose back into those pretty cheeks."

Margaret gasped. She was so shocked, she could hardly stutter, "Why, t'ank you, Mr. Sheridan."

"I don't abide separating man and wife. So go to him. I'm sure he missed you."

"Oh *t'ank* you, Mr. Sheridan!"

He nodded, dismissing her. Margaret left, her expression at once awed, grateful, and skittish.

"That was very thoughtful of you," Alana said when the servant's jib door was shut and they were alone. She could hardly believe it. Trevor Sheridan was impossible to pin down. One moment he was behaving like a rogue; the next, a saint.

" 'Twas nothing," he answered, his face again solemn.

But it was something. For the first time, she'd seen him be kind to a person other than his family. It was clear he liked Margaret despite his bullying. He'd complimented her looks and had been thoughtful enough to bring her husband up from New York.

Alana didn't want to feel the hurt that crept into her heart, but it was impossible to deny. Her husband was more solicitous and friendly to her maid than to her, his wife. She knew she should be grateful to find that Trevor loved and looked after his own. But a terrible suspicion cut her to her very soul—he would never be capable of bestowing that kind of affection on her, never allow himself to love and look after her.

Despair fell over her when she told herself exactly why that was so. In his eyes, she wasn't good enough. Margaret was good enough because she was Irish, being Irish made Margaret almost a relative, a distant relation from the family of Erin. Trevor considered there a bond between them he could never have with his own wife. Alice Diana Van Alen was an outsider, not good enough to be one of them because she had the wrong background, the wrong breeding. But just as a poor woman could do nothing about her poverty, she could do nothing about the woman she was. It was a bitter pill to swallow to think that the mess of their marriage had been spawned to gain the Sheridans' acceptance into a social set that Trevor in truth rejected out of hand. It was further ironic that he'd been concerned that a husband and wife not be separated when Alana couldn't imagine two people more distant than she and Trevor.

"Mara is waiting for us in the drawing room. She's ready to go," he said, interrupting her dark thoughts.

She watched him walk across her bedroom, careful to hide her frustration and disappointment. Defiantly, she composed herself. She couldn't be anyone other than who she was, no matter how hard she tried. So if he would never accept her, it was best to let her heart freeze over, to see this marriage as a business and get on with it. "Is Mara *dressed?*" she asked, concentrating on their talk that afternoon.

Trevor paused, then cracked a rare smile that took her breath away.

"She is. She's beautiful. I thank you."

Still angry about the *Colleen*, determined never to be vulnerable again, she nonetheless released a small sigh of relief. No doubt it wouldn't have gone well for Mara, or herself, if she hadn't been able to talk Mara into the Worth gowns. Pulling her tresses to her shoulder, she said self-consciously, trying to inject a frigid tone, "Well, thank you for the news, but I must have my privacy. I've yet to dress my hair."

"Leave it for now. Come over here." He sat on one of her slipper chairs, resting his cane on his lap. Next to all the pink satin and gold fringe, he looked overpoweringly masculine.

She picked her way across the room, careful to avoid looking too anxious. But she was anxious. His intrusion into her bedroom made her nerves fairly sizzle. She didn't want to show any feeling toward him, but her unexpressed emotion at his rejection this morning colored her cheeks a deep cherry red.

When she stood at his side, he reached into his breast pocket and drew out a long case. He handed it to her without further ceremony. "This is a token of my gratitude for helping Mara. I had it sent from Boston this afternoon. If things continue to go well, you can expect more of the same."

Her hands trembled when she opened the leather-lined case. With a sharp intake of breath, she gazed down at a necklace dripping with diamonds. It was so elaborate, she couldn't begin to count the number of stones.

"You may keep that, Alana, even after the annulment. It's my gift for a job well done."

She closed the lid. All her determination to remain cold and unemotional doomed to fail. His words were an insult, his actions worse; they gouged her heart. She wanted to shout at him, to slap his face. Instead, she collected herself, vowing he would never shatter the veneer that kept her safe. "I'm sorry. I can't accept this." She held the case out to him, her face a mask of marble. "If you'll excuse me, I must do my hair."

He hid his surprise well. In a deadly calm voice he asked, "Why are you refusing this?"

She did her best to rein in her pain and humiliation, but it was a Herculean task. She didn't like his necklace. She

hated it. For all its priceless dazzle, it was only anothe
wretched reminder of the mechanics of their marriage
Trevor Sheridan thought he could buy anything with hi
millions. It was finally time someone disabused him of thi
notion.

She met his gaze. Hers held more than a touch of repri
mand and social superiority. She almost enjoyed sayin
what she had to say. "Where I come from, Mr. Sheridan
giving jewelry isn't an intimacy to be shared betweer
strangers."

He didn't hide his surprise well this time. He answered
his tone ominous, "You're not a stranger. You're my wife."

"In name only."

He stared at her, obviously stumped for an answer
Clutching the leather case, he snapped, "So I'm to just tos
this out the window? If you don't take it, what do yo
propose I do with it, then?"

"Perhaps your mistress would find it a nice addition t
her collection." After the words were out, she could hav
kicked herself.

His eyes met hers with the serenity of a thunderstorm
Opening the case, he let the blindingly bright diamond
cascade down his hand. He taunted, "No, no. I think Daisy
has enough of these."

"Is that her name?" She cursed the tremor in her voice

"Why the interest, sweeting?"

She closed her eyes. The man was impossible. He alway
seemed to say the one thing that made her ache to slap he
palm across his cheek.

Turning from him, she said, "I really must get ready, so i
you'll—"

"No." He stood and took her arm. Without his cane, h
swayed against her, putting another hand on her waist t
steady himself. "I want to know why you're rejecting my
gift."

"Please. I must finish—"

"Tell me." He shook her, his hand tightening on her corseted waist.

She tried to pull away, but he was easily the victor. She thought of tripping him, but her logic and her experience at Delmonico's told her she was far safer struggling with him on both feet than grappling with him on the floor.

"Come along, Mrs. Sheridan," he taunted angrily while she tried to pull away from him. "Tell me why you won't take it."

"I don't like your gift because of the reasons behind it," she hissed, her restraint finally gone. All of the anger she felt at seeing the *Colleen* sail away without her gushed to the surface. "I don't like its cost. I don't like its coldness. I don't like who it's from."

He'd gotten what he'd wanted, but her words seemed to lash at him. Infuriated, he pulled her against him in a rough embrace, shoving the diamonds in her face. "That's choice, Alana. By all rights, you should love these things. Jewels as cold as these suit you."

She glared up at him, hating him at that moment. "I won't wear your vulgar jewels, Trevor. You see, there are some things even *your* money can't purchase."

His eyes gleamed with fury. "Yes, there are things I can't buy. Like the right to touch you with these common Irish hands. But don't worry, little Knickerbocker—the day may come when I might decide not to bother with buying that right. I'll just take it."

Her mouth parted in shock. She looked down at his hands capturing her nipped-in waist, and a sharp sudden fear stabbed at her.

"I get everything I want, Alana. One way or another," he whispered.

"And me?" she choked out. "Do you want me?"

He left her question unanswered. With nerves of iron, he smugly released her. He stepped to the bed and dumped the glittering necklace on her satin quilt. "Get your maid in here and finish dressing," he commanded. "We've got to take Mara to that bloody ball."

She stared at him, unable to believe he could shut himself off and on that quickly. When he met her stare with a cold one of his own, she picked up her silk skirts and ran for the dressing room. But the thought came with her: How in the world was she going to get through the evening with this beast, let alone another year of marriage?

By the time the Sheridan coach arrived at Maison-sur-Mer, the ball had already begun. The Varick mansion was also in the "Louis" taste, but whether Louis XIV, XV, or XVI, Alana was unsure. In Newport all the Louis's were beginning to blur together in a never-ending wash of gilt and marble.

The ballroom was surprisingly full for so early in the season, and the hush that rippled through the room when Alana entered on Trevor's arm told why. It was obvious that many of the guests had ventured to Newport after the Sheridan wedding to continue the entertainment. Alice Diana Van Alen's daring marriage was still considered a spectator sport.

Alana took a deep breath and put on a brave front when the butler announced loudly, "Mr. and Mrs. Sheridan! And Miss Sheridan!" This was difficult, however. After the episode in her bedroom, it had taken nearly ten minutes for her hands to stop shaking. Margaret dressed her hair in several plaits, all culminating in a smooth twisted chignon at her nape. Around her neck she rebelliously wore the Van Alen pearls.

The carriage ride had been unbearable. She'd been forced to sit opposite Trevor, and even in the dark she could feel that piercing stare that lingered with particular vengeance at her neck.

"Alana, darling! So glad you could join us tonight." Joanna Varick, one of the last great matriarchs of Knickerbocker society, stepped to the entrance and greeted her.

She was a handsome woman of fifty, wearing satin as white as her hair and the Varick emeralds, given to the family by the Marquis de Lafayette on his last tour of America.

"How nice it was to receive your invitation, Mrs. Varick. I look forward to introducing you to my new family." Alana gave Mara a reassuring smile. The girl looked terrified.

Alana then turned to Trevor. He was almost scowling. Joanna Varick was staring at him as if she couldn't quite accept Irishmen as guests in her ballroom. But when the matron turned to Alana, the glitter in her eyes betrayed just how amused she was by the scandal. "I think you know my husband, Trevor Byrne Sheridan," Alana murmured, irrationally angered by the woman's attitude.

Joanna Varick placed the facade of a greeting on her face and held out her hand. "Congratulations, Mr. Sheridan. You certainly got the best of us . . . in Alana, that is."

Alana wondered how Trevor was going to take that statement. She was surprised to see him give Joanna Varick his most wicked smile. "I entirely agree, madam," he answered. He bowed and brushed his lips across the back of the woman's hand.

Joanna Varick lifted one brow in surprise. The matron was not used to such effrontery, but Alana couldn't tell if Trevor displeased her or not. When Joanna Varick looked at her hand, Alana thought she saw a secret glimmer of pleasure soften the matron's features. Irish or not, Trevor Sheridan was an incredibly handsome man and as cool as Joanna Varick could be, blood, not ice, flowed in her veins.

"And this is my new sister-in-law, Miss Mara Sheridan." Alana squeezed Mara's arm and pulled the reluctant girl forward. Remembering herself, Joanna pulled her attention from Trevor and made to give Mara a perfunctory greeting. But Mara was difficult to dismiss. Shy and beautiful, adorned in the Worth creation with the swallows flying at its hemline, her hair demurely dressed with pearls, Mara Sheridan was a vision of innocence that even a Knickerbocker would have been proud of. Joanna Varick took one

look at the girl, and a smile escaped her lips. "How lovely
to meet you, Miss Sheridan."

"M-M-Mrs. Varick," Mara said nervously, giving a little
curtsy.

"Mrs. Anders has the dance cards, child." The matron
turned to Alana. "Shall I take Mara around?"

Alana could taste her first conquest. "That would be
most dear of you."

"It's of no account, darling." Joanna Varick gave one last
stare at Trevor, then coolly took Mara by the arm and led
the girl into the crowd of her first society ball.

"If they hurt her . . ."

Hearing the harsh whisper, Alana looked up at Trevor as
he stared at Mara and the matron making their way
through the crush.

"They won't. They wouldn't dare—now. Mrs. Varick
likes her. And while she is considered one of our eccentrics
—there was talk of a certain young man back in New York
—the Varick line is impeccable. That's enormously important to the Four Hundred."

He stared down at her. "What about Caroline Astor?"

A small smile touched Alana's lips. "Caroline Astor will
accept her. Our marriage has given her no choice."

Their gazes met. Something flared briefly in his eyes, but
whether it was loathing, longing, or triumph she couldn't
tell. "Good" was all he said before he held out his arm and
led her through the ballroom.

The evening continued to go well. Mara acquired many
admirers and had yet to sit out a waltz. Trevor's manner,
while detached, was solicitous, and Alana was content to
seat herself in a corner and watch the proceedings while he
stood behind her.

Everything went according to plan. The ball was small
enough for Mara to impress and important enough that the
impression would eventually be carried south to Manhattan. Alana was almost feeling smug when a silence fell
throughout the ballroom. Whispers and giggles slipped out

behind ostrich feather fans, and Alana stood to see the cause of the commotion. She almost fell back into Trevor's arms when she heard the butler announce, "Ladies and gentlemen, I present Mr. Anson Vanbrugh-Stevens!"

A cautious, unreadable expression froze on her face, partly because she knew a third of the room stared at her and partly because the other two-thirds were split between watching Anson and Trevor watch her.

In dismay, her gaze fixed on the entrance. Anson stood there scanning the faces in the crowd. He was a handsome man, tall and blond, with classic yet not too fine Dutch features and vivid blue eyes. When these locked on Alana, anger fairly crackled in them, tempered only by a slight petulance on his lips.

Ignoring her then, he stepped from the dais. The orchestra resumed another waltz, and the ballgoers did their best to pretend nothing had happened.

"Mr. Vanbrugh-Stevens was not at the wedding, was he?" Trevor put a hand on her shoulder. To any observer this might have looked like a nonchalant show of affection for his wife. Alana knew otherwise.

"No, he was not," she answered coolly.

He whispered for her ears only. "Could it be that he was not informed of your intention to marry?" There was no hiding the amusement in his voice.

"I would have told him," she answered stiffly behind her French fan, "but he was in Salzburg. There was no way to contact him in time."

"So that was what finally sealed your fate. You couldn't summon your Knickerbocker knight to rescue you before the evil knight brought you to the altar."

When she didn't answer, he leaned over her and whispered, "I understand he'd proposed several times. I'll always wonder why I could trap you into marriage and he couldn't."

"He wanted me as his wife, not as a tool for revenge. His intentions were completely different from yours," she hissed in a low voice so that no one else would hear her. She might also have mentioned that Trevor's offer of marriage had an out after one year. Anson's was for life.

"My intentions might not be so different." His gaze restlessly dipped to the display of creamy skin where the peacock-blue silk fell from her shoulder.

Beneath his stare she couldn't form a response. Realizing there was nothing she could say at that moment without risking Mara's future, she twisted around to afford a better view of the ballroom. To her utter shock, Anson stood in front of her, his face polite and angry.

"Mrs. Sheridan." He uttered it like a curse. He bent and kissed her hand. "May I have this waltz?"

"I'm—not sure." She glanced up at Trevor and saw instant dislike in his eyes.

"You don't mind, do you, chap?" Anson said to Trevor, pulling Alana to her feet. He didn't bother to hide the contempt in his voice.

Trevor said nothing, and that frightened her more than if he had.

She placed her hand on her husband's arm. "Let me have one dance with him, Trevor," she whispered. "Think of Mara. Everyone expects me to dance one waltz with Anson."

She watched him grip the gold head of his cane as if it were Anson's neck. Without protest, Trevor leaned back against the wall, arms crossed over his chest.

She placed a pleasant smile on her face and took Anson's arm. He gave Trevor a bitter glance, then took her by the waist and swept her into the crowd.

Alana nodded to the familiar faces on the dance floor. It seemed everyone was bumping into them, desperate to hear even a snatch of the conversation.

"It's lovely weather we're having in Newport this week. Much warmer than can normally be expected." Anson smiled politely to a matron, then turned angry eyes upon her.

"Yes," she answered, unsure where he was leading.

"I want to congratulate you, Mrs. Sheridan, on your *fine* marriage."

She took a deep breath. At least now she knew where they were going. "I know your mother sent a telegram. There wasn't time to tell you in person. I'm sorry." She felt it best to disarm him and get right to the point. Anson was as angry as she'd ever seen him. She had never known he could be so impassioned.

"I got here as soon as I could. To no avail," he added sharply.

"Please don't be angry, Anson." She looked up at him, her emerald eyes full of contrition. "There was no other choice."

"You had me as a choice!" he whispered furiously.

She watched as he nodded to Joanna Varick, who was staring at them from across the ballroom. When his attention turned back to her, Alana said, "As perfect as you are, Anson, you weren't right for me, and you know that. I told you that before."

"And that mick is?"

His words made her miss a step. She stumbled briefly, and he caught her in his strong arms.

"Alana, we had everything in common—our families, our backgrounds, our ideas. You should have married me before it was too late."

"You know nothing about me, Anson. It would never have worked."

"I know nothing about you!" His face turned thunderous. He looked around and carefully remolded his expression. "And Sheridan knows you better? In a week, he knows you better than I? I ought to kill him. I know exactly what that bloody mick did to get to know you better."

"Don't call him that," she said, her face unable to keep up the pretense any further. "Don't call him that word ever again."

He stared down at her, unable to believe her anger. "You

defend him? Caroline Astor told me you were practically dragged down that aisle to his side. She wants you to think about an annulment." He pulled her closer. "I do too."

"I'm not going to get an annulment, Anson. I don't know what else to say. I've married Trevor Sheridan. I'm staying married to him." That was, of course, only a half-truth, but she didn't want to explain that when her marriage was dissolved, she would still reject his offer. There was no point in hurting him further.

"Are you going to have that vile Irishman's baby?"

She looked up in shock, her cheeks suddenly burning with shame. "Is that what everyone thinks? That I had to get married because Trevor—"

He almost laughed in bitterness. "And what are we supposed to think? Sheridan forces you marry him, but it couldn't have been just for the money because I have money. A lot of it. You could have married me, Alana. But regrettably, I always played the gentleman." Not missing a beat of the music, he roughly pulled her around, taking the corner.

She was silent for a long time, letting herself follow him unconsciously in the waltz. Softly she said, "It's not what you believe, Anson. Things will prove differently in a few months."

"Yes, nine months." His hand roughly gripped her waist.

"I didn't marry him for that reason."

"Then why?" He tilted back his handsome blond head and laughed. His anger renewed, he pulled her against him. "Don't lie to me and tell me you love him, because I'll never believe that."

As she stared up at him, she suddenly knew why she and Anson could never have been happy. For all their superficial compatibility, they were different spirits entirely. She wanted love. He wanted what society deemed best. She wanted acceptance; he wanted perfection. She wanted to cry on a man's strong shoulder and unburden herself of all the tragedies that tore at her heart. He wanted to spare his expensive cravat.

"Go on, tell me you love Sheridan," he demanded sharply, smiling at the guests around them.

She only stared at him.

He smiled. "I knew you wouldn't." Triumph filled his deep-blue eyes. "You couldn't love a man like that."

"I'm drawn to him. I was, from the very moment I saw him." She didn't know why she felt the need to explain. She wondered if it was more for her understanding than his.

"Ah, fine. But that's not love."

"No."

"So tell me you love him, Alana, and I'll leave you alone. Don't, and I'll hound you for the rest of your days to get that annulment."

"I love him." Alana refused to look at him, suddenly overcome by a swell of emotion. It was the worst lie she'd ever told, yet it didn't feel like a lie. It felt worse than a lie; it filled her with a wild, searing panic.

Much to the guests' shock and delight, Anson stopped right in the middle of the ballroom. He grasped her to him, for the moment unmindful of scandal. "You're telling me that you've fallen in love with a common goddamned Irisher? That you've rejected me because you'd actually prefer to be with that—*mick?*" he whispered furiously.

"Yes," she gasped.

There had been very few times in Anson Vanbrugh-Stevens's life when he'd been told no. Alana supposed her rejections of his suit had been most of the reason he'd been so persistent. The idea of losing was difficult for him to accept, but watching him now, she knew he would finally have to. He'd been confident he'd get what he wanted. The worst had happened.

Without another word, he bowed to her and shoved his way through the crowds. He left, stony-faced, not bothering to even thank his hostess.

Alana felt the stares at her back as if they were knives.

With tears threatening at any minute, she fled to the balcony, taking in the sea air in great heaving breaths. She couldn't stop herself from crying. She hated hurting Anson. For all his faults, he still had a right to be indignant. She had treated him callously with her quick marriage. Now she had lied to him. But had she? More tears came, and she forced herself not to think about the reasons. It wasn't true, of course. She couldn't love Trevor; she hardly knew him. But for the first time she saw the possibility of falling in love with her husband. The idea left her breathless and afraid.

"You shouldn't fret so, Alana. Mara's success has been swift. You'll be back in his arms in no time."

The cold voice startled her. She looked up and found Trevor standing by her on the long dark balcony. Against her will, she shivered.

He gave a dark laugh. "I take it by Mr. Stevens's departure, however, that his greatest virtue is not patience."

"He wanted to marry me," she said quietly. "It was cruel not to give him notice of my marriage."

"He'll get over it."

His callous attitude chilled her. She wondered when it would be directed at her. She wondered if it would destroy her. "Anson's presence seems to have disturbed you, Trevor."

"He's everything I dislike in you, *á mhúirnín.*"

"And what *do* you dislike in me?" she asked angrily, hiding her hurt behind a well-bred facade. He'd called her something in Gaelic. Was it a curse?

"I hate your privilege. I hate the fact that you're from a set of exalted loins and therefore everything is your due, whether you've earned it or not. The Knickerbocker lack of hardship disgusts me."

She turned away, fury tautening her pale features, unshed tears glittering in her green eyes. "My family was destroyed in a house fire when I was but sixteen. My privilege did not protect me from that. Nor from my uncle, if you will recall."

He was quiet for a long time as he stared down at her in the dark. His expression was strange, as if he were torn between vengeance and mercy. "That night when Didier brought you so wet and bedraggled to my doorstep was not the first time I saw you, Alana. I'd seen you before, did you know that?"

Her shoulders stiffened. Bravely, she wiped at her wet cheeks.

"It was about a year ago," he whispered, placing both his hands on her upper arms. "I was in Delmonico's. In one of the eating salons, I can't remember which one. Lorenzo walked up in the middle of my meal. He told Eagan and me a party was arriving fresh from their boxes at the Academy of Music. In the most apologetic terms he asked that we change tables." Trevor grew quiet. "Lorenzo, of course, has great tact, but both he and I knew why we had to change tables. These people were not in the habit of being seated in the same room as Irishers." His hands felt like vises on her tender flesh. "And do you know who first entered the room upon our leaving? You and that bloody bastard who just stormed out of here. I'll always remember—when I passed you in the entrance, you didn't even see me. You were preoccupied with Anson. But I saw you. You were beautiful, probably the most beautiful woman I'd ever seen. And most definitely the coldest. I froze just looking at you." He pulled her back against his chest. "If not for Mara's sake, I would have left you alone, Alana. But by God, when I knew I had to do it, I enjoyed knocking you off that pedestal. I've finally brought this whole society to its knees. For once, *they* have to look up to *me*."

Alana listened to Trevor's story, the irony of it piercing her heart. She didn't remember the evening, for there'd been many at Delmonico's in Anson's company. If the "undesirables" had been removed, it had not been at her request, or even with her knowledge. But the worst of it was how Trevor so completely misread the situation. He'd seen her on Anson's arm and believed her to be smugly happy with her lot in life. What a lie that was. She'd been in the company of a man she knew she could never love and endured another socially brilliant night only to spin fantasies around a faceless man in a simple white house. She'd dreamed of children and home and hearth, and found Worth gowns and loneliness. It was no wonder she seemed cold. She had so much to hide. And no one to share it with.

"The pedestal was an illusion, Trevor. There was never anything beneath me but air," she whispered, her tears tracing down her cheeks.

"No," he answered confidently, "that was no illusion. Look at everyone's reaction to our marriage. Their goddess has fallen. And all because of me."

In the quiet that followed his words the strains of "The Beautiful Blue Danube" could be heard through the open doors. The music of the violins lifted on the breeze and carried the sound far out to sea.

"Why don't you go back and dance. I know this is your favorite waltz." He dropped his hands and stepped back. "I don't want to stay much longer. I think it prudent that Mara leave too early rather than too late."

"I don't dance to this waltz." She lifted her skirt and made to leave.

He touched her waist and made her face him. "Why don't you dance to it?" he asked.

"I made a promise to myself a long time ago when I first heard it played. I promised that I would only dance to it with the man I love." She unwillingly lowered her gaze to his cane.

He seemed equally aware of the fact that he would never be that person. He commented acidly, "Now that Anson's gone, there seems to be nothing more for us to do other than to depart."

"No," she whispered, despair hidden in her voice. "Shall I fetch Mara?"

He nodded. She'd never seen his face so hard.

Mara watched them from the corridor—miles, it seemed, from where they stood. Her brother and his wife were saying good night at the other end of the long hall, Mara noting every detail and expression of their parting.

The Varick ball had ended too quickly, and they'd made a silent journey back to Fenian Court. Mara hadn't understood the oppressive atmosphere, but as she peered down the hall at her brother, she began to comprehend Eagan's fears.

Trevor escorted Alana to her bedroom door. They exchanged few words, then Alana disappeared into her room, and Mara watched her brother's forlorn figure march stiffly to his. There'd been a second when Mara was sure her brother had the impulse to kiss his wife just as she'd seen him kiss Daisy. It was a movement of his hand on Alana's waist perhaps, or just her overactive imagination. Whatever, the kiss had been aborted, and the two had sought chilly solace in their separate chambers.

Mara's sapphire eyes saddened at the realization that her brother's brilliant marriage was in trouble. Her brow furrowed as she tried to think of a way to save it. When the idea came, her brow cleared, and she ran to her bedroom to write Eagan.

Her letter began: *Drastic measures tomorrow . . .*

16

Trevor came down the next morning visibly pleased to see the calling cards left on the mahogany Townsend and Goddard block-front chest in Fenian Court's enormous marble foyer. The stack of cards were proof of Mara's success the evening before, and he seemed content to sift through them, noting with satisfaction all those illustrious names.

But when he came to the last card in the stack, his expression abruptly changed. His dark moody eyes turned thunderous. Looking briefly at the writing on the back, he put the card in his pocket, summoned the majordomo, and gave him explicit instructions—essentially, to drag his wife downstairs to have breakfast with the master.

Alana awoke with Margaret standing over her bed holding out her dressing gown. The little maid informed her that her presence was requested downstairs immediately. Irritated yet intrigued, Alana dressed in a sienna-colored watered silk day gown and departed for the sunny breakfast room.

The master's disposition, however, was anything but sunny. Trevor gave her one black glance before she was assisted to her seat by the majordomo. The intimate breakfast room was hung with lime-green taffeta, the same silk and tassels festooned at the many windows. But even this cheery color couldn't wash away the pall of the master's mood as he stared at her in dead silence. The mahogany eating table sat only six, and when she went to take her napkin, he seemed to take comfort in being so close that he could see every subtlety of her expression.

Alana looked down at her plate and found Anson Stevens's calling card staring up at her as if it were a coiled snake. Her eyes briefly flickered to Trevor before she found the courage to pick it up.

"He wrote you a note on the back," he bit out.

Alana glanced up and saw the servants quietly skulk out of the room. She turned the card over and read: *I don't believe you.*

She looked up. Trevor's face was etched with anger. His eyes fairly glittered with the power of his emotions. "He seems to be confused, Alana. I'm not sure he understands the sanctity of our marriage." His barely leashed fury mocked his restrained words.

She placed the card on the tablecloth. "I'm famished. I hope we eat soon."

"What doesn't he believe?"

This question threw her. Her expression faltered. She couldn't tell him what she'd said to Anson. She'd rather die.

"What doesn't he believe, Alana?" Trevor prompted, his anger becoming more ominous.

She ignored the question. "The servants are returning soon, I hope?" It was the wrong thing to do.

Trevor took note of her noncommunicative stance, looked down at his coffee, and calmly took a sip. "If Stevens thinks he may cuckold me, you may want to mention I'll see him dead first." The words were delivered with such ice, it took a moment for Alana to think of a comeback.

Her eyes sparked with fury. "How dare you cast stones at Anson—or me. You've no right at all. Or have you forgotten our dear Miss Daisy Dumont?"

"Daisy was my mistress before I knew you," he bit out.

"And I knew Anson before I knew you. What's sauce for the gander is sauce for the goose, I say."

He stood, his chair screeching back on the highly polished parquet. "Daisy has nothing to do with this. I've always conducted my affairs with utmost discretion. Stevens, on the other hand, wants to make a fool of me. And I will not let him. Am I making myself clear?"

"Could you possibly believe that something in this world does not concern you? Oh, I know that's a shocking statement, my great Atlas, but have you ever considered that this might not be some grand plan to ruin you? Did you ever consider that perhaps Anson possessed some tenderness for me and is having a difficult time relinquishing it?"

He was obviously not immune to her sarcasm. Slowly, with barely leashed fury, he said, "I'm your husband, and as your husband I've certain rights under the law. One of them is the right to keep you from other men, even if I must beat you to do it."

Her body trembled with anger. Standing, she said, "And shall I go after you with a frying pan the first night you desire to see your little Daisy?"

"If you're planning on filling her shoes, then speak up now, and I'll have no more to do with Daisy."

His offer was clearly a dare. Her gaze locked with his for one sizzling second, and she was almost tempted to push them both over the edge and take up the gauntlet. But logic came to the rescue. She threw down her napkin, nearly running over Mara in her desperate flight back to her suite.

It was almost evening when she received Mara's note. All day Alana had paced in her room—angry, hurt, frustrated. When the girl's request that she meet her in the gazebo came, she relished the escape. She left her room, not bothering with a shawl.

Sweeping down the lawn tinted with lavender shadows of the statuary, Alana could almost feel her spirits lifted by the beauty around her. The sun was just disappearing behind Bellevue Avenue, and the sea was a deep, placid indigo.

Behind her, Fenian Court rose like a white marble monolith defying the sea to claim it.

The boathouse was empty as she made her way through. Once on the pier, she looked to the end, expecting to see Mara step from the gazebo.

Yet Trevor appeared. "What are you doing here?" he asked warily.

"Where is Mara?"

His face turned grim as he looked behind her down the dock to the door leading to the boathouse. It immediately slammed closed, and a key turned in the lock. Next, Alana saw Mara running up the lawn to the house.

"She hasn't had a whipping in years, but tonight I'll see she gets one," Trevor vowed, his face taut with anger.

"She's locked us out here!" Alana gasped.

"Eagan told her to do this. All that hand-holding business. I knew she was up to no good the evening she arrived. She lured me here with a note."

"She did the same to me." Alana looked down at the dark blue waters swirling beneath the dock. It was much too deep to wade ashore. "You'll have to swim, Trevor. I'm sorry, but of course a lady in my position . . . well, I never learned how."

He met her gaze and answered cuttingly, "I can't swim."

Her eyes widened. "How can that be? I've heard you're a remarkable yachtsman. The *Colleen* is renowned because of your skill."

"If I'm such a good yachtsman, it's because I don't want to drown," he answered through clenched teeth.

In despair, she looked around. The gazebo loomed in the foreground; she was unable to think of an escape.

"We'll just have to bide our time until the bloody brat lets us out," he said quietly.

Her shoulders slumped in defeat. He motioned toward the gazebo, and together they walked to it.

The minutes stretched like hours as the light slowly seeped from the sky. The gas was turned up at Fenian

Court, the numerous windows glittering like diamonds. It was a beautiful sight to sit in the dark and see such a grand palace illuminated on the shore—but the night air was growing cool, and she shivered, especially when she looked at Trevor, who sat in the shadows.

"Shall she keep us here all night?" she whispered, her voice hesitant.

"I bloody hope not," was his terse answer.

"You've got to explain the situation to her, Trevor. She obviously thinks our marriage is something it's not."

"I don't want her disillusioned."

"Our annulment won't disillusion her?"

He was quiet. Though she couldn't see his eyes, she knew with all her womanly instincts that they were trained on her. "An annulment doesn't quite admit the cynicism that this arrangement does."

She nodded. It was one thing to end it when there was at least an attempt at a marriage. It was another to make a marriage a farce from its inception. Depression settled over her, and she no longer felt like talking. She turned away, finding solace in the inky landscape and biting sea breeze.

"You're cold," he commented.

She hugged herself. "I didn't think I'd be here all night."

"Here." He was so close, she could feel his breath in her hair. He placed his frock coat over her, his large warm hands lingering on her delicate shoulders.

His touch paralyzed her. She couldn't face him to say thank you.

"Why didn't you marry Stevens?" he whispered, his voice inquisitive yet harsh.

Having no better explanation, she said, "Anson wasn't the man for me."

"How could anyone be more your kind than that man? He bloody reeks with good breeding."

Ignoring his sarcasm, she closed her eyes and tried to picture the man in her dreams. For so long she had imagined what he might have been, what she wanted him to be.

She could always conjure up that dream at a moment's notice and immediately feel its emotion. Now, for some reason, it was difficult. It all seemed so far away, like a memory from another life. "There are traits other than good breeding that I desire more, contrary to what you believe," she parried.

"Such as?"

She took a fortifying breath. "I want a kind man. I want him gentle, intelligent, strong. His good breeding—or the amount of money in his pocket—makes no difference to me at all."

He turned ominously silent, clearly feeling her jab. "This man you describe—is he the one you saw in Brooklyn the day before our wedding?"

She spun around, shock leaving her speechless. He knew about Brooklyn! Her heart took a leap. Had she sacrificed herself for nothing? The thought nearly killed her.

Wishing she could make out his face in the dark, she gasped, "You told me you would not delve into my affairs! Have you followed me into Brooklyn?" Growing hysterical, she cried, "I only married you because you promised me you'd leave me alone!"

"I don't know why you went to Brooklyn." In the darkness he reached out and touched her cheek. "I only know that we're married now, and with every day, I like that promise less."

"You can't renege." She turned away, disliking the feelings that his touch summoned in her.

"Tell me you won't go there again."

She pulled away, fear building in her chest. "No. I must go there again."

He paused, and even the lap of the sea against the pilings couldn't drown out the fury in his silence. "How well I now understand Stevens's frustration. Does he know about Brooklyn?"

"No one does." She grasped his arm, acutely aware of the power of the muscles bulging beneath his shirtsleeve. "I beg of you—don't delve into my life. I'm doing all that I can to help your sister. Please, just leave me alone."

"Answer me one thing. Is it this man you visit there? Have you a lover there?"

"No," she said, desperate to have his promise.

"How can I be sure? You seemed so well acquainted with this man you describe."

"Believe me, this is none of your affair. You must stay out of this and never follow me again!"

"Alana!" He shook her. "What am I to think? If you tell me nothing, I can only think the worst!"

She could no longer hide her despair. Bitterly, she said, "The man I've described doesn't exist. Don't you know that?"

"He's not Anson?"

"He's no one. He lives within my imagination, and there I fear he'll stay for the rest of my life." Her voice broke.

The silence between them was leaden. It was several moments before his hands loosened their steely grip.

"Now do you believe me?" she asked, defeated and angry.

He stared down at her in the dark. "Yes," he whispered.

"Promise me we'll never discuss this again."

"No."

She started, unable to believe his audacity. Had he no morals at all that he could break a promise so easily? "I married you to secure my privacy. We had an arrangement. If the terms have changed, you should have informed me before now."

"When I made my proposal, I had your dossier in front of me. I thought I knew everything about you. You were the classic New York elite, from your Washington Square residence to your tasteful little tea parties you held every Monday afternoon. But now I find this secret of yours eats away at me, and I can't help but wonder if that secret is the one thing that makes you human."

For one brief crazy moment she almost had the urge to

tell him about Christabel. She actually considered purging herself of her troubles, with the wild hope that he would understand and even help her in her fight to exonerate her sister. But cold reality quickly set in, and she realized how stupid that would be. It had always been prudent that no one know about Christal, and it was only more so now, given the man she had married. Trevor Sheridan was a manipulator. If she ever told him her secrets, one day he might use them against her, perhaps even against Christabel.

"I am human," she whispered. "If you just looked close enough."

"I want to." His breath feathered against her forehead. "I swear I want to."

His mouth found hers in the moment she realized she'd yet to let go of his arm. He kissed her, offering damnation and salvation in one eloquent motion. She wanted to pull back, but something stronger—his arm, she thought—pushed her farther into his embrace until she was wrapped in his warmth and strength. The frock coat slipped to the ground, but she hardly noticed as his tongue burned into her mouth, flaming her entire body, torching even the wet velvet recess of her femininity. His kiss exploded dormant emotions within her, and her hand rose inexpertly to caress his cheek.

This drove him further, his hand lifting to cover her corseted breast. She moaned, her kiss-drugged mind unable to form a protest. His thumb roughly brushed the crown of her breast, and through the layers of silk and cotton her nipple became a hard sensitive nub. Shocked, she was torn between wanting him to stop and begging him to drive forward. Anson had seldom kissed her, and she'd never allowed him to go this far. Now she knew why. He held no fascination for her. Feeling Trevor's hard demanding mouth take hers again, her only thought was that she would never summon the strength to make him stop.

His teeth gently nipped at her lower lip, and his tongue

caressed her neck. He removed his hand at her breast, and she despised the empty feeling she had when it left.

His attention went to her neck, and one by one he released the tiny buttons that ran the length of her chemisette. When the lace was parted down to her bosom, he slipped a warm hand beneath it, caressing her flesh. Helpless, she sagged against him.

"I see you're not made of ice after all," he whispered against her hair, his palm pushing lower down her bosom to cup her breast.

His arrogance drove a nail into her heart. She wanted that hand to touch her. She wanted his body to keep her warm. But she wanted them only in tenderness. She wanted it only if his heart and mind were as engaged as his body, because hers certainly were. Yet it was clear that his were not, and with a strength she hadn't known she possessed, she pushed him away from her and turned to rebutton her gown.

"Alana," he snapped, obviously feeling, as she did, that he'd just fallen into cold seawater.

"No—don't say anything. We had an agreement. You can't change it from minute to minute." Her icy fingers fumbled at the tiny mother-of-pearl buttons. She hadn't realized how frigid the night was out on this dock surrounded by the water.

"You're weren't protesting earlier."

"I was a fool. I'm not in this marriage to assuage your lust. Remember that."

"Of course," he said in a voice filled with venom, "a fine little lady like you wouldn't have gotten into this marriage if it meant you had to wrap your thighs around me every now and then."

She cried out in anger and pushed past him. Running down the planks of the pier to the boathouse, she vowed to go through the door even if she had to break it down. Wailing like a banshee and beating her fists upon the locked door, she was finally blessed by the sound of a key turning in the lock. A lantern lifted, and she came face-to-face with a surprised gardener.

"Mrs. Sheridan!" the man gasped. "I canna think how we locked ye out here!"

She didn't answer him. With the terrible sound of a repressed sob, she ran up the hill to the house, her chest heaving with unshed tears, her heart breaking in two.

17

For three days they said not a word to each other, going about their daily routine in utter silence. Alana arrived for dinner; Trevor silently watched her be seated. When Trevor announced plans for the evening, he sent a note to her suite on her breakfast tray. The soirees were the most difficult. For Mara's sake, Alana couldn't let anyone know she was anything but pleased with her husband. So they play-acted with a vengeance Shakespeare would have approved.

Mara continued her social success. But sensitive to her brother's moods, she couldn't miss Trevor's dark looks whenever she caught him gazing across a ballroom at his wife. It was worse when they spent the evenings at Fenian Court. The three of them would sit in silence, Trevor drinking his spirits, staring morosely at the fire, Alana working her Berlin wool-work as if the hounds of hell were after her to finish. Mara was beside herself. The time spent in the gazebo had done nothing to bring them together. If anything, Trevor and Alana seemed more cold and detached from each other than before.

This evening was spent much like the others, at home by the blazing hearth in the drawing room. They had dined on a magnificent turkey, but though the bird could have fed twenty, none of them seemed to have an appetite. Trevor was into his third glass of whiskey, and Alana was nervously admiring her finished needlework, a picture of Queen Victoria's pet spaniel, clearly regretting the speed with which she had completed it. Mara was just about to go to the piano and stir them up by playing a bawdy Irish tune Eagan had illicitly taught her when the devil himself walked in.

Eagan entered the drawing room with as much disturbance as possible. He tossed his top hat onto the sofa next to Alana, startling her into looking at the door. Then he sauntered into the room, his gait none too steady, for it was a good train ride from Manhattan and when he had started out, the Pullman's decanters were full. The smile on his face was dazzling, and Alana couldn't help but return it.

"Sweet sister-in-law, how I've missed you!" He pulled her to her feet and bussed her soundly on the cheek. Embarrassed, Alana blushed and looked at Trevor. He stood and, white-knuckled, clutched his cane.

"What are you doing here, Eagan?" he said, his voice low and full of disapproval.

"Mara, me love, how foin it is to see yer luvely face agin," Eagan announced, mimicking street Irish.

"What are you doing here?" Trevor asked, losing patience.

"Me own dear brother!" Eagan took the glass from Trevor's hand and kicked back the entire contents. Finished, he put his hand on his chest and stumbled back, a grimace on his boyish face. He could barely speak. "I swear, Brother, ye be drinkin' th' bloody fires of hell. Thas stuff could kill the divil hisself!"

Trevor was not amused by his brother's antics. Sternly he asked, "Why did you come here? Don't you know I'm on my honeymoon?"

"Ah well, you told me you were going on your honeymoon, but with Mara here and all, I thought to meself, 'Now what kind of honeymoon is that for me brother's foin bride?' " Eagan stole a glance at Alana and winked.

Appearing thoroughly annoyed, Trevor took Alana's arm.

She almost pulled away, but one look into her husband's eyes told her that now was not the time.

" 'Tis time to take me 'foin bride' to her room," Trevor said, the sarcasm dripping from his tongue. "We'll be saying good night, Eagan, but if you learned a thing from that 'foin' Columbia education, you'll be on a train heading back to New York this instant."

"Wonderful. So I'll be seeing ye *both* at breakfast, then?"

Alana had to bite her tongue to keep from laughing. Mara had no such restraint and giggled behind her hand. Trevor, however, looked ready to pop a blood vessel. When he looked down and saw the amusement dancing in her eyes, his face grew so furious, it was all Alana could do to control herself.

"Trevor, me brother, ye don't look so well. I niver seen such a shade o' purple.

Upon Eagan's mocking accent, the dam broke, and Alana broke into hysterical laughter. Infuriated beyond reason, Trevor took her by the arm and dragged her upstairs to her suite. She laughed the entire way.

"How goes it here, Mara?" Eagan asked, sobering only slightly when his brother and Alana had left the room.

Mara released a great sigh and slumped on the sofa. "I suppose you didn't receive my last letter. I locked them out on the dock—you know, the gazebo?"

"You did?" Eagan said, his voice full of admiration.

"Yes." Mara's face grew long. "But it didn't work. They hate each other, Eagan. I know it's not possible, but I swear it's so. And I don't think Trevor's shy at all. I think something else is going on around here."

"It's a fine line between love and hate. We just need to make them cross it, that's all."

"I don't think we can make them, Eagan. I think something like that has to come from within."

Eagan looked at her, a tenderness in his eye. "How very

stute you are, little sister. Sometimes I wonder where you
get all this knowledge."

"It's just common sense, Eagan."

"Well, you're the only Sheridan with any of *that*."

"Am I so different from you and Trevor, then?"

Suddenly not liking the direction of the conversation,
Eagan tweaked her nose and skillfully changed subjects.
"Enough of that. What are we to do about Trevor? If we
can't force him and his wife together, I'm at a loss for ideas,
and I want this marriage to work."

"They might have had a chance if we hadn't gone to the
Varicks' ball. I made them hold hands one night, just as you
told me, and by the end of the evening, they almost looked
as if they enjoyed it. But after Trevor saw Mr. Stevens at
the Varicks' ball, he hasn't been the same ever since."

"Who is Mr. Stevens?"

"Alana's old beau. He walked right up to Trevor and
took Alana waltzing. And the ire I saw in those eyes—I
swear, Eagan, I thought Trevor might punch him!"

Eagan's expression filled with mischief. His Irish accent
came back in force as he said playfully, "Is that so, me
darlin'?"

Mara nodded.

"The old plan ain't workin', is it."

Mara shook her head.

"Then you know what I think?" Eagan laughed. "I think
the brother's bloody jealous, is what I think. And you know
what, me sweeting? I think what we need now is to change
direction. Yessir, and yer darlin' brother's just the lad to do
it!" He tipped his head back and released another rather
inebriated laugh.

His dear sister Mara only looked confused.

Trevor escorted Alana to her bedroom with all the
warmth of a military procession. Still stifling her giggles,
she arrived at her door and dared a peek at him. If he'd
smiled then, she was sure his face would have cracked.

Opening her door, he gave her a crisp "Good night" and abruptly left her there. Suddenly at a loss, her laughter died, and she stood in the threshold for a moment, grappling with something akin to abandonment.

After Margaret helped her into her nightgown and she went to bed, Alana heard Trevor pacing on the other side of these gilt double doors. His step was distinctive, considering every third beat was the hollow thump of the cane on the floorboards. Lying in the dark staring at those doors, her thoughts again turned to lions, caged ones. She remembered the anger and raw power of the lions she had seen as a child in Mr. Barnum's American Museum. Now she could imagine them, pacing endlessly back and forth across the bars, every muscle, every ounce of energy, tightly leashed, silently rebelling at their captivity until that split second when backs were turned and escape was possible.

And vengeance was possible.

Trevor paced until the wee hours of the morning. Alana knew this because she lay in her bed the entire time wide awake. Thinking of lions.

18

"Good morning! It's a beautiful day, isn't it?" Alana put on her brightest smile and entered the breakfast room. To her delight, Mara and Eagan were already there, Eagan obviously nursing a grand hangover.

She went to her place and waved Eagan back as he gallantly tried to help her with her chair despite his aching head. She dropped her napkin in her lap and allowed the footman to give her a double helping of eggs.

Though she'd had little sleep the night before, for some reason she was feeling unusually optimistic. The fact that Eagan and Mara were both at Fenian Court didn't hurt. They would buffer her from their older brother, and she'd come to the realization late in the night that with their chaperonage she and Trevor might find a common ground, a place where they could be amicable, and continue in this marriage along more suitable and tolerable lines. The possibility of this cheered her considerably, and her anxieties of the night before seemed to have melted beneath the brilliant Newport sun.

"Trevor must be still abed," she commented casually, staring at the empty chair opposite her own. "I wonder if I should send some breakfast up to him?" As strange as it seemed, she warmed to the wifely duty of sending breakfast to her husband.

"You can't. He's gone." Mara was almost on the verge o tears.

Staring at her, Alana now saw her glum look. And wha she'd assumed was a hangover couldn't account for all o Eagan's grimness.

"Whatever do you mean, he's gone?" she asked Mara i her most unemotional tone. What a lie it was.

"He left for Boston before dawn. In his note he sai something about business," Eagan answered for Mara.

"I see." Alana looked down at her eggs and wondere when she had had the desire to touch them.

"What's wrong with him?" Mara lashed out, her blacl brows knitted together in a frown. "It's his honeymoor This is terrible. We three are here, and Trevor's gone t Boston—"

"Hush, Mara." Eagan nodded to Alana's still figure. "Sh doesn't need that now."

Alana hardly heard him. She couldn't think of anythin, but that Trevor had left her behind, and on her honey moon. The hurt she felt was so deep and all-encompassing she didn't know how to hide it, so she just sat very still an stared at her eggs.

"I'm sure he'll be back soon, Alana," said Eagan. "W don't own much in Boston. He can't be there forever."

She closed her eyes, unwilling to shed tears, unwilling t let him see the pain that had sprung up in their depths. B all rights, this shouldn't have hurt her. But it did hurt her terribly, and it only grew worse as she thought of the pos sibilities. "Does Miss Dumont frequent Boston?" she whis pered.

The pause was leaden.

"It's nothing like that, right, Eagan?" Mara asked, he girl's voice begging for reassurance.

"No, no—I'm sure it's not." He frowned and stared a Alana, her reaction obviously concerning him. "Look Alana, he's not doing what you think—" He stopped an turned to Mara. "Sweeting, leave us, will you?"

Mara gave Alana a concerned glance, then reluctantly put aside her napkin and departed.

When she was gone, Eagan took the chair next to Alana and patted her hand. "There's no reason to take this so hard. He's just taking care of a few business dealings while he's up here."

"You don't believe that any more than I do." She looked at him, pain and desperation etched on her beautiful face. "He's gone to *her*, hasn't he."

He was silent for a moment. "I don't know," he answered truthfully, his emerald eyes filling with pity.

"You know about our 'marriage,' then?"

"Yes."

She swallowed back her rising tears. "And does Trevor plan it to be always this dreadful?"

Eagan shook his head in disgust. "This is all my fault. I should never have come here, stirring things up. I thought Mara and I could help." He snorted in contempt. "I even thought to make him jealous, can you believe that?"

"No, this is all my fault," she countered numbly, grabbing at any rationalization that would keep her from the truth. "I should know better how to deal with this. I've—I've let it affect me because I"—her voice dropped to a whisper—"because I—"

She couldn't finish. But when he touched her hand, the tears began streaming down her cheeks, and her words came out in a sob. "I guess I wanted to believe those vows, Eagan. For one terrible, insane moment, I wanted to pretend they weren't lies."

He pulled her to his chest, and she cried as if her heart would break. He held her to him for a long time, and only after several minutes could she collect herself enough to pull back.

"Forgive me," she whispered, doing her best to wipe her eyes with her hands. He took his napkin and dabbed her cheeks. Tenderly he brushed away the strands of hair that had escaped her chignon. When he revealed her face, things happened very quickly. Their eyes met, and as if by instinct he bent down and kissed her softly on the lips.

It was over before she realized what he'd done, and apparently he hadn't been that aware of his actions either. But with realization dawning, his eyes opened wide, and a sheepish grin slid onto his face. "Sorry, *á mhúirnín*. It's force of habit for me to kiss a pretty girl."

She couldn't look at him. Her cheeks flamed with embarrassment.

Still searching for an explanation, he began, "But of course I'm not used to kissing my own sister-in-law."

"You needn't explain. Really." She braved a glance at him, hardly believing what he had done. He cracked that wonderful rake's smile.

"No, I owe you an explanation, Alana." He shook his head in a manner that could only be described as vaguely amused self-disgust. "My brother and I are two different species with two different outlooks on life. Trevor, you see, makes money and seeks retribution for the thousands of slights to our background. That is his purpose, his passion, his essence. I, on the other hand, am then left free to spend the money and chase the girls—both of which I'm shamefully adept at."

She didn't say a word.

"I wish I could say it'll never happen again, but—"

"When you have the right girl, Eagan, it'll never happen again."

A cynicism reminiscent of his brother touched his lips. "I'll never find the right girl, *á mhúirnín*. There's no girl out there for me. Believe me, I've tried them all."

She studied him. He was being honest with her. He was a rake, a bounder, a father's nightmare. If she were not so helplessly captivated by his brother, she could see how easy it would be to fall into this charmer's arms. Those wicked green eyes and that handsome Irish face must have conquered innumerable women. She was almost sorry she was not one of them. But that was impossible, and not because of her wedding vows or any fears of reprisal. It was impossible because even against her will, her heart and soul could lie no more. She longed for Trevor.

Stunned by this realization, she looked across the table to the master's empty place. Was she falling in love with her husband only to see him driven further and further away from her? He hadn't even lasted the honeymoon. How could she convince him to stay for the marriage, especially with Daisy Dumont waiting in the wings? The thought sent tears down her cheeks.

"No more tears." This time he handed her his napkin and let her dab at her eyes herself. Very gently he changed tack. "Come, Alana, it's such a beautiful day, let's forget about Trevor and my bad behavior. We'll fetch Mara and the crew and take the *Colleen* out into the sound. We'll have so much fun, we won't think about anything else."

She looked down at her hands clutching the tear-soaked napkin. Eagan's pleasure seeking might soothe his worries, but experience had told her it would do nothing for hers. "Would you mind very much if I declined?" she asked gently.

"Is there something else you'd like to do, then? Can I escort you into town? Take a ride in the country?"

"You know what I really want, Eagan? I want to return to New York. I don't want to stay here and wait for Trevor. Do you understand?"

He nodded. "I'll make the arrangements right away. Mara and I will go back with you. Trevor may not consider you part of the family, but we do. We'll stick by you, *á mhúirnín*, never fear."

"*A mhúirnín*—what does that mean?" Trevor had called her that before, and she'd assumed it was some kind of Irish profanity. She didn't expect Eagan's answer.

"It's a Gaelic endearment. It means, literally, 'my love.' "

She was stunned. "Is it used rather freely, then?"

"Well . . . yes. Why do you ask?"

Disappointed, she lowered her eyes, unwilling to let him

see how this depressed her. She answered glumly, "No reason. I heard the servants use it once, and I was just curious about it. Now, if you'll be so good as to excuse me, I must tell Margaret to start packing my things."

"Certainly." He stood and watched her go. But upon the last glimpse of her retreating back, hope sparked again in those vivid emerald eyes. "Liar," was all he said.

The Federal architecture of Brattle Street had not been sacrificed to cast-iron modernity as in Manhattan, but Trevor Sheridan was hardly the type to notice or care about such subtleties. He'd been in Boston four days, and every bit of business he could even think of had been performed twice. He'd read the morning ticker tape and in only a few hours he'd amassed a small fortune in Hudson stock. His warehouses in Boston were immensely profitable, his steamships fully booked. In short, there was ostensibly nothing that could account for the scowl on his face. But as his hired carriage rolled down the old cobbled lane, the scowl only grew blacker the more he sank into his thoughts.

According to direction, the carriage turned and soon halted in front of a brick colonial building. The tasteful gilt sign read: *Weymouth Jewelers*. Trevor left the carriage and entered with little fanfare.

When the mustachioed proprietor saw him, however, he abruptly left the customer he was attending and rushed to his side. "Mr. Sheridan! How good of you to visit us. Do tell me your lovely sister is in town. I've a pretty sapphire bracelet that's a perfect trinket for one so pure and young."

"Mara's not with me this time, Weymouth, but I want to bring her something. Show me the bracelet."

Weymouth unlocked the case, looking like a cat with cream on his whiskers. He placed the heavy gold-and-sapphire bracelet on a velvet pillow and presented it to the Irishman. "Five hundred dollars buys a priceless amount of good taste, don't you agree?"

Sheridan handled the expensive piece as if he were picking through bad lettuce. He tossed it back on the pillow and said, "Fine. Wrap it up."

"Most definitely, sir." Weymouth snapped his fingers, and a youth in an expensive suit immediately appeared to take it away. "Now"—the jeweler brushed his whiskers with his finger, wiping away the imaginary cream—"is there anything else I might get you, perhaps for that lovely Miss Dumont I've only had the pleasure to meet, regrettably, once?"

Sheridan looked the man in the eye. "I've married since that trip with Miss Dumont. I see you did not hear of it up here."

Weymouth skittered away from the subject of Miss Dumont like a cat running from a rabid hound. But a man well-versed in the art of the deal, his hopes still ran high. If the Irisher dropped a fortune on his mistress, what heavenly price would he pay to keep his wife adorned? "I congratulate you, sir," he announced. "Your wife is undoubtably a paragon of virtue and a great beauty. A discriminating man such as yourself could have it no other way."

Sheridan nodded, immune to the man's fawning.

Getting down to business, Weymouth wandered to another cabinet and began to unlock it. "Is Mrs. Sheridan fond of diamonds? I've got a—"

"No," Sheridan interrupted, his scowl growing darker. "Diamonds aren't for her."

"Sapphires, then? I've another bracelet, this one, of course, more elaborate. Quite appropriate for a married woman."

Sheridan shook his head and looked around. Ignoring the jewels, there was nothing in the shop but a collection of gold picture frames and several small music boxes set on a lace-covered table in the middle of the shop.

"I've just the thing, Mr. Sheridan." Weymouth rubbed his hands. "Mrs. Sheridan must have something special. There's a young jeweler in Russia—St. Petersburg, I think

—making endless amusements out of gold and diamonds and such. You must see it."

The man went to his safe and returned with what looked like an egg encrusted with lilies of the valley. But the egg was enameled gold, and the flowers were artfully cascading pearls. When he opened it, it contained a series of seven miniature icons, each a masterpiece unto itself. "I've just gotten this from Monsieur Fabergé—what do you think?"

Sheridan folded his arms across his chest as if he didn't know what to think.

"She'll be the only one to have something like it."

Sheridan snorted. "Well, I agree with you there." His scowl deepened. "None of this is right. I'll just take the bracelet for Mara and be done with it."

Weymouth snapped the egg closed and nodded, a decided slump to his shoulders. In a minute the young man appeared, the bracelet now nestled in a silver embossed box tied with a blue velvet bow. He rushed across the room, obviously not wanting to keep such an important customer waiting, and he bumped the edge of the table that displayed the music boxes. One fell, and as it lay on its side, the strains of "The Beautiful Blue Danube Waltz" began to fill the store.

"Let me see that," Sheridan commanded as the hapless young man fumbled to set it right. He promptly brought it to him, and Sheridan turned it over in his hands.

The music box was hardly worthy of the store's reputation for being costly and exclusive. It was a humble little piece painted with blue forget-me-nots and ivy. But for some reason, the notion struck Sheridan that it was what he'd been looking for. He turned to Weymouth and said, "I'll take this back to Mrs. Sheridan. That's her favorite waltz. Wrap it up."

"Of course," said Weymouth. "But you know, this piece is only twenty-five dollars. Are you sure Mrs. Sheridan wouldn't like something more . . . *substantial?*"

"If she's with me on my next trip up here, she can buy

the whole damned store if she likes. But right now, all I want is the music box."

"Of course, Mr. Sheridan." Weymouth snapped his fingers to have his man wrap the item. He wasn't about to risk future sales just to enlarge this one.

The music box wrapped, Sheridan took his two packages and told Weymouth to bill him. Weymouth bowed and held the door. Unable to help himself, he called to Sheridan, "I do hope we meet Mrs. Sheridan soon! On your next trip north, perhaps?"

Sheridan only laughed. It was the first time in days.

Truce

His greatness weighed, his will is not his own.
[For he himself is subject to his birth.]

—Shakespeare,
Hamlet, Prince of Denmark

19

It was a week from the day Trevor left for Boston before Alana saw him again. She and Mara and Eagan were in the drawing room of the Manhattan chateau having their after-dinner cordials. As was becoming the custom, Mara played the harp while Eagan sang in a clear Irish tenor. He'd tried to lift Alana's spirits with several bawdy tunes, but finally he surrendered to her melancholy and began a haunting love song. He sang it in Gaelic with such dark emotion, it brought tears to her eyes.

He finished, and even Mara seemed moved. No one spoke for several moments until Alana said, "What's that song called, Eagan? It's so beautiful. What do the words mean?"

He shrugged and flashed her his irreverent smile. "Haven't a clue. Trevor taught me that one. He knows what the words mean. He learned it from Father."

"It's 'Bríg Óg Ní Máille,' 'Bridget O'Malley,' and the words meant nothing with Eagan's poor pronunciation."

Alana took a sharp breath and jerked her head around. No one could mistake Trevor's deep resonant voice.

All eyes turned to the drawing room entrance. Trevor stood there, stick in hand, looking cool, collected, angry. His green-gold eyes surveyed the room with detachment, but when they found her, an emotion glittered like a jewel in them, with facets of resentment and desire.

Eagan was the first to speak. He shot Alana a concerned look, then said, "Brother. You've come back." He couldn't hide the sarcasm in his voice when he added, "All that pressing business taken care of, I see."

Trevor didn't answer. He glanced briefly at Mara's disapproving frown, noted Eagan's hostility, then returned his gaze to Alana.

She wanted desperately to look cold and uncaring, but she wasn't sure how she appeared when all she felt was hurt and despair.

"I take it, wife, that you were anxious to come here, but don't you think it would have been more appropriate for me, your husband, to show you our home . . . than my brother and sister?" There was no mistaking the contempt in his voice.

Alana put away her needlework and stood. With as much polite defiance as she could muster, she said, "You'll forgive me, but I found the waiting tedious."

Eagan laughed. "There you go, Trevor! What a prize of a wife Alana is. How brilliant of you to marry a woman with a mind of her own."

Trevor shot his brother a glance that should have knocked him dead. "Alana," he began, his voice low and ominous, "I want to speak to you. You can imagine my surprise when I returned to Newport and found my wife gone."

She put aside her hurt to say calmly, "No, I can't imagine. In truth, I hardly thought you'd notice at all."

His gaze slid to Mara. The tension in his body doubled. She could see he didn't want Mara to see their argument, and for once she and Trevor Sheridan had reached an agreement. Smiling at both Eagan and Mara, she decided to end their conversation. "I'm suddenly very tired. I believe I'll say good night."

"Good night," Mara replied, her eyes full of worry.

Eagan bowed, a small gleeful smile still on his lips.

Alana nodded to her husband in passing. She walked into

the foyer, and only when they were out of sight of Eagan and Mara did Trevor halt her. "Alana, I said I want to speak to you."

All the feelings she so desperately tried to hide surfaced. Still aching from his abandonment, she answered without looking at him. "Then do what any other gentleman would do, Mr. Sheridan. Leave your card with the butler. In the morning I'll consider it."

Stunned, he watched her ascend the marble staircase, a thunderous expression frozen on his face. He gasped something in Gaelic, and this time she didn't need Eagan to translate. She knew he'd just cursed.

Whittaker stood before his master's bedroom door, silver breakfast tray in hand. He knocked, remaining unruffled at the gruff "Enter" from behind those heavy doors.

Once inside, Whittaker placed the tray on the master's desk and laid out his linens. Trevor watched him from the shield-shaped shaving mirror perched atop his bureau. When Whittaker paused, Trevor put down his straight razor and wiped his face with a hot towel. "So what is it?" he asked, his tone indicating he knew it wasn't good news.

"You've two letters, sir. Shall I place them here on your desk?"

Trevor folded his arms across his bare chest and nodded. Whittaker did as he was told but did not go.

Trevor raised an eyebrow as if to say *So now what is it?*

His butler answered promptly. "She's going out today, sir. I thought you'd like to know. She's taking the carriage as we speak."

Immediately, Trevor turned to a window, unmindful of his limp. He threw open the enormous mahogany sash and two stories below, past the turrets and gargoyles of the Hunt architecture, Alana was being helped into the carriage.

"Shall I send someone *with* her, sir?"

Trevor faced him, an awe-inspiring sight. The wind from

the open window blew at his hair; his eyes snapped with anger. A battle played across his face as he considered his answer.

"Shall I?" Whittaker prompted.

"No," said Trevor, and turned back to the window. Furious, he watched the Sheridan carriage roll down Fifth Avenue. When he couldn't see it any longer, he slammed down the sash and vengefully pulled the curtains.

"Shall there be anything else, sir?"

"Wait here. I might need to send a reply."

Trevor snatched up the letters and ripped open the first.

Mr. Sheridan,
I'm taking Mara to the Academy of Music tonight to see Strauss's *Indigo and the Forty Thieves*. Needless to say, we won't be at home for dinner. I pray this won't cause inconvenience.

                                        Mrs. Sheridan

With a wry, almost nasty twist of his lips, he crumpled the paper in his hand and tossed it onto his leather-topped desk. Turning to the next letter, he only had to look at the handwriting on the envelope to know whom it was from and to guess what it was about. Without reading it, he placed it with other correspondence on his desk and turned a grim expression to Whitaker. "I've got to go to Miss Dumont's hotel. Bring another carriage around, will you?"

That implacable British facade almost faltered. A brief look of distaste passed across his features, but he quickly resumed his butler manner. "Very good, sir."

Trevor turned pensive. He rubbed his jaw, grimacing at every place he'd missed while shaving. "And send a note to Ebel's Florist. I want two dozen red roses delivered to her hotel before I leave the house."

"Right away, sir."

There was a long pause. Trevor's gaze fairly snapped with irritation. "I don't see your feet moving, Whittaker."

"No, sir."

"Why aren't they?"

"Pardon me, sir. They suddenly seem stricken, sir. I remember this happened once before. I am sorry."

"This happened the time I told you to send a note to Tammany Hall, and as I recall, Tweed never did get my message."

"And there went the Irish vote."

Trevor gave Whittaker a jaundiced glance. "We're not discussing my politics."

"No, sir. Of course not. The Sheridan name's been kept from Thomas Nast and the *New York Times*."

Trevor choked. "Are you blackmailing me, Whittaker?"

"Of course not, sir. I knew your father. And a good man he was. We spent many a fine night in our cups back at the old pub in Connacht."

"That's right," Trevor answered ominously.

"And of course, sir, your politics are your business."

"What do you want, Whittaker? Name your price, if that's what you're getting at."

"Oh no, sir. I don't know what you're talking about."

"Then deliver this note. Now."

"I'll do my best, sir. However, this affliction seems worse than the last one."

Trevor towered over the small elderly man and said loudly enough for a deaf man to hear, "You meddlin', connivin' old Brit, get your feet to workin', or more's the pity you were me father's friend."

"Yes, sir."

Trevor stared him down, but to no avail. Whittaker remained implacable, immovable. Finally, with anger tautening his cheeks, he warned in his full brogue, "Ye get involved in affairs o' mine, I'll have you to know I've brought a bigger man than you down."

"You're entirely correct, sir." Whittaker didn't move an inch.

Trevor raked his hand through his hair and heaved a

great sigh. He glanced at the butler one more time before conceding a tie. "You want an explanation? Is that it?"

"Of course not, sir. That is not my place."

Trevor snorted with contempt. "Well, this explanation should work miracles on that health of yours. If you must know, I've decided to allow Miss Dumont to pursue her dreams of the theater. After giving this some thought, I think it best for everyone that I send Daisy to Paris and find her a handsome, virile tutor to keep her occupied. Though I expect her vanity will soar at my artful compliments and brave show of self-deprivation in order that she may achieve greatness on the stage, I assume she'll also pout. Hence, the roses. Now have you recovered?"

Whittaker gave him an imperious glance. "Quite, sir."

With that, Trevor became so angry he forgot himself and let his Irish show. "Ye're a bloody old woman, ye are. If ye *hadn't* been a friend to me father's, I'd have left ye workin' for the Ascendency—'til ye'd met yer maker."

"Very good, sir." Whittaker bowed. When he left, it wasn't quite clear, but there was something like a smile on his lined face.

Alone, Trevor shoved his arms into a freshly starched shirt and fastened the stiff collar. From the corner of his eye a silver flash caught his attention, and he stared at the mantel where two silver boxes wrapped in blue velvet ribbon rested. A thought occurred to him, and he picked up the larger one and headed to the adjoining suite. He threw open the double doors, and the expression froze on his face when he saw that the room had not been occupied.

There were no perfumes on the dressing table, no cashmere throws on the chaise longue, no slippers by the bed. Astonished, he limped farther into the room, looking like a man duped. A noise in the hallway turned his head, and through an opened door he watched his wife's personal maid pass by. He pointed and said, "You!"

Margaret stopped, the booming voice freezing her in her tracks. She peered through the opened door, not bothering to hide the shock on her face when she saw the master of the house pointing directly at her.

"Me, sar?" she whispered faintly.

"You. Where is your mistress?"

"Miss Alana? She's gone out. I don't know where."

"Wrong, on both accounts. She's *Mrs. Sheridan* now, and I'm not inquiring where she is at this moment. I want to know why she's not staying in this room."

Margaret peered into the lush gold-and-ivory room and shrugged. "When we came down from Newport, the butler showed her this room, but she preferred another."

"Well, she has no choice in the matter. This is where the mistress of this house sleeps."

He walked up to her, not bothering to hide his limp. Margaret's eyes nearly popped from her head. If she had been frightened by the master before, now she was utterly terrified. Even the way he walked exuded violence. "You're to remove her things to this room this instant, do you understand me?" He loomed above her.

"Yes, sar! Right away, Mr. Sheridan!"

"*Deifir!* Fly!"

"Yes, yes!" She curtsied and nearly dove headlong to the carpet. Recovering herself, she straightened, took one look at his face, and within the blink of an eye she was gone.

Heaving a great sigh, he wandered back to his room and shoved the silver box back on the mantel. Disgust crossed his features, a healthy dose of frustration in his eyes.

He finished dressing, but before he left, he glanced into his wife's room. Already an army of maids were busy carrying in her clothes and toiletries. Determination hardened his face. He stood in the doorway, arms crossed over his massive chest, viewing the scene like a predator. Trevor Sheridan was a creature who survived on instinct. Now instinct demanded that inch by inch, he reclaim his territory.

As was often the case, Alana returned from her visit to Christal tired, drained, and depressed. But this time her visit had had a new edge of fear whenever she wondered if Trevor had followed her.

Christal had been in an especially bright mood, but Alana could tell it was mostly for her benefit. There were circles around her sister's eyes, and she complained vaguely of bad dreams. Nurse Steine had been even more urgent about not prompting Christal's memory for the trauma it might cause. At the rate her sister was declining Alana didn't know how long Christal would last before she indeed descended into madness. And always Alana confronted the fact that there seemed no way to free her. Her options had long ago been played out, and now she was left with an empty hand.

With despair clinging to her like cobwebs, she allowed Whittaker to take her cloak, longing for the privacy of her bedroom.

But the butler stopped her. "Mr. Sheridan's gone out, madam, to take care of unfinished business. May I get you some tea?"

She threw him a preoccupied smile and wished she could summon the strength to be more gracious. She'd liked the dignified elderly man from the moment she arrived from Newport. "I'm sorry. No refreshments for me, Whittaker. I'd just like to rest a bit before I go out this evening."

"Very good, madam. Mr. Sheridan has seen to it that your new room is prepared. May I show you to it now?"

Shocked out of her melancholy, she whipped around and pinned him with that leaf-green stare. "What do you mean, Mr. Sheridan's prepared me a new room?"

"I, of course, told him your preference for the room you were in, but he seemed to think his wife's place was beside his own. I thought to point out the flaws in his logic. . . . However, as you can see, I could find none. A wife's place is indeed beside her husband."

She seethed, unable to believe Trevor's gall. When she'd arrived at the chateau alone, she'd found justice in the fact that she'd been able to choose her own bedroom, one far from his. Now all of that had been undone with one arrogant order.

"Please summon Margaret and have her move my things back into my old room."

"Very good, madam." Whittaker bowed.

Alana nodded and waited for him to depart. He didn't move.

"Are you all right, Whittaker?"

"Yes, madam. It's just an affliction of mine. It strikes at peculiar times."

She frowned, suddenly concerned. Whittaker wasn't a young man, after all. "Shall you sit down, then? Here, let me help you to a seat."

"Oh no, madam, *you* must not help *me*. I couldn't bear the shame." Whittaker put his hand up to stop her.

"Shall I fetch someone, then?" Her gaze searched every empty corner and nook of the large marble foyer, hoping to spy a footman or maid.

"Please, madam, go about your business. If you must have your things removed from the master's suite, it is imperative you do it promptly."

"Bother that. It's you who must be attended to."

"What did you say, madam?"

"I said bother moving my things. I'm concerned about you."

Whittaker bowed. "In that case, madam, I'm quite recovered. I couldn't have it upon my head that the lady of the household worried about me." He bowed again. "Now if you'll excuse me, I must hang up your cloak and see to it that the master is ready to escort you tonight."

Her jaw dropped, and he walked away, as spry as an old fox. It took a moment for her to realize what had just happened, but when she did, she could better understand Irish animosity to the English.

That little old butler was infuriating.

20

That night the old Academy of Music was crowded with the Four Hundred, and to their barely repressed delight, the real entertainment was more gazing at the Van Alen box than Strauss's operetta.

During the first half Alana sat stiffly next to her husband, displaying a forced interest in the stage until her arm ached from holding up her opera glasses. Trevor had invited himself along, to the delight of his sister and the astonishment of his wife. Mara was to the right, her eyes wide with awe as she gazed around the exalted yet shabby gilt-and-red velvet interior.

There were only eighteen boxes at the Academy; it was cramped and inconvenient, therefore brilliantly constructed to keep out those 'new' New Yorkers the Academy shunned. Commodore Vanderbilt, considered the patriarch of the nouveaux riches, had once offered almost forty thousand dollars for one of those illustrious boxes, and when refused he'd threatened to build his own metropolitan opera house just to spite them.

The Van Alen box was at one end of the stage. The Silent Power, Mrs. Astor, sat at the other end. The matron, as usual, appeared at nine o'clock, bewigged in black and dripping in diamonds. She raised her opera glasses to take a head count and nearly dropped them when she realized the Van Alen box was occupied. Alana didn't need to see her to

know the matron's eyes must be bulging when Caroline
Astor got an eyeful of who was in the box opposite hers.

The walls of Jericho had tumbled, the final bastion of
society penetrated, the last safe harbor washed away.
Irishers, some not away from their country long enough
even to know English as their first language, were now sitting in the box opposite the Astor's as bold as brass, as if
they'd always been allowed there. Alana didn't miss the agi-
tated sawing of the matron's fan. Neither did the other
illustrious eyes.

"They're watching us, aren't they, *á mhúirnín*?"

"Yes," she whispered to Trevor, unnerved that he'd used
that endearment.

"Good."

She stared up at him in the darkness, his handsome profile taut with defiance. She was angry he'd moved her bedroom and irritated he'd invited himself along. There was
nothing to do about it now, but Alana knew that before the
night was out, she and this man she had married were going
to clash.

Eagan, who was originally to have escorted them, now
sat behind them with a companion, an actress improbably
named Miss Evangeline de la Plume. Alana had been
shocked by the woman's dress, a vulgar shiny-pink gown
with the most revealing décolletage she'd ever seen. The
woman was certainly pretty, in an overt, rather worn-out
and overdone manner, but if she had any failings, Eagan
couldn't see them for the woman's barely reined-in, all-
too-voluptuous curves.

Alana had been taught never to stare, but once or twice
during the carriage ride and their wait in the box, she'd
caught herself doing so. To make matters worse, whenever
the dazzling Miss de la Plume found Alana looking at her,
she'd wiggle her fingers in a coy wave, then giggle obnox-
iously into her purple ostrich-feather fan.

The intermission arrived, and Alana had no desire to
mingle in the lobby. Mara went with Eagan, Miss de la

Plume clinging happily to his arm. When the woman left, Alana discreetly watched her saunter away and wondered when that amazing dress would slip and the woman shame herself. She turned back to Trevor and found him staring. The gaslights were turned up, and she could see his cynical smile.

"Are you enjoying the operetta?" he asked.

She stared down into the theater, watching the milling crowd below them. "It's quite lovely," she answered perfunctorily.

"And how do you like Eagan's latest vision of lust?"

Alana glanced at him twice, then bit back an unwilling smile. "Miss de la Plume, you mean?"

"Yes."

She groped for the right answer. "Her taste in clothing is certainly . . . remarkable."

"Yes, it is." Trevor leaned back in his seat and perused her. "There are two things you should know about my brother, Alana. He likes to drink to excess. And he has abominable taste in women."

"I wouldn't call Miss de la Plume abominable."

"No?"

"No, she's just . . . just . . ."

"Just what?"

"Well . . ."

He leaned farther back in his chair. "In Connacht we've an expression for a girl like that. Perhaps that's what you're looking for."

"What is it?" she inquired politely, thinking it would be some long, drawn-out Gaelic term.

"*Whore.*"

She hadn't meant to laugh, but she hadn't expected his answer. Overcome, she put her hand over her mouth and tried to hide her smile, but her shaking shoulders gave her away.

"Ah, I see the expression translates despite our cultural barriers."

She looked up at him, her eyes tearing with laughter. His hazel ones glittered with amusement. Never had she guessed he had such a wicked sense of humor. "You are not a gentleman, Mr. Sheridan, to say such things about a lady," she admonished, still unable to wipe the smile from her lips.

"But then, I've never claimed to be a gentleman, have I?" The mirth in his eyes died. The question suddenly turned deadly serious.

Her laughter died also. "No, you haven't," she whispered, her gaze riveted to his.

"Do you want me to be a gentleman?"

His words hung over them like a cat ready to pounce. The immediate response on her lips was yes, but she never spoke it, perhaps because the answer in her heart was something different and perhaps because for the first time, the longing to become Trevor Sheridan's wife in body, mind, and soul, blossomed within her until it became almost painful to conceal.

"Why do you look away from me?" he asked softly.

She couldn't answer. The desire to cast aside the charade of her marriage was overpowering. With a need that bordered on desperation, she suddenly wanted to see passion in his eyes, wanted him to hold her, kiss her, and tell her he loved her. She wanted to destroy this wall of ice that kept them formal and distant, and even if it had to be done in his bed, she would gladly do it for just one moment of intimacy and warmth.

"My God, sometimes you're a cold woman."

The harsh words scarred her fragile heart. She wanted to prove to him that they were untrue, but she couldn't bring herself to look at him because if she did, she knew she would lose whatever control she possessed and run crying from the box.

The houselights flickered, signaling that the second act was about to begin. Behind her she heard Eagan and his companion take their seats. Mara resumed hers and began talking rapidly to Trevor, creating a nonsensical background of chatter to silence Alana's grieving heart. She didn't look at him for the rest of the evening, and when they left the Academy, he had also ceased to look at her.

They returned to the mansion after dropping Eagan and Miss de la Plume at the Hoffman House, a most appropriate place considering Bouguereau's wicked painting, *Nymphs and Satyrs*, hung in the bar. Once home, Trevor tersely bid her good night in the foyer and ascended the grand marble staircase alone. Mara and Alana shared tea in the drawing room until Mara too bid her good night.

Not ready to retire, Alana sat in the vast drawing room staring into the flames in the fireplace. Her face was an emotionless mask, her eyes the only window to her deep melancholy. She didn't know how long she had been there when she heard the loud arrival in the foyer. She looked up just as Eagan wandered drunkenly into the drawing room.

"Alana, me darlin', what are ye doin' up?" he asked, grinning like a fool.

"I couldn't sleep." She smiled in spite of herself. Eagan disarmed her as no one else could. "You're home early. Was Miss de la Plume not as hospitable as I thought?"

"She done cracked me across the cheek." He grinned and showed her his reddened cheek. "Temperamental little twa—" He bit back this last word, giving her a sheepish glance.

She shook her head, in despair of his character. The more rakish he was feeling, the more he laid on that Irish accent. It was so thick now, she could hardly understand him. "She did more than slap you, judging by that lip rouge on your collar."

"She'll come around. They always do."

"That's your problem, Eagan."

"I know it. I'm never told no . . . and I always say yes." He chuckled, poured himself a drink from some decanters on a Louis XVI table, and sat opposite her. "So Trevor's ignoring you again. He needs a good knock upside the head if you ask me."

She smiled sadly, unable to comment for the lump in her throat.

He noted her reaction and gave her a wry, lopsided grin. "Perhaps he's just having a bad night. He gets sore, you know—the leg and all."

"Tell me what happened to him. He's never told me. Was he wounded in the war?"

Eagan took a long sip of his drink. "He didn't fight in the war. Yes, he was of age, but by then he had the three hundred dollars to avoid the draft, and they wouldn't have taken him anyway. He was crippled when he was fourteen."

"Tell me," she implored. "I know so little about him."

"It's not a noble story."

"Tell me," she repeated.

He seemed reluctant. "Trevor roved with a gang of boys on the East Side. One night they broke into a jeweler's. The police discovered them. Trevor ran away. He was shot. In the back."

A heavy silence descended upon them. "He was fourteen?" she asked, her voice solemn and low.

"You have to understand how poor we were. How desperate things were. I was too young to remember much"—Eagan's mouth turned into a grim line—"but I remember the tenement room we lived in. It was one room, Alana, and we shared it with another family. Trevor, being the man he is, left at an early age to be on his own and give us more room. He took up with the 'Captain'—Isaiah Rynders—and his gang of Dead Rabbits. It's really a very common story. He wanted to help us. He thought he *was* going to help us."

She felt like crying. Her heart went out to the boy who had gone so wrong. "So he was put in jail?"

He shook his head. "No. He somehow managed to escape the police. He lay in an alley of Bandit's Roost for over a day, bleeding until someone found him. They carried him back to my mother, and she cared for him. If we could have afforded a doctor, Trevor might not be limping today. It's the shot, you know. It's still in him, lodged in his hip. It's too late to remove it now. That's why he gets sore."

Alana closed her eyes, remembering that night in Delmonico's when Trevor had fallen. It must have been painful, yet he'd borne it so well, she almost thought she'd imagined the whole thing.

"So how did he get all this?" She waved her hand at the gilded drawing room.

"It took him a year to recover. And God, what a year it was." As if to wipe away the memory, Eagan threw back half his drink. "Everything went wrong from then on. Trevor couldn't find work with his limp. He couldn't go back to stealing, for how can you do that if you can't run away? He found a job as a newsboy for the *Chronicle*. The wages were a pittance, but he worked himself almost to death trying to give us pennies." He turned even more grim and stared into the fire. "Then Mara was born."

"Your mother died in childbirth?"

"Yes. I can still remember Trevor holding Mara. She was so tiny. Do you know what her name means?"

She shook her head.

"It means 'bitter.' "

He didn't continue, and Alana respected his pause. The moment was leaden until finally he confessed, "Trevor, of course, blames himself for Mara's illegitimacy. What he'd been bringing in wasn't enough. He blames himself for what Mother had to do."

"Oh no, he mustn't," she gasped, her voice trembling with unshed tears.

"He blames everything on himself. And from the day our mother died in that tenement, his anger has been an awesome thing."

"How did he make all his money?"

"He'd read in the *Chronicle* about the huge profits in Manhattan land. He persuaded a gentleman who bought the paper from him every day to buy a tract of land—they would split the profits when they sold it. It brought a handsome sum, enough that he could buy his own land. He did his again and again until he had enough to tackle Wall Street."

"But you have to be invited into the exchange. I've never understood how they let him in."

"He sold stock in front of the exchange at one penny less than they were selling it in the exchange. When they found out about that, they were only too glad to admit him." He smiled at her. "And the rest, as they say, is history."

Alana took a deep breath, unable to get her mind off the man upstairs in his bedroom. Perhaps Trevor was in pain tonight. Perhaps his foul mood was due to his wound bothering him. The thought tugged at her heart. She felt as if she understood him better now. And suddenly she wanted very much to see him. "Is there anything that can help him when he gets sore?" she asked.

"He's never told me about it if there is."

"I had a grandfather with gout. He swore by horse liniment. Has Trevor ever tried that?"

Eagan laughed. "I'd love to see the woman who could put horse liniment on my brother."

Challenged, she smiled and tugged on the bell pull. When Whittaker arrived, she said, "Whittaker, tell the boys in the stable to bring in a bottle of horse liniment. And see that it's sent directly to my room."

"Yes, madam." Whittaker bowed, rolling his eyes only after he'd turned to go.

She faced Eagan and took his hands in hers. "I've wanted to say this for a few days now. Thank you for being on my side. I want you to know that I'll always consider you a friend, even if you aren't always my brother-in-law."

Eagan stared at her and said wickedly, "Perhaps you should have been my wife, Alana. I really think I'd mend my ways for a woman like you."

"There's a magnificent girl for you. Just you wait and see."

He nodded, staring into his empty glass. In a falsely light tone he murmured, "Well, until then I guess it's back to the Hoffman House for me."

For such a hell-raiser, he suddenly looked so unhappy Alana couldn't help herself. She kissed him full on the lip and left the room, shocking him absolutely sober.

Once upstairs, Alana was relieved to find the lights still turned up in Trevor's room. She paused in front of his doors holding the black-glass bottle of liniment and gathered her courage. This was definitely confronting the lion in his den. But what was becoming more and more clear to her was that she wanted this marriage. She had spoken the vows, and she had begun to understand the man, and both compelled her to go forward. The circumstances between her and Trevor were difficult, but could they not change? Of course they could, if one of them chose to change them. With that thought driving her, she lifted her hand and knocked.

"What is it?" came the severe response.

She nearly jumped. She'd forgotten how ominous his voice could be. "It's Alana. I—" she took a sustaining breath, "I saw the lights on and thought you might be . . . uncomfortable. My grandfather used to say horse liniment helped his joints. I . . . I brought you some."

"I'm not your grandfather," he answered in a terse tone.

His words stung. She knew he was in a foul temper, but somehow she expected something different.

Crushed, she answered huskily, "No, you're my husband."

The only thing left to do was leave, but for some reason she stayed, if only to listen to the brooding silence that emanated from beyond those mahogany doors.

There was a long pause. It didn't seem possible that he could have heard her reply, but out of the blue the commandment came down. "You may come in."

Her hand shook as she twisted the doorknob. Still in her

evening gown, she had to pull away her lavender train before she could shut the door behind her. As expected, he was lying in his bed. What was not expected was the rush of warmth in her belly when she saw that he lay there nude except for the sheet low on his hips.

"Here it is," she announced in a trembling voice, and held the black bottle up to him. She had to bring it to him, but she wondered if she could manage that when her feet suddenly felt like lead.

"What makes you think *that* will help?" he demanded, giving her a wary look that spoke plainly his distrust of the liniment, but mostly his distrust of her.

"Eagan told me about your—" She had wanted to say *accident*, but that wasn't the right word.

Before she found one, he said sarcastically, "You mean my 'wound'?"

"Yes."

"And did he tell you precisely how I got this wound?"

"Yes."

"And it doesn't repulse you? You, with your fine manners and delicate sensibilities?"

"Even I've had ugliness in my life." Her voice lowered, "Even I've had to do desperate things."

He was silent for a moment. His eyes flickered to the bottle in her hand, then slowly up her bodice to her face. Cautiously, painfully, he leaned back. "Bring me that thing."

Like an obedient child, she stepped to the bed. It wasn't a warm night, but she was suddenly hot. Her light taffeta gown clung to her like a blanket, and every step toward him seemed difficult and slow. The sight of him lying supine on the bed, his well-muscled, black-haired chest rising and falling with the pagan beat of his breath, made her almost light-headed. His skin was erotically golden, bathed in the glow of the gasolier. And then there were his eyes, eyes that glittered with promise and damnation. They turned her fear into a strange thrill. Prudently, she put the liniment on his night table and retreated.

He rolled over on his side, away from her. Without another glance, he said, "You'll have to rub it in. I can't reach behind me."

She was glad he had turned away so that he couldn't see the blood draining from her face. A wild urge to flee shot through her veins. But a stronger urge to stay made her pick up the black bottle. "Where . . . ?" Her mouth was so dry, she couldn't form the rest of her question.

"Here." He pulled down the sheet, leaving it to barely cover his left buttock.

In the ever-changing light of the flickering gasolier, she saw the scar. It was pink, the size of a New York copper penny and just to the right of his hip. It wasn't gruesome at all. In fact, if she hadn't known to look for it, she might not have seen it. Suddenly feeling more brave, she uncorked the bottle and placed a small amount in her hand.

"Christ, that smells," he growled.

She looked in the mirror over his bureau and saw his reflection. A grimace covered his face, and she suddenly knew how much it took for him to endure her helping him. He begrudgingly welcomed relief for his physical aches, but when he met her eyes in the looking glass, she wondered if he, like her, had other aches that needed soothing.

"Do it."

She nodded, glancing away, embarrassed.

Gathering her courage, she stepped closer to him and placed her hands on his hip. He was warm, like the first step into a bath, and hard, so hard she couldn't believe he was made of the same flesh she was. Her thumb rubbed over the scar. She thought she might feel the bullet beneath his skin, but she caressed nothing but bone and tight-woven muscle.

Feeling braver, she began to rub with more force. She looked in the mirror and saw he'd closed his eyes. The lines on his cheeks deepened as if he were feeling great pleasure.

Wanting to increase it, she sat on the edge of the mattress to attain a better angle. The liniment burned like turpentine in her nostrils, but she ignored it and kept rubbing. Her hands appeared small against him. His frame took the entire length of the bed; his shoulders, even as he lay on his side, were massive. She kept rubbing.

Her eyes wandered up and down his body, unused to being so close to a naked man. The sight of him sent a tingle down her spine. Touching him was like caressing a lion. She was frightened, but the delight at being allowed such intimacy with such an awe-inspiring creature was beyond anything she'd felt before. As her palms kneaded his hard body, she had to fight the urge to let them wander. She wanted to pinch the skin of his belly and see if that grid of muscle was as taut as it looked. She wanted to discover how that dark hair sprinkled across his chest felt in her fingers. And she wanted to let her thumb move down his chest before that enticing black hair disappeared in the sheet at his hips.

Still she rubbed, her mind on every inch of him, her hands on only his hip. She kneaded back and forth with all the strength she could muster until her arms grew weary and a fine perspiration glistened on her brow. She longed to change position, but to do that would require forging new territory on his body, and she instinctively knew that to be dangerous. So it was her thoughts that danced upon his back rippling with smooth skin and knotted muscle, and stroked down his legs, which she knew from the transparency of the thin sheet were hairy, long, and substantial. But her hands stayed where they were until she chanced another look into that mirror.

He stared at her like predator at prey. With hard, desirous, unflinching eyes, his gaze stopped her breath. She still wore her evening gown, and while she had thought the décolletage appropriate for the theater, it was not for this kind of activity. Whenever she moved her hands, the shadow of cleavage, modest in one position, became a deep, alluring valley in another. His eyes were riveted to that valley made even more seductive by its ever-changing geography, until they rose slowly to her face.

The shock of his stare made her hands go limp. One came to rest on his hip, and the other fell forward on his belly. His gaze captured hers, suspending time and blocking her senses to anything that wasn't him. His earthy smell mingled with the liniment, his hard male body became even harder with every second she looked at him.

If he had never moved, she might not have become conscious of what was happening, but he pinned her hand against his stomach, and that jolted her into reality. She suddenly felt what had not been there before. Though not well acquainted with the mechanics of a man's body, she still knew exactly what that hardness that was now against the side of her palm meant, and she was horrified.

But he didn't give her another moment to think. She turned shocked eyes upon him just as he put his other hand around the back of her neck. He pulled her down to him, kissing her parted lips with an ease she never expected from this distant man. His response was hot, urgent, ready, and briefly the thought flitted through her mind—*He's practiced with Daisy*—but the words were banished the second his tongue licked like a flame into her mouth.

A fire rose in her loins with his every thrust. Reason told her to pull away, to slow things down, but unable to help herself, she allowed his hand to slide down her bodice and pull away the mist of lavender netting at her neckline. The tiny mother-of-pearl buttons that streamed down the front of her bodice were next, and he broke away from her mouth to concentrate on releasing them. Panting, she looked down and saw the tangled sheet that had once covered him lying in a heap on the floor. He was naked below her, and though her knee rode between his thighs, hiding his maleness, his hand still pressed her own against it in a manacled embrace.

She pulled away, beginning to panic, but he wouldn't let

her. He again forced her mouth to his, tightening the grip on her hand until she couldn't bear it. "Please," she whispered, ripping her lips away. His male flesh burned against her until she felt she was being branded. She couldn't look at him.

"If not for this, why did you come here?" he rasped, obviously angered that she wouldn't meet his gaze, his breath coming hard and fast.

"I—I don't know," she nearly sobbed, the truth of her words overwhelming her.

"I'm not made of stone." He jerked her hand against his shaft, then repeated his words very carefully, ominously. "I am *not* made of stone."

"I know," she cried, confusion, shame, and longing warring within her.

He stared at her, and something, perhaps the worry in her ice-green eyes, moved him. Abruptly he let go of her hand, and she scrambled back, almost falling. She turned to the door, her hand holding her sobs at bay, desperate to look back at him, but she knew he lay naked behind her. And she knew he watched her, betrayal and frustration etched on those fine Irish features.

21

Alana didn't close her eyes that night. She kept picturing herself as she left Trevor's room—shocked, crying, involved. She thought she'd gone there only to help him. But when he'd asked her why she had come, she hadn't known the answer. It took all night for her to know why.

In her deepest heart, she had wanted to succumb to him. She had wanted to make theirs a complete marriage, not just a play between two people trapped by a piece of paper. There was no hiding from it any longer. She had gone to his room with the unconscious desire to consummate their relationship. Before, it had seemed wrong to make lies out of her vows, but now, when her mind and heart and soul seemed obsessed with that dark, brooding Irishman, it was a crime worthy of a grand punishment.

Lying in the dark, staring at the dim gilded ceiling, Alana forced herself to accept the truth. She desired to make their marriage whole. Even though Trevor Sheridan was not the man she believed she wanted, though his riches sometimes repulsed her, though everything about him did not seem to fit her, there was no denying it. She wanted to be his wife in every sense of the word.

The consequences of her thoughts oppressed her, the possibilities heavy and grim. If she and Trevor were to consummate their marriage, an annulment was out of the question. A divorce would be their only option if Trevor should still desire to abide by their agreement and end the marriage. But even the social stigma of divorce would be far less painful than a rejection after she'd given him everything a wife could.

No, if she dared lie with him, she could do it only with the hope that it would bind them together as man and wife and make their marriage a lasting one.

But would he think as she did? Could she seduce him into believing in this marriage? She sighed and clutched her satin pillow, thinking of white clapboard houses and children's laughter. None of those things might be hers with Trevor. They would never live a simple life unencumbered by possessions. And children—perhaps he didn't want any. She thought back to his comment at Fenian Court when Mara had mentioned the possibility of a niece or nephew. He'd told her she could have a child whenever she desired, but he'd said that only for Mara's sake. He hadn't meant it. His attention was focused on the exchange and his holdings. He wouldn't want to be bothered with the inconvenience of a family.

That last thought especially depressed her, but if she had to surrender a dream to get what she truly wanted, she would do it and never look back. For what she wanted more than anything was a husband, in every sense of the word.

Dawn broke just as she found sleep. It was late when Margaret finally woke her, bustling in with her breakfast. Alana rose and quickly dressed. She didn't bother with her coffee because she wanted to speak to Trevor, somehow to make amends for her strange behavior the night before. She wanted to apologize and perhaps show him that while she'd been confused and reluctant, she was now neither.

Tying a purple velvet bow to the back of her chignon, she looked in the mirror and was pleased with her attire. She wore a demure gown of leaf-colored silk that turned her eyes a rich grass green. She pinched her cheeks, giving them a rosy glow, and suddenly the ice princess was gone.

Before her was a girlish lady anxious to speak to her husband.

She excused Margaret and turned to stare at the doors
that separated her chamber from Trevor's. Unlike those in
Newport, these doors weren't gilded but carved with medi-
eval motifs such as Byzantine capitals, trefoils, and shields.
These doors could have been the entrance to a dark, forbidding castle.

Ignoring the tingle that ran down her spine, she knocked
and waited for Trevor's gruff voice. None came. She
knocked again and then again, but still he didn't answer.
She was about to turn away when it occurred to her that he
might be in his dressing room, unable to hear her. Slowly
she turned the heavy knob and peeked inside. His chamber
maid had yet to make his bed. It was probable he was still
dressing. She stepped into the room, unable to quash the
surge of apprehension and exhilaration that shot through
her veins. She was being very bold, but she wanted to speak
with him in private, not in the public domain of the morning room. And she didn't want to send a note. She'd been
doing that a lot lately, to cover her wounded feelings. But
now was the time for words.

"Trevor!" she called in the direction of his dressing
room, her voice suddenly turning shy. When she heard no
answer, she repeated herself, this time more loudly. The
chamber fairly echoed with the hollowness of his name
unanswered. She paused by the desk, not brave enough to
peek into his dressing room. He was clearly up and gone.
Now she'd have to find him in this maze of a house and
hope that she could persuade him to speak with her alone.

Frustrated, she turned to go, but a letter on his desk
caught her eye. It wasn't really the letter, actually, that got
her attention, but the signature, written in scrolled blue ink
that flowed across the bottom of the note. The name was
Daisy.

All her schooling, her morals, and her self-preservation
screamed at her not to read this note tossed so casually on

his desk. Her logic told her to back away, retreat to her
bedroom, hide her head in the sand. But her heart, desperate to know if there was hope for her newfound emotions,
reached for it.

My Darling Trevor,
You lied! What a vile inconvenience your marriage is
already proving to be and how put-upon I am having to
tolerate it. If you care for me at all, you'll come by today.
I am lonely, *mon cher*.

> Your angel,
> Daisy

Postscript—I know your honeymoon is over. The papers
said so.

Alana straightened, her face pale, her heart heavy. If she
hadn't been so utterly shattered, she might have laughed at
the woman's flamboyance. She could almost picture the actress—her hand swept over her brow, her figure draped
over a couch, penning this note to her paramour. But this
woman's paramour was her husband, and suddenly nothing
seemed remotely amusing about Daisy Dumont.

Alana jumped when she heard approaching footsteps.
She disappeared into her room just as the chambermaids
came to straighten the master's suite. Alone in her room,
she was desperate to talk to someone, anyone who wasn't
related to Trevor Sheridan. As she had so many times in the
past three years, she surrendered to her instinctive need to
be with her sister. Without another wasted moment, she
summoned a carriage to take her to Brooklyn.

"She's taking the carriage, sir. Shall I have someone look
after her?" Whittaker stood like a statue at Trevor's side
while the master glanced at the morning *Chronicle* at his
desk in the library.

Trevor looked up, a frustrated glint in his eye. He appeared as if he wanted to stop her himself, but thinking of past promises, he glared down at his newspaper and bit out "No."

Whittaker bowed, obviously not understanding his master's restraint but accepting it. He held out a silver salver that overflowed with calling cards. "These were left this morning. Shall you look at them, sir, or shall I give them to the mistress?"

Trevor appeared as if he were about to dismiss them but then thought better of it. He waved them over and didn't even have to shuffle through them. The card was right on top, the name Mr. Anson Vanbrugh-Stevens handsomely engraved across it, its top right-hand corner turned down, conveying a silent message that everyone knew: *I must speak with you.*

"You may go." Trevor picked up the card and crushed it vengefully in his hand.

Whittaker hastily departed. Alone, Trevor stood and went to the window. Below, Alana was just starting out in the carriage and Trevor again watched his wife depart for places unknown. When she was gone, he turned and looked at the crushed calling card in his fist, his expression rockhard.

If Wall Streeters were betting he wouldn't tolerate another trip to Brooklyn for his wife, it'd be a very bull market.

Seige

A Mhúirnín dílis geal mo chroí.

For, still imagination warm,
Presents thee at the moontide beam,
And sleep gives back thy angel form,
To clasp thee in the midnight dream.

                                    —Old Irish Verse

22

Alana arrived back from Brooklyn with barely enough time to change for Delmonico's. Mrs. Astor had made the request that she attend because the Duke of Granville had finally arrived in New York and was to make his first appearance that night. Alana was less than enthusiastic. She would have preferred to have tea and toast in her room and go to bed early, but that was out of the question. Everyone would be there at Delmonico's tonight. This was too grand an opportunity for Mara to miss.

Strengthened by her visit with Christabel, Alana dressed quickly and waited in the drawing room for the others. She steeled herself for her first meeting with Trevor, but she didn't expect the painful tug of longing in her heart when he entered the room. Cautiously they nodded to each other, and if Alana hadn't had a clear head, she might have blushed, remembering what had happened the last time they were together. But she didn't blush. The ice princess was back, frost covering her vulnerable, terrified heart.

"Mara will be right down." He stepped toward the fire, the flames glinting off his gold-headed cane. Without changing his tone, he said, "Enjoy your trip?"

Unsettled by his question and his insidious knowledge of her comings and goings, she tore her gaze away and stared at the fire. "Yes" was all she offered.

"When are you going again?"

Her eyes snapped with annoyance. "You know my whereabouts better than I. Why don't you tell me?"

The only answer was ominous smoldering silence.

Taking a breath, she said, "Are the servants spying for you? Is that how you know I went today? Is it Whittaker?"

"It's my business to know what goes on in me—" he calmed himself, "in *my* own house."

"Yes, of course. All right, you know it. I went to Brooklyn today." She turned and faced him, that note from Daisy Dumont bitter on her mind. "But I couldn't have been the only one out on the town, now could I? You were up early this morning, I see."

"How did you know that?" His gaze locked with hers.

A lump came to her throat when she thought of the hope she had had that morning and how cruelly it was crushed by that letter. "Perhaps I have my spies in this household too."

He paused, obviously not trusting her. "You missed me at breakfast. Is that what this is about? Well, I had some business to take care of. I didn't have time for breakfast."

At least not here, she thought.

"Did you come looking for me this morning?" His voice was softer than she'd ever heard it. But even its coaxing quality couldn't take away her shame. Of all the humiliations she could imagine, the worst was having to share her husband with another woman.

"I've learned never to go looking for you again." Coldly, she looked away.

"Indeed" was his frigid comment. There was nothing more between them until they left in the carriage.

Mara, as usual, was brimming with excitement over the evening's activities. She was so wound-up that both Alana and Trevor allowed her to chat away, letting her prattle falsely alleviate the oppressive atmosphere between them. But Mara finally seemed to notice their animosity and without warning quieted.

This made Alana nervous, so she began to talk. "You

look very nice tonight, Mara. Are you anxious to meet the duke?"

"I've never met a duke before. Will he be frightening?" Mara looked at her brother's scowling silhouette, then shot Alana a worried glance.

Alana tried to laugh. She wanted to say *Not as much as your brother* but answered, "Oh no, he'll probably be elderly and quite deaf. I don't think you should worry. We won't see him much anyway. Mrs. Astor, no doubt, has lots of plans for him."

"That's good." Mara smiled sheepishly and clutched her fan.

Her movement made Alana look down at Mara's hands. "That's a pretty bracelet. I've never seen it before, have I?"

"It's new," Mara answered, fingering the square-cut sapphires. "Trevor brought it back for me from Boston."

"It suits you, Mara." Alana did her best to smile, but it was painful. After all she had been through with Trevor, she didn't know why this little fact hurt her so, yet it did. Her husband had gone to Boston during their honeymoon, bringing an expensive trinket for his sister and nothing for his new wife. She'd already shown a distaste for his ostentatious jewelry, but the fact that her husband had given her no thought during his trip wounded her. Surely he had brought something for Daisy. Daisy could not go without, as the note proved. It was more than likely Trevor had bought a piece of jewelry for his mistress that could have paid for half the Confederate army, but if he had simply picked a four-leaf clover along the railroad and given that to Daisy, pressed in his coat pocket, Alana would have hated it just as much. It wasn't the cost. It was the emotions, emotions she despaired of ever being able to stir in him.

Delmonico's was fairly glittering with important personages: the Four Hundred, packed shoulder-to-shoulder with representatives from Washington and the mayor's office—all to meet this wildly prestigious duke from England. No one really knew too much about the Granvilles, except that they held a huge estate near the Scottish border, that the first duke had been knighted by Henry V, and that they were so illustrious that Victoria and Albert were said to have honeymooned in Granville Castle.

When the arrival of the duke was announced, a hush fell over the crowd. Alana stood with Mara near the back of the ballroom, Mara less interested in the old duke than the fresh young lads that flocked around them like pigeons. The real shock came when the duke appeared in the doorway—not the aged rotund whiskered gentleman most believed he would be but a fine-looking young man about Eagan's age.

"That's the Duke of Granville?" Alana blurted out in a rather unseemly manner.

"That lad couldn't be more than twenty-four," Trevor commented, getting a much better look at the man from his great height.

"He's so handsome," Mara whispered.

"He's British," Trevor said.

"He *is* handsome," Alana confirmed, ignoring her husband's remark.

"Do you think we'll be presented?" Mara asked.

"Oh yes, definitely." Alana took Mara's arm and began to lead her to the receiving line.

Trevor stopped them and pulled Alana to the side for a moment of privacy. "Fair warning, Alana. The Duke of Granville is British, and I don't want Mara getting mixed up with some damned limey."

Alana looked up at him, her mouth open in shock. "I understand the Irish have some animosity toward England, but really, Trevor, this is ridiculous. You don't even know this man."

"He's British. That's all I need to know. He's not going to be carrying on with my sister."

"How convenient prejudice is. We could take that very

sentence, transposing *Irish* for *English*, and hear it from any number of people here tonight."

He twisted his lips in a sarcastic smile. "You've a point there, but nonetheless, Mara isn't going to no Brit. That's just the way they work, you know. They see the family coffers dwindling, and they send themselves over to America to fetch home a nice young girl who can pretty up the castle along with her fat American dowry. I can tell you right this very minute, the Sheridan money ain't gonna go for fixing up some damned castle in Northumberland."

Alana listened, knowing that Trevor wasn't aware of how his accent was slipping into his speech. She said, "Mara hasn't even met this duke, and you have her married and begetting his children. Don't you think we should see if they even take to each other?"

"Oh, he'll take to Mara. Look at her—she's sweet and pretty and one of the richest here. She ain't goin' ta no Brit, an' t'a's final."

Alana artfully hid her smile behind a satin-gloved hand. She knew she was playing with fire, but after thinking all evening about Mara's bracelet, she felt it was time for a little revenge. "Come along, Trevor, surely *you*—Mr. Stock Exchange, Mr. Railroad, Mr. I-Own-Everything-in-Manhattan, Mr. I-*Always*-Get-My-Way—would like this duke. I'd think you of all people would admire a man whose relations have been able to subjugate a country for over two hundred years, even if that country is your own. After all, isn't that your modus operandi?"

He looked at her, at first shocked, but then he released an unexpected laugh. "Fine. You introduce her to Granville. But all bets are off if he wants to marry her. Our agreement does not stand."

"Of all the papers that I signed when I married you, I don't remember ever seeing the stipulation that Mara was not permitted to marry a Brit."

"I can't foresee every possibility."

"No, you can't. All bets are on, Mr. Sheridan. British or not."

Tight-lipped, he watched her saunter back into the crowd and take Mara to the receiving line.

Like an artist working with a favored medium, Alana made her way through the line. She was pleased to see the duke looking bored as he spoke with Mrs. Van Dam, an aged matron of Washington Square. It would be all the more sweet to capture his attention with Mara.

Through the crowd Alana gave Trevor a rather bold look, then grasped Mara's hand and said to the duke, "Your Grace, I'm Mrs. Trevor Sheridan."

The duke kissed her hand. There was a surprised twinkle in his eye. "Ah yes, I've heard a lot about you, Mrs. Sheridan. Your maiden name was Van Alen, was it not?"

Alana smiled, not caring that there was gossip about her. She had had no doubts there would be. "Indeed it was Van Alen, but my name is *Sheridan* now." From the corner of her eye she spied Trevor. He was almost scowling at her. She spoke loudly enough for him to hear. "And you'll be hearing more of the Sheridan name, Your Grace, because I'd like to introduce to you my sister-in-law, Miss Mara Sheridan."

The duke bent to kiss Mara's hand. As he straightened, his blue eyes met Mara's, and suddenly his air of ennui was gone. "How *nice* it is to meet *you*," he said, looking down at the blushing girl.

"Miss Sheridan is a native New Yorker," Alana interjected, "and quite fond of our lovely new park. Do you ride, Your Grace?"

"Of course, of course," he answered absent-mindedly, his gaze caught in Mara's.

Alana smiled. Everything was going quite well. The duke was struck dumb. How easy it had been. She batted her fan to regain his attention. "Miss Sheridan was just telling me that soon we must go for a ride in the park. One morning, I imagine, right after breakfast."

"That's when I like to ride."

"It *is*?" Alana put her hand to her chest as if she were astounded by such a coincidence. She turned to look at Trevor, who'd heard the entire exchange. He frowned, and she had to stifle a giggle behind her fan.

From his place in the crowd, Trevor watched his wife work her magic on the duke. She was polite, witty, and charming—all the things she'd been bred to be. If one looked closely, one might have seen pride and admiration for her in his eyes, and a healthy dose of fear.

And if one listened well, one would have heard him whisper under his breath what was most on his mind. "No, all bets are *off*, Mrs. Sheridan. Starting with your next bloody trip to Brooklyn."

"Wasn't he handsome? Wasn't he charming? I felt so clumsy when he asked me to waltz. I must have stepped on his toes four times!" Mara chattered on during the carriage ride up Fifth Avenue when the ball was over.

"Young Granville was quite a gentleman, don't you agree, Trevor?" In the golden lamplight Alana turned to her brooding husband and gave him her most dazzling vengeful smile. "I told him Mara and I would be riding in the park Thursday morning. You don't think he'd believe I was so brazen as to be dropping hints of our whereabouts so that he might 'accidently' bump into us, do you?"

Trevor scowled and said to Mara, "You needn't waste your time thinking about that lad. Caroline Astor will keep him so busy he won't have time to be calling on you."

"Oh, you're right." Mara's exuberance wilted like an overblown rose.

"Nonsense!" Alana reached over and squeezed Mara's hand. "He'll be in the park Thursday, love, I'll bet on it. And I'll make it clear he's more than welcome to call on you."

"You will?" Mara exclaimed, the joy back in her face.

"Of course I will. After all"—she gave Trevor a meaningful look as he sat stiffly in the shadows—"that's what I'm here for."

"I wish to speak to you, wife, when we arrive home," Trevor said through clenched teeth.

"Certainly, husband dear," Alana answered, having too much fun to be ruffled by his menacing tone.

When they arrived at the mansion, Trevor said good night to Mara, then proceeded to the library. Alana loved the room. She should have hated it because that was where she had made her bargain with this Irish devil so many weeks ago, but it was her favorite room in the mansion. It was like Trevor's bedroom. There wasn't a curved line to be found. This modern style was promoted by a man named Charles Lock Eastlake, and she decided if she and Christal ever had a home of their own, it would be decorated according to his *Hints on Household Taste*.

"You're encouraging this courtship just to taunt me, and I don't like it." Trevor crossed his arms over his chest and glared at her.

She breezed by a horsehair sofa and wandered to the built-in bookcases where she perused the titles. "We can't stand in the way of true love, Trevor."

"This is your exit, isn't it? You're going to get Mara into this boy-duke's clutches, and when she's married, you think you'll be able to wave good-bye, job done. But I won't let you off that easily."

She giggled. "Good heavens, Trevor, you're jumping the gun. Granville likes Mara, and I see no reason to discourage him. He seems like a fine young man who, surprisingly, lacks the prejudice that has kept a lot of Knickerbockers away. I'd think you'd be ecstatic such an illustrious young fellow has taken to our Mara."

Angered, Trevor turned away. He bit out, "Fine. Let Granville see Mara. I can deal with him should the need arise. But don't think your annulment is looming on the horizon. The man who marries my sister will have to prove his love five times to please me. Not an easy task."

Alana had had a retort on the tip of her tongue until Trevor said the word *annulment*. It wasn't going to be very long before they would get one. Mara had not yet found her mate, but it was only a matter of time. She'd proven as easy to bring out as Alana had suspected she'd be. It wouldn't be more than a couple of months at most before someone would offer for her hand.

A couple of months. Alana stared at her husband. She thought of his mistress, Daisy, and wanted to hate him. But the vile truth was she didn't hate him. Her feelings were very much to the contrary, and that was why he'd been able to hurt her so. She looked to the future, a future without the handsome angry man who stood before her. So much of it was built on dreams—dreams of white houses, freeing Christal, and shadow men who were going to one day save her—dreams as sturdy as cobwebs.

Suddenly everything she wanted to deny overwhelmed her. Her dream ran through her mind's eye with astonishing clarity—to the moment her shadow man turned around and she could finally see his face. Then, like a daguerreotype, the picture of his face froze in her mind, and all she saw was Trevor as he was now, turning to face her, his features burned into the shadows of her memory until she knew she would never forget them.

"You're not going to be off the hook that easily," he went on smugly. "Mark my words, you'll have to work a lot harder than you have been to find a man good enough for Mara."

He implied that their marriage was destined to be longer than expected, but she could only wish that that was going to be true. From what she had seen of Granville, she wouldn't be surprised to find Mara married within months, even weeks.

He asked her something, but she didn't hear him. All she could think about was how pitifully lonely she was going to be when their annulment came. She felt like Cinderella after the ball. Now that she had found her prince, her

shadow man, he happened to be the one man she would
never have.

"What, no witty set-down? No defiant retort?"

She stared at him. There was so much not to like about
him. She even hated this mansion that he lived in. It was
too big, too vulgar, too overdone. But when she thought of
finally getting her white clapboard house along the beach
and living there alone for the rest of her days, she knew
how unhappy she would be. She'd pine for this harsh, angry
man the rest of her days. The thought of never seeing him
again, never taunting him, never sitting quietly in the drawing room holding hands and listening to Mara play the
harp, made her want to throw herself to the sofa and keen
as loudly as the Irish.

"I've never seen you so quiet. Has the cat got your
tongue?"

"I—I'm not feeling well. I want to go to my room." She
put her hand to her burning cheeks and backed away. She
left the library without another word while Trevor stared
after her as if she were mad.

It was almost two o'clock in the morning when Alana
heard the banging at her door. Red-eyed and wide awake,
she wiped her tear-stained cheeks, checked that the buttons
on the neck of her peignoir were properly fastened, then
went to the door.

Secretly she nursed the hope that Trevor had come. In
the small hours of the morning she'd spent pacing her
room, she'd reconciled herself to the fact that she had
somehow fallen in love with him. What she found difficult
to accept was the hopelessness of the situation. And it was
hopeless. She could never imagine that cold Irishman loving her, not when she represented everything he despised.

With that thought giving her a grim resolve, she threw
open her door and found Eagan smiling besottedly down at
her.

"What are you doing here at this hour?" she whispered, her eyes reprimanding.

"I jus' got back from the Hoff'n House." He walked passed her into her room.

Her eyes widened, and she scurried in front of him. "You can't come in here!" she said in a loud whisper. "Don't you have any manners? This is a lady's bedroom!"

"Not to worry, Alana. I been in a lady's bedrum afore. I jus' came from one, ackshally."

"I can tell," she answered, waving her hand to clear the air of the violet water that reeked from Eagan's clothing.

He sat down on her fringed and tufted chaise longue, looking ridiculously masculine slouched against all that pink satin. It wasn't nearly big enough to accommodate his healthy frame, and every time he adjusted his seat, she was sure he was going to slide drunkenly down to the floor.

"Oh, Eagan, you're hopeless." She went to him. "What are you doing here?"

"I never had a mother, Alana. 'Least not as I can remember much. I want to talk to you like you're my mam. Can I do that?"

Taken aback, she nodded lamely.

He gave her a wicked smile, then winked. " 'Course, I feel things when I'm with you that I pray on me grave I'd never feel for me own mam."

Alana blushed and put a nervous hand to her neckline, wondering if her gown was too sheer.

But before she could do anything about it, Eagan dropped his head in his hands and sighed. "Alana, I'm tireda havin' all this fun. It's killin' me. For once I want to stand on me own two feet without Trevor behind me pullin' the strings."

The honest ache in his tone touched her heart. She knelt before him and put a hand on his head. "He doesn't pull the strings, Eagan. You just think he does. Trevor admires you. He's always talking about how smart you are."

"He's the one t'admire. He's his own man."

"You're your own man too. You just need to sober up a bit. I take it, it didn't go well at the Hoffman House with your latest—uh . . ." She didn't quite know what to call that woman she'd seen him with at the Academy. When she thought of Trevor's word, she almost giggled.

He looked up and clasped her arms. In utter earnestness he said, "For once, I want to bed a woman I love. I want to know if it's any different. If it's special."

She tried to pull away. Struck by a fit of nervousness, she said, "Oh, Eagan, why are you telling me this?"

" 'Cause I want to bed you. I want to see if I might love you. I think I might."

Shocked to her core, she sputtered, "This—this isn't what you want, Eagan. You don't love me. You just want to lash out at Trevor."

He stared at her, bleary-eyed. Taking her logic a step at a time, he finally cracked a smile. "But I do find you beautiful. Don't that count?"

"No," she said sternly.

"And Trevor ignores you somethin' terrible, don't deny it."

That truth lacerated her. She didn't comment.

"Come along, Alana, what'll he care if you kiss me?" Eagan pulled her to him until she was half sitting, half struggling on his lap.

"Eagan, stop this!" she said, unable to stifle her nervous giggle when he tried to put his lips to hers but in his besotted state kissed her chin.

"Aw c'mon, luv, many a woman'd like to kiss me. . . ."

"And has!" she answered, laughing and struggling in the same breath. "Oh, you bad man. For shame!" The words were barely out before Eagan lunged for her. That made him lose his precarious balance on the tiny chaise longue, and they both landed on the floor in an undignified heap.

Alana became nearly hysterical with laughter, perhaps because she was trying so hard to dispel her gloom over Trevor. Eagan, being the man he was, simply took advantage of her good spirits. He gripped her waist and pulled her down onto him.

He had just made an attempt to kiss her again when a voice shattered the moment, freezing both of them where they lay. "I ought to whip you like a cur, Eagan."

Terrified, Alana looked behind her and found Trevor standing in the doorway that separated their suite, his expression was hard and angry. He stared at her, and guilt seeped into her like water to a sponge. She scrambled off the floor, doing her best to pull herself together. In her peignoir, it was difficult.

"This isn't what it looks like, Trevor," Eagan said, staggering to his feet.

Trevor didn't say a word. His stare burned into his brother until Eagan visibly flinched.

"You're mistaking this for something it's not," Eagan went on. "Now I grant you, I shouldn't be here at this late hour, but it's not—"

"Get out."

It stunned Alana that Trevor could make two words seem like two hundred.

At a loss, Eagan said, "Trevor, I know what you're thinking, and you're wrong. I'd never cuckold—"

"Get out."

"Let me explain!"

"And what will you say?" Trevor snapped, glancing at his brother, then his wife, who clutched the neck of her peignoir like a terrified bride on her wedding night. "Will you say you don't find my wife attractive? Will you say you think of her as a sister? Well, I'd never see you carry on with Mara like that."

Eagan glanced at Alana, his expression absolutely sober. He said to Trevor, "It was just me playing. I meant no harm."

"You ought to be gelded for such play."

Losing control of his temper, Eagan snapped, "Your wife

might not be such a temptation if you kept her busy yourself."

Trevor moved forward, and Alana gasped. She thought they might get into a fistfight, but her husband stopped, his jaw clenched in one angry tight line. "Leave us," he growled, his temper barely leashed.

But Eagan would not leave without a final word. Angrily he said, "Admit it. It really bothers you to see Alana laughing with me, doesn't it? I don't think you even mind me touching her, but you can't stand the thought that she might be having a good time—a good time that doesn't include you."

"You're talking about my wife!"

"If she's your wife, then make her your wife!"

Trevor and Eagan stared at each other, locked in a silent battle. Alana was just about to intercede when Trevor said in an ominous tone, "Get out, Eagan. Get out now."

Eagan complied. He shot Alana an apologetic look, then stormed out of the room, slamming the door behind him.

Left alone with her husband, Alana heard the ensuing silence like the boom of a cannon. Trevor turned to her, and the room seemed to echo with his rage. She was aghast at the emotion in his eyes. Part of her quailed at the fury she found there, but another part of her, the part that had paced in her room all night and longed for a husband who loved her, rejoiced. He was jealous, wildly jealous. If their relationship held any promise, it was in that streak of possessiveness that had flared when he caught her in Eagan's embrace.

There was a long foreboding pause while he stared at her. He seemed to be contemplating his next move and going through all the possibilities before making his decision. But he was Trevor Byrne Sheridan, and once his decision was made, he acted. "Go to my room, Alana," he said quietly.

Her eyes locked with his. She knew what he was thinking. His jealousy gave her new hope, but the time for what he intended now was wrong. He was only accepting Eagan's challenge. He didn't want to make love to her because he cared for her but because of the man he was. She could see it in his eyes. He'd never let a dare go unanswered.

"No," she said just as quietly, just as firmly.

He nodded. Not a good sign. "You're my wife, Alana, my legal wife, wed in the Catholic Church. I've rights. Go into my room, or I'll get a policeman off the avenue to drag you in there."

"If you do this, there'll be no annulment."

"Then there'll be no annulment."

She stared at him, everything she wanted within her grasp yet so impossibly far away. If she refused his demand, she might never have another chance to salvage this marriage, but if she surrendered under these circumstances, would he be anything but cold and indifferent?

She thought about all that had happened to her this evening and the subsequent revelations. She had believed she loved this man. And when she looked at him, her gaze caressing his dark hair, his lean jaw, his angry eyes, she knew she did love him. Just glancing at the cane in his hand made her know it. To most, that walking stick represented fear and limitation. But she could see only strength. That stick was proof that he'd fought fear and limitation to become what he was, a rich and powerful man.

Perhaps it was only his struggle that touched her, but when she raised her gaze to him and saw the gruff, distant Irishman who had wed her, she no longer cared about the reasons for her feelings. She knew she loved him, and she knew that she'd move heaven and earth to make him love her.

"Go, Alana," he said.

"Is this only because of Eagan?" she whispered, making one last attempt at self-preservation.

"No," he rasped.

She looked at him, knowing she was going to believe

him. Slowly, she walked to his room. Behind her, she heard the door close with a click that seemed to resonate for an eternity. An eternity seemed to pass before she summoned the courage to look at him.

He stood with his back against the door staring at her as if methodically planning her seduction. She hadn't noticed before, but he was still clothed in his evening attire, his jet studs still on his shirtfront, his white piqué vest still buttoned.

In her peignoir, she felt naked standing in front of him, and his first command stopped her heart. "Go to the bed."

She turned frightened eyes to his looming tester bed. The chambermaid had long since prepared it, the creamy silk sheets pulled back forming a neat triangle to one side. Hesitating, she met his eyes. His dark hazel stare confronted her. He was not going to back down. She took the long journey to the bed.

"Take off your dressing gown."

Her hand protectively covered the column of buttons at her throat. Though she wanted this, everything seemed wrong. There was no wine, no roses, no seduction. Instead there were terse commands, long shadows from the flickering of the gaslights, and her husband's unwavering stare, dangerous and enticing.

"The dressing gown."

She lowered her gaze to the wispy garment of peach silk. The dressing gown hid the sheer nightgown he'd bought for her trousseau. If she took off her dressing gown, she'd almost be standing before him naked. Her gaze caught his. A rush of longing swept through her. It was now or never. It was love or loss. Reluctantly, her fingers began to undo the buttons at her throat. The garment slipped off her arms into a shimmering puddle at her feet. Clothed in the sheerest silk the color of her skin, her breath quickened, and she watched him from the shadows of the enormous tester bed.

Taking his own torturous time, starting at the bottom where the hem of her nightgown trailed behind her in a small frothy train, his gaze moved upward to the suggestion of shapely calves and lush thighs alluringly molded by the translucent silk. From his expression, the womanly curve of hips was apparently approved before he took in the silhouetted nip of her waist. Hungry now, his gaze wanted more, but the show was interrupted by her crossed arms. "Put your arms down," he whispered in a harsh steady voice.

She didn't move, didn't even look at him. She just stood there, frozen with fear and an inexpressible need. They'd been playing a game of dare, and she'd gone as far as she could.

To equal the score, Trevor leaned his stick against the door and walked toward her, his gait stiff and uneven. Letting her see him like this was his way of sharing an intimacy, and her guard came down a little as she watched him go to a table near the bed and pour himself a drink from one of the crystal decanters.

The scent of the cheap raw whiskey burned her nostrils. She wondered if he was going to pour her a drink too, and she hoped so, not only because it might strengthen her but because drinking together would be another intimacy shared.

He took two large swallows before turning. She was disappointed to see he had only one glass. But then he held the glass out, his eyes beckoning her to take it. Her hand trembled as she reached for it. Sharing the glass with him sent an ominous tingle of excitement down her spine. This was only a foretaste of things to come, of what they would eventually share.

Her lips touched the rim, and she relished her small taste of the whiskey. It was as strong as she remembered, but it warmed her, and the flavor reminded her of his kiss. The whiskey tasted of him.

She handed the glass back to him. He accepted it and looked down at her, his eyes taking in everything he couldn't see before. Her arms weren't covering her any longer, and her breasts thrust against the mist of peach silk, her soft dusky nipples in plain view.

His eyes darkened, and he took the rest of the glass in one gulp. Grimacing, for the whiskey had to burn like acid, he slammed the glass down on the night table. She was just about to clutch her arms to her chest again when he whispered, "No." He laced her hands in his and kissed her, not permitting her to fight, not permitting her to touch him.

They kissed, his mouth taking hers in a wild ritual of domination. She could barely breathe, but he seemed to have the power to take away her need for air, leaving her with only her need for him. She tried to touch him, but he wouldn't let her, forcing her hands to her side until she ached with the desire to cup his handsome face in her hands.

"Acknowledge me," he groaned against her hair when he pulled his lips from hers.

Confused, she shook her head, not understanding and too drugged from his kiss to respond.

"Say my name," he insisted. "Not Eagan . . . not Anson . . . *my* name."

"Trevor," she gasped.

"That's it. *Tá sé agat anis.*" After that enigmatic sentence, he released her hands, thrust his arm beneath her bottom, and lowered her to the bed.

His lips and body crushed her into the softness of the feather mattress, and his hand roamed, but not where she thought it would. Bracing herself for his touch on her breast, she was shocked when he moved lower, rubbing his thumb through the peach silk across the triangle of deep gold hair that covered her womanhood. She gasped, but the sound was muffled by the heat of his tongue. Shuddering, she pulled back from his exquisite torture, but there was no escape. He'd captured her, body and soul, her entire being in his hands, a fragile butterfly to be crushed or stroked according to his whim.

Pulling the sheer gown above her thighs, his touch went

deeper until he elicited an unwilling response. Overwhelmed, she lay beneath him, the well-bred, high-born girl aching to let this Irishman master her body. His method was ceaseless until she nearly sobbed with pent-up excitement, but she fought her desire, almost hating him when he toyed with secret places she hadn't known existed.

Then he slowed. He pulled off a stud from his shirtfront and pulled down her gown from her shoulder. Inch by wretched inch, he undressed himself, then undressed her. When his vest and shirt lay in a heap on the carpet and his trousers were unbuttoned, her gown was but a small band around her chest. He amazed her with his control. The last thing he needed to remove was his trousers, and he did this gracefully, sliding them down his hips without even sitting up.

He rolled naked to her side, and she expected he would rid her of her clothing with the same exacting expertise. But a spark flared in his eyes when he looked at her, a spark that seemed to burn away his control. Suddenly he no longer took his time. His hand stroked her skin, golden in the gaslight, and his eyes met hers, her own as dark with passion as with fear. He pushed her gown away from her breasts, and those same hands that had been gentle ripped the gown in two.

The violence frightened her, but he saw her stiffening and knew the cure for it. His mouth drew on hers, and he made her forget everything except how his skin burned against hers, how the hair on his chin and chest and thighs dragged sensually over her smooth body, how his tongue tasted of that potent unforgettable whiskey.

A lady, she had believed the liaison between a man and woman in bed was something akin to holding hands in the parlor. She'd dreamed of her husband-to-be and had always thought their joining would be soothing, gentle, and quiet. But she had never imagined her husband as Trevor Sheridan, had never imagined anything could be like this.

He took her with a passion as raw and strong as his drink.

When he wanted her, he gave no time for persuasion but
joined with her in one swift movement, his expression almost expecting a cry of surprise and pain as he entered.

But she didn't make a sound. She watched him, his wild,
primal movements exhilarating her and terrifying her in a
single, never-before-experienced emotion. When he bent
down and covered her aching nipple with his hot wet
mouth, rocking furiously within her, the feeling spun out of
control until she craved him with a passion she knew she
would never feel for another.

He lifted his head, and his mouth again captured hers,
creating more heat between her thighs. The pleasure he
gave her was like a band of rubber being pulled until it
snapped and she fell, twisting in the air until he caught her,
his hand beneath her hips to hold her closer, to make her
pleasure complete.

"Trevor," she moaned, chanting his name in surrender.

It drove him over the edge. He seized her and bit out the
word, *"Jeysus,"* then fell against her, sated.

Lying beneath him in the long quiet minutes afterward,
Alana impulsively reached up and touched his cheek. With
what she knew now, the questions for her had become simple. Could she live without her dreams? Without waltzes
and white houses and simplicity? She smiled a bittersweet
smile. The answer was obvious. It was yes. Absolutely yes,
for to live any other life would mean to live without this
wild, unforgivably brazen Irishman, and that was impossible. There were no other men like Trevor Sheridan. It was
he, or it was no one. And she'd already lived with no one.
After her parents had died and she lost Christal, she'd had
three long wretched years without anyone to love. Now
that she loved him, she would do so with a passion she
would take to her grave.

There was only one question left, one that haunted her
with his every retreating movement. Would he ever find a
way to love her?

She felt the cool air touch her body as he drew from her. The night had not seemed so cold before. Now it was rigid.

Trevor rolled to his back and stared up at the coffered ceiling. She didn't know what he was thinking, and it terrified her. He was not a man of pretty words; she didn't expect them now. They were never going to be a couple who cooed and billed at each other in their bliss.

But she wanted words. She wanted to know what was going through his mind, and in her desperation she spoke first. "Is it always like this?"

He turned his head and looked at her. "Like what?" he asked solemnly.

"So . . . unrestrained." Her phrasing was inadequate. There were no words to express what had just happened. It had been savage and uncivilized . . . beautiful.

He didn't answer. His gaze flickered over her nudity, and she thought she saw guilt in his eyes. When he took the sheet and covered her breasts, she knew it.

Holding the sheet to her, her fingers turned to ice. She didn't want to cover herself. She wanted him to hold her, to keep her warm and caress her with all the tenderness of a lover until she fell asleep in his arms. But that wasn't to be. Something was wrong, and her foreboding spawned such a feeling of dread, it turned her heart to stone.

He closed his eyes as if he were fighting something inside him. When he spoke, his words were anguished. "I'm not a man who takes his bargains lightly. Nor do I like those bargains changed. I deal in numbers. But this is something else entirely."

"But was this so unexpected?" Her voice took on an edge of panic. "After all, I'm your wife."

"When I made this agreement with you, I never really believed this would happen. I certainly thought I could control myself. Avoid these entanglements."

"Is that what this is, an 'entanglement'?" she asked, unable to hide the hurt and accusation in her tone.

He was silent, as if he could think of no response.

"A vulgar word, *entanglement*," she whispered, feelin
him pull away. "I've never heard it called that before. **}**
must be that the Irish do it differently." She knew he woul
take that as an attack, but the way she was beginning t
hurt, she wasn't sure she cared.

He stared at the ceiling once more. She could see he wa
angry. Finally he said, "The words may be different, bu
trust me, the Irish do it just like the Knickerbockers."

She was silent, inexplicably wounded. He said nothing
just stared up at the ceiling. Soon she began to tremble
finding her hopes as crushed as the pillow beneath he
head. They were in his bed together, but his words were s
cold, so distant. He thought it all a mistake. Just as sh
feared, he'd acted from jealousy and competition wit
Eagan. He felt no emotion for her, none at all. Excep
regret. He'd broken their agreement, and now he feared fo
Mara's future. Perhaps he regretted that she was not hi
Daisy. Unlike his mistress, she'd been a virgin. She'd prob
ably come off as awkward and inexperienced, and she'd dis
pleased him. Despite all her wild, passionate feelings, she'
seemed cold. But then, maybe she *was* cold. She'd wrappe
herself in that cocoon after her parents' death and perhap
never emerged.

She closed her eyes, holding back the tears that threat
ened to spill onto her cheeks.

He spoke again, not looking at her. "We can still get a
annulment. I'll give you that if you still wish to fulfill you
part of our agreement."

"How—" She swallowed, determined not to show hin
how destroyed she was. When she spoke again, her voic
was cool and accusatory. "How can we have an annulment
after what we've done?"

"We won't be the first to lie about such things. Trus
me."

She pushed the curtain of blond hair out of her face

Searching for her peignoir, she stiffly rose from the bed, then pulled it to her.

"Did you hear me? Where are you going?" he asked, not bothering to hide his nakedness. He rose from the bed, a splendid example of angry manhood.

"No more lies. I can't take any more lies," she whispered.

"What are you saying?"

"I'm saying I won't lie to get you out of this marriage."

His jaw tightened. "Then how do you propose we end this marriage? How do we fulfill our bargain?"

"We'll have to get a divorce."

His face was hard as marble. "The Catholic Church does not permit divorce. That's out of the question."

She glared at him. "We made this agreement on the basis that we would separate at the end of it."

"I never said we could divorce. I only mentioned annulment. Divorce is not an option. I cannot get one. You'll lie and have your annulment, or you'll have nothing."

"I won't lie anymore before God," she said. "This marriage began as a lie. It will end with the truth."

His eyes glittered with fury. "You're telling me—a woman of your station—that you'd prefer the ugliness of a divorce?"

Her defiant spirit saved her at last. "No," she answered coolly. "What I truly prefer, Trevor Sheridan, is a husband better than you."

He stared at her, too enraged to move. She walked from his room, and he started toward her, but she was too quick. She slammed the door, and his walking stick that leaned against the wall clattered to his feet. He snatched it up and began his slow pace back to the bed. But then whatever passion simmered in his soul suddenly came to a boil. He stared in self-loathing at the cane in his hand, and with unusual violence, he snapped it in two and threw it across the room, making a sound that seemed like a harsh, repressed sob.

23

The next morning Eagan found himself alone at the breakfast table. Mara was slow to rise, and Trevor and Alana were breakfasting in their rooms—in their separate rooms—he'd heard from the servants.

Disgusted with himself and the world, he shoved away his eggs and studied his coffee cup. Stepping to the sideboard, he took a decanter from a silver tray and laced the coffee with a drop or two of brandy.

He sure had a heavy case of the Irish melancholy. Nothing seemed to make him happy anymore. Last night he'd taken his usual sojourn down Broadway from Madison Square—Gentleman's Walk, it was called—after dark. The *nymphes des paves* were out in force—beautiful, well-dressed, and well-spoken women, each a different kind of candy to tempt a bored and restless spirit. He'd made a "chance meeting" with one, a petite, glorious redhead, and followed her back to her house of assignation. There was nothing of note about the evening. For a man of his station to visit a temple of love was commonplace. The parlor houses were so out in the open, they were even listed in *The Gentleman's Directory* and that went so far as to include the number of female "boarders" and whether it was a first- or second-class establishment.

But the night had soured. After he'd done his duty by the lady, he leaned back in the bed and stared at her, for the first time completely at a loss. The realization seeped in that he had nothing to say to this girl, nothing to say, really, to any girl of his acquaintance. If he and the woman of the moment weren't in the process of satisfying their physical needs or building to that process, there was nothing between them. He couldn't think of a girl he could just hold in his arms, lie in the dark, and talk to.

He'd ended the evening early, giving the girl twice her rate, leaving her satisfied in more ways than one. Then he walked and drank until he found himself at the Battery. He'd watched the lights of Governor's Island, thinking, thinking, until his brain hurt. Trevor's wife came to mind more than once. She was definitely a girl to hold in the dark. But he knew she wasn't for him more than she did. He wasn't blind, and he knew Trevor was building a passion for her that was just about to overflow the dam of his withdrawn personality. And when that dam burst, neither of them would ever emerge.

But that was what he wanted. He wanted obsession. Seduction. He wanted a girl he could hold in the dark. For the first time in his long debauched life, Eagan finally wanted something he couldn't have.

Drunk and depressed, he'd gone back to the mansion, hoping to ease his sorrows by sharing them with Alana. That had turned into a mess, and now, taking the last sweet drop of his morning coffee, letting it distance the woes of last evening, he decided that perhaps the best thing would be for him to lose himself for a few days. Trevor could cool his head, and in the meantime he could take up residence in Newport or find some sport down at the Jersey shore.

Eagan left the mansion and refused a carriage, thinking the walk to the Commodore Club would do him good. His mood didn't seem so dark in the thin light of the morning, and by the time he'd downed a couple of brandies at the club, he was actually feeling optimistic. After all, his life wasn't so terrible. And those girls, well, they were a mighty fine lot, so fine that by half-past four in the afternoon, he'd

decided to go to Lord and Taylor's and buy Miss
Evangeline de la Plume a little gift to apologize for being so
brash the other night. That would baste that bird pretty
well, he thought rather lecherously, knowing that Miss de
la Plume was no different from the *nymphe* he had had last
night, except that her price was a little higher and it took a
little longer.

He rode a hack up Broadway to East Twentieth Street
and the dazzling five-storied, cast-iron-front department
store. Potted palms and French gilt mirrors met him on the
first floor, hiding the fact that this grande dame of a store
had started out as a harness shop. The paintings, frescoes,
chandeliers, and particularly the endless miles of cold marble made him almost sentimental about home. If it weren't
for the rainbow colors of hats and gloves stacked upon polished mahogany display counters, he'd be damned if he'd
have known the difference.

Sauntering through the marble rotunda, he debated
whether to splurge on an emerald brooch or just have one
of the shopgirls wrap up a fur. Deciding on the fur—it
would make a bigger impression, and Miss de la Plume
might be so grateful she'd let them *both* lie on it—he paused
by the ornate doors to the Otis vertical railway and rang for
it to take him to the fifth floor.

The clock in the rotunda struck five, and shoppers
streamed out the etched-glass doors. The store was closing,
but he rang again for the lift with the confidence that the
minute his face was recognized, they'd stay open all night if
need be. Minutes passed, and he rang the bell again for the
elevator. Impatiently, he tapped one polished black shoe,
the sound echoing through the empty rotunda.

Bored and ready to sprint for the stairs, he noticed a
figure out of the corner of his eye. Thinking it might be a
store manager who could fetch the fur for him, he swung
around to summon him, but he stopped in his tracks.

It wasn't a manager. It was a scrub girl, obviously, from
the bucket and mop hanging in her hands. She stood at the

foot of the curved marble staircase, close enough that he could make out the details. Her hair was blond, held in a neat bun at her nape. Her face was pretty despite the smudges of dirt that marred each cheek—proof of how long and hard she'd been working. She was small in stature, her clothes gray, worn, and patched yet clean, except for her hem where it had dragged in her scrub puddles.

He might not have looked at her twice—in his years in New York, he'd seen a thousand of her—but she paused at the bottom of that monstrously grand staircase, looking hesitantly up at those hundred steps, her hand resting on her swollen belly in a gesture of grave uncertainty. She was very, very pregnant.

The bell dinged as the elevator operator pushed aside the doors of the cage. Recognizing Eagan instantly, the tiny wiry young man straightened his bow tie and asked, "What floor, Mr. Sheridan? Are we buying jewels or furs today?"

Eagan snapped his head around to look at the attendant. "Furs, I think, Billy. Take me to five."

"Very good, sir." The attendant stepped aside to let him enter.

Eagan didn't move. He watched the petite young woman rub the small of her back and stare at the intimidating stairs. Though she couldn't have been more than eighteen, her face was careworn. In a few years that look would be there permanently, eating away at whatever prettiness she once had. Her little figure moved him, and he gave way to impulse. "Madam," he said, the word echoing across the empty rotunda. "Madam," he repeated until she realized he was speaking to her.

She turned and faced him with the clearest blue eyes he'd ever seen. They were like the sky over Ballinlough from a forgotten childhood memory. They made the breath catch in his throat. "Madam, would you like to ride?" he said solemnly, holding out his hand to the elevator.

Those incredible eyes widened, and while it appeared

that she very much wanted to, she shook her head and glanced around her as if she expected trouble.

"Come here." He waved her forward.

She did as he asked, her bucket and mop grasped fearfully in each hand.

"Don't you want to ride instead of walk?" He took her arm and led her into the elevator. She pulled back, but Eagan insisted, his strength easily settling the issue.

Billy coughed. "Ah, hem, if I may, sir. . . . This girl's the help," he pointed out, clearly disapproving of a scrub girl in his vertical railway.

"I see that," Eagan answered. "But surely Lord and Taylor would not want her to be taking the stairs in her condition, now would they?"

The customer was always right, but a man with Eagan Sheridan's pocketbook was God. Billy smiled his most cheerful smile and said, "Of course not, Mr. Sheridan. Let the lass ride to her floor. I'll drop her off just as soon as I get you to five."

"Thank you, Billy." Eagan shook his hand and discreetly lined his palm with a ten-dollar note. At that price, Billy would have carried them both on his back.

Going about his business, Billy closed the cage and pulled on the rope that ran through the ornate car. Eagan flashed the girl a wry grin, and those unforgettable eyes stared back at him with gratitude and something uncomfortably akin to distrust. They were on their way, but the ride to the fifth floor was not destined to be. After they passed three, a loud crack resounded through the shaft, and the vertical railway stopped dead between floors.

Billy, shaking his head and murmuring something about the damned thing not working right all day, tugged mercilessly on the rope for almost a minute, but nothing happened. Apologizing to Eagan, he cupped his hands and shouted upward, "Harper! Crank the shaft! Crank it!"

Nothing happened. Billy shouted again for his partner.

There was no answer but the resounding echo of his voice that rumbled through the shaft.

Mildly amused, Eagan took the cushioned bench that lined the perimeter of the small ornate car and prepared to wait. He offered the girl a seat, but she refused, looking frightened.

"It'll be all right," he told her with a smile.

She didn't appear to understand him, and he wondered if she had just come off the boat from some Scandinavian country.

Billy, meanwhile, fiddled with the rope and shouted again for Harper, who was obviously shirking his duties now that the store was closed. "I'm sorry, Mr. Sheridan," Billy said anxiously, at a loss with no assistance from above. Frustrated, he glanced up at a door fixed in the elevator ceiling, and an idea came to him. "Mr. Sheridan, I won't be but a minute. I'll go up the shaft to four, and we'll get this thing moving again without wasting any more of your time."

"Fine. I'll stay here and man the fort." Eagan gave a wry twist to his lips.

Billy laughed nervously, not sure what to make of that comment, then leapt to the bench. He was small and wiry, but even he had a difficult time squirming through the tight ceiling door. Eagan's broad shoulders would have never passed through it. While Billy monkeyed through the hole in the ceiling, Eagan almost laughed. This adventure was proving amusing after all. But then Billy disappeared, and he was alone. Except . . .

His gaze turned to the girl. She held on to the wall, trying to appear brave, but she was trembling in spite of herself. Eagan looked down at the girl's belly. For some irrational reason, it appeared twice the size it had been when she first stepped into the car. Suddenly his palms went clammy.

In reaction to his stare, the girl huddled back against the wall and put a protective hand on her belly. She was clearly wary of him. But in truth, she was the one scaring the hell out of him.

"Damn, damn, damn!" Eagan ground out, punching his hand into his palm. He looked up at the hole in the elevator ceiling and called, "Billy! Goddammit! Come back here!"

It had been over an hour since the attendant disappeared. The girl had finally sat down, and she rested her head against the etched glass, tracing the Greek key pattern with her finger.

"Goddammit, somebody answer me!" Eagan shouted at the dark endless hole that neither could fit through.

Still no answer. He slumped to the tufted bench, tapping his shoe. The girl was frightened, but she was tired too, so tired that her fatigue seemed to numb her fear.

It didn't numb his. He thought of himself as a rather brave man. But every time his gaze slid to that girl's belly, he could feel the blood drain from his head. What if she needed something? Water, for example. How would he get that for her? Billy was the only one who could fit through that bloody hole. And where the hell was that puny little bastard anyway?

He ran his hand through his hair, unwilling to think of Billy never coming back. He'd come back, all right, or Lord and Taylor's store was going to have its butt kicked with the biggest lawsuit it'd ever seen. Eagan stole a glance at the girl. She was rubbing her belly in a strange, pensive way, as if she were comforting the baby within. He felt that he should do something for her, but the best thing he could do was get them out of there.

He stood to shout through the hole again. Suddenly a tinny voice came down through the hole, sounding far away. "Mr. Sheridan? Mr. Sheridan?"

"We're down here! Billy?"

"No," the voice sounded back, "Name's Harper."

"Where the hell did Billy go?"

There was a long pause. "Mr. Sheridan, you must not lose patience. We are doing everything we possibly can."

"Where did Billy go?" Eagan demanded.

"He went to find Mr. Otis," the voice answered, obviously trying to stay calm.

"Mr. Otis!" Eagan struck his forehead. "Are you telling me we're *that* stuck?"

"We've been working on it, but the thing's got us confounded. Mr. Otis understands this newfangled contraption. He designed it. He'll know how to fix it."

Eagan glanced at the girl. His agitation was frightening her more than Harper was. He made a heroic attempt to cool his temper. "Fine. We'll wait, then. After all, how long can this take?"

"That's right, Mr. Sheridan," Harper soothed. "It won't take long. In the meantime, we're lowering you a basket of necessities."

"Why don't you come down here and serve us yourself?" Eagan snorted. "Better yet, tell Mr. Lord and Mr. Taylor to come down here. I'd like to talk to them."

"I'm afraid Billy's the only one who's going to fit through that hatch." The voice chuckled. "The wife's cooking, you know."

Eagan groaned. "Well, you can lose a few pounds chasing after Billy. I want me and this girl out of this cage in an hour, understood?"

"I understand, and the management relays their regrets, sir."

Eagan rolled his eyes.

Fifteen minutes passed with absolute silence between them. Eagan stared at the girl, and she stared at the carpet, her face a mask of worry.

"What's your name?" he finally asked, wanting to know. She'd been so quiet through this whole thing. It wasn't natural. He knew a girl in her position was forced to defer to her "betters" and keep her mouth shut. But in this situation he wanted her to talk to him.

She looked up, her blue eyes questioning.

"Your name?"

She said something in a soft, melodic, vaguely familiar tongue. Then she said, "I cannot be speakin' moch English."

She looked at him. "*Ochone*," she whispered, and then he knew where she was from. His knowledge of Gaelic was limited, but that word meant "Oh dear."

"You're from Ireland?" he whispered.

She looked at him, her expression wary. "Aye."

He wished to God he'd taken more interest in his brother's Gaelic. If anything should happen, he could at least speak in her native tongue and reassure her. As it was, the best he could do was sing "Bridget O'Malley," and a fat lot of good that would do for either one of them. "My family's originally from Connacht. You?" He looked at her.

Her eyes cleared, and she said something in Gaelic, but he shook his head. Smiling, he said, "Sorry. I guess I've been here too long. I only know English."

She nodded. "I can't be speakin' moch English."

He'd gathered that. The girl must come from the far western regions of Ireland. Despairing, he glanced up at that black hole in the ceiling.

"The time?" she asked.

"You mean, how long have we been here?"

She nodded.

He opened his gold pocketwatch and grimaced. "Over two hours." A thought occurred to him, and he paled. "Is anything wrong? Do you need anything? Should I do something for you?"

She didn't quite understand him, perhaps because he was speaking so fast and his accent was unfamiliar.

"Is someone coming for you? Your husband?"

This last word she seemed to understand. She stiffened

and slowly drew her right hand over her left, trying to hide the fact that she had no wedding band on her fourth finger.

But Eagan noticed. He met her gaze, astonished by the hurt and betrayal he found there.

Falling silent once more, they let the minutes tick by, unmarred by conversation.

Another hour went by, and there was no news from above. Eagan was just beginning to wonder how he could punch out the hatch to make it big enough to accommodate him when a familiar voice rang down.

Eagan grimaced. "What is it now, Harper?"

Harper paused, and Eagan swore that when he got out of the elevator, he was personally going to wring the man's chubby neck.

"Sir, we're going to get you out of there. It just may take a bit longer. Billy couldn't find Mr. Otis. It seems he's gone to New Jersey. Billy just sent a messenger from the ferry. He's going to fetch him, so have a little of the supper I sent down, and—"

"New Jersey!" Eagan ran his hand down his face. "Christ, we'll be here all night!"

"We'll get you out at the first possible moment! As soon as Mr. Otis—"

"Make him fly, Harper. Do you hear me? Put wings on that bastard and get him here because I've taken all I'm going to take!"

"Yes, Mr. Sheridan. And again, on behalf of the management, sir, we apologize for the inconvenience."

Eagan released an exasperated sigh. He went to take his seat again, but he noticed the girl was glancing at the basket that had been sent down, her eyes large with hunger. Ashamed, he handed her the basket and motioned for her to take whatever she wanted. He watched her timidly take a roll, leaving the silver dish of caviar, the pastel-colored petits fours tucked in white linen, and the Dom Perignon for him. It was obvious that he was the only reason the basket had been sent down, and it angered him to think that if she had been stuck in this vertical railway by herself, they probably wouldn't have sent a thing to her.

She ate her bread, clearly embarrassed that her condition left her a slave to physical needs. He continued to look at her, her vulnerability touching him. She really was a pretty girl. Her skin was Irish skin, like a child's—soft, pink, and flawless.

Misunderstanding the reasons for his stare, she nervously handed him the basket. He put it aside and thought about having a drink. He had a flask with him, but for some reason he just wasn't interested. He was much more interested in her. He couldn't come to terms with the fact that some man had taken this pretty girl to his bed, done what he'd done to her, and abandoned her without a fare-thee-well. He was no saint, he'd had his share of women, but if one of them had come to him in trouble, he would have worked to the bone to see the mother of his child taken care of, not let her out in the world scrubbing endless marble floors nine months pregnant—like his own mother had.

Of course, the girl's lover might have died before he'd gotten her to the altar. He'd heard of things like that happening. But that wasn't the case here. Though they hadn't communicated much in words, she'd told him all he needed to know. He'd looked into those breathtaking eyes and seen the betrayal.

"What's your name? Mine's Eagan Sheridan," he tried again.

Recognizing an Irish name, she looked as if she trusted him a bit more. She answered in English with a little difficulty, "Me name's Caitlín O'Roarke."

"Kathleen. That's a beautiful name."

She just stared at him.

"Somebody must be worried about you, Caitlín," he said softly. "Where's your family?"

She looked away. "T'ere's no one worryin' about me."

"You came to America alone?"

"Here's better for the babe." She put a hand to her belly. Still she wouldn't meet his eyes.

Eagan leaned back on the tufted bench and thought again about his mother. Trevor had seen her suffer. Trevor remembered much more than he did. Now he remembered too. Caitlín was living proof that their mother's plight continued to be repeated too often.

"The child's father—is he an American?" Eagan knew he was prying, but he had the irrational urge to look this fellow up and make him sorry for what he'd done.

She stared at the carpet and looked as if she were making her confession to the priest. "He's Ascendency."

So the girl had been seduced by one of the British landholders. Trevor's hatred of the British suddenly became Eagan's hatred too.

"Did you ever tell him?" he asked gently, becoming desperate to find a solution to this girl's wretched fate.

Caitlín closed her eyes. "He was marryin' another. A lady from London." Her voice lowered and grew thick with unshed tears. "He gave me ten pounds to come to Americker. An' so here I am."

Eagan grew quiet and let her collect herself. He didn't know what he could do, but if they ever got out of this bloody elevator, he was going to try to help this girl. He could place her with the other servants in the mansion. The Sheridans were good employers. She would be better off under their wing than here, out in the world, mopping floors until she dropped from exhaustion.

"Where do you live?" he asked, this time without hesitating.

"Baxter Street," she whispered.

He inwardly cringed. In the heart of New York's worst slums. He didn't need to ask more. "Would you like—" He was about to ask if she would like to come work for him when she took a deep breath and held it, as if she were in pain. "Caitlín?" he whispered, afraid to articulate the rest of his thoughts.

The moment passed, and she turned to him. She mus
have seen the panic in his eyes because she said, "It'
noothin'. Me back's sore today."

Desperate to believe her, he looked up into the hole. He
shouted for Harper to get an update on the situation, bu
Harper wasn't at his station. Anxious to do something, he
handed her the basket. "You must be hungry. Eat. Go
ahead."

She took the basket, but then her knuckles went white on
the handle. Eagan watched her, the pit of his stomach falling to the first floor of the building.

"Ochone," Caitlín whispered, and gripped her stomach
She tried to get into a better position, obviously believing
that might relieve the pain, but when she tried to stand, her
water broke and seeped into her skirt.

Eagan noted her sopping skirt and knowing nothing
about the birth process, believed she had embarrassed herself, being confined to the elevator with no water closet. He
felt for her, but at the same time he couldn't squelch the
rush of relief that her behavior had nothing to do with her
enormous belly. Until she reached out and put a viselike
grip on his arm. She said something in Gaelic, then, "Mr
Sheridan, the babe's comin', and t'ere not much I can do
about it."

"How do you know?" he asked stupidly, his face ghost-
white.

"Me water's broke. Me water's broke," she whispered
again fighting off a spasm of pain.

Eagan stared at the wet skirt. Her baby was being born
Everything he feared was coming true. His hand swept
back her hair, and he tried to soothe her, fighting his own
panic. Mechanically, he removed his jacket and put it over
her shoulders. Then he screamed for Harper.

"Yes, Mr. Sheridan?" came the blessed voice from above
and Eagan knew God had a sense of humor.

"Get a doctor down here immediately. I want a doctor
and Charles Otis here on the double!"

"We're doing what we can. Billy isn't back from New Jersey."

"I need a doctor! This girl's going to have her baby. *Now!*"

Silence followed these words. Then Harper gasped, "Yes, sir. Right away, sir. I'll send someone for a doctor this minute." Harper walked away so quickly, he stumbled into something and cursed.

When there were no more footsteps, Eagan turned his gaze to Caitlín. She was in the throes of another spasm, her features screwed up tight, her hands gripping her belly.

"Everything will be all right," he whispered. But there was no reaching her. Slowly he looked down at his shaking hands. He had lived his entire life from one dissolute moment to another. His biggest complaint had been a vague sense of annoyance that he was rarely if ever needed. But now this girl needed him, her baby needed him, and there was nowhere to run, no way to find help. It was up to him and him alone. If he had any heroic qualities, now was the time to prove them.

He cautiously removed his gold cufflinks etched with the Connacht shield and began rolling up his shirtsleeves, just in case the doctor didn't arrive down the shaft in time. He watched Caitlín. She released a low guttural moan, and a tear slipped from the corner of her eye as she held back her pain.

Eagan Sheridan wasn't the sort to pray. But he was praying now.

An hour later, the baby still had not come, and Eagan had hopes that a doctor might arrive in time. Caitlín lay on his frock coat, her brow beaded with sweat from her work, his handkerchief wadded in her small hand. He'd removed his silk vest now that her pains were coming so close together. They needed something to put the babe in when it came. He knew instinctively it was going to be soon.

"Caitlín," he whispered, grasping her hand tightly.

"You're doing well, girl! You're a brave lass. The father of this babe didn't deserve you."

Caitlín gave him a weak smile before her pains began mounting again. Taking long, deep breaths, she held fast to Eagan's hand until the worst of it was over.

But what they considered the worst was fleeting. With each pain, the contractions grew closer and closer until there was no talking to Caitlín. She merely lay on the floor clutching his hand, whimpering like a suffering animal while Eagan ran his forearm over his brow, wiping away his sweat.

When he knew he could avoid it no longer, he carefully pulled up the girl's skirts. He'd seen the anatomy of a woman before, but in this instance, he felt as if he were trespassing on holy ground. Caitlín was a mother about to give birth to her first child, and there was no place for a man at her side now. She needed other women who'd gone through the same, not some rake whose only function in life had been to get women into such trouble. Loathing himself at that moment, he pushed up her knees.

And gasped. The child's head had appeared, and it had dark hair, obviously like its father's. He squeezed Caitlín's hand and crawled back to her head. "You're gonna have to push, sweeting. Can you push?"

"*Tá mé an t-uirseach. Tá mé an t-uirseach*," she mumbled.

He couldn't understand her, but he knew she was exhausted. He had to get her moving again. "Caitlín!" he whispered sharply, "I can see your baby. Your baby has dark hair. Not at all like yours. But I cannot tell you whether it's a girl or boy unless you push."

"*Mo croi*, dark hair," she murmured.

"That's right. Dark hair. Do you want to see?"

She nodded weakly.

"Then push, sweeting, push!" He squeezed her hand until he was afraid he might crush it. She did as she was told, using her last strength to bear down on the baby. And just when Eagan was sure the entire thing was impossible and that they were all doomed, her belly contracted. He grasped the baby by the shoulders. The baby slipped out and released a wail that nearly knocked Eagan onto his backside.

In wonder, he looked down at the life squirming in his hands. The baby was as slippery as a fish, but he held on to it as if he held the world in his hands. Counting every perfect finger and toe, he could hardly believe this tiny bloody creature had the power to make him feel utterly alive and utterly humble.

"What is it? What is it?" Caitlín gasped weakly, trying to ease herself up to see.

He looked down at her, her blond hair hanging in sweat-matted hanks, her clothes unspeakably soiled, her face drawn with fatigue and strain, but the joy in those glittering blue eyes made her the most beautiful woman he'd ever seen.

"It's a girl, Caitlín—sweeting—she's a beautiful girl," he whispered, in awe of the bawling creature he held in his arms, in awe of the woman who had created it.

"A girl?" Caitlín whispered, too weak to prop herself up to see.

He carefully brushed the sticky tendrils of Caitlín's hair out of her eyes so that she could better see her baby. He laid his vest on her belly and placed the baby within it, deciding to leave the cord for the doctor to cut. Caitlín was too weak to hold her, so he sat behind her and pulled her against his chest, wrapping his arms over her arms to cradle the newborn. They lay there for a long while, and Eagan felt the strain catch up to him. But sitting there holding both of them gave him such a deep satisfaction, he would have given his last breath to do it again.

"She's a beautiful *coilín*, isn't she?" Caitlín whispered.

He nodded softly against her blond hair, the babe quieting now that it was secure in its mother's embrace.

Tears cascaded down Caitlín's cheeks. "Aye, she is beautiful."

He looked down at her and gently wiped the tears away. "What shall you name her?"

"I'll be namin' her Siobhan."

Shivhan. It was a lovely name, and he liked it, especially the way Caitlín said it.

"Oh, but she's so wee," she moaned, more tears slipping from her eyes. "And she deserves so much. . . ."

Eagan wanted to comfort her, but he didn't have the chance.

They heard noises from above, and finally Harper's voice greeted them once more. "Everything all right, Mr. Sheridan?"

Eagan smiled blackly. "Sure, sure, Harper. Where the hell have you been? And when are we going to get out of here? When this babe is out of finishing school?"

"I've got a doctor with me, Mr. Sheridan. And Mr. Otis is in the shaft. We're getting it started up now. The doctor will meet you here on four. It'll just be another minute, I promise."

"Promises, promises!" Eagan retorted, and squeezed Caitlín, who smiled.

They looked down at the babe, who had fallen asleep against her mother's breast. Caitlín was just about to stroke her fine, downy head with her finger when the elevator lamp burned out, depleted of kerosene. They both laughed, as if to say "And what else can go wrong?" They laughed in relief that they were being rescued and that Shivhan was now with them, alive and healthy.

They waited in the dark to be rescued, Caitlín holding her babe and Eagan holding Caitlín, knowing for the first time what his life had been missing.

24

It was almost dawn when Whittaker informed Margaret that she was wanted in the master's library. Poor Margaret turned sheet-white at this news. She left the servant's common room inconsolable, believing the master's notoriously mercurial mood had now resulted in her termination.

At the library door she gave a timid knock and nearly jumped from her skin at Sheridan's booming "Come in!" Her hand shaking and sweating, she turned the silver doorknob and crept into the room. The library was in darkness. The green velvet drapes had been drawn, and no matter the light color of the woodwork, the imposing room threw long dark shadows.

"I want to talk with you, Margaret."

The little maid cast her worried gaze respectfully toward him. Sheridan sat near the fire looking rumpled and unkempt, as if he'd not been to bed for several nights. By his side was an empty glass next to an empty decanter. He'd obviously been drinking, but at that moment he seemed stone-cold sober.

"What—what have I done, sar?" she whispered in her lilting accent.

"Sit down." He nodded to a green velvet armchair.

Surprised by his solicitousness, yet terrified by his tone, she numbly took the armchair.

"Margaret, you and Kevin are the only servants Mrs.

Sheridan brought with her when she left Washington Square, isn't that correct?"

"Yes, sar," she answered, her voice trembling.

"Why is that?"

She bit her lip. When she couldn't think of an answer, she blurted, "Is me and Kevin gettin' the boot, sar?"

He appeared surprised. But far from comforting her—after all, he was a man of facts and logic—he only said, "No" and kept her pinned to her seat with that piercing gaze.

"So why did she only bring you and Kevin to my household?" he demanded.

The maid swallowed, her accent becoming more pronounced with her nervousness. "Well, sar, I suppose because she wasn't very trustin' of the other sarvents. Miss Alana's always been one to keep to harself."

"Why is that?"

"Well, I suppose it's because of the fire that killed her family. She's never gotten over it, sar. In fact, well . . ."

"Go on."

"She's rather obsessed with Miss Christabel, sar. I mean, it seems she's gotten over the death of her parents, as best as one can, but her sister, she's always thinkin' of Miss Christabel, and to my mind it ain't healthy. Sometimes I've heard her whisperin' to that picture of her sister as if the girl was standin' right next to her."

"I've never seen that picture," he mused, a disturbed expression on his face.

"Oh, sar, she keeps it with her always, but she's very secret about it. She doesn't like people knowing about Miss Christabel."

"Odd behavior. Mrs. Sheridan has always struck me as being very levelheaded."

Margaret whitened at his words. "I'm not gossipin', sar. It's only because you asked—she is levelheaded—"

Sheridan waved away the rest of her babble, silencing her. He rubbed his unshaven jaw as if he were deep in thought. "She trusts you, Margaret. You know some of her secrets. I have one very important question to ask you before you go, and I want you to tell me the truth. Upon your faith as a Catholic, I want you to tell me the absolute truth, do you swear it?"

"Yes," she whispered, wide-eyed.

"What was your mistress doing the night of Mara's debut?"

"The night of the Sheridan ball?" Margaret looked around the library and tried to remember. "I don't recall her doin' anything out of the ordinary. . . ."

"She was just stayin' at home that night, then?" Sheridan prompted, his face hard, his accent no longer calculated.

She looked at him. "Oh no, sar. She weren't stayin' at home. She were dressin' for the ball." She shook her head. "And I remember it was rainin', and I had to run upstairs with her cloak."

"You mean my wife was going to attend Mara's debut?" Sheridan's voice was as quiet as a prayer.

"Yes, sar. She was dressin', just as she would to go out for any other night. I was helpin' her. . . ." Margaret paused. "Then, acourse, her uncle found out what she was doin' and put a fine stop to that. He locked her in her room, and for hours I could hear her cryin' in there. It broke me heart. It fair broke me heart. And the next day she had a nasty bruise on her cheek. We had a fine time tryin' to hide it."

Sheridan sat back, his face grim, his eyes glittering with some unnamed emotion. "You swear to this, Margaret? You swear you're telling me the truth?"

"May I die tomorrow and never have children!" Margaret vowed.

Sheridan ran his hand through his hair. He looked worse now than when she'd first arrived. He seemed older, somehow. The lines on his face had deepened, almost as if with remorse.

"You may go, Margaret. And I'll take you on your word that you won't speak a word of this to your mistress."

"Yes, sar." Margaret rose and curtsied. She left the library overcome by the sadness of his figure. To her mind Mr. Sheridan looked as if he'd lost everything he'd ever wanted in the world.

As planned, Alana and Mara took the basket phaeton out to Central Park on Thursday. The tulips were already blooming, and they rode by bed upon bed of vibrant, sunlit pinks, yellows, and reds. Purple wisteria climbed the sinuous lines of the gazebos designed from knotted tree branches. In the distance a girl sat by the lake reading a book, her figure as placid as a Rembrandt.

They hadn't seen the duke, but Alana was sure they would meet him. She'd had years of training in society; she knew an unspoken assignation when she heard one.

Mara was quiet today, her concentration too tightly wound around seeing her young duke to spend it in conversation, which suited Alana just fine because her thoughts were centered on her husband.

It was now the second day that Alana hadn't seen Trevor. Yesterday she'd stayed all day in her room, refusing to go out for the smallest errand. It had taken her that long to gather the courage to face him again. But when she'd emerged that morning, Trevor had already gone downtown to see to his stocks.

Or so the servants had informed her. Perhaps he had really gone to see Daisy. That thought had sent her tumbling into despair. But she put her armor into place once more and rode along the park in the open phaeton looking as placid and cool as the lake on this windless day, though deep in her soul, she was bleeding.

She had surrendered to him in an attempt to save her marriage. But still the lies were piled like the stones of a fortress around them, and the tragedy was that out of those lies one truth had emerged to render the final blow: her love for her husband.

Trevor had taken her body without whispers of love,

without even the seduction of false commitment. After they had finished, it was business as usual, his only thought how to chart his way out of the mess their lovemaking had caused. And he'd come up with the perfect end to their crime—another lie, this time for an annulment.

The very idea made her blood run cold, but she knew if he insisted, she would have to accept it. In a fit of anger she'd spoken of divorce, but she didn't think she could go through with it. Trevor was right. Divorce was too ugly. It would harm all of them, even Christal. And what would be the point? Alana would still lose him. She couldn't force Trevor to care for her. One person could not make a marriage. It was both of them, or it was nothing.

She turned to Mara, who anxiously looked around, hoping to see the Duke of Granville riding across the Mall toward Bethesda Fountain. Watching her, Alana's heart grew even heavier. She'd grown to love Mara, and it was painful thinking how expendable she was in Mara's life. Trevor had used her only as a matchmaker for his sister, and it was now obvious he cared nothing about his wife's feelings or her attachments. When her task was completed and Mara well married, he no doubt expected Alana Van Alen to shed her married name like a satin cloak, pack her bags, and never see any of them again.

But she would have to see Mara again. Eagan too. They were the only family she'd known in years. Alana had grown to care for them too much. Trevor might feel she was nothing more than a chain around his neck, something he had to endure to get what he wanted, but she prayed that Eagan and Mara felt differently.

"He didn't show," Mara suddenly announced like a death knell.

"It's still early," Alana comforted, patting Mara's kid-gloved hand with her own.

"No, let's go home. I've waited before. I'll never do it again. . . ." Mara turned away to hide the pain in her eyes.

Alana felt a lump come to her throat. On the verge of

tears herself, she instructed the driver to head back to Fifth
Avenue.

They had barely passed the Terrace when they were bar-
raged with the thunder of hoofbeats. Both women turned
around and found the Duke of Granville and his entourage
closing the gap between them, the duke sporting a brilliant
smile on his face at seeing Mara. "Good day to you, Mrs.
Sheridan!" He reined in his shiny black Thoroughbred and
doffed his top hat to Mara. "And good day to *you*, Miss
Sheridan."

Alana was, appropriately, the first to speak. She exchanged words with the duke like an actor in a well-rehearsed play. "Why, Your Grace, how coincidental that we
should bump into you here at the park."

"Yes, I was thinking the same." He nearly winked.

"Would you like to ride along with us before we return
home?"

"If that wouldn't be presumptuous."

"Of course not." Alana smiled. "But would you ride at
Mara's side? I've developed a crick in my neck and would
much prefer you at my right."

His Grace nodded, an appreciative smile on his lips. He
pulled his steed along Mara's side of the phaeton and gazed
almost hungrily down at her as if he were afraid he might
not see her again.

Mara threw him several shy glances. As always, she
looked like an enchantress of demure innocence, dressed
today in deep blue velvet the exact color of her eyes.

The duke hadn't a prayer.

Alana led them into an innocuous discussion about the
Greensward, and quickly Granville took Mara into a conversation of their own, letting Alana sit back and play chaperone. During the slow trip back to the bustle of the city,
the duke invited them to join him at a soiree in his honor
given by Mrs. Astor, and Alana nearly clapped with glee at
the triumph.

By the time they arrived at the mansion, Mara was infatuated, the duke entranced. And Alana was depressed as she had never been. No matter how thrilled she was at Mara's conquest, there was no denying what that conquest would cost her. Any chance at happiness would die with her annulment. She must accept the agreement her marriage was built upon, but it agonized her to think that the day Mara married was the day she would be sentenced to having her thoughts dwell forever in lonely places. Forever haunted by Trevor Sheridan.

Bríd Óg Ní Máille

Oh, Bridget O'Malley, you left my heart shaken
With a hopeless desolation, I'll have you to know.
It's the wonders of admiration your quiet face has taken,
And your beauty will haunt me wherever I go.

The white moon above the pale sun,
The pale stars above the thorn tree,
Are cold beside my darling, but no purer than she.
I gaze upon the cold moon
'Til the stars drown in the warm sea,
And the bright eyes of my darling are never on me.

25

"Who died and left you all alone to sit at the wake? Don't you know it's a beautiful day?" That same afternoon, Eagan entered the library and shoved back the heavy green draperies. A stream of afternoon sunshine fell on the grim face of his brother, who sat by the hearth.

"What do you want, Eagan?" Trevor growled, squinting in the light.

Eagan cracked a smile. "I came to learn some Gaelic. I found out last night that it definitely can come in handy."

"What are you talking about?"

"You'll never guess what happened last evening in Lord and Taylor. . . ." Eagan recounted the story in a couple of minutes. When he finished, he grinned.

"So where's this girl and her babe now?" Trevor asked, as if, by Eagan's grin, he needed to.

"She's downstairs with the other servants. When she's up and around again, I promised her a job. I knew you wouldn't mind."

"No, I don't mind." Trevor scowled at his empty glass and poured himself a drink. "I do find it particularly ironic that you'd take a girl in trouble under your wing, especially since you're the type who gets them into trouble." He held out a fresh glass. "Drink?"

Eagan declined. "But you should see this baby, Trevor. She's really special. She's beautiful."

"I'm sure she is."

"Come see her, and come meet Caitlín. You can talk to her in her own tongue. That'll comfort her. I know she's frightened, but by God, she's a brave girl."

"I'll go downstairs when I finish my drink."

Eagan paused to examine him. Trevor hadn't shaved in two days, and his wrinkled shirtfront had long since worn away its starch. He couldn't remember seeing his brother so unkempt since the days down at Mott Street. "You look like hell," he commented.

"Do I?" Trevor snapped, gulping his whiskey.

"This has to do with what I did the other night, doesn't it. I promise you, Trevor, Alana and I aren't—"

"It doesn't matter," he growled. "Just get out, Eagan, I'm in no mood for this."

"What's happened?"

Trevor grew silent.

"Tell me."

Trevor swallowed a large burning sip of whiskey and became even more morose.

"I know it has to do with Alana. . . ."

Slowly Trevor said, "You should have never been in her room the other night. You interfered with our marriage, and because of that, the consequences may be grave."

"The way I see it, I saved your marriage."

Trevor looked up. From the look in his eye, if there hadn't been a fraternal bond between the two men, the conversation might have turned violent.

"That's right." Eagan stood his ground. "You finally consummated it, didn't you? And high time you did, too."

Trevor's words were ominously low. "I consummated the marriage because I was pushed to do it by your stupid antics, and now we must lie to get an annulment."

Eagan was shocked into silence.

A muscle bunched in Trevor's jaw, hinting at his agitation. "I never meant for my marriage to last. I never meant to get this—involved. The last thing I ever wanted was a society woman for a wife."

"But you are involved, so why throw your marriage away?"

He released a long, bitter sigh. "What would you do, Eagan, if you'd set out to take revenge on a number of people and in doing so, you'd discovered you'd hurt someone completely innocent? What would you do?"

"I'd apologize . . . I'd make restitution. . . ." His gaze scanned Trevor's morose figure and especially the glassful of whiskey held tight in his hand. ". . . I'd feel guilty."

Trevor closed his eyes as if he felt a pain in his chest. "I've found out—Alana was truly going to come to Mara's ball."

"I knew it." Eagan shook his head. "So what stopped her?"

"It's just as she told me. Her uncle forbid her to go, locked her in her room." He took a deep gulp of whiskey. "All this time I've looked upon my wife as embodying every kind of evil—prejudice, oppression, injustice—and I punished her for that. But in the end it looks like she was the only one defiant enough, brave enough, to lash out at them and attend Mara's debut."

"So now that you know what a wonderful woman she is, why are you insistent about this annulment? Do you think patting her on her head and saying 'Sorry, my mistake' will make everything all right?"

Trevor's voice rose in anger. "What else can I do? Do I betray her again, bind her to my side, force her to stay with a man she loathes?"

"She doesn't loathe you," Eagan answered quietly.

"She's said as much" was his grim answer. "She's told me she wanted a husband better than me."

"But every option that would ease your guilty conscience would in turn break your heart, am I not right?"

Trevor shot him a look that could kill.

Eagan sighed and again shook his head. "For all your

scheming, you've finally caught yourself in a scheme of your own making."

"And I'll disentangle myself yet, never you fear," Trevor retorted.

Eagan smiled blackly. "What strange justice—to fall in love with your wife, the one woman you can never have."

Trevor rose and poured himself another whiskey. A double.

Two hours later, Trevor was still drinking whiskey, still in a foul mood. He'd spoken to Whittaker about sending to Newport for the *Colleen*, thinking a long sail might do him good, but after he gave those orders, he turned moody and closeted himself, this time in the drawing room. There he drank some more and tapped out the tune to "Bridget O'Malley" on the Steinway, as if either might assuage his melancholy.

At precisely four o'clock Whittaker knocked on the drawing room doors and entered carrying a gold salver. Trevor growled, "Leave me alone," but Whittaker ignored him. He walked up to his brooding figure and held out the salver.

Trevor needed only to glance at the card to know whose it was. "Is he here?" he asked Whittaker, anger supplanting his morose mood.

"Yes, sir. I thought you might just want to speak with him this time. He sent Mrs. Sheridan a note." With a white-gloved hand, Whittaker turned over Anson's card. He'd written the words *Meet me*.

Trevor stood up, in control despite his hours of drinking. "Send him in here."

"*Very* good, sir," Whittaker announced.

Whittaker promptly led Anson Stevens into the drawing room, closing the door behind him. Alone with his wife's former beau, Trevor stared him down like a Yank confronting a Reb at Little Round Top.

"Is Alana not at home? Forgive my bluntness, Sheridan,

but I'd come to call on her, not you." Anson tightened his lips, clearly surprised and displeased to see him.

Trevor took a calming sip of his whiskey, but his anger churned like a steam engine. "Stevens, what gives you the right to come calling on my wife as if she were some unwed debutante fresh from her mother's arms?"

Anson smirked. "Welcome to society, Sheridan. I guess New York isn't like Ireland, where a biddy marries a mick, gets saddled with twelve children, and that's the last that's heard from her."

"You're not going to ever have my wife, Stevens."

"Oh?" Anson raised a fine dark-gold eyebrow. "Caroline Astor thinks differently. In fact, I've heard rumors that an annulment is forthcoming."

Sheridan's words were calm. "What makes you think an annulment is possible?"

The hatred in Anson's cold-blue eyes glittered like shattered glass. "Your marriage with Alana has been nothing but a facade. Everyone can see it. Alana has all but admitted it."

Trevor gave him a nasty smile. "In the eyes of God and the law, I am Alana's husband. What is or is not done in our marriage bed concerns us and only us. Take that message back to that witch on Thirty-fourth Street."

In his fury, Anson grasped at any straw. "If an annulment is not possible, there's divorce. . . . I'll see Alana out of this mess no matter what must be done or said."

"And why is she your cause?" Trevor snapped. "Are there no other young misses in the Four Hundred for you to concentrate your well-groomed rutting instincts on?"

Anson's tone was like poison. "Caroline Astor and I consider ourselves missionaries. Alana is a girl of breeding, a rarity that shouldn't be squandered on the likes of you. It's our duty to save her from your dirty Irish money and your dirty Irish hands."

Trevor slammed his drink on the Steinway. "You go back and tell your keeper that Alana Sheridan is a lost cause. I've put my 'dirty Irish hands' on her, and I'm keeping them on her."

"She doesn't love you. She only wants something from you, and when she gets it, I swear she'll leave you. After all, she's a decent girl."

Trevor took that last comment like a blow to the jaw. But he recovered quickly. "Meaning no decent girl would stay married to me?" He paused long enough to let Anson squirm. Then he went for the kill. "Let me tell you something, boy-o. Alana may have her complaints about me. But one place she does not complain is in the bedroom."

Anson's control snapped. He strode over to Trevor, put his full weight behind his fist, and swung. Trevor ducked, adept at brawling from his years on the streets, then sent Anson careening into the Louis XV commode with his fist.

Blood streamed from Anson's nose, and he looked around, dazed. Trevor took this as the cue to send for the footmen. The green-and-black-liveried fellows arrived and discreetly dumped Anson back into his carriage while Trevor gave explicit instructions in Gaelic where to send him.

When the ride in the park was over and the duke had bid his farewell, Alana went to her suite to change for dinner. She had still not seen her husband, and the longer the time they were apart, the more she dreaded that first glance into his eyes. She made it to her rooms without incident. Margaret hadn't arrived yet, and Alana reveled in being alone, the quiet allowing her a few moments to prepare herself for what she knew would be a trying evening.

She threw her kid gloves on the bed, hardly glancing at it, but then the card caught her eye, tossed across her satin coverlet as if in anger. Her hand trembling, she picked up the card and saw that it was Anson's. She turned it over and paled at what was written there. Crossed out were Anson's words *Meet me* and in their stead, in a bold, commanding hand, was written, *Shall I give you the words to Bridget O'Malley?* The card fluttered to the bed.

Trevor had again proved he was jealous, and Alana could have cried with the irony of it. Once she'd believed that a man must love to be jealous, but she'd forgotten that one can also be jealous over a possession. Love need not be involved. The other night had proved it. Trevor might not want her, but until she was no longer his property, he would kill rather than let another have her.

She touched the gold border of the card. Her husband was a crafty sort, but she was beginning to understand his manipulations. He meant something by these words on Anson's card, and no doubt they were his way of hurting her.

"Mrs. Sheridan?"

Alana looked behind her and found Margaret standing there holding a flannel-wrapped bundle, an enormous smile on her face. "Oh, Mrs. Sheridan, I had to show you. Caitlín let me bring the babe up here. Has there ever been sooch a darlin' little girl?"

Alana walked over to the bundle. There, nestled in a pink blanket, was a newborn infant. The baby's features were perfect, her tiny head was dusted with a sprinkling of black hair. "Oh my," Alana whispered, and touched the tiny chin. The child made a face, and both women laughed.

Margaret held her out. "Would you like to hold her, Mrs. Sheridan? We never had a babe to care for, you and me, did we. I wonder if Kevin and me will ever . . . Well, enough of that! Here. Hold the child. I knew you'd love her."

Alana colored with excitement. She could hardly remember the last time she'd held a baby in her arms. When the child was placed there, so warm and soft and fragile, her heart tugged with love and protectiveness. "When did she arrive? I don't remember any of the servants expecting," she said.

"Mr. Eagan found the lass. The mother, Caitlín

O'Roarke, was stuck in a lift with him. Mr. Eagan delivered her."

"I don't believe it!"

"Oh, it's true, Mrs. Sheridan. And Mr. Eagan, he's in love with the child, don't you know. He can't do enough for her—or her mother. Brought her here and gave her a job, he did—that is, when she's feelin' up to it."

"I always knew Eagan was a good soul. I could see it in his eyes. He's got such warm, caring eyes."

"Yes, Mrs. Sheridan." Margaret stroked the baby's dark downy head. "Well, I'd best bring the child back below-stairs. . . ."

"Let me come with you. I'd love to meet her mother. And I want to hold her for a little while longer." Alana smiled at the baby. "What's her name?"

"Siobhan," Margaret whispered.

"What a beautiful name. Well, little Shivhan, let's take you back to your mama." Margaret held the servant's door, and they took the steep steps to the lower quarters.

Through a maze of passages and servants' rooms, they arrived at the mother's bedroom to hear an intense voice coming from it. "In a few days, after you're stronger, you can be up and around. Until then, when the doctor has given you permission, you will stay here."

Alana and Margaret entered the room just as Eagan picked up a young woman in a white cotton nightgown and placed her gently back in bed.

"But I should be workin'," the girl said, her face pale from her ordeal of giving birth, her eyes wary of her sur-roundings, obviously suspicious of her good fortune.

"No, Eagan's right," Alana broke in. "You can't even think about working now when you've this dear child to care for." She smiled down at the bundle in her arms. Shivhan was fast asleep.

Caitlín looked at Alana in awe. By her dress, Alana was clearly the lady of the house. Caitlín couldn't seem to be-lieve she would bother with the likes of her.

Eagan made the introductions and said, "That's telling her, Alana. The baggage won't stay in her bed." He looked down at Caitlín, Caitlín chanced a glance back at him, and suddenly Alana was struck by the intangible bond between them. If she didn't know better, she'd think Eagan was rather taken with this girl he'd saved from a life of shame on the streets. And she'd think that shy, smiling glance Caitlín gave Eagan was filled with hero worship. Maybe something more.

Eagan nodded to Alana. "I must say, Mrs. Sheridan, you look good with a babe in your arms. Trevor should take note."

Alana paled and blushed at the same time—if that was possible. Eagan's comment frightened her and compelled her. The possibility of a child was beyond the realm of her and Trevor's relationship, and yet, because of the other night, it was more of a possibility than she cared to think about.

The baby saved her from having to comment. Shivhan startled, awoke with a cry, and Alana's attention turned to her. She rocked the newborn in her arms. "I think it's din- nertime," she said softly.

Caitlín offered to take the infant, but before Alana could hand Shivhan to her, a voice sounded from the doorway saying something in Gaelic. Trevor stood there, sporting a new walking stick, an Irish blackthorn. He'd just bathed. His hair was still wet, slicked back as if with Macassar oil. His jaw was freshly shaven, his vest a brilliant scarlet, his paper collar crisp, white, and new.

Again he said something to Caitlín in Gaelic. It made the girl nervous, and she turned her eyes warily to Eagan. Trevor laughed.

"Must you frighten her? She's just had a baby." Alana didn't know where she'd found the courage to say that, especially after Trevor's gaze captured hers, his eyes re- counting all the passion, guilt, and fury that they'd spent on each other two nights ago. He lowered his gaze to take in

the picture of her holding the baby. Approval crossed hi
face, then worry, then anger, in that order.

"I only asked the girl if she were some kind of Celti
princess. I expect so, since she's holding court here in he
room."

Alana could tell he'd been drinking. He didn't loo
drunk, but there was something in his eyes, an unnatura
gleam. The baby wailed, sensing the tension. Alana rocke
her. She stepped to the mother and said, "It must be sup
pertime. Margaret, will you stay here and see if Caitlí
needs anything? I'll take away the men, so she may fee
Shivhan."

"Yes, Mrs. Sheridan."

"Gentlemen," she said woodenly, "will you follow m
upstairs?"

Trevor didn't say a word, so Eagan spoke up. "I've go
business downtown." He looked at Trevor. "She's all yours
Brother o' mine." With a salute and a fond look at Caitlír
Eagan left the tiny servant's room.

Caitlín struggled with Shivhan, waiting for privacy be
fore baring her breast. Alana angered at Trevor's lingering
She gave him a lethal stare, then left the room.

"Wait." He caught up with her in the corridor. He too
hold of her arm just as a maidservant curtsied and scurrie
by, clearly unnerved at finding the master in the help'
quarters.

"What!" she hissed, snatching back her arm.

"We have to talk."

"You're drunk. And isn't this a little tardy? What's ther
to discuss?" She laughed bitterly, unable to civilize he
pain. "Oh yes, I suppose it's time to orchestrate our Gran
Lie for our annulment now that Mara's taken with th
duke."

"Mara's seen Granville again?"

"What a coincidence. We saw him in the park. Imagine."

His gold-green eyes lit with anger. "Fine. Let Mara se
him. As I said, I've my own ways of handling him."

"As usual, you've got everything under control. So if you'll excuse me—"

"No." His hand tightened on her arm; his voice turned soft. "We've got to talk."

She pulled at the manacle of his fingers. "I know this will come as a great shock to you, Mr. Sheridan, but I don't want to talk to you."

"Well, you must talk to me. And where will it be—here in the servant's passage or upstairs in the privacy of the drawing room?"

"You've obviously been drinking. I don't have conversations with drunk men. There's nothing to discuss."

He pulled her closer. She smelled the liquor on his breath, but her desire for him struck her like an arrow, his smell of whiskey and soap seducing her.

"You say there's nothing to discuss, but you're wrong," he rasped, obviously trying to be more rational than his drunken state would allow him to be. "Let's just begin with your physical condition. . . ."

She stiffened, her cheeks flaming with anger and embarrassment.

He added, "The symbolism of little Siobhan in your arms hasn't escaped me. Are you ready perhaps to be holding your own in nine months?"

His words cut her. He made a mockery of their relationship and their lovemaking. To him, the possibility of their having a child seemed like nothing but an inconvenience. She let loose her fury. "Oh, and that would destroy your plans, wouldn't it." He tried to interrupt, but he couldn't break through her indignation. She continued. "I can just see you, saddled with a Knickerbocker child. How revolting! No wonder you're panicking. Do you want me to pay a visit to Madame Restell?"

"I'd kill you if you visited that woman."

She didn't doubt he meant it. Suddenly she was filled with so much irrational anger that all she wanted to do was beat him until she dropped with exhaustion. He was the

cause of all her problems, and that he dared instruct her on
anything but how to help Mara was more than she could
endure. She tried to pull away again to avoid a scene, but he
wouldn't let go. She pulled again and again until her anger
overflowed.

Out of control, she slapped him hard across the cheek—
once, twice, three times—while he just stared down at her,
hard and dispassionate. "Are you done?" he asked rigidly
when she began to cry.

"I hate you," she whispered through her tears, now not
caring if the whole world saw her. "I can't wait for that
annulment."

"That annulment may not be possible."

"Why?" she lashed out, crazy from anger and her soul-
wrenching hurt. She wanted to love this man, but everything he did drove her to despise him. He toyed with her
like a cat with a mouse. The rules changed constantly until
she could no longer endure the emotional upheaval.

"The babe that was in your arms should tell you why."

"I won't be having *your* baby."

He chuckled blackly. "Oh? And how do you know that?
Does that pristine womb of yours reject the idea of spawn-
ing a child by the likes of me? Well, more's the pity, because you may have no choice." He jerked her against him.
"And don't get any ideas in that sophisticated society head
of yours. I'll know if you're pregnant even if I must monitor
your laundry and interview your maid daily."

"You crude man."

"That's right. I am a crude man. A pagan in this civilized
world of yours. Don't you ever forget it."

"How can I?" she retorted, hysterically wrenching her
arm from his hold. "You remind me of it at every turn. No
wonder you can't buy acceptance. I don't care how much
money you have—nothing could sweeten your kind of hy-
pocrisy and prejudice. You've mastered those two things all
too well. But then, why should that surprise anyone, since
you're a victim of them yourself!"

"I'm no victim," he growled.

"Oh?" she said, staring boldly into his eyes. "I think that's exactly what you are. You're a victim of society, Trevor Sheridan, so you think that gives you some divine right to hurt anyone in your path. But what you're really a victim of is your own twisted thinking, and because of that, you'll be a victim forever."

He looked as if he wanted to raise his brand-new walking stick and hit her with it. Instead, he shoved her away. "No one could take such a woman as you. You're just like a diamond, Alana, beautiful but cold. More's the pity you don't like diamonds, because they do become you all too well." He shook his head in disgust and looked at her. "This marriage is a curse and has been from the beginning."

"Yes, it's a curse, and I can't wait to escape it!" she cried.

"Then don't cross my path again," he said ominously. "If you play temptress as you did the other night, I'll see you back in my bed, and if we escape this time without a babe, you may bank on the fact that next time you'll not be so lucky."

"Even if I have your baby, I'll leave you! And being Catholic, you've more to fear from a divorce than I!" She stared at him, the ghost of a triumphal smile on her lips.

He crossed his arms and accepted her challenge. "You don't understand, á mhúirnín. There's no way to divorce me. Our marriage vows are binding till death do us part. No matter if you run, you'll still be my wife. And unless there's an annulment, you'll remain my wife until you breathe your last breath and are cold in the grave."

She stared at him, shocked by the enormity of his words. If she was pregnant and there could be no annulment, she could move from Trevor Sheridan's household, but she would never be free to marry, to have any children but his, to be with any man but him. And how could she have his children, how could she endure his intimate caress, when he looked at her with only anger and hatred?

Deathly pale, she turned and walked away, trying desperately to absorb this latest soul-wrenching news. It was ironic, but the symbolism of her dream had finally come true. She knew who her shadow man was. But instead of saving her, Trevor Sheridan was the last thing she saw before she drowned in the sea of his wealth.

26

"I—I can't stay too long. . . ."

"I don't care. I just wanted to see you. You were an angel to meet me. Can we walk together?"

Mara Sheridan looked behind her to her groom and driver, perched on her phaeton. "I can't go very far."

"That's all right. We'll stroll across the Mall and back. Will they approve?" The duke shot a glance to her carriage.

"We can do that. I've got an hour."

The duke held out his arm. "Then let's be off, shall we?"

Mara paused, then hesitantly accepted the duke's arm. They walked for several minutes, chatting about all things New York: Delmonico's, the Academy of Music, Wallack's Theater. They had just finished a discussion about how brilliant the actor Edwin Booth was and still treasured despite his brother's hideous crime when Mara fell silent, a worried look creeping into her eyes whenever she glanced at him.

"What is it that has you so quiet? Have I the pox?" Granville chuckled.

Mara shook her head. The pox he didn't have, no indeed. The Duke of Granville was a sternly handsome young man with fine English features, cropped blond hair that turned a pale shade of red in the sun, and laughing blue eyes, the color of which she'd seen only once when Trevor had taken her on the *Colleen* down to Montserrat. She'd never forget the Caribbean Sea. She saw it every time she looked in Granville's eyes.

"Why are you so quiet, Mary?"

She looked away, not even noticing he'd used the anglicized version of her name.

"Are you angry at me?"

"No, no," she blurted out, shocked that he might think such a thing.

"Then what?"

"It's just that—that—well, I'm just not sure why you're paying me attention." There, she'd said it. She could hardly look him in the eyes now.

He put his head back and laughed. "And why do you think that's so strange? Is it you think I'm too old for you, Mary? Well, I'm only twenty-two. Does that ease your mind?"

"It's not that," she said hastily, "although Trevor thought you were twenty-four, and this should ease his mind. He almost turned blue when Alana introduced us. He doesn't approve of you, you know."

Granville let out a boisterous laugh. "You asked me why a chap like me would want to court you. Well, it's comments like that, Mara, that never cease to be entertaining. You American girls—you say just what's on your mind."

"Not everything that's on my mind. . . ." Mara again turned quiet.

"Then what is it?" His laughing eyes turned somber.

She faced straight ahead, her face a mask of stone. "Have you heard from anyone about my debut?"

"Yes."

She searched his face for something that would betray him. Finally she said, "What did you hear?"

"That these colonials you New Yorkers call the Four Hundred did not attend." He brushed away a dark lock of her hair that had blown onto her cheek. "And I heard it was because you're Irish."

"And you're British. Trevor says we should hate the British because they hate the Irish even more than the Four Hundred do."

Granville's smile was at once mirthful and bitter. "Don't let anyone tell you to hate, Mara. That's always a bad practice. And as for me, I don't hate the Irish. My grandmother was Irish. Old Granville was one of the Ascendency from County Clare, and he stole my grandmother right out of the kitchens of his estate. They were married for fifty years and had ten children and thirty grandchildren. Do you hate me?"

Mara closed her gaping mouth. "No. I was just afraid that you might . . ."

"Hurt you?"

She nodded.

He touched her cheek again, this time not bothering with the pretense of brushing away a curl. "You know, we Granvilles are a strange set. Every one of us dukes married his wife within weeks of meeting her. Old Granville was the worst. One week his wife was a scullery, the next a duchess. Some say he was so dazzled by her, he proposed the day he met her, but she refused, believing him either mad or drunk."

"And was he?"

"I don't know. Do you think I'm mad or drunk?"

She shook her head and looked into those incredibly vivid blue eyes.

"Good," he whispered. When he was assured no one was looking, he kissed her lightly on the lips. "When shall we wed?"

She blushed. "Well, maybe you *are* just a wee bit mad."

He smiled. "I've got another four weeks. I'm warning you, I know how old Granville felt when he saw the duchess in the scullery. And I believe a long slow sail back to England would make the perfect honeymoon."

Mara just looked at him.

* * *

Alana sipped her champagne and watched the waltzers spin around the ballroom of the Fifth Avenue Hotel, the women in the arms of their black-clad partners turning like gaily painted tops. Mara floated by, led by Granville, her face serene and happy. Alana was glad. She hadn't been sure of the duke—Nigel, as he now insisted the family call him. She had just wanted the social coup of introducing Mara to him. Now she could see on his face how Mara entranced him, and Alana believed with all her heart that it was real.

She glanced at Trevor, who stood next to her, a pain searing through her heart when she had the fleeting wish that her husband might one day look at her that way. But wishing for things like that was futile. Even now his face was set with a grim expression as his eyes followed the dancers on the parquet floor.

"They make a lovely couple, don't they?" she said, trying to get him to talk to her. They hadn't spoken since that time in the servant's corridor, and for some strange reason she missed his biting comments. Even that was better than his cold, brittle silence.

He looked at her, his eyes trailing down to the necklace she wore. She'd been so angry after their last encounter that when she dressed for the cotillion tonight, she'd stumbled upon the diamond necklace he'd given her so long ago. She saw it, and his words burned into her memory. *No one could take such a woman as you. You're just like a diamond, Alana, beautiful but cold. More's the pity you don't like diamonds, because they'd become you all too well.* Vengefully, she pulled the gaudy thing out of the drawer and clasped it to her neck. If he thought her a cold woman, she'd take great pleasure in proving it.

But now the necklace stood between them like a wall of cannon. He knew exactly why she'd worn it. She'd seen it in his eyes as she descended the staircase that evening. His frigid disparaging glance took note of how she despised his gift and how she was using it to mock him. They hadn't had a cordial moment since then.

Alana regretted it. They were forced to be in each other's company, and it was bitterly uncomfortable not to have a pleasant word with the man she'd slept with. "They make a lovely couple, don't you think?" she repeated.

"Who?" he asked, surprising her.

"Why, Mara and Nigel, of course." She looked at him, confusion crossing her face. He hadn't taken his attention from the ballroom floor since they'd arrived. If he wasn't thinking about Mara in the arms of that Englishman, then what?

"You haven't danced all night. Why is that? Is Stevens the only man here who is willing to waltz with you?" he asked, his comment seeming to come out of the blue.

"What?" she exclaimed, taken aback.

"What's wrong with these gentlemen? Everyone knows you love to dance. Why hasn't someone asked you?"

"Trevor, what are you talking about?" She looked at him as if he'd gone mad.

But he hadn't gone mad. What he'd been saying suddenly became all too clear to her when his gaze moved to his blackthorn. Angered, he abruptly excused himself and went to the bar for another brandy.

She watched him go, his stiff artificially formal gait tearing into her soul. He rarely showed his insecurity about his wounded hip. Though she didn't know why it irritated him so much tonight, when he took his drink from the bar and walked into an adjoining room to brood, she was compelled to go to him.

She found him in the reading room, a lone figure standing by the open windows on Fourteenth Street. There were few others in the room—an old fellow snoring in a leather chair, a busboy clearing away some used glassware. She walked up to him, unsure of what to say. "Dinner will be served soon. I'll need an escort," she said quietly.

"Stevens won't do it?" He eyed her, his face taut with distrust.

"Do you want me to be escorted by Anson?" Her voice grew husky.

He was about to answer her when a loud group of young men burst into the room. They went right to the bar, laughing raucously and ordering brandies from the bartender.

". . . so the Irisher says, 'Brace yourself!' " The man who delivered the punchline slapped a friend on the back, and they all burst into renewed laughter.

"Oh no—I've got one better than that!" one man cried. The others chanted for him to speak.

"Well, the biddy runs to her mother and says, 'Moother! I'm pregnant!' "

The men waited, their faces alive with anticipation.

The man chuckled. "And then the biddy's mother says, 'But, Bridie, are ya sure it's yourn?' "

Howls of laughter echoed through the room. The men slapped each other on the back as if they'd just won an election. Alana stood perfectly still, barely able to look at Trevor's face. He had been in a foul mood when he came into the room. Now his face was cast in stone, hiding what had to be an awesome rage.

"Fairchild, me boy-o, how's t'at steel mill of yours runnin' these days? I understand the stock's doin' well!" Trevor called out in his thickest brogue.

The men turned around, and one by one the color drained from their faces.

"Sheridan." The man who'd delivered the joke stepped foward. He said almost sheepishly, "We didn't know you were in here."

"T'at was a funny joke you just told. But we've a lady present here. I t'ink you owe me wife an apology."

Fairchild's gaze shot to Alana. It was obvious he was more afraid of having offended her husband than her, but he nodded and said, "Forgive me, Mrs. Sheridan. I didn't see you here. I shouldn't have told such a vulgar joke in front of you."

Alana didn't answer him. Her eyes turned to her husband.

"Very good, me man. You're excused." Sheridan scanned them all, clearly taking note of all their names. The men left like whipped hounds, tails between their legs, mentally counting the precious funds in their bank accounts and wondering when Sheridan would drain them away.

After they'd gone, silence rained like hail. Summoning her courage, Alana touched his arm. "Trevor?" she whispered, aching for him to speak to her. "They didn't mean it. They were just stupid young men having a good time. Don't waste another minute thinking about them."

He nodded, still not looking at her. His voice was tight with fury. "I didn't want any of this, you know. It's Mara and Eagan I've fought for. I've never had any desire to socialize with people like you."

"I know that," she answered, hurt by his "people like you," yet understanding it.

"Sometimes I've hidden what I'm most proud of because I didn't want my background to hurt them."

His insecurity moved her, blossoming almost to tenderness. "You mean your brogue? You're not using it now, you know. You only use it when you're angry . . . or when you forget." She thought of the time in bed when he had forgotten. He'd slipped into his brogue and proved he couldn't be the iron-willed creature he wanted to be all the time. For one aching moment, his emotion had run high, and he'd been forced to let down his guard. And she had reveled in the power it had given her.

He heaved a sigh and ran his hand through that dark hair she secretly longed to touch again. "I shouldn't have spoken like that to them. Now they've seen I'm no better than their servants. That won't help anybody."

"You're an Irishman. Why must you speak like someone else? You should speak like yourself."

"Mara and Eagan are Americans. They speak like Americans. I'll be damned if my brogue will hold them back."

Her voice fell to a whisper. It was foolish to say what was on her mind. She knew better than anyone else that her husband was like a wild cat, purring one minute, poised for attack the next. But in the end she relented to his stark handsome profile and her heart. "I—*like* your brogue, Trevor. I wish—I wish you'd use it, even if just to speak to me."

His surprised questioning gaze met hers and held it. But she could see the distrust there, hewn from so many years of fighting poverty and injustice. "So you can feel yourself superior? As they did?"

"No." She wanted desperately to wipe away his suspicion, wanted him once and for all to see she didn't care how anyone else judged him, indeed had never cared. He broke her heart at times, but still she saw things in him, noble things that were worth defending. He'd proven his nobility in his treatment of Mara, and for that alone he was more than worthy of the Four Hundred. Her only despair was that in his eyes she would never be worthy of him.

"Go on to dinner," he said. "I'm sure after that scene you'd prefer to be on someone else's arm for a change." He turned back to the windows, his gaze amazingly steady and unfeeling.

"Take me to dinner," she whispered, determined to show him that she didn't judge him by what others thought. They might get their annulment, their marriage might be doomed, but it would never be because he was Irish. "Give me your arm and escort me there. Please."

Slowly he turned to stare at her. His gaze was filled with uncertainty and distrust. Hesitating, he held out his arm. She took it, her grasp tight and trembling.

"I don't think I'll ever understand you," he murmured almost to himself, still looking down at her as they proceeded to the ballroom. "You've done so many things I don't understand."

She smiled, near tears, nodding to a matron or two in passing and holding proudly to her husband's arm. It was difficult to speak the truth. "You don't want to understand, Trevor. That's the source of all your troubles."

He didn't answer, and the rest of the evening he drank heavily. More than once she caught those unsual green-gold-brown eyes brooding upon her, but every time, just as her gaze caught his and she searched for a current of under-standing, he would shutter his eyes and like the cold Irish-man he was, he would look away.

27

Mrs. Astor's soiree was becoming the social event of the century. In three weeks her ballroom was to be transformed into a miniature version of Versailles. The matron was going, appropriately enough, as Marie Antoinette, and Backhouse had even bought her a suite of jewels that had once belonged to the notorious Queen of France.

But Alana hardly cared to attend. If she did go, it would be to hear the duke say his farewells and to read the stunned expressions on the faces of Four Hundred when he announced his engagement to their outcast Mara Sheridan.

That he was going to propose was almost a certainty. A week had gone by and the duke had been at Mara's side at every opportunity. Alana did her best to chaperone them around the city, but she suspected Mara was meeting Granville during her buggy rides, and she had no doubt both were as smitten as Eagan and his fallen angel.

Eagan had shocked everyone with the Irish girl. Though neither he nor Caitlín would admit a fondness for each other beyond the realm of employer and employee, it was obvious to those watching them. Caitlín was not working in the household yet, but had been given every kind of luxury. Shivhan had a bassinet with pink satin bows, a layette of fine Irish linen sewn by the nuns at St. Brendan's, and most absurd of all, a nanny that Eagan demanded when he rationalized that Caitlín was too weak after her ordeal to care for her babe.

But that was untrue. Caitlín was as strong as a horse and almost needed to be strapped into her bed to be kept from beginning her duties. She was obviously desperate to repay this man who had saved her and her baby, and clearly embarrassed by his gifts and attention. Alana even suspected she was frightened by him. Caitlín, for all her worship of Eagan, didn't quite trust him. And the more doubts she displayed, the more Eagan showered her with gifts to dispel them, only creating more doubts.

Alana tightened her lips. She didn't know how the budding relationship between Eagan and Caitlín was going to turn out. Eagan could go back to his strumpets at any time, but somehow she couldn't see him doing that. Shivhan's birth had affected him. He looked at women in an entirely different light after that experience in the elevator. He'd seen their victimization up close and he'd seen their strength. Now he looked at Caitlín with a reverence in his eyes that Alana had never seen him display with any other woman.

"Your carriage is ready, Mrs. Sheridan," Whittaker announced, breaking into her thoughts when he stepped into the drawing room.

Alana stood, already dressed in her dark blue traveling suit, the one she always wore to go to Brooklyn. She'd been so engrossed in Eagan and Mara's problems that she'd forgotten her own. "Thank you, Whittaker," she said, and as an afterthought, though she doubted anyone would notice, especially the master of the house, who had virtually ignored her since they returned from the cotillion, she added, "If anyone should ask, I'll be back for supper."

"Very good, madam." Whittaker held the door and watched her walk across the marble foyer past the cast-iron statuette of Cupid ready to shoot the first arrow. The elderly butler saw her to the carriage, then went back into the house. His aged feet carried him across the same marble foyer, past Cupid, and paused at the open entrance to the library.

"She's in the blue traveling outfit, sir, surely off to Brooklyn. I've taken the liberty of readying your carriage."

With a grim set to his face, Trevor picked up his black-thorn and departed for Brooklyn.

"She's not doing well, Mrs. Sheridan. I urge you to re-turn to Manhattan. We'll send a note when she is more amenable to company." Nurse Steine tightened those thin lips and peered down her nose at Alana.

"What's happened?" Alana asked, clutching her small beaded purse in fear.

"She's deluded herself into thinking she's remembered the night your parents were killed. She's had to be sedated. We've given her morphine. Now is not the time for a visit."

"I must see her! She needs me now," Alana cried, beside herself that Christabel was going through such hell. "Where is she?"

"Mrs. Sheridan, I urge you to calm down and recon-sider," the nurse commanded.

Alana began to cry. With tears streaming down her cheeks, she said, "Does she believe she killed them, then? Is that why you don't want me to see her?"

"It's worse than that. She's delusional. If you go in there, she'll probably accuse *you* of killing them. Now I strongly suggest you return to your carriage and spare both her and you a dreadful experience."

"No," Alana stated flatly. "I want to see her. She needs me."

"We'll have to have the physician's approval. And he's not here right now. It may take all day for him to return." Nurse Steine's lips disappeared altogether.

"Then I'll wait." Alana removed a linen handkerchief from her sleeve and dabbed her eyes. Her chin took a defi-ant set.

Nurse Steine looked at her, her lips pursed in disapproval. "Very well—"

A scream cut off the rest of her words. Startled, Alana looked down the corridor. A transom was open over a closed door, and she could hear a woman struggling with two attendants. "That's my sister," Alana snapped. "The doctor be damned, I'm going in there!"

"You cannot!" Nurse Steine shouted as Alana ran to the room and threw open the door.

What she saw nearly destroyed her. Christal was a ghost of her former self, rail-thin and wild-eyed. She fought to rise from her bed as two blue-and-white-gowned female attendants held her down. Next to her on the night table morphine salts and a used syringe revealed that she had just been drugged.

The morphine was already taking effect. Christal's will to fight soon gave way to apathy. The attendants were able to tighten the bed straps to her arms and legs. Finally Christal just lay there, a dull, glazed sheen on eyes that had once sparkled with life and happiness.

"Oh God!" Alana choked out, going to her. She touched Christal's matted blond hair and wept.

"You see, this isn't helping her," said Nurse Steine.

"Why is this necessary?" Alana grew furious. "She's never needed treatment like this before."

"We warned you this was coming, should she ever remember."

"But she didn't remember. You said she was delusional."

Nurse Steine faltered, but she quickly composed herself. "Yes, but she believes what she remembers is true, and because of that, there's no rationalizing with her. To her, everything she thinks is as real as you or I."

"What does she remember?"

"I've already told you, it's nonsensical. She accuses everyone."

Alana had the distinct impression Nurse Steine was lying, but she believed it was because the woman was trying to justify her sister's treatment. "I want her out of this institution immediately. In fact, pack her things. I'm taking her today."

"You cannot do that, Mrs. Sheridan. The superintendent of police allowed her to be put in here. Only he can withdraw her to another institution."

"I will get his permission. Until then, prepare her to come with me."

Nurse Steine turned cold and hard, and to Alana's shock, she looked at Alana as if she hated her. "When you have a signed letter from the superintendent of police that Christabel Van Alen is to be released into your custody, she will go with you. Until then, I've a duty to your uncle and the people of New York to see that she is here where she was intended to be."

"But you've a greater duty to be humane! Can't you see?" She began to cry again. "Christal's only sixteen! She *can't* be treated like this!"

"She's a danger to herself and to others." Nurse Steine pierced her with her icy gaze. "So I suggest you leave now, Mrs. Sheridan. And until you have that letter in hand, I pray you will have the sense not to return."

Alana stared at the woman as tears streamed down her cheeks. Christabel, now peaceful, moved only her lips in silent protest. Swamped with impotent rage and frustration, Alana ached to free her, but when she looked back at Nurse Steine, she knew the only way to save her sister would be to get the letter—an impossible task.

"Good day, Mrs. Sheridan," the nurse prompted, showing her the door.

Furious, Alana kissed Christabel on the cheek and ran from the room, her hysteria building to a fever pitch. She thought the cool air would calm her down, allow her to think, and she burst out the main door, gasping for breath between sobs. If her last day on earth had to be spent petitioning the superintendent to allow her custody of her sister, she would do just that. But in the meantime the idea of

Christabel enduring this treatment was enough to drive her mad. All these years Park View Asylum, the most modern and expensive sanitarium in New York, had pretended to offer her sister humane care, but now when Christal was most fragile and vulnerable, they did nothing but tie her and silence her, a throwback to the Dark Ages.

Feeling betrayed, Alana burned for retribution. But when she looked at the drive for her carriage, the threadbare strings that held her senses together suddenly snapped. For there, not five yards away, stood her husband, arms crossed over his massive chest, leaning indolently against his black-lacquered landau, the only clue to his emotions a rather grim twist to his lips as he met her gaze.

She'd been betrayed twice.

Nothing moved for an entire second. Even the birds ceased their twittering in the elms that lined the drive.

"I asked an attendant. She told me that there is a patient here named Christabel Van Alen." His voice became as gentle as a whisper. "She's your sister, isn't she?"

Alana stared at him, despising everything about him at that moment—his handsome Irish face, his blackthorn walking stick, his vulgar foreign mannerisms. "You lied to me. You promised never to follow me here. You're a liar. Liar!" she rasped, pelting him again and again with that word.

He walked to her, his expression hard, as if he'd expected her rantings.

She wanted to beat him away. All her defenses were shattered, all her secrets revealed. She didn't know how she would make things right again, or how she would protect herself and her sister now that Trevor Sheridan knew every vulnerability. She said venomously, "You're despicable. We had a bargain. You promised never to follow me. You promised—"

"Alana!" He harshly cut her off. "I had to know. I couldn't let you trot off another day without knowing. It was something I had to do."

"You're a liar," she repeated as if the word could wound him.

His features hardened to stone. "Yes, I lied. But I couldn't stop myself from coming here."

"What are you going to do with this information now that you have it? How are you going to hurt me with it?"

"I didn't come here to hurt you."

Panic swelled in her. "Don't hurt my sister," she said quietly. "Don't hurt Christal. I'll do anything to protect her—I'll give you anything to protect her—you can have—*anything*—just don't hurt her!" Her thin emotional armor clattered to the paving stones. All the horrible ideas of what he could do now to her played through her mind. Her life was falling apart. Everything seemed beyond her ability to repair. She buried her face in her hands and began to weep again.

She barely felt his hesitant touch. As her crying continued, he took her into his arms, his cane against her back as he held her. But she was hardly aware of any of this. The agony of Christabel's situation overwhelmed her, and defeat loomed like an insurmountable fortress on all sides. There weren't tears enough for her sorrow, frustration, and hopelessness, and for one moment she was forced to succumb to her pain so that she might find the strength to continue.

Minutes ticked by, and her tears abated. Reality came back to her in small doses until she realized he was holding her, his walking stick pressed uncomfortably into her spine, his hand stiffly stroking her shoulder. For a moment his arms seemed so strong and so safe, she almost believed he wanted to help her, but her sanity returned. She knew that his embrace could lie.

"I didn't come here to hurt your sister," he whispered. "I want to help if I can."

She started to cry again, and unwilling to let him see her fall apart again, she turned away.

But as before, he proved quick and agile. He took hold of

her, pulling her to him by the waist. "Tell me how to help her," he whispered.

Sobbing, she didn't answer right away. Finally she surrendered. "She's ill. They're mistreating her. I've got to get her out of there . . . they'll kill her, kill her. . . ." She broke down in sobs again, and before she could stop him, he pulled her against his chest, letting her tears fall unchecked onto his silk paisley vest.

"Who do you need to see to get her out?" he prodded gently while she cried.

"Th-the superintendent of police." She wept.

"All right. I'll get her out. I can get her out."

"H-how?" Breathless, she looked up at him in shock and expectation.

He almost smiled. "Think about it, *á mhúirnín.* There are more Irishmen than Knickerbockers among the police."

She stared up at him. "That's true," she said slowly.

"Then let me take care of your sister. I'll even enjoy it." He gave her a bitter smile. "This may be the only area where I have more influence than you."

"You're really willing to help us?" she whispered, clinging to this salvation but afraid he might snatch it away at any moment. He nodded, so she asked, "But why?"

"Because I like it when you need me."

Her gaze riveted to his, and a strange charge of excitement went down her spine. In his own austere way he might have just told her that he was beginning to feel something for her. Then too, his words hinted at something darker, revealing the side of him that she'd seen too much of, the side that must dominate and win at all costs.

"I do need you," she whispered, conceding anything to get her sister out of the hell that surrounded her, and ironically confessing what was deepest in her heart.

"Good," he answered simply, a mysterious satisfaction gleaming in those dark Celtic eyes.

*   *   *

When the Sheridan carriage departed, Nurse Steine stepped away from the window where she'd been watching them. She went to her desk and quickly penned a note, addressing it to Mr. Baldwin Didier, Hotel Athena, Troy, New York.

"Take this and see that it goes first-class," she told a male orderly who was just passing her office.

The orderly nodded and glanced at the letter.

"How is she?" the nurse asked.

"Sleeping," the orderly answered.

"Go, then. Waste no time. Mr. Didier was adamant that he be contacted immediately should anything like this happen."

"Yes, ma'am." The orderly shrugged out of his white jacket and into his black serge one. Nurse Steine watched him go. Then she looked in on Christabel.

The girl's lips were still moving, proof of her strength even under the influence of the morphine. Dispassionately Nurse Steine watched on while Christabel gave a muffled cry and writhed in frustration at the ties that held her down.

With nothing left to do for her patient, the nurse turned to go. Walking away, she didn't hear her patient moan, "I saw you . . . I saw you . . . don't . . . Don't! Oh please, I beg of you, *don't, Uncle Baldwin!*"

28

When they arrived back at the chateau, Alana was drained. Trevor had set off immediately for the superintendent's office, so she went to her suite to rest and sort out her overwhelming emotions. Christal's dangerous situation weighed on her mind, but so did Trevor's words. Alana knew her husband well enough to realize he would extract some kind of payment for his good deed, and the tune to "Bridget O'Malley" kept playing in her head, its indecipherable words a warning and an invitation.

After a brief restless nap she rose and went to the bell pull to summon Margaret. She undressed with the maid's help and was just about to order a bath when she changed her mind. Abruptly excusing Margaret, Alana wrapped herself in a pink satin dressing gown and went to the adjoining bathing room.

She had never used the room before, though it connected to her bedroom and was meant for the lady of the house to share with her husband. She had heard Trevor going through his daily ablutions in it, but she had always had a bath sent to her dressing room as she had done in Washington Square. After all, she was a Knickerbocker, schooled to turn up her nose at modern luxuries like indoor plumbing. But today she was willing to lower her standards. The temptation of all that hot water showering down on her sore, stiff muscles was more than she could resist. With

Trevor gone, she saw no reason not to relax. She would need to rejuvenate for the Van Dam soiree that night and to face whatever news Trevor brought from the police.

The rainbath, as it was called, stood in the middle of a large marble room. Billowing curtains of oiled linen surrounded the perimeter of the marble tub to keep the water inside when it sprinkled down from the box on the ceiling. Operation was as simple as turning the gold-plated handles and adding cold water to adjust the temperature.

She dropped her satin robe, unplaited her hair, and stepped into the tub. Soon her only fear was that she would never want to come out. As the hot shower pounded her back and scalp, her problems seemed to drain down the tub like the water. A sense of optimism rushed through her, and she began to believe things might work out. Trevor would get Christal free. He was the master in situations like this. He could get anything he wanted; he'd proven that again and again.

And, she thought, her heart pounding with a strange excitement, wasn't there at least a chance that his unsolicited help with Christal meant that he cared for her more than he showed? She closed her eyes as if in prayer, hoping that they might turn their marriage around. The nightmare of having to leave him, even if their marriage was properly annuled, was becoming unbearable. Trevor was not the wit that Anson was, nor was he the flirt Eagan was. But she was less lonely with him than she had been with anyone, even Christal. Something in his soul beckoned her. She had seen it that very first night, and it had bound her to him, a kindred spirit. It was what had made him move heaven and earth for his sister, and Alana had understood it, even in their worst moments, because of her love for Christal.

But it was tragic that his love for his family kept her on the outside, kept them from creating a family of their own. She didn't want to relinquish her marriage without a fight, but she couldn't surrender her pride and beg him to love her. She needed that pride of hers because that was what

ould hold her together in all the lonely years that loomed
ead should their annulment go through.

The water pounded on her like a drumbeat. Steam
eaded on the oiled linen. She reached for the soap in the
old shell-shaped holder. It smelled like him, a faint herbal
ologne milled into the bar. When she closed her eyes and
haled, the picture of Trevor was so immediate, she felt as
she could reach out and touch him.

She quickly lathered the bar in her hands, unwilling to
dmit how disturbed she was by the idea of rubbing it over
er naked body. Determined to be rational, she washed her
ms, but as the scent permeated the shower, she was less
d less able to forget Trevor. He was everywhere around
er, in the scent, in the air. Secretly she might have reveled
it, but it frightened her too. It made her body react with
a animal response, and she could feel herself melting,
eating, aching for him in a way she didn't want to admit.

Shaking herself, she concentrated on lathering a sponge.
he ran the sponge down her breastbone and squeezed it,
tting the white musky lather coat her bosom like a layer
icing. She rubbed, and suddenly she couldn't take it any-
ore. What should have been a perfunctory task was turn-
g to torture, made all the more painful by a desire that
as destined to burn undoused.

Moaning, she pulled her head beneath the water, hoping
would wash away the scent and her excitement. She
ayed there for almost a minute, eyes closed as if willing it
away. But it didn't go away. Her nipples remained hard,
er thoughts tantalizing. Her mind, body, and soul were
rapped around her husband, and deep down in her own
rivate hell she knew that was exactly how she wanted it.

A noise intruded, a strange distant sound like rain beat-
g on paper. Her eyes opened, and through the blurry
ush of water she saw that the linen curtains had parted and
figure stood watching her, the rainbath pelting droplets
nto his starched shirtfront.

With trembling hands she wiped the water from her

eyes. Trevor watched her from the parted curtains, his ex
pression a mixture of surprise and deep, hardened lus
Stunned, her fantasy by some strange magic made real, sh
was unable to snatch the curtain and hide her nudity. Sh
couldn't even think of the questions she knew she must as
about Christal. Before she could utter a sound, he took he
by the back of the neck and pulled her mouth against hi

A moan escaped her, but it was not a moan of protes
Protests were useless now—worse, hypocritical—for ho
could she lie to him and herself that she didn't want th
when she did, so badly that it had become like a hunge
that must be sated or she would die.

His tongue, hot and strong, thrust again and again int
her needful mouth, a wild accompaniment to the thrum o
the shower. Demandingly, he cupped her breast, his pal
brushing the steam droplets that clung to her nipples lik
diamonds. He flicked open the buttons to his trousers.

She was hardly aware of what he did next. Her only sen
sation seemed to be his mouth on hers and the overridin
instinct that he wanted her, ferociously.

He lowered them both to the floor of the large marbl
tub and pulled her, naked, on top of him. This man wh
was so cold and totally in control had finally been cut fror
his bindings, and she could see in his gleaming eyes tha
nothing was out of bounds. For the first time in their mar
riage, the possibilities were endless.

In a daze, drugged by the hot pounding of the rainbat
on her back, the even hotter desire that ignited them, an
the overriding desperation to seize this rare intimacy, sh
pushed aside his wet shirtfront and ran her hands greedil
through the slick dark hair of his chest. He liked her bra
zenness because the corner of his mouth lifted in a dar
smile. He caressed the soft pale thighs that straddled hir
before he twisted his hand in the length of her wet gol
hair and pulled her down for another desperate kiss. Hi
arm went around her hips, and he eased her onto him.

His flesh filled her to the womb, and she arched back lik

cat. Panting, he showed her how to move, and yearning to ease him, she proved an apt pupil, particularly when his thumb caressed her at their joining where dark gold hair met jet black. It didn't take long for her to respond, and her moan set his hands in motion. He pulled her down for another kiss, then took her breasts in his palms. He thrust up inside her again and again, and just when she saw the havoc this dangerous game was playing in his expression, in this man who needed control like a drug, she cried out, embracing her pleasure as if she were afraid it would be taken away.

A second passed, or an hour, she didn't know. Weak and gasping for air, she looked down at him as he still moved inside her. Her hands roamed his sodden clothes, his slick hair, his heaving chest, his pleasure-taut face, and she suddenly found she reveled in her power. For all her fears, she knew that Daisy had never had Trevor Sheridan like this. Her husband's rigid facade was gone, and in its place was a wild animal that wanted her with a greed that took her breath away.

She heard his groan, felt him shoot up inside her, and she wanted to cry, to laugh, to express any deep emotion that would equal the one she felt now. It was her first taste of power, and power was an insidious drug. But so was love, and she gloried in both because for one brief roaring moment she was a lioness.

At five thirty Margaret stood in the corridor in front of Alana's door and stared at Mr. Sheridan's valet, who stood before the master's door. Her mistress had not been in her bedroom or the bathing room where Margaret had left her. The master's rooms were all locked, and by instinct neither of them, not even Mr. Sheridan's elderly valet, dared to knock.

Margaret looked at the old man expectantly, an expression on her face that said "Now what?" The valet simply nodded and turned on his heels. With an embarrassed pink

in her cheeks, Margaret did the same, rationalizing that i
Mr. and Mrs. Sheridan forfeited supper, they could still b
dressed and ready for the Van Dam soiree at ten.

Alana lay in Trevor's arms in sheets damp from thei
shower and lovemaking. Trevor's clothes lay in a wet tra
to the bed. When he'd taken her there, he'd taken her twic
again, more slowly but with no less fervor.

And in the silences they held each other, Alana, lying o
her belly, gently toying with the dark hair on his chest
Trevor, lying on his back, quietly stroking the gentle curv
of her waist. They both seemed to fear words. Words wer
always the villain between them. They said too much, the
not enough. So when it was time to speak, Trevor spoke i
Gaelic, in soft tones she couldn't translate but understood
She kissed him when he wanted kissing, he caressed he
when she needed assurance, and finally when she whim
pered beneath him, his pounding body within the carna
embrace of her legs, she came to the rhythm of his whis
pered pleasure as he said again and again *"tar-cionn"* unti
he could speak no more.

29

"I want to marry Mara. I plan on taking her with me to England when I leave next week. I—" the duke hesitated, then spoke his mind, "I would hope to have your approval."

Trevor stared at Granville, who sat opposite him in the library. It was early the next morning, Alana still asleep in his bed. They had never gone to the Van Dam mansion. He rubbed the growth of beard on his jaw. The duke had arrived before he'd had time to shave, and there were a million things he needed to discuss, none of them with this impudent young Brit.

"How does Mara feel about you?" he asked cursorily, his voice gruff and unwelcoming.

Nigel paused, choosing his words with care. "I believe and pray that she returns my sentiments."

"She's only sixteen, you know. Far too young, in my opinion, to marry."

"In Ireland they marry younger."

"This is not Ireland." For the first time Trevor smiled. The duke became visibly tense. "You know, *Your Grace*," said Trevor, "I'm quite aware that as damning as it is, there is no doubt the Irish love a lord. My father named me after the earl who owned the land he plowed. Such a high compliment. However, that was the same earl who let my mother starve when my father died. So I have no love for the Ascendency. Pardon me if I don't slap you on the back and say 'Welcome to the family, me boy-o.' "

"The Granvilles have never been a part of the system in Ireland. We agree with you that it's wrong and unjust.' The duke lifted his chin imperiously. For his twenty-two years, he suddenly seemed much older.

"Fine. Then when it's corrected, you shall marry my sister." Trevor rose as if dismissing him.

But Nigel was not to be bested that quickly. "Shall you have her elope, then? Because I swear that's what we'll do if we must. Even though I know she wants your blessing."

"But you're the one who's come for it. I find that amusing."

The duke spoke slowly. "If the truth be known, I don't give a fig about your blessing, Sheridan. I can stand on my own. I don't need you. I just want Mara to be happy."

Sheridan laughed. He clutched his walking stick. "You want Mara to be happy," he mimicked. "What you want is all that American money that goes with her. Come along, boy-o, we're not stupid. Tell the truth."

"I love your sister, Sheridan, not her money. And I'll make a good husband for her, I promise you that."

Trevor turned dangerously pensive. "Granville," he said slowly, "I want Mara to marry well, and I've done near-Herculean things so that she may have that opportunity. You must know, I didn't do any of it to see her marry some impoverished duke who only wants her because her umbilical cord is attached to the Bank of New-York."

Nigel lost patience. "If you and I cannot come to an understanding, then I at least know I tried. I don't want Mara because of her money. In fact, I don't need her money, but since I cannot convince you of that, I'll take my leave. But I must tell you, I plan to announce our engagement at Caroline Astor's *bal masqué*. And after that, as they say, it's between you and your maker, Sheridan."

Sheridan laughed again. "Let's up the ante, shall we? You announce your engagement to Mara, and I'll cut her off without a thin dime. If you want to marry an Irisher, Granville, then you'll marry one. When you take her to wife, he'll be as poor as her mother when she came through Castle Garden."

"Poor or rich."

"Then you'll have no trouble announcing the engagement, will you."

"None whatsoever." Angry, Nigel took his top hat, nodded tersely, and left.

Trevor's smile became more cynical. "You'll never know," he flung to the closed door.

Alana rolled over and slowly opened her eyes. Sunlight streamed in from four enormous windows, four unfamiliar windows with drapes pulled aside and sashes thrown open. Though two stories up, she heard the noises of Fifth Avenue. The omnibuses rattled along, queuing for passengers; a man cursed at another for smashing into his brougham.

She closed her eyes, remembering she was still in Trevor's bedroom. She thought of last night and savored each stormy detail. Every muscle seemed to ache from their lovemaking, but there was a particularly wicked ache between her legs, one that made her wish her husband were still in bed with her.

Had she ever thought him cold and detached? A secret smile played on her lips. He'd been anything but last night. Now it was morning, even later perhaps. Would he continue the intimacy between them, or would he move away, back into that fortress he'd built around himself? Her smile faded.

She rolled over and looked at the other side of the room. Surprised, she found Trevor staring at her from a leather seat by the fireplace, his blackthorn across his lap.

"I didn't know you were still here," she whispered, held captive by his penetrating stare. His gaze lowered, and she looked down, finding the sheet so low on her bosom, it was ready to expose one dusky nipple. Self-consciously, she pulled the sheet up nearly to her neck. "Have you been u long?"

He nodded, and for some reason the lines and care wor into his face appeared heightened in the daylight. Perhap it was because of the sweet fury of the night before, but a he stared at her, he looked every day of his thirty-two year. "You make a pretty picture asleep in my bed, *á mhúirnín*, he said quietly. "So serene, so childlike—so different fror the woman you were last night."

Alana felt a blush on her cheeks. She couldn't refute hir Her passion had surprised even her.

He removed a letter from his vest pocket. He stood an walked to the bed, looming over her as he handed it to her "Here is the letter from the superintendent. Your sister i to be released into your care. All you have to do is show : to them at the asylum."

She took the letter and looked at it, holding it with trem bling hands. Her dreams had come true. Christal would b freed into her care. Alana was ready to run to her bedroor to dress so that she could be in Brooklyn by noon. At las everything was going to be all right.

She looked up at Trevor, her face a mask of unspeakabl joy. "Thank you," she whispered. "You'll never know hov much this means to me. I'll be in your debt forever."

"You erased that debt last night."

Her thoughts were so caught up with Christal, it too her a moment to realize what he'd said. He walked away his blackthorn silent upon the carpeting.

"If you think last night was payment for my sister's free dom, you're mistaken," she said to his back.

He stopped. He did not turn around. "It was paymen Why else would you be waiting for me as you were in th rainbath?"

"I—" *wasn't waiting for you*, she'd been about to say, bu she couldn't tell him that their encounter last night was a accident. Even she didn't believe that. Some force ha pulled them together and whether or not she wanted to g along with it, she did because it was too strong for her to deny. That was why she'd been so impelled to try the rainbath for the first time last night. She hadn't known she'd been waiting for him, but somehow she'd known he'd come to her.

"As I thought," he said quietly when he had no answer from her.

"No, it's not as you think. Last night had nothing to do with Christal." She rose on the bed, clutching the sheet over her chest. "I did it because I—" Her breath caught when she realized what she was about to say.

"Why did you do it?" he asked, a scowl on his face when he finally turned around. When she didn't answer, he said, "I'll tell you why. Because you've discovered the arts of seduction and loveplay, and you now know how to get anything you want."

"That's not why!" she cried out in disbelief that his thinking could be so skewed.

"Then why?" he demanded.

She looked at him, her face ravaged with emotion. "Why do you *think* a woman like me would become as wanton as I was last night?" Her voice lowered to a whisper. "A woman like me, Trevor, would only do that for the man she loves." The words were out, and she found relief in finally speaking the truth. There was no hiding it any longer.

He stared at her as she kneeled on his bed, the sheet artfully draped around her nude body. His expression was blank. Even his eyes shuttered what he felt. Finally he said, "You say you love me, Alana. But why would a woman like you ever love a man like me? Give me one earthly reason why."

Tears threatened as she saw him withdrawing. "There are no 'earthly' reasons for love, Trevor. I don't even want to love you. You've nearly ruined my life, and you've hurt me. All I know is that I do love you, and though you push me away with both hands, I believe a small part of you loves me as well."

He said nothing, his emotions cloaked in steel. His lack of a response hurt her, but she was willing to be brave. She would fight for their marriage. She would be patient and give him time. He liked to be the master of the situation. For once in his life he was embroiled in something beyond his control.

"Stevens would make a better husband than I, Alana. As much as I despise the fellow, I admit it. You're from his world, not mine." His voice seemed to catch for a moment, and his dark eyes turned stormy.

His words panicked her. She could see him slipping away. Her tears fell in earnest now. She wanted to shake him and force him to say what she needed to hear. "My God, Trevor, can't we ever be equals? Is there something so lacking in your character that you cannot put aside *who* I am for *what* I am? I've been able to do it with you. I see you not as an Irisher up from the gutter but the man I desperately want to love!"

He stood, the emotion on his face no longer hidden behind a mask. "No, you don't see me, Alana." His words were laced with bitterness and anger. He made no effort to hide his accent. "T'e man you want to love is still inches from the gutter. I see that every time we go to those cotillions, every time Caroline Astor looks at me with distaste. The man you beg for is not much of one. He cannot even be askin' his own wife for a dance. And why is that?" He looked into her eyes, and she swallowed a sob. "I'll be tellin' ye why. Because the man you want for a husband was shot thievin' in Five Points and canna be waltzin', ever!"

He turned and walked to the window, not bothering with his cane, his movements stiff, awkward, oddly violent. She watched him, tears streaming down her cheeks, a dark hopelessness seeping into her soul. He didn't think their marriage would work because he didn't think himself good enough for her. He would never accept her because of his insecurity, so their marriage was doomed before it had begun. The pain of that revelation was beyond her tears.

A knock sounded, shattering the silence. Trevor barked "Not now!" at the closed door, but Whittaker's muffled voice said, "A telegram has just arrived, sir. It's for Mrs. Sheridan. I thought it urgent."

Trevor looked at Alana. She wiped her cheeks and pulled the sheet around her more closely. He went to the door. When Whittaker departed, Trevor handed her the telegram.

She wasted no time opening it. The color drained from her face as she read:

> Christabel Van Alen disappeared Park View 5am. Believed to have run away. Searching. Prognosis not good. Will contact you when found.
>
> Mrs. Mathilde Steine

Numb, Alana lowered the telegram. The sheet had slipped, but she didn't notice.

He took the telegram from her limp hand and read it. When he was through, he said, "I'll find her. I've men who can look. Pinkertons."

Grief etched on her features, she refused to look at him. All she could think of was Christal—fragile, vulnerable Christal, her only relative besides Didier, out on the streets with no one to care for her.

"Have you heard me?"

She raised her head, too distraught to find the words to answer him. In one brief interlude she'd lost the man she loved and her sister. "Why did she do this? Just as I had her freed . . ." she said numbly.

"I don't know, love. I don't know why she did this."

"She didn't do this." Her anger surfacing, she felt tears again spring to her eyes. "Christal would have never done this without a reason. I don't care if everyone thought her mad. She wouldn't have left me without a good reason. I know it. I *know* it!" She searched wildly for a wrap so that she could flee.

"Where do you think you're going?" he demanded.

"I'm going to Brooklyn! I'm going to find her!"

"There's nothing that you can do that I can't do a hundred times over with Pinkerton men. I'll have everyone look for her. How are you going to make a difference?" He held her. The sheet slipped altogether, and she was left naked and struggling in his embrace. "Be reasonable, Alana. There's nothing you can do right now."

Her anger flared. He'd rejected her love, and now he was keeping her from her sister. Unable to get away, she lashed out at him. "Let me go! I'm the only one who can help her. After all, isn't it odd that you discover my sister one day and the next day she disappears?"

"What do you mean by that?" he asked, pushing her onto her back and pinning her to the bed.

She nearly spat. "I mean, after all, even *you* have to worry about your reputation. Perhaps finding out about my mad sister made you see that it might sully Mara's social conquests. And with all your effort behind her success, I can see why—"

"You're not thinking clearly, and you know it."

"Let me go," she said quietly, too quietly.

"Your sister was ill. You told me they'd had her drugged. She was confused and escaped in the early hours of the morning. I'm sure she'll turn up. I'll have everyone I can hire looking for her."

"Will I ever see her again?"

Almost as if he felt chastised, he eased his grip on her arms. "I'll do everything I can to find your sister. It's a promise." He stared at her, her expression far away, filled with pain and bewilderment. "Look at me," he said softly, his hand resting on her thigh.

She wouldn't. Her mind was snapping. She was too bewildered to think of anything but Christal. She wondered where she could be and whether she was all right. Silently she begged that her prayers be answered, that Christal would come to the mansion. When she thought she might never see her sister again, she gave a terrible sob.

"Alana," he whispered, his hand reaching out to comfort her.

"No, don't touch me! Don't touch me! If you don't love me, you cannot touch me!" She leapt from the bed and took the sheet. Holding it over her front, she ran toward her room.

He stopped her, his arm encircling her narrow waist.

"Oh God," she sobbed, breaking down, "please let her be all right. I beg of you . . . I beg of you."

"Hush," he whispered, again trying to comfort her.

She pushed him away and stared at him through teary pain-ridden eyes.

"I'll find her. I promise." There was an edge of desperation in his voice.

"Your other promises are all broken, though, aren't they?" Pain seared through her heart. "This agreement, this marriage—you've never kept any of your other promises to me."

He stared at her, his face stone-hard. "I'm the one who can help you, Alana. I'm the only one."

She turned away, unable to look at him. Running and tripping on the trailing edge of the sheet, she fled his bedroom while he stared after her, a terrible grief of his own ravaging his features.

30

"No, no, I cannot be doin' such things," Caitlín insisted

Eagan stared down at her, a frustrated frown on his handsome mouth. She was juggling the baby from shoulder to shoulder while Shivhan cried softly. "But you've got to do something more than just be a servant. Think of your child."

"Me mam was a sarvent. And her mam before that What's wrong with t'at?" she said irritably.

"But why do that when I can set you up in a shop and you can do more? Think of the babe. She should go to school and make something of herself. How will you do that on servant's pay?"

Caitlín went to the basement window and looked through the ornate black grille that kept the thieves away. She bounced Shivhan against her chest. "It's not right, I tell you, to be acceptin' such a thing from a man."

"You can pay me back."

"I'll never be able to."

"But I don't care, so why should you?"

She shot him a glance, then returned her attention to her baby. "I cannot be doin' it. I cannot."

Eagan ran his hand over his jaw. Everything had been so simple for him. Then Caitlin had come along, and now everything was impossible. "Sometimes I think you don't like me very much."

She spun around. "T'at's not true! You've been a saint to us." She looked at Shivhan, and her eyes clouded.

He stood by her side. "Then what is it?"

"You wouldn't understand."

"Make me understand."

She was quiet, patting her little baby against her shoulder. Just when she was about to say something, Shivhan burped like a beermonger.

Amazed that such a loud noise could come from such a tiny creature, they were both stunned into silence. Eagan was the first to chuckle, then Caitlín. Shivhan had ceased her fussing—no wonder—and she merely looked at Eagan with a sleepy, glazed stare.

Still laughing, he reached out and took Caitlín's chin in his hand. She stopped smiling just as his lips met hers.

By Eagan's standards the kiss was brief and respectful. She seemed to enjoy it because her mouth became soft and pliable, just the response he had wanted. But when he was through, he felt guilty just looking at her. Her expression warred between accusation and betrayal, with a small glimmer of desire thrown in.

"You're angry," he whispered.

"I'll be leavin' here today," she said quietly. "You speak of Ireland as if you think we have t'at in common. But we have nothing in common." Her gaze roamed the kitchen. Even that room had more luxury than she had seen back in Ireland. "Only the Ascendency lives in houses like this one. You're the American Ascendency, Eagan." She started crying. "And I'll not be havin' your babe so you can put me out on the streets too." With that, she wrapped Shivhan into her receiving blanket and fled to her little room.

His mouth open in shock, Eagan just watched her go, helpless to stop her.

By three in the afternoon, the Sheridan men were drunk. Eagan had arrived in the library shortly after lunch and helped himself to Trevor's whiskey. The stuff was torture to get down his throat, but he already felt tortured, and he could get more drunk more quickly on a couple of shots of that Five Points whiskey than he could on the V.S.O.P.

Two hours passed, and neither man spoke much. Trevor tapped his stick against the grate and stared morosely into the cold coal-blackened hearth while Eagan kicked back more drinks than were wise.

Finally Eagan swilled down one last shot and slammed the glass on the table. "I got pro'lems," he announced, slurring every letter that could be slurred. "You're me big bad brother, Trevor boy, Brother o' mine. What would you do in me shishuation?"

Trevor crossed his arms over his chest and peered at him, nonplussed. If his own speech hadn't been a fraction off, he might not have appeared drunk at all. "Wha's the situation?"

"Women, Trevor, women."

"And don't I know it." Trevor downed his own shot.

"Caitlín's driving me crazy. I think I love the girl."

"Don't fall in love."

Eagan seemed taken aback by this warning. "Too late. 'Sides, she needsa husband. Shivhan needs a father." He fingered the rim of his whiskey glass, his eyes defiant. "No —arguments?"

"No."

"Well, thas a surprise. Wha's got into you? I thought you'd want me to do—better . . ."

"I did better. Look what it got me."

Eagan studied his brother's melancholy figure.

"Marry a girl beneath you, Eagan. Otherwise there'll be no end for your pain."

"Alana loves you, Trevor—loves you."

Trevor gave him a dark glance. His answer was as succinct and poetic as it was hopeless. "How do you mix whis-

key and champagne? How do you sing *"Bríd Óg Ní Máille"*
to the tune of "Blue Danube"? You know how you do it?"
The fire in his eyes died. "You can't, that's how. You just
bloody can't."

31

Alana sat in the chateau's palm court with her morning coffee. A pleasant green fragrance surrounded her, and a fountain gurgled in the middle of the glass-and-iron enclosure, but none of it cheered her. The hours ticked away as slowly as an unwound clock. The mansion was as quiet as a mausoleum, a marble prison where she waited for news about her sister.

No news had come. Her sister, it seemed, had left without a trace. Though the asylum had searched frantically and detectives were at the chateau at all hours reporting on spurious leads, there was nothing. Christabel Van Alen had disappeared into thin air.

Depressed and anxious, Alana nonetheless had time to think about her harsh words to Trevor. When she'd gotten the news of Christal, she'd been pushed beyond her endurance by the joy and pain of her relationship with Trevor. He had always made her feel vulnerable, but after the intimacy of their lovemaking and her confession of love, hearing about Christal's disappearance ravaged her. Her instinct had been to fight back.

Now there was only numb silence between them whenever she glanced at him at the dinner table or spied him in the foyer. Her accusations made her feel foolish. There were so many detectives reporting to the mansion, they were wearing a path to the library door. If it was all show, her husband was doing a brilliant job.

She fingered one of the lush palm leaves surrounding her, knowing she had to apologize. Her heart was already torn apart by Christal—she couldn't bear losing the only man she would ever love too. Now they were separated more profoundly than at any time before, even when he was forcing her to marry him.

"A letter for you, Mrs. Sheridan." Whittaker entered the court.

"Thank you," she said anxiously, taking the letter and the gold opener. She looked at it, and her hands began to shake. The handwriting on the front was Christal's.

"Madam, are you all right?" Whittaker inquired.

"Fine . . . fine . . ." she mumbled, trying to get the envelope opened. Her gaze devoured it.

My dear, *dear* sister,

How painful it is to be writing you like this, so far away, unable to speak to you about what weighs so heavily on my mind. By now, you know of my departure. I understand it was wicked of me to run away, but I swear to you, Alana, there was no other choice. I would have perished at Park View. But not for the reasons you think.

This will come as a great shock to you, Sister. And knowing what I know now, I thank God every day that you have stood by me and defended my innocence against all odds and all reason. I know you've felt Mother and Father's death in some ways more deeply than I. I, at least, had confusion to numb me. You did not. Forever, I will remember your bravery because of this.

I did not kill Mother and Father. And yet their death was indeed no accident. I know this now because one week ago, I awoke with such clear memory, I weep to regain the bliss of forgetfulness. My memory is a terrible one, Alana, but it frees me. No longer must I carry the guilt of a heinous crime, for now I know who killed our parents.

And that is why I must flee. Didier is still out there, Alana. And he will come after me, as surely as I know you will. But if he finds me, he will kill me. I know after the shock of this sinks in, your first reaction will be to seek our uncle out and accuse him of his terrible crime. But always, *always* remember this: You too are at risk. You must not shout accusations, even though your suspicions are correct, since you have no evidence. You only have my word, and though I know you believe me, Sister, others will not. I've been in Park View Asylum for three years; our case is lost.

But do not cry for me, Alana. I've gone to seek a better life, no matter how bleak it may look now. I've managed by selling my jewelry, and that money will suffice for a very long time. You must believe that to stay would have meant a far worse end than the anonymity I've chosen.

My situation is dire, Alana, but my real pain now comes from having to be separated from you. I love you. In the years to come, when the threat is gone, I make you this promise: I will appear at your doorstep. Just when all hope is gone, I will come. I'll embrace you, and I'll never let go. We will regain the years snatched from us now, and the years to come will be sweeter for it.

Do not look for me, Alana. You will not find me. I must run far away because I fear for your life too. Remain ignorant. When the time is right, Justice will find us. In the meantime, know that I always think of you. I pray for your fine husband and the nieces and nephews I will someday meet. And I pray that you believe this had to be and that you know I am happy at last.

> Your adoring sister,
> Christal

Alana stared at the letter, unsure if the drops that smeared the ink were from her tears or her sister's. The handwriting became rushed at the end, and she wondered when Christal had penned it. The postmark was Manhattan, but where? She pictured her sister at a dock or a train station, alone and frightened, traveling far out west or even to the Orient to escape the demons left behind in New York.

The pain of losing her, of perhaps never seeing her again, clawed at her heart. But worse was the seeping horror that the real criminal had escaped, unpunished for his heinous crime. And because of their uncle, Christabel had been put through unspeakable mental agony. She'd had to grow up early. Even the letter seemed written by a girl much older than sixteen, much wiser, more burdened. It had been a crime to put her through such trauma, and the thought that this could have been avoided if justice had ever looked favorably upon them made Alana want to scream in rage.

But she remained silent. Her fury, her lust for retribution, would stay dormant until she knew the most effective thing to do. Christal was right. For now, at least, she could make no accusations. She must get help, but to do that, she needed her husband.

Desperate to find him, she smoothed the letter and held it for one reverent moment to her breast. The letter might be the last she would ever see from her sister, and she fought to hold back her tears. Someday, she promised Christal, they would have vengeance for what had happened. Somehow justice would be found, if it took the rest of Alana's life.

Collecting herself, she turned and looked at Whittaker, who still stood quietly in the entrance, lines of concern written deep in his face. "Where is Mr. Sheridan?" she asked softly.

"He's in the library, madam."

She nodded.

Once in the library, she found Trevor working at his desk, pondering the stacks of documents about Christal's whereabouts that the Pinkerton men had generated. He looked up when she entered. "Whittaker told me a letter arrived for you," he said.

She looked at his harsh features, half of her wanting to beg him to help her, the other half wanting to run away, shamed by his refusal to admit he might love her.

"Have you had news of your sister, then?"

"Yes." She stared at him, unsure how much of the letter she wanted to reveal. "She ran away, as you said. She couldn't take the asylum anymore. There are no clues to her whereabouts. The postmark is local."

"May I see it?"

Reluctantly she handed it to him. He read it, his mouth a grim line. Finally he muttered "bastard," and she knew he was talking about Didier.

"Can we find my uncle too?" she whispered.

He was already writing those instructions for the detectives.

"I have one last request." Her voice shook. It was time to confront the lion for the last time. Trevor looked up, and their eyes locked. They had been at an impasse ever since they'd last made love. Now that Christal's future was in the hands of the Pinkertons, Alana knew she must focus on saving, or dissolving, her marriage.

"And what is your request?" he asked slowly, as if sensing her grave mood.

She cleared her throat. "After this moment, I'll never speak of this again. The duke is going to announce his engagement to Mara at Mrs. Astor's ball. I shall leave it up to you, Trevor. All I need is evidence that you want this marriage as much as I do. If I get that, you know I will stay" —her voice wavered—"forever." She swallowed, refusing to break down in tears. "However, if you continue to insist that we cannot remain married, I must tell you that after Mara's engagement I shall be moving to other quarters, and I'll expect you to bring about the annulment precisely after that."

"I don't like being given ultimatums." His eyes flashed darkly.

"I know you don't," she said.

"And I'll have you know, Granville is not going to make that announcement, so this little speech of yours is wasted. I doubt Mara will be engaged for a long time yet. You'll not shed me that quickly, I fear."

She raised her chin and collected herself, amazed that she could do so when she was so shattered inside. She loved him. She considered him her husband in every sense. They had shared a bed, and his desire for an annulment cheapened what to her had been a mysterious and powerful act. He thought he was buying time by assuming Nigel wouldn't go through with his engagement to Mara. But he was wrong.

She had no choice but to put an end to the emotional turmoil that was destroying her. "When Mara's engagement is made, if the man I love can't love me, the marriage must end." She searched his face to see if her words had any effect. For a brief, wishful moment, she thought she saw pain cross his face, but quickly it disappeared, replaced by the same distant expression she knew all too well. She turned to the window, cursing the tears that had suddenly sprung to her eyes. She'd lost Christal, and now she was going to lose him. She couldn't bear the finality of it.

She cleared her throat again so he wouldn't know how close she was to sobbing. "I'm—I'm afraid I must be completely mercenary. I need help to find my sister. If we part, I hope you will continue to—"

"I'll find your sister. Regardless."

She couldn't allow him to see how devastated she was. "Thank you," she answered tightly, her heart turning to stone. When all that had to be said had been said, she swept back the demi-train of her gown, and walked out of the room.

Treaty

Parting is all we know of heaven,
and all we need of hell.

—Emily Dickinson

32

Alana's monthly time came the day before the Astor ball. Margaret didn't understand why her mistress burst into tears when she instructed her to fetch the cloths, but the little maid knew something was wrong. Margaret had gone through a similar experience, for she and Kevin had prayed for a child every day of their marriage. But Mrs. Sheridan certainly hadn't been married long enough to worry about being barren. Helpless, Margaret nodded at her mistress's request and left for the laundry.

Chastising herself, Alana wiped her tears, thinking of all the things she had to do for tomorrow's ball and remembering her vow not to cry. She refused to wallow in her depression. She and Trevor had hardly seen each other in the past few days. There had been no confessions of love from him, and now there was no possibility of a child between them, her last hope of keeping them together.

Placing the armor back around her heart, she went into her dressing room and surveyed her costume. Of all the designs she could have asked her seamstress to make, she'd picked the most defiant. She was going as Maeve, the legendary Queen of Connacht. Her gown was green satin with shamrock embroidery on the hem, and the costume was topped by a crown of emeralds. Mara had helped her with the design. Mara was going as the fabled pirate queen

Grace O'Malley. She would be gowned in emerald velvet and wielding a sword.

Margaret returned and helped her with her toilet. That completed, the maid delivered the message that Eagan wanted a word with her in the palm court. Alana rushed downstairs, wondering what could be the trouble, but when she saw Caitlín, she knew the news was good. Caitlín was dressed in a costly gray brocade traveling dress, a gown that far exceeded a servant's pay. On her finger was a diamond wedding band.

Alana didn't need the announcement. "When did you do it?" she gasped, her face opening with a grin.

Eagan chuckled. He looked a bit paler than usual. "This morning," he replied. "We wanted to stop by with the news before we left on our honeymoon. We're going to Ireland to tell Caitlín's mother."

He's scared to death, Alana thought as she kissed him. She also thought he looked happier than she'd ever seen him. So there was justice somewhere in the world. "Wonderful! Wonderful!" Alana kissed Caitlín and held her hand. "Your mother will love Shivhan. You must be beside yourself waiting to show her off." She smiled at the babe in her mother's arms. Shivhan was dressed in a fine pink linen gown and looked every inch the spoiled little miss.

"T'ank you for all your help, Alana. Your visits belowstairs meant everything to me. Eagan was right about you." Caitlín impulsively hugged her.

Alana laughed. "Pooh, what was a visit or two? I was just jealous of your babe, that's all. I'd love to have a child as sweet and beautiful as Shivhan."

Upon hearing that statement, Eagan suddenly turned quiet. Alana stared at him, her pain glittering in her eyes. Eagan knew. Suddenly it took all her will not to cry.

Eagan kissed his wife and asked her to wait for him in the library. Caitlín and Alana said their final farewells, and Alana was alone with Eagan.

"Have you told Mara and Trevor about your marriage?" Alana asked, wanting to gloss over her troubles.

"Yes, they know. I just spoke to them." Eagan finally spoke his mind. "What's going on between you two? There were two or three times I thought your marriage was going to last. Now it's all busted apart."

Alana didn't cry. She couldn't allow herself that anymore. It was time to fight. "I'm afraid Trevor will never accept me, Eagan."

"But why not?"

Just three little words, and suddenly those forbidden tears were pooling in her eyes. "Because I'm not Irish." She gave a black little laugh. "I must be the only person in this whole city of a million who wishes she were."

He rubbed her arms. "He just can't take you off that pedestal, can he."

"He's the master of every situation. He's done what he wants."

"I don't think so. Not this time."

Alana shook her head. "Eagan, if he cared for me, there would be one hint, one tiny piece of evidence that would prove his feelings. If anything, he's always gone out of his way to make sure I know I'm an outcast."

"He thinks about you all the time." He ran a hand through his hair. "No one can say *you* didn't try, Alana."

She nodded. "But I can't stay here and play at marriage alone. He must meet me halfway." She looked up at him and gave him a brave smile. "You'll always be dear to me, Eagan. Now don't leave your bride and daughter waiting. Have a delightful trip, and I'll come visit just as soon as I know where I'll be living."

Eagan sighed. "I wish it were otherwise."

She laughed and cried at the same time. "I do too."

The Croton Reservoir stood on the west side of Fifth Avenue between Fortieth and Forty-second Streets. Atop its enormous walls was a promenade favored by society.

They could stroll, see and be seen, and take in the sweeping view of the ever-changing city skyline not yet dominated by buildings other than church spires.

Alana went there to get away from the chateau, to think to clear her head and force herself to contemplate what seemed inevitable: She was never going to have Trevor Sheridan.

Their marriage was definitely going to end as soon as Mara and Nigel announced their engagement. With her emotions caught in Trevor's web, she wished fervently that they had never met. It was unbearable to watch something she'd nurtured and hoped for die a premature death. Living with only a memory was a hollow future indeed.

She stopped at the northwest corner and stared at the countryside past Sixtieth Street. In her depression, she was hardly aware of the man who stood next to her.

"Why, Mrs. Sheridan! What brings you up here with only your groom for company?"

Alana glanced over, surprised to see Anson. "Hello, Anson," she said, turning back to the promenade railing without really acknowledging him.

"What a chilly reception."

She looked at him. He looked dashing in a gray morning coat and ruby cravat. She wondered why he was still bothering with her when any other lady would love his company. "I'd have thought you'd be the one giving me the cold reception," she commented. "I heard about your row with Trevor."

Anson laughed. She didn't quite trust it.

"Don't be angry with me, Alana. Your husband's the one who started that fight. I was there for a simple visit, and he turned it into a boxing match."

"He's not *that* much of a hothead."

"But look what he has to protect. Can you blame him?"

He was paying her a compliment, but her suspicions were raised because she didn't know why he was doing so.

"Are you attending the Astor ball?"

She nodded.

He smiled. "May I escort you? I see Sheridan hasn't attended too many functions of late."

She looked at him incredulously. He just couldn't leave well enough alone. "You know that would only irritate him."

Anger tautened his face, though he did a valiant job hiding it. "That's precisely it, my little Irish rose. He threw me out of that house like a drunken sailor ejected from a barroom. I think I have the right to irritate him a little . . . and enjoy your company, of course." He smiled. He was so transparent, she almost laughed. That last comment was clearly thrown in as an afterthought.

"You shouldn't be placing me in such a position, Anson," she reprimanded, looking again over the railing.

"I've never seen you so glum, Alana. What is it? Did you marry the wrong man?"

She steeled herself and didn't answer.

"May I escort you to Caroline Astor's ball? It's almost certain your husband won't be attending, with his obvious dislike of Granville. It's a crime that you of all women should go unescorted."

She released a deep sigh. "If my husband isn't attending, I'll send you a note, and you may escort me. Will that suffice?"

"Fine! Fine!"

"But I know you're only doing this to anger Trevor." What she didn't say—her greatest fear—was that it wouldn't work, that Trevor wouldn't care if she attended the ball with Anson.

"I'll wait for your note" was all he said.

The detectives still filtered in and out of the mansion, and Alana prayed every night that one might find a clue that would locate Christal. They were also on the trail of Didier. Christal had told her not to; it was dangerous and there were no accusations she could fling at him that she

could substantiate—yet. But she wanted to know where he
was. She was terribly disappointed to find that he too had
disappeared.

Alana had only to deal with the silent dark figure that was
still her husband. She and Trevor had hardly said a word to
each other for days. She ached to be near him, to experience those warm moments they'd had in bed, but the ball
was in his court. She'd bared her soul. There was nothing
left for her to say. The only solace she had was that it was
easy to be cold and uncommunicative if the conversations
weren't long. And recently they hadn't been.

But now it was time to talk. Mara was becoming distraught about Trevor's disapproval of Nigel, and as the Astor ball neared, she begged Alana to speak to him.

When she knocked, Trevor was again in his cups in the
library, a habit these days. Alana thought it just as well. If
she had to approach such a beast, perhaps it was safer while
the beast was inebriated.

"Who's there?" he growled at her from across the room.

"I knocked. There was no answer," she said coolly as she
opened the large library door.

"What is it?"

His tone set her back on her heels, but she chose to
ignore it. "I wanted to talk to you about Mara. Nigel and
she plan to be married, you know—despite your attempts
to ignore the fact."

Trevor stared at her as if he didn't quite trust her visit.
"They won't be married," he answered smugly. "I'll cut her
off if she does. Granville's bluffing."

"I don't think he's bluffing."

"He is. He won't announce that marriage, I'll bet on it."

"Mara wants your approval."

"I don't want to hurt her, but this is the only way. When
he doesn't announce their engagement, she'll see I was
right."

"You could be wrong."

He stared at her, anger in his eyes.

"Your lack of faith in her judgment disturbs her greatly. I almost think she's willing to give up Nigel just to please you."

"Then she should."

"I said *almost*." Alana gave him a chilly smile. "Your sister has a mind of her own. I suspect she'll marry her beloved whether you like it or not."

"He won't marry her if she's penniless."

"What if he does?"

"Then I'll recant what I said about cutting Mara off." He leaned forward, nearly sloshing the whiskey in his glass. "But he'll drop her. Mark my words. The bastard's only going after her for her money."

"Well, for once, you're not being a hypocrite. You finally admit there's no possibility that one can love another for the person inside, but only for the assets that can be brought into a marriage." Each word dripped acid.

He watched her, his eyes brilliant with anger and guilt. "What you fail to understand, Alana, is my decision that our marriage cannot be based on love. It's based on right and wrong. It was wrong of me to use you the way I did. It's up to me to correct the wrongs and see that you're better off for this—deviation in the course of your life."

She laughed. "Is that how you describe our marriage? 'A deviation'?" She almost wept, the hurt drove so deeply into her heart. And she was furious. He wouldn't allow himself to love her because he was too obsessed with their stations in life. He'd built a wall around himself, and there was no allowing her in.

Retreating, she turned her back on him and with shaking hands poured herself a whiskey.

"What are you doing?"

She took a deep breath. "I thought we should have a toast, Trevor." She turned around, facing him, then lifted her glass. "I think it's appropriate, don't you? After all, we've been through a lot together in this marriage, as brief as it's been, and I think we should end it with dignity."

He stared at her, a white-knuckled grip on his black-thorn.

"To you, husband," she began, her wounds shielded from his view. "I've seen you lie, cheat, and steal to get ahead. But you've gotten everything you wanted, and I admire—"

Before she knew what he was doing, he violently knocked the glass from her hand. She gasped as it shattered against the marble fireplace.

"Don't mock me," he said through clenched teeth.

"I wasn't!" she shot back, her eyes blazing with fury. She cared not a whit about his feelings when hers were so mortally wounded. "That's right. I was telling the truth. I admire you—"

"And you hate me."

She said nothing, wanting to hurt him just a fraction as badly as he had hurt her.

"Hate me, then," he rasped. "You have that right after all I've done, but you won't mock me."

"You know all too well how I feel about you." Their gazes met, and she no longer bothered to hide her emotions. She loved him, and if he couldn't see it in the way she looked at him now, by the hurt in her eyes, in the vulnerable way she had held out her heart in her hands for him, he would never see it.

There was a long silence. Neither seemed to know what to say. Finally she said, "The ball is at eight. Are you attending? Mara and I need an escort with Eagan gone."

"No," he answered adamantly. "Mara expects an announcement of her engagement, and I won't watch your people hurt her again."

His words stung her. In soft tones she said, "Anson has offered his escort. I'll have him take us."

Quietly he bit out each word. "Stevens is taking you to the Astor ball?"

She was desperate to maintain her composure. "I'd think you'd be grateful."

He turned from her, his face rigid and cold. Cursing, he

whispered, "Ah, these sophisticated times. . . ." Then he pushed away from the decanter table, refusing to look at her.

For some irrational reason, his apparent lack of jealousy, of caring, hurt her more than anything he'd done before. Anger froze her unshed tears, and she quickly left, never hearing the sound of his whiskey glass as it shattered against the library wall.

33

It was truly an auspicious affair when the sexton of Grace Church, the "glorious Brown," consented to play castellan for the arriving guests. The man stood underneath the white canopy at the front of the Astor house, dressed in immaculate tie and tails, supervising the drivers with his silver whistle, ushering in the ladies with his silver tongue.

A light rain misted the sidewalks, graying the city to a ghostly translucence beneath the gaslamps. Carriages were lined up all the way down Thirty-fourth Street to release their passengers, the Stevens brown coupé among them. It soon pulled up, and Alana alone was helped down. Mara was not with her because the duke had wished to escort her and had called early. Believing them soon to be engaged, Alana allowed Mara to go on without her, and she had waited for Anson.

Anson had disapproved of her Celtic costume at first sight, but his disapproval gave Alana an odd tingle of delight. Her only disappointment was that Trevor had not seen her as the Irish queen Maeve. Perhaps deep down she had thought to gain some acceptance by dressing as a Celt, that if he'd seen her dressed this way, he'd see her in a different light. But he had never emerged from his library, and Anson had arrived to take her to the ball.

In the foyer a footman took her green velvet cape, and Anson nearly scowled when he took in the sight of her gown once more. Nonetheless, he held out his arm and strolled with her into the picture gallery where society had gathered. The crowd was thick, the gallery stuffed with the Four Hundred, who mingled like preening pigeons on a New York rooftop. Handing her champagne from a passing footman, Anson said, "Have you heard the rumor that the duke will announce his engagement to Mara Sheridan? Isn't that absurd? And he's British!"

Irritated, Alana accepted the champagne. "My sister-in-law is a sweet young woman, beautiful and accomplished. Why shouldn't Granville want to marry her?"

"I know what he wants from sweet young Mara, so why would he shame himself by announcing an engagement to her? The one doesn't have to do with the other."

She halted, fury burning on her cheeks. "You mean money?"

Anson looked down at her and said smugly, "No, my dear, he wants the exact thing I want from you—if I could get it without doing the same."

She almost spat, she was so angry. "I always suspected you were a cad, Anson, and now you've just proved it."

"Well, a cad is better than that trash you've been saddled with. And who knows, if you ever do get an annulment, your pedigree may induce me to overlook your dubious virginity and marry you anyway."

"How dare you!" she whispered, pulling away from his arm. They hadn't been at the ball five minutes, and their false accord had already disintegrated.

"Careful, Alana. You're making a scene." He locked her arm back in his, and no struggling was going to take it from him. "After all the trouble and humiliation you've put me through, tonight you'll behave. The least you can do for me is to act respectable."

"What are you, my keeper?" She dug her nails into the flesh of his upper arm. Finally he let her go rather than risk a scandal.

"Where are you going?" he snapped under his breath.

He laughed cruelly. "Are you off to seek out that husband of yours? Oh, I forgot. Wasn't he invited? Or was he with those other Irishers that were handling the stables tonight?"

"You couldn't shine my husband's shoes, Anson." She gave him a look of disgust and was just about to walk away when Trevor Byrne Sheridan was announced at the door.

The entire ballroom fluttered nervously, like birds with a predator in their midst. From the doorway Sheridan surveyed the room, appearing austere and unapproachable in black tails and a white barrel-knotted tie. Every person in the room seemed to flinch back, as if to say "I hope that look isn't for me."

But not Alana. She stood her ground, her gaze violently meeting his, though they were half a room apart. They stood there saying nothing, dueling with glances, until the music seemed to start again and the crowd relaxed, filling the distance between them.

Shaken, Alana looked up and found Granville at her elbow. He asked her to join him in the German cotillion, a dance that took nearly two hours. It was a tradition passed down by Caroline Astor's mother, Mrs. Schermerhorn, who thought polkas, redowas, schotisches too wild. Alana almost fell to her knees in gratitude for the long diversion. She accepted quickly and was fortunate not to spy her husband again in the crowd during the entire dance.

But when dinner was announced, Alana did see Trevor again. Her heart nearly stopped to find him sitting in a parlor in a "comfortable," a plush upholstered armchair, the latest rage from Paris, Joanna Varick perched precariously on the arm of the chair, both laughing at something Trevor had just said. Her husband's smile was blinding, and Alana felt her breath catch in her throat when he turned it on her. But when their gazes met, that wonderful smile faded, replaced with a grim expression until he turned his eyes away once more.

Alana could hardly bear to look at them. Joanna Varick,

with her Teutonic paleness, was a striking contrast to
Trevor's dark, menacing good looks. It wounded her to see
him having such a grand time. Though she had wanted to
gain his acceptance into society, she could see quite clearly
it had gone too far. He was hardly ostracized now. If anything, the women fluttered around him like gaily feathered
peacocks, curious and excitable, all too willing to embrace
him.

With this picture burned into her mind, it suddenly came
to Alana that none of the Sheridans needed her any longer.
It was just a matter of time before Mara was settled with
her duke, and Trevor, who scorned this society, was a part
of it now, whether he cared about such things or not. Caroline Astor might still be eyeing him with contempt from
her gold chair on the dais, but Joanna Varick's eyes held
something different altogether. The Four Hundred had finally been penetrated by the Irish, and if they let the Irish
in, could the Vanderbilts be far behind with all their vulgar
new money? The change Alana had predicted was happening. She was no longer needed as the bridge to a new society. A new society had been born when she had not been
looking.

She glanced at her husband once more. His dark gaze
held a gleam of wickedness that any woman would find
attractive. Joanna Varick certainly did as she touched his
arm in a gesture of intimacy. Hopelessness threatened to
engulf Alana, but soon Granville was at her side again, asking the honor of her company at dinner.

Dinner consisted of twenty-three courses of such things
as *aspic de canvasback*, forequarters of lamb with mint sauce,
turtle soup, salmon, asparagus, and truffled ice cream, but
Alana could hardly touch any of them. Her appetite was
severely diminished every time she looked down the long
table and saw her husband enjoying himself.

After dinner the ladies soon rejoined the gentlemen, and
once more Alana had to endure Joanna Varick's attentions
to her husband, who seemed to ignore the fact that his wife

was in the room. Alana became so miserable finally that she
decided to leave, but before she could, a voice stopped her.

"Caroline wants a word with you, darling."

Alana missed the arrow of her husband's stare as she
found Anson at her elbow. She had never seriously considered him a prospective husband, but now just seeing him
made the prospect of losing Trevor that much more excru-
ciating. "I don't want to speak with her, Anson. I'm not
well. In fact, I'm going home."

She tried to turn away, but he took her arm. "Come
along, *me darlin'*," he mimicked.

Unwilling to fight, she let him drag her to the dais to
speak with Mrs. Astor.

"How are you tonight, Alice?" the matron asked, falsely
solicitous. She lowered her feathered mask, revealing a face
much like Marie Antoinette's, complete with white wax
makeup and a patch seductively placed to the left of her
upper lip. "I was so hoping you would honor me with a
visit."

Alana kissed her, knowing full well she was the one supposedly honored by being allowed on the dais with the matron.

Alana was about to make an inane comment about the
wonderful ball when from across the room the duke stood
upon the threshold to the ballroom, clanging a spoon
against his champagne glass. "Everyone! I have a very important announcement to make." The duke stared down at
Mara, who looked up at him with glowing happy eyes.

Alana held her breath. The announcement of their engagement was going to happen after all. Though she was
happy for Mara, she felt time slip helplessly through her
fingers.

The duke continued. "I must tell you, first of all, that I
will always remember my visit to New York with great
fondness. You are a most gracious people, who've done
nothing but see to my every whim and desire, and for that I
am most grateful." Nigel then turned to Mrs. Astor on the

lais. Every head turned in her direction. "Mrs. Astor, I salute you. You are a renowned hostess, and I will sing your praises to the queen herself."

Everyone clapped, and Mrs. Astor nodded, the flush on her cheeks either false modesty or relief that the duke hadn't lived up to that vile rumor about wanting to marry that Sheridan girl.

"I have another announcement. One that eclipses this one."

The room sank into utter silence. Those rumors could prove true after all. Mrs. Astor tensed. Alana's gaze shot to Trevor. Judging from his expression, he was surprised.

Nigel gazed down at Mara. Their eyes locked, and he raised his champagne glass. "New York has been doubly kind to me, for not only have I found matchless friends, I've found the woman I want to be by my side into eternity. Thank you, New York." He looked through the crowd to where Trevor was sitting. "Before I make my final toast, I must take the time to thank a man, one whom I admire. I toast him because in this wretchedly modern age, he is a man who has shown me that noble passions such as loyalty and devotion to one's family still exist. His sister would not be the girl I know without having grown up in his shadow. And so I thank you, Sheridan." The duke raised his glass to Trevor, who sat in his chair absolutely still, obviously waiting for whatever came next. The duke obliged. "I want to say that at precisely seven o'clock this evening I was wed. Would you all toast the bride, my beautiful wife, the former Miss Mara Sheridan, Her Grace the Duchess of Granville."

The room uttered a gasp, and Alana felt as if she'd just been knifed. She wanted to smile and run to hug Mara, but she felt as if the rug had been pulled from under her feet. She'd expected the engagement. She'd made her promises that when Mara was engaged, she would leave Trevor. Now Mara was married. Everything she loved was soon to be lost forever.

She looked to Trevor to see his reaction. Even from

across the room she could see him mouth the words "I'll be damned." She looked at Caroline Astor who was so shocked and appalled, she appeared as if she were ready to fall into Anson's arms in a dead faint.

The duke ignored the pandemonium around him. He drank to his bride while Mara simply looked up at him, a becoming blush to her cheeks. Any other girl might have circled the room gloating over her catch, but it was clear Mara had considered none of that when she wed her duke. Her happiness seemed to stem only from the fact that she finally had the man she loved.

"Oh, this ruins everything!" Caroline Astor flung aside the smelling salts proffered by her maids, her anger reviving her. "How dare Granville do such a thing after all I've done for him!"

"Why would a duke of the realm consent to marry some immigrant Irish biddy from New York?" Anson muttered, bewildered.

Alana stared at them, disgusted by their words but pitying them too. Their secure little world was changing, leaving them terrified. But they weren't the only ones whose world had changed this night. Alana's had shattered before her eyes. Tomorrow the rift between her and Trevor would be permanent. There wasn't another thread to keep her by his side: no baby, no Mara, no social ambitions, and now no time.

From the dais she watched Trevor move through the crowd and begrudgingly shake Nigel's hand. He hugged his sister, and Alana prayed that he would turn and search the crowd for her. She ached for him to come to her, to tell her that time had caught up to both of them and that he indeed loved her and desperately needed her to remain his wife. But the crowds thronged around the duke, and soon she could hardly see Trevor's dark head among the well-wishers. Her heart heavy, she stood numbly at the dais realizing that tomorrow she would pack her bags and go. If she was ucky, her husband might be gracious enough to hold the door for her departure.

"And this is all your fault, Alice!" the matron said, turning on her. "Your mother must be turning in her grave to have raised such an upstart! None of this would have happened if you hadn't married that—that *man!*" Mrs. Astor flicked a glance at Trevor.

Desperate not to fall apart in front of these two, Alana snapped, "Well, if you don't like it, Caroline Astor, then the devil take you!" She left without saying another word, Anson and the matron shocked into silence that such a vulgar Irish retort had just come from the mouth of one of their own.

Stumbling, Alana found her way through the crowd to one of the exits. She wanted to congratulate the newlyweds, but she knew that if she didn't flee immediately, she would become totally unglued. Outside, she procured a hired carriage from Brown and rushed back to the chateau.

It was quiet there. She walked through the marble foyer, every footstep echoing off the polished walls. Lifting her now-hated green satin skirts, she ascended the grand staircase, her heart as heavy as the stone of the walls. For the first time in her life, she wondered what she had left to look forward to. Christal was gone, perhaps in far worse straits than when she'd last seen her. And now her husband was gone too, the man she'd grown to desire and love.

Every step to her room was slow and difficult, her mind filled with memories of Trevor. She pictured his face, handsome but never serene, his expressions varying from intense pride to deep passion. She mourned that never again would she have the joy of lying in his embrace watching his expression as they laughed and shared a tender moment.

"If only you'd let me go with you, Christal," she whispered, flinging herself on her bed. She lay there for an eternity, it seemed, burdened by a heart and soul too weary to allow her to cry.

After nearly an hour, she rose, hearing Margaret's knock

at the servant's door. Alana decided it was just as well the
maid had interrupted because she wanted her to begin
packing. It was imperative she leave tonight. To make a
drama out of departing tomorrow seemed unnecessarily
painful.

She was just about to give Margaret her instructions
when the maid held out a small music box. "The master
came home, Mrs. Sheridan. He asked me to give this to you
as soon as I saw you."

Alana took the music box. With a trembling hand, she
stroked the naively painted lid of forget-me-nots, thinking
how refreshingly pretty it was against all the preponderance
of gilt in her room. Nervously, as if she were afraid of
putting too much store in its symbolism, she opened the lid
and watched the mechanism chime out "Blue Danube."

The music touched her, haunted her, because it was so
beautiful and because she had never waltzed to it in her true
love's arms. And never would.

The thought sent a small crystalline tear cascading down
one cheek. She wiped it away so that she could read the
note inside.

Alana,
    You once told me there'd come a day when I would
regret making you marry me. I do regret it now, Alana,
with all my heart. For tonight I've seen the joy on a
willing bride's face, and I regret that I was never able to
see that on yours. I mourn the sorrow I now understand
that I've brought to you, but if you leave me, I'll mourn
my own sorrow at losing you infinitely more. Let these
words assure you that in this world of injustice, God's
sword is ruthless upon the wicked. If I lose you, one man,
this man, got what he deserved.

                                                   Trevor

Breathless with sobs, she could no longer read the tear-
stained ink of his letter. His words touched her soul, saying

everything she had ever wanted him to say. Desperate to see him, she wiped her cheeks and looked around, bewildered. Then, without hesitation, she ran from her bedroom.

She didn't have to go far. From the top of the banister she looked down and watched Trevor walk with tired stiff movements to his library, then shut the door. She wanted to run down the stairs and rush into his arms, but she squelched the impulse, knowing instinctively that wasn't the way to approach a lion. She had to do it cautiously, warily, to take each step with care and thought.

She made her way down the stairs and through the foyer, her eyes never leaving those austere library doors. Once there, she thought to knock but decided not to give him the option of refusing to see her. She entered and closed the door behind her.

He stood at the hearth staring into the cold ashes, his broad forbidding back to her. His blackthorn was clutched in his hand as if he needed its support even more tonight. She watched him, wrestling with her options, her emotions. She cleared her throat, unsure how to begin. Finally all she said was "Trevor."

He stiffened but didn't look up. She could almost picture his frown.

"Are you sorry you hurt me?"

He turned finally and caught her gaze. His voice was husky and low. "I never meant to hurt you."

She stared at him, the man she'd grown to love. Everything about him was contradictions. He hated the British, but she knew he would accept Nigel into his family because Mara loved him. He hid his background in that forced, overly mannered speech, but he burned with pride to keep his heritage alive in songs like "Bridget O'Malley." He was a man who could hate and love with equal ferocity, but he was never reduced to mediocrity. Life in society had surrounded her with senseless chatter or vacant silences, but never had her soul heard a roar. Until she met him.

"I want a man who loves me. Are you that man?" she whispered.

The silence became leaden. He turned away to stare at the cold hearth.

"Do you *love* me?" Now the answer was simply yes or no, and she could act accordingly.

"I want you to have the right man, Alana."

She shook her head and said again to that unyielding back, "Do you love me?"

"I've never been in love before. I don't know what being in love is like."

"I'm asking you. Do you love me?" Her voice caught with unshed tears.

He paused as if thinking through each word. "I've nothing to compare it to, but if love is obsession, if love can be so powerful it overtakes a man's reason and his will, if love is the feeling that one would rather die than live only to grieve its loss—" He turned, and she could see the desolation on his face. In one sweet rough whisper, he said, "Then yes, I love you, Alana. I'm doomed to love you. I'll always love you."

Tears streamed quietly down her cheeks. The tension between them stretched taut, the seconds passing with no words. She groped for the right thing to say, the way to express just how much he meant to her, how desperate she'd been at the thought of losing him, how much she needed him, loved him.

But when the words would not come, she did the only thing she could that would ensure he would never leave her. She picked up her skirts and ran to him, flinging herself into his embrace. With a gasp of relief and joy, he held her with both arms, his walking stick clattering to the marble floor, at long last useless.

Epilogue

How many loved your moments of glad grace,
And loved your beauty with love false and true,
But one man loved the pilgrim soul in you,
And loved the sorrows of your changing face.

—William Butler Yeats

"Wintertime" came the feminine whisper, muffled in the huge walnut tester bed, "Christal and I would go sleighing in the park. What a wonderful time we'd have. Father bought us a sleigh one year, and it was a beautiful sleigh, in the shape of a seashell, painted a deep green and lined in red velvet. It was small, only big enough for two girls, and I remember one snowy afternoon when Father followed us with his trotters, grooms in tow, and we drove through Central Park, the cold ruddying our cheeks, snowflakes clinging to our hair, the sharp liniment smell of our ponies comforting us in the midst of all the ice. Our feet were frozen, our hands too—we never wore our muffs—but we didn't want to return to Washington Square, though Mother had promised us chocolate upon our arrival." Alana touched her husband's bare chest, reveling in his warmth and hardness. She smiled at him, a wry smile but one very much like the secret, intimate smile of a wife. "I must seem so spoiled to you."

He didn't answer, so she playfully tweaked his chest hair. "Tell me your best childhood memory—I know you have one. Tell it to me."

Trevor stared up at the high canopy. The gaslight flickered shadows over his pensive face. "Perhaps my best memory is that of my father."

She was quiet. He spoke so little of his former life, she listened with rapt attention.

"We had family in Connemara, and summers me father and I would go out on t'eir boats with the other men to catch rockfish from Galway Bay. . . ."

She watched him dreamily, his accent, which he used often now, softening the hard edges of his English. He spoke of innocent childhood tasks, hero worship for his father, the simple joy of riding the waves high in the *curragh* and being counted one of the men. When he was through, her soul mourned for the child that was no more.

She rested her cheek against his chest and stared out the windows of his bedroom in the chateau, noting every frozen windowpane of February. She grew quiet, her eyes taking on a misty faraway look.

"You're thinking of Christal, aren't you?" he asked softly, stroking her back.

"I'm thinking of Christal and dreams." She was quiet for a long while. "Will we ever find her? Or Didier?" Her voice had an edge of unresolved sadness.

"The last we heard, your sister was in Bolivia, but you cannot go there, love, and you know it. So promise me you'll let me find her. It may take some time, but I swear to you I'll do it."

"I know you'll find them. I just wish it were soon."

"You said you were thinking of Christal and dreams. What are the dreams, *á mhúirnín?*"

She smiled softly. "Before I was married, I used to dream of a simple white clapboard house, and a man, and children. I yearned for the simplicity of another life, a poorer life."

"Are you sorry I can never give you that?"

"You've already given me that. Rich or poor, I want the man I love, a family—not the trappings, be they simple clapboard houses or mansions by the sea."

Suddenly he frowned. "You've startled."

His fierce stare, the one that once made her jump, now made her smile. "The baby's kicking. He's just like his father, you know." She placed her hand over his, and together they felt the sharp little punch against her belly.

"How do you know it's a boy? It could be a girl just as well."

She smiled. "Oh, he's a boy, all right. He's kicking and screaming to get into this world, and will no doubt come early just to be difficult. I told you, he's like his father."

He kissed her then, a searing tender kiss that left her aching for more. "Tyrant," she whispered. Then he kissed her again, proving her correct.

Afterward she snuggled into the crook of his arm, relishing the weight of his thigh as it covered hers.

"I love you, *á mhúirnín*, do you know that?"

Their eyes locked, and she looked at him, every emotion written clearly on her face. "Yes," she whispered. "I knew it when I saw your letter. I've never doubted it since."

His gaze didn't release her. "I want you to rest this next month. I don't want anything to go wrong. You mustn't worry about your sister."

"I just hope Christal is out there somewhere, finding a happiness as deep as mine."

"And are you happy?"

"I love you, Trevor. Does that answer your question?"

It did. He leaned over, cupping her breast, kissing her mouth. Her hand drifted up to his hip, and she tenderly fingered that small round scar. She'd been foolish ever to grieve over his inability to waltz. She thought that now as he began the waltz of lovemaking again.

Read these faint runes of Mystery,
O Celt, at home and o'er the sea;
The bond is loosed—the poor are free—
The world's great future rests with thee!

Till the soil—bid cities rise—
Be strong, O Celt—be rich, be wise—
But still, with those divine grave eyes,
Respect the realm of Mysteries.

—The Book of Orm

YOU WON'T WANT TO MISS IT
ANOTHER SPECTACULAR ROMANCE FROM

MEAGAN MCKINNEY . . .

RIFLES AND ROSES

COMING FROM DELL IN 1993

1

June 1875

It was a bad hanging.

And if there was one thing Doc Amoss hated, it was a bad hanging. He surveyed the seven white-draped bodies laid out in his small office. Even these men, the infamous Dover gang, had deserved the respect of a sharp snap to the neck and a swift journey to damnation. But this hanging hadn't been clean. At least, not at the end.

Doc shook his head, pushed up his spectacles, and went back to work. He'd spent all day with the Dover gang, first watching them hanged, one by one, until their seven bodies dangled from their nooses, limp and solemn in the haze of dust kicked up by the horses. Afterward he'd helped cut them down and haul them to his office. The small town of Landen didn't have an undertaker, so it was Doc's job to ready them for burial. It'd taken all afternoon to wrap five of them. He was now on the sixth.

Doc leaned toward the spittoon, missed it and left a pockmark in the dust on the naked floorboards. Outside, beneath the peeling sign *Haircut, bath and shave, 10 cents—Surgery done Fast* he could see to the end of town where seven men dug seven graves in the anonymous brown sweep of eastern plain.

The shadows grew deep in his office. It was late. He pulled off the sixth man's boots and checked his mouth just in case the fellow had some ivory teeth the town could sell to pay for the hanging. Doc wrapped him, then crossed off his name on the list.

Now there was no avoiding it. The last man had to be attended to. The seventh and worst.

Macaulay Cain. Just the mention of that name made a chill shiver down Doc's spine. He'd seen it on enough wanted posters to spell it backwards and forwards. He'd never wanted to mess with the likes of that notorious gunslinger. God and his sense of justice. Just when the hanging went bad, it went bad on Macaulay Cain.

Doc reluctantly looked over to the seventh white-draped figure. In all his days he'd never seen a man so difficult to put atop a horse and get a noose around his neck. Cain had required every one of the sheriff's deputies and even at the end, when his face was covered by the black bag and the men were ready to put the whip to his horse, Cain struggled and demanded that they wait for that telegram, the one he claimed was going to clear him.

The one that never came.

"Sonofabitch." Doc hated a bad hanging. It made a man feel right uncomfortable inside just thinking about the horse rearing and Macaulay Cain twisting in the wind, no broken neck to put him instantly out of his misery. When all was done, the deputies had brought Cain to the office. They cut the hands free and crossed them over his chest in a reverent manner. But Doc was the one to take the black bag off the head. No one else would do it. In a really bad hanging the tongue gaped out and the expression was frozen into a mask of terror as the poor bastard struggled to breathe while the noose tightened around his neck. The deputies visibly flinched when Doc removed the bag, unsure of what they might see. But before the sheet went over Cain's head, they all were relieved to see the expression loose and peaceful beneath the outlaw's scruffy growth of beard.

Resigned to his task, Doc walked over to the last body. The sheriff would be there soon to take the gang away for burial. He'd best be quick.

He bent to get a length of rope to tie the shroud. The room was quiet except for the buzz of green flies against the windowpanes and the sound of Doc's breathing. He leaned over the body, hand outstretched to grasp the sheet.

Then he felt it.

Another man might not have taken note of the small drop of blood that plopped onto Doc's black store-bought shoes. A man less trained in the medicinal arts might have never given it a thought, but John Edward Amoss had spent forty of his sixty-odd years learning one thing: Dead men don't bleed.

Sure, in a hanging there was always some oozing around the neck, but not enough to run off the table and plop right onto his toe.

The hairs on the back of Doc's neck rose. His hands itched to remove the sheet, but his feet were wiser. He stepped back.

Too late.

The hand shot out from beneath the sheet and clamped around his neck. Doc squeaked like a prairie dog caught by a coyote, but no one outside heard him. The townfolk had all gathered on the prairie waiting for the burial.

A long moment passed while neither man moved, Doc and the infamous gunslinger poised like statuary. In the silence Doc heard the man's labored scratchy breathing as Cain greedily filled his lungs.

Unable to help himself, Doc croaked, "You coming alive just now, son?"

The outlaw swept the sheet from his face. He looked bad. Too bad for a miracle. "Yeah. Sure. I'm the Second Coming," he grunted.

Doc nodded, too scared to laugh.

"The telegram. Where's the goddamned telegram?"

"Nobody cleared you, son. No telegram came." All the while Doc said this he kept thinking about the twelve men the Dover gang had been convicted of shooting and wondered how many of those men were this one's doing. He wondered too if in the end the final toll wouldn't be thirteen. Cain's hand tightened around his neck. Doc could hardly swallow.

"You lying to me?" The outlaw's features tightened, already pale from loss of blood.

"I wouldn't lie to you at a time like this, son."

Cain looked straight at Doc. Then he smiled, the smile never reaching his eyes. "I reckon, I'll have to take you with me, Doc. I'm hell-bent to get outta this hanging town. One way or the other." The man quit smiling. His wrists bled, his neck bled. And by God, thought Doc, he has cold eyes.

Doc swallowed. Not easily with the man's steely grip on his throat. "They ain't going to hang you again. They owe you. We all agree. It was a bad hanging."

"Bad all around," the man spat.

Doc didn't answer, his eyes drawn to the man's neck. The rope sure made a bloody mess.

"You got a horse?"

Doc drew his gaze away from the wound. "Yep. Out back. Good solid Indian pony. Take her."

"Gun?"

"Ain't got one. Don't rightly believe in them. Being a doctor and all."

"Then I'll take you with me after all. An outlaw's gotta have some insurance." The man swung his long legs over the side of the wake table. The fringe of his chaps was almost all sheared off, a sign of a renegade. Men running from the law sure as hell couldn't waltz into town to repair a harness. They used their fringe for everything from buckles to bootlaces.

Doc swallowed, conscious of the hand on his throat, the hand that at any minute could close and choke the life out of him. Fear made the blood drain from his face. "How far do you think you'll get with me dragging behind you?"

The outlaw stared. Those frigid gray eyes assessed Doc's paunch and balding head. "I need time" was all he offered.

Doc understood. "I won't tell. Not for a while anyways. That'll buy you some time. Get on out of here."

Those eyes narrowed, reminding Doc of a wolf's he once saw in the dead of winter. "Why would you do that for me?"

"I don't believe in hanging a man twice is all. You survived it. Must be for some reason. I ain't playing God."

The man pinned Doc with those eyes as his hand pinned him by the throat. "I need five minutes," he finally rasped. "If I don't get it, if you don't give it to me, I'll come back from the grave to get you."

"I swear you'll get your five minutes if I have to barricade the deputies from the door." Doc nodded as best he could.

Cautiously the man slid to the floor, his hand still clamped to Doc's throat. Together they walked over to the back door. For one brief second the two men looked at each other, a strange understanding passing between them. Just like that wolf, Doc thought, remembering how he'd lowered his rifle and the wolf ran off, leaving only the memory of those shattered-ice eyes.

The outlaw was at least a foot taller than the doctor, lean, hard, and capable from years in the saddle. There was no reason for Doc to say it, but he whispered it anyway, his throat still constricted from the power of the man's grip. "Good luck to you, Macaulay Cain."

The outlaw glanced at Doc, his expression startled. He looked as if he were about to say he didn't need any good luck from a man who had tried to hang him. But instead he took his moment, like the wolf, and he cleared the back door in a dead run. He leapt onto the startled Appaloosa in the corral and hightailed it west as if he were part Indian, with no need for a saddle or bridle to take him to the mountains that jagged up from the blue horizon.

And Doc watched him. Strangely anxious to see him free and gone, like that wolf in the snow.

July

When traveling she always wore black. Widows were never questioned. They said all that needed to be said in the color of their weeds. Because of that Christal Van Alen had learned to wear black. She had learned the trick of wearing the black cotton gloves so no one would see she didn't have a wedding ring and therefore no late husband. And she had learned to wear the long black netting over her face, labeling her as a widow, veiling her features, obscuring her age. Dressed as she was, she rarely got inquiries, or conversation. It was safer that way. One would think that a woman traveling alone would want the friendly solicitations of her fellow passengers. But she'd learned too in her time out west, that the only thing more dangerous than a renegade band of Pawnee, was a stranger too inquisitive about her past.

The Overland Express coach hit a rut in the road, shoving Christal into the sharp corner of an object. She looked next to her and eyed the small replica of a bureau that was the pride and joy of the hefty furniture salesman who held it.

She straightened, almost envying the salesman his wide girth. The stage accommodated six passengers, but the man next to her had been charged double fare because of the room needed for his samples and his large size. Squeezed between him and the side of the stagecoach, Christal could barely keep her skirts from being crushed. Her petite stature was no help. While the salesman was so heavy he hardly bounced around at all, she was thrust onto the corner of that tiny bureau with every jolt.

Clutching her grosgrain purse, she resumed her position, sitting primly, ankles crossed, hands placed one on top of the other in her lap. The ride grew smoother and she had the chance to look at the other three passengers who had got on the coach with them at Watson.

One was an old man with a placid grandfatherly face. She thought he might have been a preacher when he reached inside his breast pocket and pulled out a book of Scripture. But then she noticed that the book was carved out to hold a small metal flask, which he eagerly swilled from, and she wasn't so sure anymore.

The one next to him was a young man—a kid, really—who anxiously looked out the window as if he were ashamed of riding in the coach instead of doing the manly thing, pulling his weight alongside on a cowpony. His traveling companion might have been his father, a grizzled character with a faded indigo vest and a large wiry gray beard that would have benefited immensely from a pair of shears.

No one chatted. The "preacher" drank; the man in the blue vest dozed; the salesman stared at his little bureau as if thinking of his next account. Another jolt of the coach sent her once again into the vicious corner of the bureau. This time Christal sat back rubbing her ribs.

"Name's Mr. Henry Glassie, ma'am."

Christal looked up to find the salesman smiling at her. Thankfully, it had taken him a long time to converse, especially considering that for most of the ride she'd practically been sitting in the man's lap.

"And you are . . . ?" Mr. Glassie raised his eyebrows.

"Mrs. Smith," she answered in a low voice.

Mr. Glassie's smile widened. "A lovely name, Smith. So proudly democratic. So easy to remember."

She almost smiled. He'd all but said her name was common,

which it was. That was why she had chosen it. Yet Mr. Glassie made her feel complimented. He was certainly a smooth character. From his presentation, his fashionable verdigris suit, and the large pearl stuck in his black four-in-hand tie, Christal could believe he was very successful at what he did.

But poor widows didn't buy much furniture, and conversation quickly trickled away, much to her relief. She was left once again to look out the window at the ironing board-flat prairie. Every now and again she removed her handkerchief, reached beneath her dark veil, and dabbed the perspiration that beaded along her brow. The sun burned overhead, and dust blew in the open windows, coating her gown with a gritty blond powder. They had just started out. Noble was a long day's ride. She was anxious to get there.

She'd heard a lot about the town of Noble the last three years. All her hopes now rested there. It was a good place to hide, she'd heard. A lot of gambling, a lot of women, and nobody asking questions. There was once a time, way back in the olden days of a life she hardly remembered anymore, when a word like vice would have never entered her vocabulary. Words like vice weren't in her family dictionaries. In her world, vice was kept permanently untranslated and unexplained. It was as meaningless a word as something written in Latin. The irony was, she probably would have learned Latin, for that subject was taught at Miss Bailey's Conservatoire for Young Ladies, the exclusive girl's school on Fifth Avenue where once her destiny had mockingly led her. Now, instead, she'd learned the word vice, because she'd spent three painful years trying to avoid its clutches by refusing to sell anything but dances, as she had back in Laramie. But she knew with each desperate hour, those fingers tightened around her, beckoning her to quit fighting and relinquish her lust for revenge on her uncle, the man who had forced her into this low existence, and surrender to another kind of lust altogether.

"Oughta be riding shotgun, too, Pa. Them Sioux—never know when they gonna act up." The boy looked at his pa, who was trying to sleep beneath his hat.

"You're a genelman now, Pete. We got money. We don't ride shotgun no more. Soon as we get to St. Louie, we gonna buy us some clothes and be genelmen once and fer all."

"We ain't got no escort, just the driver and the shotgun. What if we get stopped? This is Sioux territory. And them Cheyennes, everybody knows they're all riled up—"

"Noble's spittin' distance from here. They don't need you, Pete. That's what we paid 'em fer. And what you gonna do when we get on that there locomotive in St. Louie? Try and push it fer 'em?"

"Aw, Pa," Pete groaned. He gave an embarrassed glance in her direction, then, as if he were glad for her veil, he turned to the window, appearing to scout for braves.

Indians. Christal had heard enough stories in the years she'd been out west to make her scalp tingle every time anyone even said the word. In the territory she'd crossed she'd heard about the Kootenai, Flathead, Shoshone, Blackfoot. They were bad stories, stories that gave her nightmares. But she'd come to realize that nightmares weren't so bad when one was living a nightmare. Even Indians would be hard pressed to do to her what had already been done. She wasn't afraid.

Then the coach stopped.

At first no one knew what had happened. There was just a silence, a stagnant pause that held nothing but the flavor of anxiety. A pair of boots thudded against the top of the stage, but Christal realized that was only the man who rode shotgun shifting position.

"Why have we stopped?" Mr. Glassie asked, clutching his bureau and looking around as if someone inside the coach would know the answer.

"We ain't spose to stop at Dry Fork." The grizzled man in the blue vest frowned, then poked his head out the window. He opened his mouth to shout at the driver, but for some reason the words collapsed in his throat. When he drew back inside the coach, the muzzle of a rifle was pointed directly at his nose.

Christal gripped her purse until her knuckles were white. Suddenly all those stories of Indians and outlaws came back to her with an immediacy that left her stunned. Her mouth went dry. Through the mist of her veil she saw the preacher slam close his Bible, shock, not inebriation slackening his features. Pete looked as if he were foolishly about to take on whoever held his father at gunpoint. Outside she heard the horses stamp, nervous with strangers in their midst. A second later the sound of a scuffle battered the top of the coach. There was a sudden silence; then a rifle thudded to the ground.

A hand, a very un-Indian grimy white hand, reached inside the coach and unlatched the door. Christal drew back in fear. A scuffed boot came up to rest on the threshold, and its owner leaned on the knee. "Howdy, folks." The man smiled, showing a mouthful of bad teeth. He was unshaven and dirty, with mean dull eyes that quickly surveyed the passengers. When he saw his threat registered, he laughed.

"Is this a holdup?" Mr. Glassie gasped, holding his miniature bureau like a shield.

From behind the black veil Christal watched the outlaw, her heart hammering in her chest as if it would break free of her corset.

"Cain!" the outlaw shouted, lowering the rifle. "They want to know if'n this is a holdup!" He laughed again and pulled his bandanna over his face to mock them.

"See here," Mr. Glassie blustered, but before he could get out the words, the outlaw was pulled aside, and another took his place.

Christal had never seen such a man before. As an outlaw, he looked much like the other one, taller perhaps and more broadly built, but he was unshaven, with several days' growth of dark beard on his chin. His shirt was dusty and worn, a faded scarlet bandanna was tied around his neck, available to cover his face should the need arise. But he was different, memorable, more dangerous than the other man. His eyes made her heart stop. She had never seen such steely eyes, eyes that made it feel like January in July.

"Men outside," he grunted. Those eyes turned to Christal, pinning her to her seat. She knew he couldn't see her face beneath the veil, but that was small comfort as she squirmed beneath that chilling gaze.

To her relief he turned away to direct the male passengers. Her shoulders slumped after the assault of that stare and she expelled the breath she hadn't even realized she'd been holding.

"Is this a holdup?" Mr. Glassie persisted, unwilling to remove himself from the coach until the situation was more clear. "As you men can see, we've a lady on board. We can't just trot off this coach and leave her behind without someone—"

"I said men outside." The outlaw with the cold gray eyes blessed Mr. Glassie with a glance of ice. The salesman didn't need more than that to convince him to relinquish his bureau and get out of the stage.

One by one, they filed out. Pete kept a defiant look on his face, as if to say "I ain't afraid of you." His father looked anxious, as if he'd come so far only to have all his dreams dashed in a robbery. From the window Christal looked at the preacher. His hands were shaking as he held them over his head. Her own hands were slick with cold sweat as she held on to the window.

She looked in the distance, hopelessly seeking help. The bridge at Dry Fork was obviously where these outlaws had been hiding as their target had rolled toward them. Christal spied their horses tied beneath the bridge. She counted five.

". . . am a representative of the Paterson Furniture Company of Paterson, New Jersey, and my company shall hear about this outrageous treatment, my good fellows!" Mr. Glassie announced as the first outlaw searched him for weapons. The second, the one with the steely eyes, patted down the old man's blue vest while Pete glared.

"I'm a poor man, a poor man, mister," Pete's father chanted while being searched. "Ain't no need in stealing from me 'cause I'm a poor man."

"No weapons, Cain," the first outlaw called out.

Cain, the man with the steely eyes, nodded. He lifted up Pete's coat. Finding a six-shooter stuck in the waistband of the boy's jeans, he took it and pushed the boy aside.

"Listen up." Cain shot a couple of times into the air. Everyone gave him his full attention, including the driver and the man who rode shotgun, who were now on the ground. "You men'll be walking the rest of the way. Just follow behind the stage." Cain looked to a couple of riders who were galloping up from the Dry Fork bridge. "The boys'll see you get there."

"Where?" Pete asked bravely.

Cain shot him a stare. "A town called Falling Water. You ever heard of it, kid?"

Pete hardened his chin. "Sure. It's a damn ghost town. Nobody been there for years."

"That's right. But you'll be seeing it."

"You kidnapping us?"

"Yeah."

"Why?"

Christal clutched the door, waiting for the answer. The situation was escalating out of control. What was at first a simple holdup was getting more and more complicated and frightening. Her mind played out one scenario after another as reasons for this. The worst was that somehow, some way, she'd been found by her uncle.

"The Overland Express has its payroll coming in Tuesday. We're holding you all for ransom." Cain stuck the kid's six-shooter into the waist of his own chaps. "So you men walk behind the stage. If you get outta line, Zeke here's got permission to bullwhip you." The man named Zeke edged his sorrel toward the group. In his right hand was an enormous wicked-looking whip, the kind that could easily flick the skin from a man's back.

Christal watched the numb horror seep into the other passengers' expressions. She was petrified too, but she took small consolation in knowing that her uncle wasn't behind any of this. If Baldwin Didier had found her, she wouldn't live to see tomorrow. With these outlaws, she had some chance.

"You can't hold us that long! Tuesday's almost a week away!" Mr. Glassie exclaimed, obviously thinking of his accounts.

Cain shrugged, obviously not caring.

"Who are you, my good man, that you think you can do this to us?"

"Macaulay Cain."

Pete gasped. "Macaulay Cain! Macaulay Cain was hung in Landen over a month ago!"

"Some say that."

"And some say Macaulay Cain got out of the hangin' and met up with the Kineson gang. Is this here the Kineson gang?" the boy's father inquired, dread on his face.

"It could be, and if you're right, you'd best not be acting up." Cain's words were so low, Christal wouldn't have been able to hear them if he weren't standing right next to the stage. The menace that edged the man's raw voice sent a chill down her spine. She quickly saw she had been too confident. These men were outlaws. They'd done awful things, perhaps even killed men. They were wanted, desperate. And she was a woman alone.

Another rider rode up from the bridge, leading the last two horses by their reins. He hitched the two to the coach and fell in with Zeke. She was nearly hanging out the window when Zeke pushed the six men, including the driver and the shotgun, to the back of the coach to walk.

Christal bit her lip. If there were two horses hitched, one of them belonged to the outlaw who would be driving the carriage. That left one other gang member to either walk or . . . ride in the carriage with her. Her dread-filled gaze slid to Macaulay Cain.

A sudden overwhelming panic seized her, and she wanted to run out of the coach and fall in with the other passengers. She didn't want to be alone in the stagecoach. More than that, she didn't want to ride with one of the outlaws, particularly the one with the cold gray eyes.

"You better treat that widow right. We ain't gonna stand for you mistreatin' her" she heard Pete demand from behind the carriage. His words tugged at her heart. He was brave to say such things. She couldn't remember the last time a man had cared about her welfare.

The sound of a high-pitched laugh crawled down her spine. Christal believed it was the man who first opened the stagecoach door. "She'll be all right. She's going to ride with me."

"I'll be riding with her." The second voice brooked no debate.

There was a long resentful pause before the other outlaw said, "Sure, Cain. You go ahead and get a peek at her. She's probably too old to fiddle with anyway."

The coach creaked as the iron-clad wheels ached to roll again. The number of horses had doubled, and there was that much more jangling of harnesses. Zeke cracked the bullwhip, but it must have been for intimidation because none of the passengers cried out. Still, the sound reverberated over the open prairie like a gunshot.

Christal prayed the man called Cain would forget about her. But after a moment the coach door opened, and he jumped in, rifle and all. He slammed the door behind him and knocked twice on the roof with the butt of his rifle. The stagecoach lurched to a start, and he slouched down on the dusty velvet seat opposite her, kicking Mr. Glassie's prized bureau to the center of the coach so he could stretch out his legs on it.

She stared at him through the veil. He terrified her. The rifle rested across his knees, drawing her eyes to the length and power of the man's legs. He wore chaps, the leather rubbed smooth along the inside of the thighs from long hours in the saddle. He was dirty, covered in dust and sweat. She expected a bad animal odor from him, as she would have from that first outlaw, who had the rotten teeth, but he didn't smell like that. His presence filled the carriage with the scent of fired gunpowder which stained his hands and shirt. He was sweating, and she could smell that, but there was a musky kind of man smell to him that repelled her and seemed to seduce her at the same time.

It was hot in the carriage. The sun was now at high noon, and the dust kicked into the window with a new ferocity. Christal longed to pat away the perspiration on her face, but she didn't, not wanting to call the man's attention to her. She watched him covertly beneath the veil, letting the sweat trickle down her temples and between her corseted breasts.

He gave her hardly more than a glance. His attention was taken by the window and his thoughts. She wondered what he was thinking, what plans he had for them. Uncontrollably, she shivered, imagining what this man might be capable of.

She watched him rub the sweat from his eyes with his thumb and forefinger. He pulled at the faded scarlet bandanna, untying it so that he could wipe his face. She gasped. The man's neck was circled with an angry ragged scar. She could think of only one thing that could give a man a scar like that.

Unfortunately her gasp did exactly the thing she wanted to avoid. That cold, steely gaze riveted on her. He touched his neck, then flashed a cynical smile, revealing strong white teeth.

He leaned toward her. She certainly had his attention now.

"You ever felt the noose around your neck, ma'am?" His laugh was rumbling and husky.

She just stared at him, shocked and frightened. Unconsciously her hand went to her neck. She swallowed, not wanting to think of her past, of her uncle. But even her past and Baldwin Didier seemed less of a threat when coupled with the hard outlaw in front of her. For three years she'd been running from one danger. She wondered if she had landed in a worse one.

The outlaw sat back and perused her black-clad figure. She cursed herself. She'd certainly caught his interest now.

Without warning, he raised his rifle and pointed it at her. Her heart stopped dead. She waited for him to pull the trigger, but he put the muzzle beneath her veil and began to lift it.

Her gloved hands gripped the barrel to stop him. She needed the protection of that veil. Just looking into those eyes told her so. She didn't want him to see her face. She didn't want to be that vulnerable.

She slapped away the gun, but he held it firm. Too terrified to move, she stared at him, still hidden by the veil, now noting the rope scars on his wrists. He held the rifle in front of her and tipped up the veil. In a flash, the veil was up and off her face.

It was his turn to be surprised. She knew he expected an older woman, not a nineteen-year-old girl with a face bred of the aristocracy of New York. Her Dutch ancestry was only too apparent in the gold of her hair and the crystalline blue of her eyes, eyes that clashed defiantly with steely gray ones.

He didn't say a word. They stared at each other for one long moment, each assessing the other. She was afraid of him, but experience had taught her never to show fear. She presented a face as haughty and cold as marble.

He wasn't intimidated. He just stared right back, an enigmatic expression in his eyes. And by her expression, she dismissed him as easily as she would a servant. She turned her face away and gazed out the window. But she had not counted on that rifle he still pointed at her. He placed the barrel against her cheek and forced her to turn her head. Her eyes glittered with anger and fear. She met his gaze once more. His eyes were as cold and steely as the smooth rifle barrel laid across her cheek.

Then he did the strangest thing. Slowly he lowered his rifle.

Her heart lurched when he reached over, but he did so only to cover her face once more by the veil. He sat back, gave her one inexplicable glance, and again looked out the window, absorbed in thought.

"Why did they hang you?" she gasped, desperate to know, and finding courage behind her veil.

He turned back to her, his gaze slamming into hers as if the veil were no longer there. She believed his every word. " 'Cause maybe I needed hanging."

Terrified, she drew back against the seat, her fear a small choking sound in her throat. He gauged her reaction, his smile mirthless and satisfied. Then he resumed looking out at the wide stretch of prairie dismissing her as if she were no longer there.

I live in a 110-year-old house in New Orleans. From the front of my house I can watch the streetcar roll along palm-lined St. Charles Avenue. My witty and charming husband, Tom, is an attorney, and we have just recently been blessed with a handsome little boy, ingeniously named after his father. My hobbies are horseback riding (I *still* have the horse that I had when I was twelve), visiting with friends, and caring for the many stray animals that have been gracious enough to adopt us. My greatest wish is for people to have their pets spayed or neutered so that my husband and I won't have to have any more, as my father puts it, furry freeloaders.

It's not easy combining the careers of mother, zookeeper, and romance novelist, but I juggle them as best I can. My husband knows how much I love to write, and his support has made all the difference. I hope you enjoy *Lions and Lace*. If I can provide a reader with a few hours of enjoyment, then I feel that all those long hours at the computer have paid off.